Praise for Pam Hillman

"*The Road to Magnolia Glen* is a sweet story filled with romance, adventure, and Southern charm. A beautiful and redemptive theme comes together in a satisfying ending that will leave readers pondering the extent of true love."

HEIDI CHIAVAROLI, AUTHOR OF *FREEDOM'S RING*

"*The Road to Magnolia Glen* is historical fiction at its finest. Intrigue. Romance. Faith. Author Pam Hillman combines all these elements into a story you won't want to put down. You'll root for Kiera and Quinn while booing and hissing at the evil Le Bonne—and finally cheer at the end after an explosive finish. All this and a history lesson too. Win-win."

MICHELLE GRIEP, AWARD-WINNING AUTHOR OF THE ONCE UPON A DICKENS CHRISTMAS SERIES

"Romance, danger, and courage are woven through a backdrop of tension as thick as the Mississippi humidity. . . . Quickly embracing Connor and Isabella, readers will remain fully invested in the outcome of their story, savoring each word and maybe even forgetting to breathe a time or two along the way. The first book in the Natchez Trace series is perfect for fans of Tamera Alexander, Laura Frantz, and Lori Benton."

ROMANTIC TIMES, 4½-STAR REVIEW, TOP PICK

"Hillman breezily weaves together colorful details, romantic tensions, and suspenseful plotting in this fun historical romance."

"In the first of her new Natchez Trace series, Hillman carries readers to antebellum Mississippi in an entertaining tale. Greed, murder, and glimpses of the slave trade give it depth, while the subtle Christian themes provide hope."

"Hillman's series launch set in antebellum Mississippi effectively mixes intrigue and suspense with a healthy dose of romance and historical details."

"Pam Hillman has done it again—stolen both my sleep and my heart with a breathless novel unlike any I've read. From a Natchez auction block to a timeworn Mississippi plantation, this is a journey richly written and historically alive, a unique and gentle love story that is truly a promise kept."

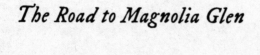

The Road to Magnolia Glen

THE ROAD TO
MAGNOLIA GLEN

A Natchez Trace Novel

PAM HILLMAN

Tyndale House Publishers, Inc.
Carol Stream, Illinois

Visit Tyndale online at www.tyndale.com.

Visit Pam Hillman's website at www.pamhillman.com.

TYNDALE and Tyndale's quill logo are registered trademarks of Tyndale House Publishers, Inc.

The Road to Magnolia Glen

Designed by Jennifer Phelps

Edited by Erin E. Smith

Published in association with the literary agency of The Steve Laube Agency.

Scripture quotations are taken from the *Holy Bible*, King James Version.

The Road to Magnolia Glen is a work of fiction. Where real people, events, establishments, organizations, or locales appear, they are used fictitiously. All other elements of the novel are drawn from the author's imagination.

For information about special discounts for bulk purchases, please contact Tyndale House Publishers at csresponse@tyndale.com, or call 800-323-9400.

Library of Congress Cataloging-in-Publication Data

Names: Hillman, Pam, author.
Title: The road to Magnolia Glen / Pam Hillman.
Description: Carol Stream, Illinois : Tyndale House Publishers, Inc., [2018]
  | Series: A Natchez Trace novel
Identifiers: LCCN 2018000556 | ISBN 9781496415943 (sc)
Subjects: | GSAFD: Christian fiction.
Classification: LCC PS3608.I448 R63 2018 | DDC 813/.6—dc23 LC record available at https://lccn.loc.gov/2018000556

Printed in the United States of America

24 23 22 21 20 19 18
7   6   5   4   3   2   1

The Road to Magnolia Glen is dedicated to my youngest son, Darin.

They say still waters run deep, and that is true with Darin. On the surface, he's an easygoing young man who goes through life charming everyone around him with his ready smile and agreeable nature.

This is the young man who carries packages without having to be asked, opens car doors for women (young and old alike), and never, ever loses his temper unless someone is being bullied. I can count on one finger the time he truly lost his cool as a teen (spats with his brother don't count)—and it was in response to some young ladies who were verbally accosted by strangers while in his presence.

With such a generous spirit, caring attitude, and the ability to relate to young and old alike, is it any wonder he chose a career in the medical field?

The heart of a gentleman is alive and well and can be found in Darin Hillman.

Prologue

THE *LADY GALLANT* IN THE MIDDLE OF THE ATLANTIC OCEAN
JANUARY 1792

"Keep your brother away from my sister!"

Quinn O'Shea spread his feet wide and tried to keep his balance on the deck of the *Lady Gallant*. After weeks on board, he'd just begun to get his sea legs. A violent storm had kept all the passengers confined for days on end, the coffin-like spaces in steerage hardly fit for pigs, let alone humans.

But now the storm had passed . . . well, except for the one that stood in front of him, blue eyes blazing, strands of blonde hair blowing in the wind, and pale cheeks stained cherry apple red.

She was sky blue and golden, from the top of her head to the peach-and-cream silk gown she wore. He'd seen her on deck twice before, but her kind didn't mix with the masses stacked like cordwood in the belly of the ship.

He grinned. "Ah, now which o' me brothers would that be, lass? Rory or Patrick?"

In response to his teasing, her brows, three shades darker than her hair, descended into a frown. She stood taller, looking down her haughty little nose at him.

"Don't tell me there's more than one of the scoundrels?"

Her tone and the tilt of her chin gave her the look of sniffing something foul on the wind. He scowled. Her accent was British with a wee hint of the homeland that she tried hard to hide. One of those, eh? Just enough British aristocracy flowed through her veins that she'd squashed her Irish heritage to death, much like the British landlords had done to him and his.

"Scoundrels they be, fer sure." Quinn stepped closer, his gaze on hers. She blinked, stepping back. "And aye, there's more than one. So I shan't be knowing which of the rascals you're referring t', now shall I?"

Two well-dressed gentlemen taking a constitutional around the deck stopped nearby, eyeing Quinn with suspicion. One turned to the girl. "Miss Young, is this—" the middle-aged man tossed a condescending glance toward Quinn—"*gentleman* bothering you?"

"No, Mr. Marchette." Her day dress rustled as she dipped into a curtsy, the creamy skirt falling in silky folds across the deck, then pooling over Quinn's broken-down boots. "He was helping me look for my sister. But thank you for your concern, sir."

"Of course. Good day, miss."

Before they were out of sight good and proper, the haughty miss whirled back to Quinn. Like a dog worrying a bone, she didn't miss a beat. "I don't know your brother's name, but ever since the storm broke, the two of them have been roaming this ship from stem to stern, and I'm at my wit's end."

"And I'm supposed t' keep him away from her? Mayhap your sister needs t' keep her distance, eh?"

"I'll see that she does." Her blue eyes snapped. "And if you would be so kind as to—oh!"

The ship lurched sideways. She grabbed for the railing but missed. Quinn snagged her around the waist just before she pitched forward onto the rough planking.

Those blue eyes stared into his, no longer narrowed in anger, but wide in shocked surprise. Her full pink lips rounded into a surprised O before just as quickly compressing into a thin line, her displeasure returning full force.

She pulled away, straightened her dress, and crawled right back on her high horse. "My sister is too young—" Twin spots of color polished her porcelain cheekbones. "She oughtn't be dallying with boys."

"Ya mean poor Irish trash?" In spite of his teasing, Quinn held his temper in check.

"I never said any such thing." She sighed. "Look, Mr. . . ."

"O'Shea. Quinn O'Shea." Quinn touched his hat and gave a short nod.

"Mr. O'Shea. The truth is that within a few weeks, we'll land in Natchez, and well, I'm to be married, you see, and . . ." She bit her lip, the fire in her gaze banked to a worried simmer. "Megan's already a handful, quite the tomboy, and the less drama I have from her, the better off we'll all be."

"A tomboy? And you're worried about her and me brother Rory?" He squinted at her. "Just how old is this sister o' yours?"

"She's eight—"

"Eight?" Quinn threw back his head and laughed.

"I fail to see anything funny about the situation." The glare returned with full force.

"As I said, I have more than one brother, and I do no' think ya should worry o'er Patrick and the lass. They're both eight. What harm can they do?"

"That's where you're wrong. Do you even have a clue where either of them are right now?"

He frowned. "Well, no—"

"So they could have fallen overboard and you wouldn't even know it—"

"That's a wee bit far-fetched, Miss . . ."

"Young. Kiera Young." She crossed her arms. "And on the contrary, it's very likely. Do you know where I found them yesterday?"

"Where?" Quinn asked, not sure he wanted to know, but just as sure that she was going to tell him.

She stabbed a finger toward the mainmast. "There. Halfway up the rigging. Now, tell me that your brother is a good influence on my sister?"

Quinn's lips twitched, but he did his best to keep a straight face. "My humble apologies. I shall do everything in me power t' keep me rascally brother away from yer—ah—delicate wee sister."

"Please see that you do."

And with that, she whirled and was gone.

Chapter 1

THREE WEEKS LATER
NATCHEZ UNDER-THE-HILL ON THE MISSISSIPPI RIVER
FEBRUARY 1792

"Stay close."

Eyes on the bustling wharf, Kiera held tight to Megan's hand, ensuring her adventuresome sister didn't disappear into the crowd.

"But, Kiera, I wanted to say good-bye to Patrick."

"That snotty-nosed lad?" Sixteen-year-old Amelia wrinkled her nose. "Really, Megan, he's simply not the kind you should be associating with. Gutter—"

"Amelia, that's quite enough." Kiera kept her tone even,

nervously searching the wharf for a glimpse of the man who might be her intended.

Amelia sniffed, then looked away, as poised and regal as Megan was wild and untamed. Sometimes Kiera felt like the two of them pulled her so hard in opposite directions that she would be torn asunder.

She didn't know which one she worried about the most—the one who never met a stranger and never backed down from a challenge, or the one who seemed bent on following in the footsteps of their flirtatious half sister, Charlotte.

Kiera sighed. If there was one thing to be grateful for about being shipped half a world away from her beloved home in Ireland, it was putting an ocean between Amelia and Charlotte.

It was terrifying how much of Charlotte's personality Amelia had taken on in the last two years. Kiera had spent many a night in prayer over the impressionable sixteen-year-old's future. Amelia would have stayed in Ireland, but Charlotte's husband hadn't given her a choice. When Father died, God rest his soul, Charlotte's husband had decided to sell the family holdings in Ireland in order to finance his own dealings in London.

Since George was married to the oldest sibling and all their father's property fell to him, it was his right to do with as he saw fit. But that still didn't stop Kiera from pining over the loss of the only home she'd ever known.

Only a few short weeks after George had cheerily announced that he was disposing of her father's legacy, he'd dropped a startling piece of news. He'd arranged an advantageous marriage for her in the colonies. With Charlotte's blessing, they'd agreed it was best that Amelia and Megan travel with Kiera across the ocean to the Natchez District.

Not for the first time, her stomach roiled at the thought of her upcoming marriage to a stranger, and with great effort, she pushed the panic down. She wasn't the first woman to enter into a marriage of convenience with a man she'd never met, and she wouldn't be the last.

She should be thankful George had arranged a marriage for her and allowed her sisters to accompany her to the colonies instead of just throwing them all out in the streets. As a British nobleman, he had no obligation to his wife's half-Irish half sisters.

Everything had happened so fast after that.

Or maybe she'd simply ignored the inevitable during the long ocean voyage from Dublin.

But now they were here, and she couldn't ignore it any longer.

Her gaze panned the wharf, the dockworkers in tattered clothes unloading the ship, the other passengers disembarking, some never pausing on the crowded thoroughfare but walking quickly away toward waiting carriages, greeting friends and relatives. Others, like her, stood at the railing, unsure where they were supposed to go or what they were supposed to do now that they'd arrived.

Each conveyance wove through the crowd and up the steep incline that led to the city spread out on the bluff above the wharf. Even from here, she glimpsed several spacious homes nestled among the trees, the full-length verandas facing the river to catch the summer breezes. Wouldn't it be grand if her intended owned one of those homes with the fancy scrollwork and porches that stretched from end to end? But she wouldn't fret over that. If her husband was a man of God and of sound moral character, she'd call herself blessed.

She searched the wharf once again, frowning as one by one their shipmates went on their way. The noon hour was far gone, and they needed to be settled before nightfall. Why wasn't her intended here to greet her and her sisters?

She spotted the boy, Patrick O'Shea, and his two older brothers threading their way through the crowd, Quinn O'Shea's broad shoulders and forceful march breaking the tide and allowing them ease of passage toward their destination. He left his brothers in charge of a meager pile of baggage and, without hesitation, entered a small building tucked against the base of the cliff.

She read the sign.

James Bloomfield, Esquire. Attorney-at-Law.

Bottom lip pulled between her teeth, she eyed the door that led to the lawyer's office. Making a quick decision, she motioned for two stevedores to carry their trunks to shore and headed toward the gangway. "Girls. Come."

As they stepped foot in a strange land where she knew no one, she squelched another surge of panic. She breathed a prayer as a pair of drunken sailors pushed past, almost pulling Megan out of her grasp. *Be with us, God.*

Even her unknown intended had to be better than the fetid smell of dead fish, unwashed bodies, and debauchery found along the waterfront.

Without bothering to carry their belongings any farther than necessary, the stevedores dumped their trunks at the end of the gangway and rushed away, no doubt in search of strong drink and comfort in one of the rough buildings lining the wharf.

She squared her shoulders. Surely Mr. Bloomfield could give her directions to her destination. She caught Amelia's attention. "Keep an eye on our belongings. I'm going to secure a conveyance."

Amelia huffed. Kiera sighed and bent down to Megan's level. "Stay with your sister. And no matter what, do not run off."

Megan nodded without taking her eyes off the chaos surrounding them. "Yes, ma'am."

Kiera threaded her way along the crowded wharf. She mounted the steps, tossing a quick look toward her sisters. They both sat on one of the trunks, Megan openly watching everything while Amelia pretended not to.

She ducked inside the lawyer's office, hoping to get her questions answered posthaste and be on her way. She pushed the door shut, then turned.

Quinn O'Shea stood next to a balding man wearing eyeglasses. Both men looked up, questioning, but it was Quinn's arched brow that set Kiera's face aflame.

Quinn took in the freshly pressed dress made of something soft and satiny, the pale hair pulled up and away from Kiera's face, the white bonnet trimmed with a blue ribbon that matched her eyes.

"Miss Young."

"Mr. O'Shea."

"Good day, miss." Mr. Bloomfield nodded a greeting, then looked to Quinn for introductions.

"Mr. Bloomfield, meet Kiera Young, a fellow passenger on the *Lady Gallant*."

"Miss Young, it is a pleasure." Mr. Bloomfield motioned toward Quinn. "Do you mind if Mr. O'Shea and I conclude our business? We'll only be a moment."

"Not at all. Please, continue." She moved to stand by the window, giving them some privacy.

Quinn turned back to Mr. Bloomfield. "You were saying?"

Bloomfield smiled. "We've been expecting you and your brothers. As soon as I heard you were on board the *Lady Gallant*, I sent word to Thomas Wainwright—"

"Thomas Wainwright?"

"Yes, the Wainwrights, good friends of your brother and his wife's family, have a home here in Natchez." Bloomfield searched through some papers. "As soon as the runner returns, I'll have him escort you and your brothers there until you head to Breeze Hill."

"Why do we have t' wait?" Quinn scowled. He'd been

cooped up on a ship for almost three months, and he saw no need to sit and wait when he could just as easily go straight to this plantation his brother had married into. "Just point me down the road t' Breeze Hill, and I'll be on my way."

"No, no, you can't go alone. The Natchez Trace is too dangerous. It would be much better if you wait and travel with Wainwright's party."

Quinn tamped down his impatience. "I see."

Someone knocked and Bloomfield called out, "Come in."

A man old enough to be his father entered, followed by the distinguished gentleman who'd asked about Kiera's welfare aboard the *Lady Gallant*. The second man nodded politely in Kiera's direction, then turned toward Quinn. After a brief pause, he inclined his head in recognition.

"Mr. Wainwright. I didn't expect you so soon." Bloomfield sounded pleased. "I haven't long sent a boy to fetch you."

"Poor lad." The man called Wainwright chuckled. "His trip will be wasted. As soon as I spotted the *Lady Gallant*, I came to welcome Mr. Marchette to our fair city." Wainwright motioned to his companion. "My business associate from London, Alistair Marchette."

"Of Marchette Shipping?"

"You've heard of us?"

"Of course, my good man." Bloomfield smiled, then cleared his throat. "Perhaps you could join me for dinner this evening? I have several clients who have need of a reputable shipping company in London."

"That's why I'm here." Marchette spread his hands, returning Bloomfield's smile. "I'm at your disposal, sirs."

"Splendid." Hands behind his back, Bloomfield addressed Wainwright. "Thomas, I'd be pleased if you'd join us."

"I'd be honored."

Bloomfield turned to Quinn. "My apologies, Mr. O'Shea. The prospect of an alliance with Marchette Shipping made me forget my manners. Thomas, meet Connor O'Shea's brother, Quinn O'Shea."

"Mr. O'Shea, it is a pleasure to meet you at last. A pleasure indeed." Wainwright shook his hand. "My son is a friend of your brother. Actually, my daughter-in-law and your brother's wife are sisters-in-law."

Quinn's confusion must have shown on his face because Wainwright laughed and clapped him on the back. "It's complicated. You'll get the gist of it by and by. I promised Connor I'd be on the lookout for your ship and would arrange transportation to Breeze Hill."

"Transportation, sir?"

"Yes, it's a day's journey to the plantation."

"I see."

"Mr. O'Shea, if you'll just sign these papers, you can be on your way." Mr. Bloomfield handed him a sheaf of papers and stepped back. "Excuse me, sirs, while I attend to Miss Young."

Quinn made his mark where indicated, then turned to the next page. When he was done, he set the papers aside.

"I trust your passage was uneventful?" Wainwright asked.

"It was—"

"The Blue Heron? Are you quite sure, miss?"

Quinn turned at Bloomfield's distraught tone.

"Yes, sir." Kiera Young glanced toward him, then turned her attention back to Mr. Bloomfield. "Is that a problem?"

"Well, miss, the Blue Heron isn't exactly the place for a lady, if you'll pardon my saying so. And you have two younger sisters, you say? I'm afraid—"

"Mr. Bloomfield, my brother-in-law sent me to Natchez with the understanding that I'm to be married. The address given was the Blue Heron." She gave the solicitor the same look she'd given Quinn on board the *Lady Gallant*. "Might someone please secure a carriage for us?"

"Yes, but . . ." Bloomfield glanced around helplessly.

"Is there a problem, Miss Young?" Marchette interrupted, coming to her aid once again.

"No thank you, Mr. Marchette." Kiera's face bloomed with color. "A misunderstanding, perhaps."

The lawyer pulled out a handkerchief and mopped his forehead. "Miss Young, you seem to be acquainted with Mr. Marchette and Mr. O'Shea. May I introduce one of our leading citizens, Thomas Wainwright?"

"My pleasure, miss." Wainwright dipped his head. "Welcome to Natchez."

"Thank you, sir."

"Miss Young, if you would permit me, Mr. Bloomfield is right to be concerned over your welfare. The Blue Heron is not the type of establishment a young lady should rendezvous with her intended." Wainwright's smile was filled with fatherly concern. "Perhaps you're mistaken—"

"There's no mistake, sir. My brother-in-law made the arrangements, and—"

The door flung open and Patrick barreled inside. "Quinn. Hurry. That man's taking Megan and Amelia."

"Taking them? Where?" Kiera lifted her skirts and rushed toward the door.

Quinn hurried after her, pausing briefly on the porch to search the wharf for Kiera's sisters. In spite of the lengthening shadows, Natchez Under-the-Hill still crawled with humanity. There. At the end of the gangway. His own brother Rory was wielding a broken board, the two girls cowering behind him. A hulking brute of a man with a wicked-looking knife advanced on Rory, the sixteen-year-old no match for the giant.

"Megan! Amelia!" Kiera ran across the wharf, skirts flying.

Quinn sprinted after her, grabbed her arm, and pushed her behind him. "Get out o' the way, lass." Palming a knife, Quinn shoved his way between Rory and the brute, his left hand held palm out. "Wait. What's the meaning o' this, man?"

"Get out of the way, *monsieur*. This is none of your affair."

Quinn crouched, knife at the ready. Looked like he and Rory were in for it, and he didn't even know what had caused the ruckus. Rough men, silent and watchful, gathered round. Women in rags and children with dirty faces jostled for position. No one offered to help or to stop this.

"Quinn, he—"

"Hush, lad," Quinn growled at Rory to keep quiet. The man-mountain circling him wasn't in the mood to talk about whatever had set him off. And from the scars crisscrossing his face, he'd been in enough fights to bury Quinn ten times over.

Dear Lord in heaven, protect me this day. Don't let me have come all this way t' spill me guts on me first day in the New World.

"Claude. Enough." A voice with a heavy French accent cut through the tension. The crowd parted, and a well-dressed man inserted himself between Quinn and the brute with the knife. He turned, his emotionless black eyes boring a hole through Quinn. His craggy face would have been unremarkable, and might have even been considered handsome at one time, but a long, jagged scar ran from his temple to his jawline. His thin lips curved into a sardonic half smile. "My associate is correct. This is none of your affair."

Quinn didn't take his eyes off the Frenchman or the thug with the knife.

"He said Amelia belonged to him, that he was going to take her to a tavern and force her to—" Rory's voice broke over the horror of what he'd heard—"to . . ."

"It is true. These *filles* are my charges." The Frenchman stepped forward. "The captain of the *Lady Gallant* has accepted payment for their passage. My apologies for any confusion my man caused with his limited English. Claude." He snapped his fingers. "Load up their belongings and let us be on our way."

"*Oui*, Monsieur Le Bonne."

"No." Rory swung, and in one quick move, Claude caught

the board, wrested it from Rory's hands, and had the knife at his throat before Quinn could stop him. Wide-eyed, Rory stared at him.

Quinn crouched again, his attention jerking from the thug to the well-dressed Frenchman, his heart in his throat as his brother's life hung by a slender thread. Slowly, he put down his knife, then held up his hands, palms forward. "The lad meant no harm. Just—just let him go."

The Frenchman lifted his hand, and a hush fell over the crowd. Quinn's stomach dropped, and he knew he was looking death in the eyes. One word, one snap of the Frenchman's fingers, and Rory would be dead.

Kiera pushed in front of Quinn before he could stop her. "Monsieur Le Bonne?"

The Frenchman's gaze raked Kiera, like a merchant giving his stamp of approval on goods received. Quinn barely resisted the urge to strike out at him. Only the knife at Rory's throat held him in check.

"Please, have your man put away his knife." She fumbled with the drawstring on her purse. "A letter. Here's a letter from my brother-in-law." She held the letter out, hand trembling. "I'm—I'm to be your wife."

Chapter 2

HIS WIFE?

Not much caught Pierre Le Bonne off guard, but that did.

The idea was laughable, but the three Irish beauties standing before him were willingly giving themselves into his safekeeping.

Oh, the irony.

Did she not know the real reason her brother-in-law had sent her and her sisters to him?

He fingered the letter in his pocket delivered to him by the captain of the very ship that had brought Kiera Young and her sisters to him. He snapped his fingers.

With a wicked flick that drew a spot of blood, Claude

jerked his knife away from the young whelp's throat and gave him a shove. Gasping, the boy stumbled and fell, his hand at his throat. Irish grabbed the boy and pushed him to safety behind him.

Pierre allowed a satisfied smirk to surface. He should have no more trouble out of these poor crackers fresh off the boat from Ireland. Claude and his knife had that effect on people.

He turned his back on them, took Kiera Young's hand, and bowed over it. "*Mademoiselle.* You are as lovely as your brother-in-law said you were. Welcome to Natchez."

"Monsieur Le Bonne." She offered the letter once again. "From my brother-in-law, Lord Manderly of Devonshire."

Pierre remembered the man not with fondness but with the full extent of his ire. The repayment of his debt had been a long time coming. He took the missive, raising an eyebrow as he slit the seal. "You have not read the letter, *mademoiselle*?"

Her porcelain cheeks pinkened, and honey-colored lashes lowered over her azure eyes. "It wasn't my place."

"How commendable." Pierre scanned the letter, reading empty words about how Manderly's wife would miss her sisters, but knowing that Kiera would have an advantageous placement justified the arrangement. Manderly ended the silly little letter with the words that he hoped Kiera and her sisters would be more than happy with Le Bonne, charging him to treat them kindly.

Kindly, indeed.

Interesting that even though Manderly had told the girl

she was to be married, the letter was extremely vague. So vague in fact that marriage wasn't mentioned at all.

Which was as it should be.

He turned his attention to the two girls standing behind her, their coloring close enough that he had no doubt the three were all sisters. He smiled. "And these are your sisters?"

"Yes. Amelia and Megan."

Pierre folded the letter and stuck it in his pocket. He spread his hands, faced the crowd and the two Irishmen who'd defied him. "Now that we've established that these lovely young ladies have been given into my safekeeping by their brother-in-law, are there any objections to us going on our way?"

Silence met his question.

"Very well." Pierre took up the reins of his horse, mounted, then turned to Claude. "Take them to my place. I'll meet you there."

As darkness descended, Quinn watched Le Bonne's henchman hand Kiera and her sisters up into a carriage, then load their trunks and strap them down.

Kiera looked out the window, her gaze meeting his. She smiled, trying to look brave. As the carriage rolled away, he had the sudden urge to run after it, to stop it.

But that was crazy.

She'd come to America to marry the Frenchman, as unsavory as the thought might be.

One lass—no, three—weren't worth relinquishing his dream. As soon as he got the boys to Connor, he would be free. He could go to sea or work his way across the colonies as a blacksmith. Anything other than work underground. He didn't know if they had coal mines—or any other mines—in the Natchez District, but he would never set foot in another one as long as he lived. He'd gone down the shaft at the age of ten, and he'd had enough of being buried alive before the end of the first week. It was just by the grace of God that he'd been picked by the mine boss to apprentice with old Seamus at the smithy three years ago. He'd shown an aptitude for the work and hadn't looked back.

The only wretched thing to come out of his good fortune had been his brother Caleb's jealousy.

"Come on, lads." He led the way to Bloomfield's office. Mr. Wainwright, Mr. Marchette, and Mr. Bloomfield stood on the porch, watching as the carriage disappeared into the fading light.

"I don't like it. Not one little bit." A frown knit Thomas Wainwright's brow. "What do you know of this Pierre Le Bonne, Bloomfield?"

"Le Bonne showed up a few months ago. He purchased the Blue Heron and quickly established himself as boarding master responsible for providing sailors for ships. And let's just say his methods are highly suspect. Unless I'm terribly mistaken, he is not going to marry that girl. He's going to put her and her sisters to work in that brothel, and the poor child hasn't a clue."

Rory stuck his nose in Quinn's face. "I told you—"

"There's nothing we can do." Bloomfield shook his head. "Her brother-in-law sent them to Le Bonne as indentured servants—or wards, I suppose. It's a legal matter between the two of them."

"Legal? Bah!" Marchette's face showed his disgust. "If you're correct, there's nothing legal about what this Le Bonne has planned for those girls."

"We have no proof—"

Quinn glared at the lawyer. "I need t' see for myself. Where is this tavern—brothel—whatever it is?"

"I'll take you there." Wainwright nodded. "Maybe we're all wrong, and Le Bonne isn't as terrible as I've heard."

"Do you mind if I accompany you?" Mr. Marchette tugged on his gloves. "I grew quite fond of those girls on the voyage over. They remind me of my own daughters back in England. I'd hate for misfortune to befall them."

"Of course." Wainwright turned to Mr. Bloomfield. "Would you be so kind as to take the younger boys to Wainwright House? Tell Mrs. Butler I'll be along shortly."

"I'll be more than happy to." The lawyer cast a glance over the darkening streets. "It's time I closed up shop before the rowdies come out."

Rory's chin jutted out. "I'm goin' with you, Quinn."

"Me, too." Determination laced Patrick's young voice. "Megan's my friend."

"No, Patrick. Ye'll go with Mr. Bloomfield."

"But—"

"I do no' have time t' argue, lad. Not if I'm going to make sure Megan and her sisters are all right." Quinn put a hand on the boy's shoulder. "Just do as I say."

Patrick dropped his head. "All right."

"Kiera, I'm scared." Amelia's voice trembled.

"I know." Kiera held her sisters close as the carriage rumbled along the wharf. Twilight had fallen, and the scene outside the vehicle turned her stomach. Row after row of squalid inns, taverns, and brothels flashed past the conveyance. She hoped and prayed they left this seedy part of town soon.

"I don't like that man." Megan wrapped her arms around Kiera, her hands like ice.

"It's going to be all right. Monsieur Le Bonne was just . . ." Kiera swallowed, remembering the craggy, scarred face of her intended. She reached for a lap quilt on the opposite seat and wrapped the dark fur around her sister, rubbing the warm softness against her sister's chilled skin. "He was just protecting us."

"But we didn't need protection from Patrick and Rory."

"He—he didn't know that, now did he? I'll be married shortly and all will be well."

"You're going to marry him?" Amelia's voice was filled with horror.

Kiera sighed. "I don't have a choice, sweetheart. George arranged it."

Monsieur Le Bonne—Pierre—wasn't what she'd envisioned as her future husband, but maybe the events on the wharf had colored her impression of him. After all, perhaps he truly had been trying to protect them. Even Quinn O'Shea and young Rory had come across as fearsome and willing to shed blood over the incident. Men and their misunderstandings. They tended to act before they asked.

Regardless, her stomach roiled again at the thought of marriage to a man she didn't even know. Mayhap the wedding could wait, and she could get to know her intended a little better, before—

The carriage came to a halt, and Kiera's heart sank. Her prayers that they'd leave the wretched wharf far behind before reaching their destination had gone unheeded.

The door to the carriage opened. Quelling the sudden urge to shrink into the dark corner and cover her head with the lap quilt, she allowed the same hulking man who'd held a knife at Rory's throat to assist her from the carriage. While the two-story building in front of them was somewhat set apart from the others, it was just as dark and dreary as every other building she'd seen so far.

Amelia and Megan alighted, staying close to her.

The giant of a man motioned them forward. "This way."

Kiera wanted to take both her sisters and bolt into the night, but there was nowhere to go. She feared she'd made a terrible mistake in agreeing to go with Le Bonne, but what could she do? She'd been afraid for Rory's life. The boy had simply wanted to protect them. Surely . . .

Their escort opened the door, then moved out of the way to allow them to precede him. Gingerly, Kiera stepped inside, her sisters on her heels. Claude slammed the door behind them, his bulk blocking the exit.

The three of them huddled together, staring at the rough interior of the establishment. One glance and Kiera knew she wasn't in anyone's home. Far from it. She'd never been in a tavern or a bordello or anything of the sort, but she knew.

The hour was young, and there were few patrons, but the men who stared at them from the tables scattered around the room made her skin crawl. Kiera blushed at the sight of a scantily clad woman seated on a man's lap in the far corner. She shifted, blocking Megan's view of the lewd display.

"Up the stairs," the giant's voice rumbled, and Kiera went willingly, pulling Megan along behind her. Anything to get her sisters out of here.

At the top of the stairs, he opened a door, moved aside, and they entered. Pierre Le Bonne sat behind a desk, a cigar in one hand and a smile pulling at his thin lips. A smile that didn't quite reach his black eyes.

"*Mademoiselles.* Welcome to the Blue Heron."

Megan and Amelia crowded closer. Kiera had to do something. And soon. "Monsieur Le Bonne. May I have a word with you?" She glanced pointedly at Megan. "In private, if you please?"

"Of course." He waved the cigar. "Claude, please show . . . *Pardon*, Mademoiselle Kiera, I do not recall your sisters' names."

"This is Amelia. And Megan."

Both girls bobbed a curtsy.

Le Bonne chuckled as if amused by their show of manners. "Claude, please show Mademoiselles Amelia and Megan to their room and have their trunks brought in."

"That won't be necessary." Kiera lifted her chin. "We can't possibly live in a tavern."

He stood, rounded the desk, and approached her, his eyes glittering with something that sent a cold chill down her spine. "Of course you can."

Faster than a striking adder, he took her by the arm and yanked her toward him. Amelia screamed and Megan grabbed for her.

Kiera clawed at Le Bonne, but he turned her around and held her fast, his forearm cutting off her oxygen. She gasped for air, her sisters' horrified faces swimming before her eyes.

Claude grabbed her sisters, and Le Bonne jerked his head toward the stairs. "Take them to their room and lock them in."

"Please. No." Terror filled her as the man hauled Amelia and Megan away.

"Kiera!" Megan screamed as she fought against his hold.

Kiera whimpered as the door clicked shut behind her sisters. Le Bonne pushed her into a chair, and Kiera was thankful for the support. She doubted she could stand on her own.

"Let us get something straight." He plucked her letter out of his pocket and held it over a candle. The paper went up in flames. "While I was greatly amused to find that you traveled all this way to become my bride, I must inform you that the truth is not quite as—shall we say—romantic?"

He pulled out another letter. "Now, this letter tells us the truth about why you're here."

He held it out, but Kiera didn't take it. Instead, she curled into a ball in the chair, watching him with wary eyes.

He smirked. "Do you not want to know the real reason your dear brother-in-law sent you and your pretty little sisters to the colonies?"

In a daze, Kiera shook her head.

"Take it." He barked out the order, and she jumped. With trembling fingers, she took the letter.

She read, shock rendering her speechless. Her brother-in-law had sold her and her sisters in order to settle a debt. She wasn't meant to be a bride, but a . . . a prostitute.

Panic threatened to choke the very life out of her. She had to get out of here. She had to find her sisters. They had to get out of this place.

"Please, just let us go," she whispered.

"Let you go?" He laughed. "*Ma chère*, that is simply not possible. The three of you are worth a lot of money to me."

"The three of us?" Kiera died just a little inside. "Meg—Megan's just a child."

"True. But it's of no consequence." By the look on his face, the way his eyes showed no emotion, she knew he meant it. He would have no compassion on her, nor on Amelia or Megan.

She fought the tug of a dark abyss that threatened to pull her under. What had her half sister and brother-in-law done to them?

"Please. I'll do anything. But—" her voice broke on a whisper—"not my sisters. Not Megan. I beg of you."

His lips curled into a satisfied smile. "I thought you'd see things my way, *mademoiselle*."

Chapter 3

QUINN WAS NO STRANGER TO A TAVERN, but this place turned even his stomach. Rory stared, eyes round, jaw slack. He should have made the boy go with Bloomfield, but he hadn't expected Wainwright to lead them to such a squalid establishment.

Surely Le Bonne hadn't brought Kiera and her sisters to this place?

Scantily clad women worked the room and ale flowed freely. He spotted more than one sailor who'd been aboard the *Lady Gallant.* As soon as they'd drawn their pay, they'd come ashore and started spending their coin on strong drink and women.

"Rory, lad, wait outside." Quinn's tone brooked no argument, and his brother bolted for the door.

Quinn spotted Le Bonne on the other side of the room. Nudging Wainwright, he jerked his head toward the tavern owner. "I'm going to find out where they are."

But before he made it to Le Bonne's side, the tavern owner pulled out a pistol, aimed it at the ceiling, and pulled the trigger. The din in the room ceased immediately.

"*Messieurs!*" Le Bonne called out. "I have a special surprise for you tonight."

He snapped his fingers, and the brute named Claude appeared on the balcony above, clutching Kiera's arm. White-hot anger shot through Quinn. The composed young woman he'd left at the docks was gone, and sheer terror was stamped on her features.

Where were her sisters? His gaze swept the balcony that ran along the left side of the tavern. Were they up there somewhere?

Catcalls broke the silence as Le Bonne's associate forced Kiera down the stairs. She stumbled on the last step. Claude jerked her up like a rag doll. Quinn's gut clenched at her whimper.

"On the block. Put her on the block so we can see her."

Men started pounding tin cups against tables, and over the din he heard them call out, again and again until his ears rang with the bile-inducing demand, "The block! The block! The block!"

Kiera screamed when Claude spanned her waist and lifted her to a platform two feet off the rough-hewn floor.

Quinn pushed forward, but a hand clamped like a vise on his wrist.

"Not now, you fool," Wainwright hissed, his voice of reason penetrating Quinn's hot-blooded zeal.

Le Bonne jumped up on the block, leaned down, and said something to Kiera. Just as quickly as she'd shown fear, she clamped her trembling lips together and stared straight ahead, on display in front of men who were no better than animals. It was all Quinn could do not to charge forward when twin tracks of tears rolled down her cheeks, but she stood like a statue, not moving, not screaming, not reacting.

He wanted to hit someone, anyone, and he didn't care what Mr. Wainwright thought. He plowed against the beasts in front of him, his only thought to get to Kiera before Le Bonne carried out whatever torrid scheme he had in mind. Wainwright shoved in front of him. "If you want to live out this night, and you want that girl to do likewise, you'll do as I say," he muttered, eyes glittering. Marchette stood shoulder to shoulder with Wainwright, the two men blocking his view of the scene across the room.

Chest heaving, Quinn gave a short, quick nod.

Motioning toward Kiera, Marchette whispered frantically in Wainwright's ear. The man nodded, and Quinn saw the flash of coin as it changed hands. Marchette began working his way toward the front of the crowd.

Blood pounding through his veins, Quinn focused again on Kiera, his heart torn to shreds at her eerie silence, at her acceptance of what was about to happen. Then it dawned on him. She'd sacrificed herself for her sisters. But he was under no illusions. It was only a matter of time before Le Bonne decided to use the two younger girls in the same manner. The thought was too repulsive for words.

Dear God in heaven, stop this madness.

"How much, Le Bonne?" someone yelled out.

"All in good time, *monsieur*." Le Bonne grinned, his complexion dark and sinister in the dim light.

"It's as I figured," Wainwright spoke quietly. "He's going to sell her to the highest bidder. Marchette plans to be that man. As soon as the deed is done and we see where they take her, we'll go around back. Pray that Le Bonne doesn't have bars on the windows."

"Give me the coin." Quinn growled through gritted teeth, hand on the hilt of his knife. If he could get close to that platform, close to Claude and Le Bonne . . . "I'll do it."

"No. Le Bonne saw you. Marchette is the logical choice."

Le Bonne grabbed Kiera's hair and jerked her head up. Quinn's hands curled into fists. "*Mademoiselle* is fresh off the boat."

"French, is she?"

"Unfortunately, no. But she's still a lovely Irish rose, is she not?"

"Irish, you say?" Disgust filled the voice. "Bah, I don't want no Irish gel."

Le Bonne shrugged. "I'm sure everyone doesn't feel that way, *monsieur*."

"Show us the merchandise, Le Bonne."

A hungry hush fell over the room, and the tavern owner eyed the crowd, his aloof silence designed to heighten the tension—and the final offer for the first time with Kiera. Le Bonne snapped his fingers, and Claude moved toward the dais. Men stood, surged forward, crowding around, their lust and base intentions sickeningly evident. The henchman reached for Kiera's bodice. She gasped, eyes going round as she jerked away. "No. Please no."

The clank of coins on the dais rang loud in the silence. "No need in exposing the girl to those who can't—or won't—pay for the privilege."

Marchette.

Le Bonne glanced at the coins, then at Marchette's tall, imposing bearing. Quinn held his breath. Le Bonne smiled, if one could call it that. "Gentlemen?"

When no one else topped the offer, he nodded. "She is yours, *monsieur*. For the night."

Le Bonne's henchman jerked Kiera off the platform and pushed her toward the stairs. She stumbled again but regained her footing. Marchette followed, looking neither to the left nor the right. Their fun at an end, the crowd returned to their drinks and their slow descent into debauchery, but Quinn stood in the shadows, watching as Kiera was led up the stairs and along the balcony.

Someone tapped him on the shoulder, and he turned. Wainwright clasped him by the shirtfront, grimaced. "Sorry to do this, but—"

Then he drew back and slammed a fist into Quinn's face.

Kiera huddled in the corner of the room, trying to make herself as small as possible. The broad-shouldered man stood at the door, his back to her.

Swallowing the bile that rose in her throat, she uttered a silent prayer. *Please, Lord Jesus. Please . . .*

She heard him advance one step toward her, then another, and her prayers turned to audible pleas forced through cold, nerveless lips. "Please, sir, have mercy."

He stopped. "Miss Young, you have nothing to fear. It is Alistair Marchette. We met on the *Lady Gallant* and again this afternoon at Mr. Bloomfield's. Remember?"

"Mr.—Mr. Marchette?" She sobbed out his name and took a good look at the man, feeling weak with relief. In her distress, she hadn't paid any attention to who'd thrown the coins on the dais. And in her state of shock, it was doubtful she would have recognized him regardless. "How? Why?"

"Never mind that. We don't have much time." He glanced around the room, spotted her trunks. "Yours?"

"Yes."

Grabbing a pillowcase, he tossed it at her. "Stuff as many of your belongings as you can in this. And hurry."

The sound of shouts and splintering wood reached her from below. She scrambled to do as he said. "What's going on?"

"Wainwright and O'Shea are creating a diversion." He moved to the door, hand on the latch. "Ready?"

"Yes. My sisters?"

"Where are they?"

"I—" Everything was a blur. She closed her eyes. "Down the hall. Corner room."

"Good girl. Stay close to the wall and out of sight from below."

He cracked open the door and, crouching, ran along the balcony toward the back of the tavern. Kiera followed. When they reached the corner room, she collapsed against the wall, heart pounding. A rope held the latch securely in place, and Mr. Marchette fumbled with it, trying to undo the knot.

He jerked his head toward the rear stairs. "We'll go that way. Understand?"

"Yes." Her voice trembled.

From below, the brawl escalated, and she could see a bit of the far corner of the room. A chair splintered as one man brought it down on top of another's head. Men slugged each other; women screamed. The door swung open, and she scrambled into the room. Megan and Amelia fell on her, sobbing. But there was no time to comfort them.

"The stairs. Hurry." Mr. Marchette shoved her out the door, pushing her sisters along with her. As they reached the stairs, she glanced back, saw Le Bonne and Claude rushing at them from the other end of the hallway.

A shot rang out and she screamed. Crimson bloomed on Mr. Marchette's shoulder. He drew his pistol and urged her down the stairs. "Go. I'll hold them off until you can get away."

Kiera did as she was told, wrenching open the door to

blessed freedom. She burst outside and fell headlong against a hard chest.

"I've got ya, lass."

Nothing had ever sounded as good as Quinn's Irish brogue.

"Where's Marchette?" Mr. Wainwright shoved Amelia and Megan toward Rory.

"Inside. He's been shot—"

Mr. Marchette stumbled out the door, slammed it behind him.

"Quinn, Rory, get them to the carriage and wait for us there." Mr. Wainwright whipped out his pistol as Mr. Marchette fumbled to reload.

"But—"

"Do as I say, man. We'll be right behind you."

Quinn lifted Megan in his arms and took off at a near run. Kiera grabbed Amelia's hand and followed, Rory bringing up the rear. Quinn led them down an alley, then another. Soon, an enclosed carriage appeared, a wide-eyed youngster holding the horses. Quinn jerked open the door. "Get in before someone sees you."

"But what about Mr. Marchette and Mr. Wainwright?"

"They're behind us—" He broke off as Mr. Wainwright appeared out of the darkness.

"Get in. We must go. Hurry, Jack."

Quick as a wink, the stable lad jumped to the driver's seat and had the horses in motion almost before Mr. Wainwright was seated.

Kiera found herself squished between Quinn and Megan. Mr. Wainwright, Amelia, and Rory sat facing them.

"Mr. Marchette?" Her voice warbled.

"We became separated. Pray that he finds his way to safety until I can return for him."

Hours later, at the Wainwright home high on a bluff overlooking the Mississippi, Kiera felt anything but safe and secure.

A log fell in the fireplace, and she jumped, her gaze automatically jerking to where Megan snuggled next to Amelia, both finally sleeping. They'd both refused to leave Kiera's side, even when Patrick had allowed Mr. Wainwright's housekeeper to lead him off to bed.

When her sisters didn't stir, she turned back to the window. What was taking them so long? Quinn, Rory, and Mr. Wainwright had left hours ago to search for Mr. Marchette. Surely . . .

Her heart pounded. With each passing hour, her worry increased. In the background, she could hear Mr. Wainwright's housekeeper turning the pages of the family Bible, alternating between reading and praying softly. But not so softly that Kiera hadn't heard her pleas and the Scriptures she read from the Psalms.

"Deliver me, O my God, out of the hand of the wicked, out of the hand of the unrighteous and cruel man."

Kiera wrapped her arms around her waist as an image of Pierre Le Bonne flashed through her mind. If anyone was unrighteous and cruel, it was he. She shuddered, thankful she and her sisters had been delivered out of such an evil man's hands. But at what cost? At the cost of the lives of the men who'd rescued them?

Please, Lord, no.

Tears sprang to her eyes as she battled with the desire to fall down on her knees and thank God for His mercy, for His deliverance, while all the time, her mind screamed, *Why?* She'd faced tempests before—the death of her mother and the child who would have been her father's heir. But she'd persevered, holding on to Father and her sisters for comfort, and yes, to God, who was her strong habitation.

But then her father had died a scant two years past, and her life had unraveled from that point forward. She should have realized that Charlotte and George would sell the family holdings in Ireland, uprooting them from the only home they'd ever known. She'd hoped that her half sister and her brother-in-law would stay in London and forget about the small plot of land in Ireland and the stepsisters who resided there.

The truth of what her brother-in-law had done was shocking beyond comprehension. In her worst nightmares, she'd never imagined that anyone could be so cruel as to do what her own kinsman had done. Yet George's brand of cruelty was but a drop in the bucket to what Pierre Le Bonne intended.

Mrs. Butler patted the settee next to her. "Come, child, sit here by me. Worrying over the men will do no good. They will return in good time."

Ashamed that she'd been wallowing in her own fears and

regrets while Quinn and the others searched the streets, Kiera left her vigil by the windows and sat on the edge of the settee, too keyed up to relax.

She twisted her fingers in her lap, her attention straying to the windows yet again. "How can you be so sure?"

A faint smile graced the housekeeper's aged face. "Faith. And trust in God. That is what sustains us in times of trouble."

Mrs. Butler froze when the whinny of a horse reached them. Standing, Kiera rushed outside, toward the stables, the portly housekeeper close behind. Hope sank as the men dismounted and she realized Mr. Marchette wasn't with them.

"You—you didn't find him?"

Quinn shook his head, and fear shot through Kiera.

What had happened to the man—hardly more than a stranger—who'd risked his life to save hers?

Chapter 4

RORY AND PATRICK LAY SPRAWLED ON THE BED, sounding like the bellows from the smithy back in Kilkenny.

Quinn had opted for the hardwood floor, nothing he wasn't already used to. And besides, Mr. Wainwright's housekeeper had provided so many thick quilts that he felt like he was lying on the finest feather bed.

And still he couldn't sleep.

Worry over the fate of Mr. Marchette as well as what would happen to Kiera and her sisters played tug-of-war with his thoughts. But Mr. Marchette was smart. He'd probably holed up somewhere safe until morning, when he could get word to Wainwright that all was well.

Mr. Wainwright and Mr. Marchette, both men of means, would see that Kiera and her sisters were taken care of. One less worry before Quinn could move on with his own plans.

Plans that had been delayed yet again.

He'd intended to depart on the next ship out of Natchez, but he hadn't known the plantation was a day's ride into the wilderness. He'd have to deliver the boys to Connor and face his eldest brother even though that was the last thing he wanted to do.

Clenching his jaw, he rolled onto his side and bunched the pillow up under his head. He'd go to Breeze Hill. He'd face Connor and make sure his brothers were settled; then he'd shake the dust of Natchez and the memories of Ireland off his feet.

He drifted off, only to be jerked awake moments later by a frantic pounding on the bedroom door. He threw back the covers just as the door flung open, slamming against the wall. Wainwright stood there, faint light from a single candle casting eerie shadows over his face.

"Marchette is dead."

Rory sat up, glancing from one to the other. Quinn swept the cobwebs from his brain. "How—?"

"His battered body was found in the river. A trusted confidant sent word."

A knot of alarm balled in Quinn's stomach, and he glanced at Patrick. The boy was still asleep. Not even the slamming door or Wainwright's distressing news had disturbed his little brother. He stood, motioned Wainwright to the hall. Rory joined them, and Quinn pulled the door shut. No need in Patrick waking and hearing the worst.

"Do you think Le Bonne killed him?" Quinn kept his voice low.

"I can only assume Le Bonne and his henchmen are the culprits. The question remains whether Le Bonne knows where the girls are. We can't risk him getting his hands on them."

"What are you suggesting?"

"I'm sending you—all of you—to Breeze Hill tonight. Now. Jack knows the way and can lead you there. It's dangerous, but it'll give you a head start."

"What about you and Mr. Bloomfield?"

"If Le Bonne shows up here, I'll plead ignorance. Bloomfield knows nothing other than that we went to the tavern. He's worked under the hill long enough to keep his mouth shut." Wainwright pinched the bridge of his nose. "With Miss Young and her sisters safely out of the way, I'll try to find out if Le Bonne has any real claim to them. If so, I'll talk to Connor. Maybe he could buy their papers from him."

"They do no' have any papers. Kiera didna sign anything saying she wanted t' be indentured t' Le Bonne." Quinn scowled. "Maybe we should stay and fight. Running isna going t' do any good."

"The only way we'd win in a fight would be to kill Le Bonne outright. And even then, I'm not sure we'd win if anyone contested our claims. I need time, and the only way to get that is to get those girls out of Natchez. The sooner the better."

Mr. Marchette was dead?

Even now, after hours on the trace, Kiera could hardly believe it. If she'd had any doubts about Pierre Le Bonne's cruel and barbaric nature, the news of Mr. Marchette's demise had banished them.

A man had died to save her and her sisters, and she would never forget his sacrifice.

Shivering, and not just from the chill of darkness, she pulled her borrowed cloak tighter, thankful for Mrs. Butler's generosity.

Fear and worry wormed their way through her thoughts again. *Lord, keep Mrs. Butler and Mr. Wainwright from harm.* If Le Bonne knew they'd played a role in helping her escape, he might do to them what he'd done to Mr. Marchette. Kiera didn't know if she could stand to have more deaths on her conscience.

Hour after hour, Jack led them farther into the wilderness. Because of the distance and urgency, Mr. Wainwright had insisted they travel by horseback instead of his carriage. As dawn neared, the stable boy pulled off the main road, looking frightened.

"Mount Locust is just up ahead. We'll skirt around, being extra quiet. Master Wainwright said it was better not to let anyone know we came this way."

"How far is it to Breeze Hill?" Quinn asked.

"About two hours."

Amelia groaned, and Kiera felt like groaning with her. None of them had ridden in months. She gripped the reins and held on to the saddle horn. She'd do what had to be done to protect her sisters.

"Jack, a wee break t' stretch our legs might be a good idea, don't ya think?" Quinn's attention swung from the stable boy to her, then to her sisters and his younger brothers.

Jack shook his head. "Master Wainwright said to press on until we got to Breeze Hill. It's too dangerous to stop at Mount Locust. No telling who might be stayin' the night there. They're liable to chase us down and murder—"

"It's all right. We can manage for another two hours." Kiera threw a glance in the direction they'd come, every shadow just as frightening as when they'd first set out, hours before. What if Le Bonne and Claude were behind them at this very instant? She shivered, then urged her mare forward. "Lead the way."

Quinn nodded at Jack. "Let's go, then. Everybody keep quiet."

They rode single file, keeping to the shadows. On a hill to her left, through the trees, Kiera spotted a dogtrot cabin silhouetted against the skyline. She could see several out-buildings, as well as a group of wagons clustered underneath the trees just down the hill from the cabin. Most likely travelers who'd overnighted at the inn. She let the others pass until the only one behind her was Quinn.

As they drew adjacent to the inn, a dog started barking and was soon joined by others. As the dogs raced down the hill toward the road, Jack spurred his horse, and they galloped away, leaving Mount Locust far behind. They'd gone a good mile or more before Jack slacked his pace.

Heart thudding against her rib cage, Kiera rode close to Quinn. "Jack seems truly frightened of the travelers at Mount Locust."

"He has reason t' be scared out o' his wits."

Kiera swallowed. "Because of Le Bonne?"

"Not just Le Bonne." He turned in the saddle, searching the road behind him. The saddle creaked when he faced forward again. "I heard the men talking on the ship. Merchants and plantation owners from up north float their goods down the Mississippi, sell everything, then walk back up the trace toward home. Outlaws lie in wait, ready to kill them for a bit o' coin."

Kiera eyed the shadows. Had she landed her sisters in a more dangerous situation than before? "Maybe we would have been better off staying in Natchez."

"With Le Bonne?" The rising sun peeked over the horizon, bathing the land in a pink glow.

"No, of course not. But . . ." She spoke softly, not wanting her voice to carry. "But what do you know of this Breeze Hill? What do you know of the people who live there?"

"I know me brother is married t' the owner's daughter."

"Your—" she cleared her throat—"brother?"

He arched a brow, his blue eyes boring into hers. "You sound surprised."

"I . . ." She paused. The news *had* surprised her, and it

shouldn't have. She didn't know enough about Quinn O'Shea and his brother to make a judgment about them. And this land was the land of opportunity, where a man could become anybody he wanted to. "I'm sorry. I didn't mean to offend."

"No offense taken. My brother's been in the colonies for nigh on nine years. As a matter of fact, Connor was indentured t' the master of Breeze Hill, then ended up marrying his daughter. And he helped save the governor's intended. In appreciation, the governor paid for our passage." He chuckled. "Under other circumstances, my journey t' the colonies would have ended with a seven-year indenture, if it had started at all."

"Like mine."

He reached out and grabbed her horse's reins, pulling her mount to a stop beside his. His gaze searched hers. "There are no circumstances that should have put you and your sisters in the position you were in this past night."

Tears pricked her eyes, and she nodded, the horrific experience too raw to speak of it.

Scarcely two hours later, Quinn took in the wide, sweeping expanse of the plantation home that was the centerpiece of Breeze Hill.

Situated on a hill, surrounded by a grove of moss-draped cedars, the white house with black shutters boasted a long porch from one end to the other. A more compact second story with a breezy balcony sat centered atop the main floor, a spindled widow's walk running the entire length of the house.

Fallow fields stretched to the left beyond a grove of trees. To the right, the hill sloped gently downward toward a well. Various outbuildings—a barn, a row of cabins, a corncrib, a smokehouse, a smithy—dotted the landscape underneath shady oaks and tall pines. And beyond the buildings, a tree-shaded lane led toward more fields, more outbuildings.

While not as impressive as the Wainwrights' home in Natchez or some of the homes he'd spotted before boarding the *Lady Gallant* in Dublin, it was still beyond anything he ever hoped to call his own.

Just the idea of his brother dwelling in such luxury when they'd fought for survival in a hovel in County Kilkenny made his blood boil.

Patrick rode up beside him. "Would ya look at that, Quinn? Ain't it grand? Are we going t' live there?"

Glancing at his little brother's openmouthed astonishment, Quinn took a deep breath, then let it out slowly, like the air escaping from a deflated bellows. "I reckon so, Patrick. Would ya like that?"

Patrick grinned. "You bet I would."

Quinn shifted, pointed toward the cabins scattered among the trees. "Mayhap ye'll be required t' live in one o' those. After all, ye're the poor relation come from Ireland."

Patrick scowled. "Connor wouldna do that t' us. We're his brothers."

Quinn turned away, his attention captured by a dark-haired woman and an older man standing on the front porch. He prayed Patrick was right, and Connor wouldn't do that to them. He'd put aside his feelings toward Connor and do what was right by Rory and Patrick. The boys deserved a better life than what he'd been able to provide back home in Ireland. If Connor and his wife's family could provide that life after he was gone, who was he to complain?

They stopped at the porch, and the young woman helped the older man down the steps. In the face of their clean, pressed clothes, he felt dirty, rumpled, and as poor as he really was. But it was of no consequence. If this was Connor's wife, she'd have to accept the poor relations from Ireland or send them packing. For Patrick and Rory's sake, he hoped she was kind.

The older gentleman lifted his head and Quinn sucked in a breath. His face was puckered and scarred, pink and white and pulled to one side. Quinn had seen men who'd escaped mine fires with scars that looked like this.

Kiera's gaze jerked to his, her eyes wide. He gave her a reassuring smile.

"Jack, is that you?" The scarred man lumbered down the steps, his gait uneven. The young woman held his arm.

"Yes, sir."

"Welcome, son. Where are you traveling to this fine day?" His gaze ran over the party, resting on Quinn, then continuing to encompass all of them.

Jack dismounted, and Quinn followed suit, then lifted Kiera to the ground. When he turned, Rory had already helped Amelia dismount, but Megan jumped off her horse in a flurry of skirts. Losing her balance, she landed in a flounce of petticoats.

Patrick cackled, and she leapt up, dusted off her clothes, and glared at him. "Patrick O'Shea—"

"O'Shea? Are you—? You're Connor's brothers." The dark-haired beauty pressed a hand to her bodice. She looked first at Quinn, then at Rory, before settling on Patrick. "You're Patrick. I can see Connor in your eyes."

Patrick tilted his head, a quizzical look on his face. "I look like Connor?"

"Very much. He's going to be so excited to see you." She stepped forward, smiled at Quinn. "I'm Isabella Bartholomew O'Shea, Connor's wife and your sister-in-law. Welcome to Breeze Hill."

"Madam."

A tinkling laugh escaped. "None of that, now. We're family. Please, I'm Isabella, and this is my father, Matthew Bartholomew." She looked around, a frown marring her smooth forehead. "There's supposed to be four—"

"Quinn?"

Quinn's heart stuttered in his chest. He closed his eyes. He hadn't heard that voice in nine years. He turned and saw his brother standing at the far end of the porch, his shirt sweat-stained, his exposed forearms and breeches covered in sawdust.

Rory and Patrick moved to stand close to Quinn, and they waited together as Connor walked toward them. Twenty feet, then ten, close enough Quinn could see the muscle jumping in his clenched jaw.

Quinn lifted his chin. If Connor wasn't pleased to see them, he should never have allowed the governor to pay for their passage.

At five feet, Quinn could see the tears in Connor's eyes and realized the scowl on his brother's face wasn't from displeasure, but from an effort to keep his emotions in check. Connor closed the last few feet and grabbed Quinn in a bear hug. Awkwardly Quinn put his arms around his brother. Seeming to come to himself, Connor stepped back.

"You're here. You're finally here." He took a deep breath, blinked, before turning toward Rory. "Rory?"

Rory nodded. "Yes, sir."

Connor chuckled and reached out his hand. When Rory took it, he pulled him close and wrapped one arm around his neck, then held him at arm's length. He looked Rory up and down, shaking his head from side to side. "You're the spitting image of *Da*, God rest his soul."

Quinn wanted to tell him that mention of their *da* was sacrilege, especially given the fact that Connor hadn't even been there when the old man had passed over. But he held his peace. Now wasn't the time or the place to remind his brother that they didn't speak of the dead.

Patrick stepped forward, angled his head to squint at Connor. He pointed at Connor's wife. "She said I look like you."

Connor lifted Patrick up high, and the two of them stared

into each other's eyes, green upon green. "What think you, young Master Patrick?"

"Maybe." Patrick shrugged. "But do I have t' call ya Master Connor? That don't seem right. I've never called Quinn or Rory that, and they're me brothers."

Connor threw back his head and laughed. "Connor will do."

He glanced around, saw Kiera and her sisters, but his perusal passed over the Young sisters and returned to Quinn. He let Patrick slide to the ground, the joy and lightness in his face turning to stone. "Where's—where's Caleb?"

"He took off about three years ago." Another sticking point with Quinn. But he shrugged as if Caleb's desertion were of no consequence. "Said he wanted t' see the world."

Connor swallowed, the muscles in his throat contracting as he digested the news. His wife moved to stand beside him, placing a hand on his arm. "Is he—is he dead?"

"We haven't heard from him since."

"I'd hoped . . ." Connor's eyes closed.

After a moment, he opened them, the grief palpable on his face. Quinn almost laughed out loud. Grief? Grief over Caleb seeking his fortune on the high seas when Connor himself had abandoned the family much the same way all those years ago?

The two of them were peas in a pod. Looking out for themselves while Quinn had taken on the role of caretaker for their parents, and later as mother *and* father to the younger boys after their parents had died.

Why all the caring now?

Connor's wife turned to Kiera, smiling. "And who might this be? Your wife, perhaps?"

"No, ma'am. I have yet to take a wife." Quinn choked on a snort of amusement. He stepped back to include Kiera in the circle. "This is Kiera Young and her sisters, Amelia and Megan."

"Pleased to meet you, Mr. and Mrs. O'Shea. Master Bartholomew." Kiera curtsied, every bit the prim and proper young lady she'd been raised to be. Her sisters dipped as well, though Megan's wee bob was more than a bit wobbly.

"Young?" Connor sounded strangled. "Are you related to Charlotte Young by any chance?"

"Charlotte is my half sister."

"I see."

Every drop of warmth and welcome had fled, leaving Connor's clipped words cold as ice.

Chapter 5

Kiera didn't see. She didn't see at all.

But one thing she did see and see quite well was the cold stone mask that settled over Connor O'Shea's face as well as the shock that leached all color out of his wife's face.

Something was terribly wrong, and it had to do with Charlotte. Didn't it always?

Drawing a deep breath, she took the bull by the horns. "Mr. O'Shea. I can see that the news has caught you by surprise. Do you mind telling me why?"

His attention flitted to Megan and Patrick, who were both watching the exchange with great interest. His jaw hardened. "Now is no' the time."

"No time like the present." Kiera kept her voice low. Quinn had said his brother had been in the colonies for nine years. What did he know of Charlotte and her shenanigans?

Mistress O'Shea moved toward the children. "Patrick—and Megan, isn't it? The cook just pulled some bread out of the oven. Would you like some?"

Megan scowled, her attention bouncing from Kiera to Connor. Mimicking her sister's stance, she replied, "I'll be staying right here, but thank ya anyway, mum."

Kiera resisted the urge to tell Megan to speak proper English. There were more pressing matters to deal with than Megan's propensity to let a bit of Irish brogue slip now and then. Without taking her eyes off Connor O'Shea, Kiera ordered, "Go on now. Be a good girl."

"But, Kiera—"

"Do as I say."

Mistress O'Shea held out a hand. Huffing, Megan ignored her and flounced inside. With a worried glance over his shoulder, Patrick followed.

Mr. Bartholomew stepped forward, put a hand on Mr. Wainwright's stable boy's shoulder. "Jack, let's you and I take these horses over to the stables. They could use a good currying, don't you think? And I'd like to hear all the goings-on in Natchez."

"Yes, sir." Jack gathered the horses' reins and they disappeared down the drive toward the stables.

Rory glowered at them all, looking as if wild horses couldn't drag him away.

Amelia moved to stand beside Kiera. Quinn shifted a bit closer to her, the movement so subtle that Kiera almost missed it. Arms crossed, he scowled at his older brother. She didn't get the impression Quinn had sided with her as much as he'd sided against his brother.

Sided against him over what?

"You don't remember me, do you?" Quinn's brother scrutinized her.

Her mouth gaped. "Should I?"

"I suppose not. It was a long time ago." He shrugged. "Ten years past, I was a stable hand at your father's country estate in Ireland. Your favorite pony was Cinnamon."

"How . . . ?" She tilted her head, trying to remember. She hadn't spent much time at the stables, mostly because Charlotte was always there and usually sent her away in tears. But she did remember Cinnamon. After Charlotte married and moved to London, she'd enjoyed the stables and her rides on the pony. "You really were one of our stable hands? And you knew Charlotte? How?"

He sighed. "Do ya really want me t' go into detail, lass? Suffice it to say that when all was said and done, your sister was engaged to be married to the future Lord Manderly, and I was on a ship bound for the colonies as an indentured servant."

Like a bolt of lightning, the truth hit Kiera. Charlotte had been a minx. She still was. As much as it shamed Kiera, she knew that Charlotte had taken lovers even after her marriage to George. Many times over the years, Charlotte had summered in Ireland, leaving her husband in London. While she could merely speculate on the mischief George got into while his wife was away, she knew all too well what Charlotte was capable of. She suspected her despicable brother-in-law wasn't much better. She supposed that was why they were so well suited for each other.

No wonder at the hard mask that had shut her out the moment Quinn's brother heard her surname. He'd send them packing the first minute he could. She fisted her hands in the folds of her skirt. She wouldn't give him the chance.

"I'm sorry. I—I didn't know." She lifted her chin. "We'll go back to Natchez with Jack."

"No." Quinn snapped to attention, eyes blazing. "Over my dead body."

His brother stared at him, face like stone. "Quinn, you know nothing of the matter. It's probably best for everyone if Miss Young and her sisters return to Natchez just as she suggested."

"Best for who, Brother?" Fists clenched, Quinn stalked toward his brother. Connor straightened but kept his arms at his sides. The two were matched for height, both broad-shouldered, muscled from hard work. A ball of worry knotted in Kiera's stomach. Surely the two wouldn't come to blows over her and her sisters. "Best for Kiera or for you? Does your wife know why ya had to leave Ireland?"

"She knows."

"Does she now?" Quinn sneered. "I doubt she knows that the affair was just as much yer fault as Charlotte's."

"My wife knows everything," Connor gritted out through clenched teeth. "I kept nothing from her."

"Quinn, please. We don't belong here." Kiera shook her head. "If I'd known, we wouldn't have come in the first place."

"Kiera? We can't go back!" Amelia grabbed her arm, pure terror stamped on her face. "That man. He—"

"Connor, ya think Charlotte wronged ya?" Chest heaving, Quinn squared off with his brother. "Well, what she did t' ya is nothing t' what she did t' her own sisters."

"Quinn, don't." Kiera's face flamed as Connor O'Shea stared stoically at his brother, then at her. He didn't care what Charlotte had done to them. He only cared what she'd done to him. "There's no need—"

"There's every need." Quinn jabbed a finger at Kiera and Amelia. "Their sister—their own flesh and blood—allowed her husband t' ship them t' Natchez, all the while making Kiera think she was on the way t' an arranged marriage. Marriage? Ha! When they got here, they were forced t' go t' a tavern."

Connor's jaw clenched. "How'd you and the lads become involved?"

Quinn quickly outlined the events that had led up to them getting away from Le Bonne.

"Mr. Marchette lost his life rescuing Kiera and her sisters from that madman. They canna go back. Not until Mr. Wainwright has time to look into the matter."

Kiera glared at them both. "Don't I have any say in the matter?"

"Nay," Quinn shot back.

Connor blew out a puff of air, then faced her. "Miss Young, I won't deny that having you and your sisters here is very uncomfortable. To tell you the truth, I'd hoped to never hear the name Charlotte Young again in this lifetime, let alone play host to her family members."

"Then—"

He held up a hand. "Be that as it may, I won't be party to sending you and your sisters back to an establishment such as the Blue Heron against your will. You're welcome to stay here until Mr. Wainwright gets this mess straightened out. My wife will see to your needs."

Hands clasped so tight her fingers hurt, Kiera nodded. "Yes, sir. Thank you."

With one last look at Quinn, Connor turned and left, his long strides taking him to the end of the porch and away as quickly as he'd come. Quinn stared after his brother, his scowl still in place, his jaw as hard as a rock.

Tears sprang to Kiera's eyes. Connor O'Shea had waited nine years to be reunited with his brothers. Nine long years of separation. And in the space of a few minutes, a few words, she'd managed to destroy their reunion.

"Here it is. I hope you'll be comfortable."

Quinn, followed by Rory and Patrick, trailed their sister-in-law into a room as large as their whole house had been back in Ireland.

"There ain't no beds," Patrick stated baldly.

"That's because this is the sitting room." Isabella motioned to two doors. "There are only two bedrooms, I'm afraid, so you will have to share."

Rory disappeared into one bedroom, and Isabella led Quinn into the other, Patrick following close behind. The smell of fresh-cut lumber permeated the space. Quinn pivoted. The bedding, the pegs, even the curtains over the window looked new. "This hasn't been built long."

"A fire destroyed this wing of the house a year and a half ago. That's when my father was injured. Connor came and rebuilt, making it a two-story so that we'd have plenty of rooms for guests." She pushed back the curtains, letting the feeble winter sunlight spill into the room. "My sister-in-law was supposed to have the downstairs suite of rooms for her and the baby, but she's since married William Wainwright and moved to the Wainwright plantation half a day's journey north." She smiled. "It was a difficult time, but in the end, it all worked out. And now you're here."

Quinn wanted to ask what had happened to Isabella's brother but didn't want to pry.

"We met Mr. Wainwright." Patrick peered at her, brow scrunched. "But he was old."

"Yes, that was William's father."

"He helped get Megan and her sisters away from the tavern." Patrick took a running start and jumped on the bed. "Megan says that the women wore—"

"Patrick, off the bed with ya now. Ye'll soil the nice quilt with yer filthy clothes." Quinn grabbed his little brother and propelled him back to the sitting room. Keeping a tight grip on Patrick's collar, Quinn frowned at Connor's wife. "This is much too nice for us. Is there somewhere else? Something smaller? We'd be glad t' stay in one o' the cabins—"

"No, Quinn. You, Rory, Patrick—" Isabella stepped forward, put her hand on Quinn's arm, her dark eyes filled with pleading—"you're family. Everything Connor's done for the last nine years has been to bring you and your brothers to the colonies. This is your home now. At least until little Jon comes of age. But by then, Connor will have rebuilt Braxton Hall. . . ." She paused, then gave a soft laugh. "But that will be many years down the road. For now, this is our home and yours."

A home? What would Connor's wife say if she knew he planned to leave as soon as Patrick and Rory were settled? Patrick pulled against his hold. He let go, and Patrick promptly headed outside to the veranda. From habit, Quinn followed, keeping an eye on the lad.

Now that the time had come, could he leave? Who would keep Patrick safe? And would he feel that Quinn had abandoned him just like he'd felt abandoned by Connor and Caleb?

He turned away, scowling. He wasn't abandoning Patrick and Rory. Not like Connor and Caleb had. He'd delivered the boys halfway around the world to their oldest brother, the one who should've taken responsibility for all of them years ago.

"Patrick?" Isabella held out a bucket. "Would you be so

kind as to fetch a bucket of water for your room? There's a cistern right there by the kitchen. No need to go to the well."

Patrick grabbed the bucket. "Yes, mum."

As Patrick clattered down the steps, Connor's wife moved to stand beside Quinn. "I want you to feel at home. And Connor does too."

Instead of answering her, he gripped the railing and sucked in a breath of the fresh February air. He eyed the courtyard of the U-shaped house. "I've never seen a house built like this."

Every single room opened onto the courtyard, shrouded in winter gray, dried leaves, and wilted flowers.

"It's a nod to my mother's Spanish heritage. And you'll be happy to have the veranda during the hot summer months. You can open the doors and the windows and get a nice breeze."

Patrick returned with the water, the bucket half-empty from where he'd spilled most of it coming up the stairs. Quinn reached for it, set it beside the door. Patrick tugged at his coat, pointing at the barn nestled among the trees. "I saw Jack at the barn. Can I go see the horses?"

"Go on, but stay out o' trouble, ya hear?"

"I'll watch after him." Rory slid past Quinn and doffed his hat at Isabella. "Ma'am."

"If you'll excuse me, I need to check on our other guests." Isabella turned to go. "If you're hungry, Martha has a pot of stew cooking. Just follow your nose."

"She doesn't—" Quinn stopped at Isabella's raised eyebrow. Then he nodded. "Thank ya, ma'am. I'll let the boys know. But I'd better warn you. Patrick and Rory might eat you out o' house and home."

"Not to worry. I suspect they'll be doing their share to put food on the table in due time."

Quinn eyed the fallow fields, the lack of activity around the house. Besides Jack and the younger stable boy, and the faint sound of Martha humming in the kitchen, all was quiet. "Doing what?"

His sister-in-law laughed. "Believe me, there's plenty to do. As soon as the weather permits, Mr. Mews will start the plowing. And see that building in the distance?" She pointed in the direction Connor had gone. Quinn could just see the roof of a cabin with a thin wisp of smoke curling skyward. "That's the sawmill. Connor has kept busy all winter sawing lumber to take to Natchez. You'll have your pick of work to earn your keep."

After she'd gone, Quinn stood uncertainly. The sun hung high in the sky, and he didn't know what to do or where to go. Never in his life had he had a spare moment to call his own. He'd worked long shifts digging for coal, until the mine boss had pulled him to work as an apprentice in the smithy. While the work was hot, backbreaking, and the hours were just as long, at least he'd been aboveground and could see the beauty God had created every day instead of being buried underground and rarely, if ever, seeing the light of day.

Uncomfortable just standing around, he went in search of his brother. He skirted the grape arbor, the vines dormant and covered with straw until springtime. Rory, Jack, and the redheaded youth let Mr. Wainwright's horses out to pasture. Where was Patrick? Finally he spotted his brother and Kiera's youngest sister talking to a redheaded girl, a puppy cradled in her arms. When she handed the pup to Patrick, Quinn knew he didn't have anything to worry about. The puppy would keep Patrick occupied for the rest of the day.

Next to the outdoor kitchen, he spotted a large vegetable garden. While most of it lay fallow, several rows of what looked like winter greens had been banked with straw to ward off the chill.

He passed the row of cabins he'd spotted from the veranda, most unoccupied and falling into disrepair, then headed down the tree-shaded lane toward the sawmill.

When he came out into the open, he paused. Half a dozen logs waited to be sawn into lumber, and several stacks sat around the clearing, curing. But there was no one at the sawmill.

Quinn retraced his steps, pausing at the smithy. The cabin was rustic but had two wide doors that could be opened to let in a cooling breeze or closed off during the winter months. From what Quinn had seen of winter here, he couldn't imagine ever needing to close the doors, but they were closed now. The doors creaked as he slipped inside the darkened space. All was quiet, and dust motes danced on the air.

He walked around, picked up a set of tongs, and hefted them for weight. Hammers, from small peen to large flat ones for pounding metal, lined the walls. Bent, broken, and damaged tools—shovels, an adze, a pickax, and hoes—lay in a heap in the corner.

A moth-eaten leather apron and a pair of gloves hung on pegs near the forge. He fingered the apron, stiff and brittle from disuse. From the looks of things, the smithy hadn't been in operation for some time, which was surprising, given the number of broken tools that needed repairing.

He palmed a piece of iron not much bigger than the span of his two hands. Someone had started flattening a blade to make a hoe but never finished it. With a good hot fire, he could finish all these projects in a few hours.

He'd need an assistant. He could probably get Rory or Patrick to man the bellows.

Maybe . . .

He tossed the half-finished blade back onto the table, the clang loud in the silence. What was he thinking? He wasn't going to be here long enough to get the smithy up and running again. He'd be gone long before the field hands would need hoes, and if Connor needed a blacksmith, he'd hire one.

Clamping a lid on his enthusiasm for working with iron, Quinn pivoted, walked outside, and headed toward the barn where he'd last seen Patrick.

Chapter 6

KIERA FOLDED THE FEW ITEMS OF CLOTHES she'd managed to stuff in the pillowcase, along with the cloak Mrs. Butler had given her. She'd had no idea what she'd managed to salvage, and the results were paltry indeed.

She'd only grabbed one pinafore for Megan. Frowning, she turned, then hurried into the sitting room in the suite Mistress O'Shea had allotted to them.

"Where's Megan?"

Amelia shrugged. "I don't know. I haven't seen her since we got here. That girl—the redheaded one—said something about showing her some puppies."

"I'll go look for her." Kiera grabbed her wrap, eyeing her

sister as she lay curled up on the settee. "In the meantime, Amelia, I suggest you go find Mistress O'Shea or Martha and offer your services."

Amelia yawned. "She said to call her Isabella. And besides, there's nothing to do right now. It's winter."

"There's always something to do. I noticed you didn't offer to help with the dishes after the lunch hour."

Amelia shrugged. "That's Martha's job."

Kiera strode across the room, knelt in front of her sister. "Amelia, just because the O'Sheas are allowing us to stay here doesn't mean that we're on par with them. Our own sister allowed her husband to sell us to a brothel to pay off his gambling debts. There's no going back to the way things were before."

Amelia picked at a thread on the worn settee. "Do you think she knew what he intended?"

Her whisper was filled with pain, and Kiera reached out and smoothed back her blonde hair, a few shades lighter than Kiera's own. "Who knows the workings of Charlotte's mind? But what's done is done, and we have to make the best of it. Whatever happens, we don't want to go back to Le Bonne. Is that understood?"

Amelia's face blanched white. "Yes."

"Good. Perhaps you could see if Martha needs help in the kitchen. If she doesn't, then ask for a bucket of water and some dust cloths and dust our rooms. We don't want to make more work for the woman than we have to."

"All right."

"I'll be back as soon as I find Megan."

Kiera walked outside to the veranda and searched the courtyard. No sign of Megan. Sighing, she pulled her wrap closer and started toward the barn.

Surprisingly, the weather was quite nice for February and the light wrap was more than sufficient. But she'd been told that the weather could change overnight, which wasn't all that unusual. The weather back home was just as unpredictable.

She searched along the path that led toward the grape arbor, then poked her head in two or three run-down cabins, wondering at their emptiness. When she didn't find her sister, she headed toward the stables, pushed open the heavy door, and paused inside, letting her eyes adjust to the darkness.

"Megan?"

No one answered, and she turned back toward the door. Stepping into the sunlight, she ran into Quinn. He reached out to steady her, and she sucked in a breath. "Quinn. You— you scared me."

The corners of his eyes crinkled as he smiled. "Sorry, lass. Didn't mean t' startle ya."

"I was looking for Megan. Have you seen her?"

"I was doing the same, lookin' for me brother." He shrugged, a hint of amusement playing about his mouth. "At least there's no rigging for them t' climb."

Kiera winced. "You're not going to let me forget that, are you?"

"Not likely." He chuckled.

"Amelia said that the redheaded girl—I think her name's Lizzy—was going to show them some puppies, but she didn't know where." Kiera plopped her hands on her hips. "I just don't want Megan to get into any trouble."

"Same with Patrick. If I canna hear him, then it doesna bode well. Come on. Let's go check the smokehouse. Mayhap they're o'er there."

At the smokehouse, the puppies were snuggled in a hole dug under the foundation, fast asleep. There was no sign of the children. Kiera wrinkled her brow. "I wonder where they've gotten off to?"

"Listen."

Kiera heard giggles, and she and Quinn followed the sound toward the corncrib. The three children sat on the steps of the crib with an Indian woman, surrounded by half a dozen other children, all with lighter skin but straight black hair like hers.

Megan saw them and ran to Kiera, smiling. "Kiera, come meet my new friends."

Kiera allowed herself to be led to the group. "Good day, ma'am."

The woman stood, head bowed. "I am Mary Horne, mistress."

"Kiera Young." She motioned to Quinn. "And Quinn O'Shea."

"Master O'Shea. Mistress Young."

"Quinn'll do, ma'am."

"As you wish, Master Quinn."

Quinn scowled but didn't correct the woman a second time.

Megan sat down between Lizzy and Patrick. "Would you tell us another story? Please?"

The woman dipped her head and returned to her seat on the steps. Silently she reached for another ear of corn. As she shucked, Megan frowned and glanced at Lizzy. "Why isn't she talking?"

"She'll only tell stories if everybody's shucking corn." Lizzy handed Megan another ear, and Megan started shucking along with the rest of the children.

"The little *loksa*, or terrapin . . ."

As Mary's singsong voice mesmerized the children, Quinn leaned close and whispered, "It seems t' me that Mrs. Horne could teach us a thing or two about keeping Patrick and Megan occupied. Would ya no' agree, Miss Young?"

Kiera smothered a giggle. "I do believe you are right, Mr. O'Shea."

Quinn didn't see Connor again the rest of the day, so he made his way to the sawmill before daylight the next morning. He might not be staying long, but he'd earn his keep as long as he was here.

A small band of light peeked over the eastern skyline when Connor appeared. Quinn eased up from the steps and swiped at the sawdust on his breeches.

"Quinn." Connor nodded a greeting. "You're up early."

"I'm no' used t' lying abed." Quinn shrugged, eyeing the fog-shrouded morning. "*Da* would have me hide."

"That he would." Connor opened the door to the cabin, grabbed a peeling iron, hefted it, then offered it to Quinn. "You up for a bit o' work this morning?"

"That's what I'm here for." Quinn took the peeler. "Where's the rest o' the men? I figured they'd all be here come daylight."

"They'll be along shortly. No need in heading into the woods until full daylight."

"Yet you're here."

"I'm here." Connor grasped another peeler and headed toward logs at the edge of the clearing. "I like a bit o' quiet time to myself every morning. Sometimes I work on a piece o' furniture; sometimes I peel bark. Sometimes . . ." He took a deep breath. "Sometimes I just sit and pray, thanking God for His blessings."

Quinn hefted the peeler in his hands. "So what do we do with these things?"

"Come on. I'll show you."

Connor scored a log from one end to the other, then reached for the peeler. "Once ye cut the log, you slip this spud under the bark and jab at it until the bark loosens. Then you just keep peeling until the whole thing is slick as a greased pig."

Quinn followed Connor's lead, trying to keep from breaking off pieces of bark and having to start over. But the straight blade kept gouging the log and chipping tiny pieces of bark instead of the long, smooth sections that Connor managed to break loose. Regardless, he got the hang of it soon enough and debarked one log and moved on to another.

"This would be easier with curved blades." Connor scored the second log. He cupped his hand along the curve of the log. "Just a wee bit of curve on the blade makes a world of difference."

"'Twould make the work go faster."

"It does. I saw some peelers like that in the Carolinas. Much easier t' work with." Connor positioned himself at one end of the log, and Quinn at the other, his boot on the log to hold it steady.

Quinn inspected the flat peeler. "I could make one o' those."

"You can forge steel?" Connor threw him a glance. "How'd you learn to do that?"

"Remember old Seamus? He was getting on up in years and needed an apprentice." Quinn shrugged. "I was available and glad t' get out o' the mines."

He'd been more than glad. If he'd had to spend one more day underground, he wasn't sure he would have survived it.

"Breeze Hill hasn't had a blacksmith since I've been here. You're welcome to take over the task if you'd like."

"What about Mr. Bartholomew?" Quinn concentrated on making a smooth, clean peel. "Shouldna he have a say in who does what around here?"

"Isabella's father isn't well. He turned the plantation over to me until his grandson comes of age. Then little Jon will inherit Breeze Hill."

"Even if ya and Isabella have children?"

A pained look crossed his brother's face. "Aye, even if we have children. I didna want Isabella t' think I married her for Breeze Hill."

"But it worked out, didna it? Isabella said something about a place called Braxton Hall." He chuckled. "I never thought I'd see the day an O'Shea would become a land-owner. What'd ya do, rescue another damsel in distress?"

"Yes." Connor's jaw clenched. "Isabella."

Feeling like an *eejit*, Quinn swallowed. "I'm sorry. I didna know—"

"Nolan Braxton was a thief and a highwayman." A hard-ness laced Connor's voice. "He killed Isabella's brother, almost killed her father and her sister-in-law, and wanted Breeze Hill to further his thievery, and he planned to get it through Isabella. After he was killed, the governor awarded me his land."

Quinn squinted at his brother. "Did ya kill the man yerself?"

"No." Connor shook his head, his attention straying toward the house. "No, but it wasn't from lack o' trying."

The rasp of the peelers was the only sound between them for several minutes.

"So tell me about Caleb." Connor filled the void. "Why'd he decide to take off?"

Quinn jabbed the spud at the log. "He said he'd had

enough o' working in the coal mines. Said he wanted t' see the world."

"I can understand that. I hated the mines myself."

Quinn grunted. At least that was one thing he and his brothers had in common.

Connor was quiet for a long time. "He left you to care for Rory and Patrick?"

Quinn's spud slipped, gouged into the log. He clenched his jaw, pulled the peeler out and jabbed at the log again, the day Caleb had left still fresh in his mind all these years later even though the bruises from their fistfight had long since faded. "Nothing was different. Caleb was never much help even when he was around."

"I wish I'd been there to help. All these years and . . ." Connor leaned on the handle of the peeler, staring at Quinn. "Our reunion isn't what I'd always dreamed it would be."

Quinn scowled. "What did you expect?"

"I don't know. For things to be like they were when we were lads, when *Mam* and *Da* were alive."

"Things haven't been like that for years." Quinn gouged at the log, long-held resentment seething just below the surface. "You can't go back."

A dozen men walked down the lane toward the sawmill. Connor stared at the approaching workers, looking unhappy with the interruption. "I suppose not."

Just like Quinn couldn't go back and undo the damage of taking the job that should have been Caleb's.

A choice that had caused Caleb to despise him and leave Ireland and their family behind for good.

Isabella barged into the kitchen. "Where's Martha?"

"Gathering eggs." Kiera ducked her head and continued to chop onions for the stew Martha had started for the noon meal. The cook hadn't said yea or nay when Kiera had shown up in her kitchen before daybreak, but the woman hadn't stopped her from helping either.

Kiera was determined to prove her worth. Otherwise, she and her sisters would be sent back to Natchez and to Pierre Le Bonne.

"That husband of mine is going to be the death of me. Martha said he didn't eat breakfast, and I'm certain he didn't break his fast with the camp cook, Lafitte, not when he could eat Martha's cooking instead." Isabella glanced around the kitchen, hands on her hips, her brows drawn into an irritated frown. "Connor knows he can't work all day without nourishment."

Kiera blinked against the sting of the onions, hoping the flush on her face could be attributed to the job at hand. She knew why Connor had skipped breakfast. She'd met him on the path on her way to the kitchen. With a silent nod of greeting, he'd stridden on by, headed toward the sawmill without so much as a by-your-leave.

"And that brother of his, Quinn. I haven't seen him either."

Isabella grabbed a basket off one of the shelves. "Kiera, did you see Connor or Quinn this morning?"

"No, ma'am. I mean—" Kiera swallowed. "Yes, mistress. I saw Mr. O'Shea. I mean Master Connor."

Isabella sighed, crossed the room, and sat down next to Kiera. "There's no need to be so formal. Connor isn't your master, and I'm certainly not your mistress. You and your sisters are our guests."

"I'm not sure your husband feels the same way. He's not happy we're here." Tears sprang to Kiera's eyes as she cut into another onion. Blinking, she shook her head. "Not after what my sister did to him."

Isabella patted her arm. "What Charlotte did has nothing to do with you. And from what Quinn tells us, she and her husband did you and your sisters an even greater disservice. I, for one, am glad that Quinn and the Wainwrights were there to help you. I shudder to think what would have become of you otherwise."

"He—your husband—wouldn't even look at me when I met him on the path this morning. That's why he didn't come to breakfast." She lowered her gaze. "He couldn't stand to be in the same room with me."

"That's not true." Isabella shook her head, annoyance creasing her brow. "He skips breakfast all the time. So you can get that thought right out of your head, you hear me?"

"Yes, ma'am."

"Good. Now, to scrounge up something to feed him and

that brother of his." Isabella stood and marched across the kitchen. "I'll be right back."

Kiera swiped her nose on her apron, being careful not to get onion juice in her eyes. Squinting against the sting, she finished chopping as quickly as possible, then dumped the onions in the stewpot.

She appreciated Isabella trying to make her feel better, but she'd heard the anger in Connor's voice when he'd found out who she was. And one day wouldn't have changed his opinion of her. He wanted her and her sisters gone, the sooner the better.

The door opened and Isabella reentered, holding a round of cheese. "Oh, good. You're through with the onions." She handed Kiera the cheese. "Slice this while I fry up some ham. And there's bread in the pie safe. Cut several pieces of that as well. They've been working all morning, so they'll be hungry."

Kiera did as she was told, laying out the bread, cutting and wrapping the cheese as the aroma of fried ham filled the kitchen.

Soon Isabella forked the ham onto the bread, then wrapped it up to keep it warm. Placing the food in a basket, she grabbed her shawl, hoisted the basket over her arm, and headed toward the door. Turning back, she smiled at Kiera. "Aren't you coming?"

"I don't—" Kiera broke off when Isabella arched a brow. "Yes. Let me get my cloak."

Isabella wasted no time on the shaded path that led past the derelict cabins. Kiera stayed close as they drew near the sawmill. Crews of two stood atop saw pits sawing logs; some stacked lumber, while others used horses to drag logs across the clearing.

A tall, skinny man doffed his hat at them. "Morning, Miz O'Shea. Miss."

"Good morning, Mr. Horne." Isabella nodded a greeting, then leaned toward Kiera. "That was Mr. Horne. You'll meet his wife and daughters soon."

"Mary?"

"You've met her?"

"Yes. She had the children shucking corn yesterday."

"Telling them stories, no doubt."

"Yes, ma'am."

"She does have a gift for keeping them entertained." Isabella laughed. "The Hornes have ten children. The youngest is five months old, just a few weeks younger than my nephew. You'll enjoy Sunday services. Mary and her daughters create beautiful harmony, and Mr. Horne is a very animated preacher."

The chaos around them didn't seem to faze Isabella, and she plowed straight through the workers. Quinn stood atop a saw pit, feet braced apart. Drenched in sweat, his worn homespun shirt clung to him as he pushed and pulled the saw blade back and forth, the steady rasp of his saw creating a soothing singsong melody. He paused and swiped at his brow with the kerchief knotted about his neck. His blue eyes met hers, and she blushed, looking away.

Connor crouched beside the log, pounding a wedge in

to hold the cut apart. He glanced up, spotted them, then handed the hammer off to one of his men. He strode toward them, his face the image of a thundercloud. But his attention was focused solely on his wife, not on Kiera.

When he reached Isabella, he took her by the arm, pulled her to the side. "You shouldn't have walked so far from the house, Wife. It's too soon after—"

"I'm perfectly fine, Connor. Stop worrying."

"Whoa! Whoa, you *dunderhead*!"

Kiera whirled as a horse's frightened whinny rang out right behind her. The horse reared, its hind legs tangled in the harness and chains attached to a log. Kiera backed away, stumbling on the uneven ground.

The large draft animal lunged upward again, jerking the lead rope out of its handler's grasp, hooves slashing the air mere feet away. Suddenly Kiera was swept off her feet and out of harm's way. Men rushed toward the horse, calming the animal as they unhooked the log and untangled the chains.

Kiera looked up into Quinn's deep-blue eyes.

"Are ya all right, lass?"

"I'm—I'm fine." His arm, like a band of steel, wrapped around her waist and held her upright. Heart pounding from the near miss with the horse—or was it from Quinn's nearness?—she pushed him away.

"Björn!"

Kiera jumped as Connor brushed past her toward the commotion. Quinn pushed her toward Isabella and followed his brother.

"What happened?" Connor barked at the hapless man holding the lead rope. The horse, now freed of the chains, stood quivering but docile enough.

"I do not know, Master O'Shea. One minute the horse was leading along like a good girl, and the next she were fighting like the devil himself."

"Well, you almost got my wife and—" Connor's angry glare jerked toward Kiera—"and Miss Young killed."

"I am sorry." Björn crushed his hat between beefy hands. "It will not happen again."

"If ya canna control that animal, I've got no use for ya here at Breeze Hill." Connor's voice cut through the silence.

"But I did nothing—"

"He's right, Connor." Quinn hunched down next to the log, the chain in his hands. "It wasna his fault. One o' the chains broke."

"Let me see that." After examining the broken link, Connor ripped off his hat and scraped a hand through his hair. Then he glanced at the muscular Swede, standing there, eyes downcast.

"My apologies, Björn." He waved a hand at Isabella and Kiera. "My concern for my wife and Miss Young caused me t' overreact."

The man lifted his head. "I still have a job, *ja*?"

Connor chuckled. *"Ja."*

The man grinned, plunked his hat on his head, and hurried away, leading the horse, muttering about what a *dunderhead* she was.

Chapter 7

Quinn squinted up at Connor. "No' much good his job will be t' him if these chains are no' fixed."

"You've trained as a smithy. Can't you fix it?"

"I do no' think that's a good idea."

"Why not? Ya told me yourself that ya apprenticed with Seamus. And there's a smithy just waiting for someone with the know-how to get it in operation again."

Quinn dropped the chains. "I'm no' going t' be here long enough t' start up the smithy."

"Not be here?" Connor jerked his head up, the shock in his tone and on his face evident. He looked away, toward Isabella and Kiera, then toward the men who'd wandered back to their work. "I see. Should we talk about this in private?"

Quinn stood. Maybe it was time to clear the air. If he didn't, the anger and resentment deep down inside would continue to fester.

Isabella eyed them both before handing over the basket of food. "Well, you might as well eat while you're at it."

She linked arms with Kiera and strode off, leaving Quinn and Connor standing there staring at each other. Connor jerked his head toward the dogtrot cabin. Out of sight of the other men, he plopped the basket on the porch, ignoring the food.

"What's this all about?" The scowl on Connor's face reminded Quinn of his *da* when he'd been angry. "If you're still mad about the girl, I've already said my piece about her."

"This has nothing t' do with Kiera and her sisters."

At least his desire to be on his way had nothing to do with them. But on the other hand, it had everything to do with them, with taking on the responsibility of others to the point that he forfeited his own dreams.

"Then what is it? I thought . . ." Connor blew out a long, slow breath. "For a long time, returning to Ireland and being reunited with my family was all I thought about. After *Mam* and *Da* passed on, and there was nothing left t' hold any of us in Ireland, I started dreaming of bringing you and the lads to America. It's almost as if you wish you'd never come here."

The faint sound of saws biting into wood and the call of

the drovers as they headed back into the forest carried on the morning breeze, the peaceful tranquility of the sounds in direct contrast to the tension between his brother and himself.

"It's no' that I didna want t' come." *It's that I do no' want to stay.* "Tell me something, Connor. Are ya going t' abandon Rory and Patrick like ya abandoned all o' us nine years ago? I need t' know straight-out if ya are, so me and me brothers can shake the dust o' this place off our boots."

A muscle jumped in Connor's jaw. "What makes you think I'd abandon them?"

"Ya did once. Ya left. Just like that." Quinn snapped his fingers. "Ya were gone. For more than a year, we didna know if ya were dead or alive."

Connor looked away, his eyes on the sun as it bathed the land in a new day. Finally he looked back at Quinn. "It wasna my choice t' leave Ireland—"

"It was yer choice t' dally with Charlotte Young, it was."

"A choice that has haunted me all these years. And now with her sisters here, it continues t' haunt me." Connor looked at him. "But the worst of it is that I wasn't there for you and the little ones, and I'm sorry for that. Can you forgive me?"

Quinn wanted to say yes, but . . .

Sucking in a calming breath, he stalked toward the woods, then turned back toward Connor.

"Ya know, I hated ya for what ya did, for leaving me t' take care of *Mam* and *Da* and the little ones. But I canna even feel the hate anymore. I just want t' know if you're ready t' take responsibility for the little brothers now. Rory is about the same age I was when ya left. Patrick is still just a lad."

"You'd leave your brothers?" In spite of the softly spoken question, Connor's hurt came through loud and clear.

Put like that, Quinn's longing sounded selfish, but he'd been tied down for so long. "All I've ever known was working in that coal mine, then later sweating in the smithy. At night, on me bed, all I could think about was what you and Caleb were doing, the places ya were seeing, and I wanted that for meself."

"Caleb was always prone t' wayfaring."

"But no' you?" Quinn scowled.

"It never crossed my mind t' leave Ireland until I was forced to." Silence fell between them, and Quinn was reluctant to break it. They'd said all that needed saying, hadn't they? After a long moment, Connor spoke, all the fire gone out of his voice. "I won't try to stop you. Patrick and Rory have a home here, and it's my turn t' see that they're cared for."

His words elated and terrified Quinn all at once. He could leave Patrick, couldn't he? Rory was old enough to strike out on his own should he want to, but Patrick was still a wee lad and couldn't even remember his mother. Quinn was the only parent Patrick had ever known.

"I daresay ya need a bit o' silver before ya strike out on yer own, aye? Nobody else can run the forge, and I could use the help."

Quinn clenched his jaw. His brother was dragging him

right back into family obligations yet again. But Connor was right about one thing. He had nary a coin to call his own. "Till spring, then."

"And if you do leave—" Connor put a hand on his shoulder—"know that you're always welcome back."

Quinn stiffened at his brother's touch. It wasn't that easy to erase years of resentment. "I'll remember that."

Connor reached for the basket, then held out a wrapped bundle. The enticing aroma of ham wafted toward him. "In the meantime, we'd better do as my wife suggested and eat. Otherwise, she'll have my head."

But the ham and cheese tasted like sawdust in Quinn's mouth.

Now that the freedom he'd longed for was at hand, he wasn't sure he could go through with it.

Pierre placed both hands on his desk and glared at the three men standing before him. "No sign of them?"

"None, *monsieur*."

He eased back in the plush leather chair he'd imported from France, eyeing his hired goons. Claude stood stoic, looking neither to the right nor the left, but the other two fidgeted, glancing sideways in his direction. Their sniveling grated on Pierre's nerves.

"Do you mean to tell me that three beautiful *filles* have disappeared without a trace?"

"Yes, *monsieur*."

Pierre stood, fury sweeping over him. The man who'd purchased Kiera Young for the night had been a stranger to him, and even after Claude had tortured him to reveal his name and where the girls were, he'd remained steadfast in his silence.

"And what of our recent guest who took a swim in the river? Has anyone inquired after a British shipping magnate?"

The three men stood silent before him, blinking like owls. *Imbéciles!* Did he have to tell them how to do everything? Could they not think for themselves?

"A well-heeled, well-dressed Londoner doesn't just disappear without someone raising an uproar." Pierre spread his hands. "No questions means that he wasn't operating alone. Find out who that man was. He had connections in Natchez. Somebody knew him, and that someone has those girls, and I want them back." He looked at each man in turn. "That is, if you don't want to join our British friend at the bottom of the Mississippi."

Connor kept himself busy all day, not letting his thoughts dwell on the conversation he'd had with his brother.

But when night fell and he returned to his bedchamber, Quinn's words came back to haunt him.

He sat on the bed and blew out a long, slow breath.

"What was that all about?" Isabella paused, her brush motionless, watching him from her place at the vanity he'd made for her as a wedding present.

"It's been a long, long day." Connor took off his jerkin and tossed it over a chair.

"The trouble with the horse this morning? Truly, Connor, Kiera and I were unharmed."

"I know. I just lost my head for a few minutes." He shook his head. "It's not that."

She arched a brow. "And did you eat as I asked?"

"Yes, madam, I ate."

She put down the brush and joined him. "Then what is it? Is it Quinn? The two of you looked like two bears after a long winter of hibernation. Of course, neither of you had bothered to eat, so it's no wonder . . ."

"All these years I wanted nothing more than to be reunited with my brothers, to enjoy life like it was when we were lads." Another sigh. "But Quinn wants nothing to do with me. He blames me for leaving him and the little ones in Ireland."

"Talk to him. Tell him that if you could redo the past, you would."

"I don't think he wants to listen." Connor ran both hands through his hair. "And it doesn't help that he brought that woman and her sisters here."

"Connor O'Shea, he didn't know they were Charlotte's sisters, and even if he had, would you have him leave them in a brothel?" Isabella's eyes flashed. "I think not."

Connor kept his head in his hands. She was right, but he didn't have to like it. Just the thought of Charlotte's sisters brought back memories that he'd believed were long dead and buried.

"Quinn will come around. Give him time."

"I don't know if he's going to stay on long enough for that."

"He wants to leave? But he just got here."

"Yes, he's planning to leave. He wants to travel, to see the world, to do all the exciting things he thinks Caleb and I have experienced." He pulled off his boots and tossed them into the corner, their clunks loud in the silence. "If he only knew."

Isabella reached out to push a lock of hair off his forehead, her touch never ceasing to quicken his pulse. "What? You haven't had any excitement, my love?"

Connor chuckled, then grabbed her wrist and pulled her closer. "Woman, I've had more excitement since I met you than in all my years on earth combined."

"There you go. Breeze Hill is not as dull as one would think. If one knows where to look." She wrapped her arms around his neck and smiled. "We'll just have to help Quinn look in the right places."

"What's that supposed to mean?"

But he truly didn't care, not with his wife's arms around him and her lips nibbling his ear.

As a matter of fact, he didn't care to think about Quinn at all.

Chapter 8

THEIR FIRST SUNDAY AT BREEZE HILL turned out to be a cold, wet, drizzly day. After a short prayer service on the veranda, everyone retired to their living quarters for a day of rest. Except for Amelia, who whined that there was nothing to do. But she'd turned up her nose when Kiera suggested she accompany her to the kitchen to help Martha.

Martha glanced up from her never-ending chore of baking bread. Without asking permission, Kiera donned an apron and turned toward the cook. "What can I do?"

"Well, if you want to be of help, missy, you can go draw some water." Martha jerked her head toward the empty bucket. "Take your cloak. It's quite nippy out there."

"Yes, ma'am."

Kiera wrapped her cloak around her and grabbed the bucket. As she opened the door, her eyes fell on a party of travelers filing down the lane toward the grove of trees beyond the house.

"We have visitors." She motioned toward the travelers.

Martha leaned around the door and peered out. "Ack. Who'd be traveling this time of year?" The cook went back to kneading dough. "By late summer and fall, there'll be a party every day or so, sometimes asking to spend the night at Breeze Hill."

Kiera eyed the strangers, remembering Jack's fear and Quinn's description of the dangers along the trace. "Do you think they might harm us?"

"Oh, it isn't *them* you need to be wary of, girl. It's the highwaymen. Groups of lawless scum who won't lift a finger to do an honest day's work, but prey on hapless travelers instead." She stopped kneading, her hands idle for a moment. "Dear Master Jonathan—Miss Isabella's brother—lost his life coming home from Natchez. We thought it was robbery, but turns out he was kilt for Breeze Hill."

"Murdered for Breeze Hill?" Kiera stared at the cook. "C—Master O'Shea didn't kill him, did he?"

"Oh no, not Connor." Martha sounded shocked at the very idea. "I never got the full story, but it was a neighboring plantation owner, that no-account Nolan Braxton. Unbeknownst to anyone, he was the ringleader of a vicious group of highwaymen, but Breeze Hill stood between him and the trace, and he wanted the land so his men could move about freely. He was about to marry Miss Isabella when it was discovered he wasn't who he pretended to be."

"Surely he's not still nearby. Not after killing Isabella's brother."

"He's not. Everything happened so fast, but there was a storm. Miss Isabella had gone to Braxton Hall, and Master William and Connor went to fetch her. Nolan Braxton—I refuse to call him master—almost killed them all, but a tornado ripped the place apart, and he was killed."

"Goodness, that's a horrible way to die."

Martha's gaze settled on her. "Truth be told, I heard he didn't die from the tornado, but that one of his own men slit his throat."

Kiera felt the blood drain from her face.

"Oh, dearie, I didn't mean to get so morbid. But it was a terrible time. But all's well that ends well. The governor awarded Connor the deed to Braxton Hall, and Connor ended up marrying Miss Isabella, and everything is return-ing to normal around here. Even Mr. Bartholomew is almost back to his old self. We can thank the Lord for that." Martha scraped the dough off her hands. "Now, where's that water?"

"Oh, I'm sorry, Martha; I forgot all about the water."

Kiera hurried toward the well, shivering when she spot-ted several men making camp on the cold, damp ground. A heavy fog hung in the air and the temperature had been dropping steadily all day. It would be a miserable night for these travelers, for sure. Thankful for a warm place to sleep, she drew water and turned toward the kitchen.

"Miss?"

Glancing up, she spotted a well-dressed gentleman standing nearby, a lit pipe in one hand, a Bible in the other. He looked on her kindly. "Might I have a word with you, miss?"

Kiera glanced toward the kitchen.

"The Reverend John Summers at your service." He motioned toward the ramshackle row of cabins. "Are any of these cabins available for the night? My wife and I would be obliged for warmer—and drier—accommodations."

"I'm not sure, sir. I can fetch Martha for you."

"Please and thank you." He smiled. "I'm willing to pay handsomely."

"I'll tell her."

"Thank you, miss."

Kiera hurried to the kitchen. Isabella sat at the table, nursing a cup of tea and nibbling on a crusty piece of bread.

"Martha, a traveler wants to know if he and his wife can stay in one of the cabins for the night. What should I tell him?"

Martha scowled. "We ain't no inn."

Isabella propped her hand on her chin. "We might as well be, Martha. Everybody stops here regardless." She looked at Kiera. "Most travelers heading north stop at Mount Locust for food and lodging, but some push on; then when they realize they won't make it to the next inn, they decide to spend the night here."

"We passed Mount Locust on the way here." Kiera bit her lip, thoughts whirling. "Have you thought of opening an inn here?"

"Heavens, no." Martha set out her pans to form loaves of bread. "Breeze Hill is a working plantation, not a stand for travelers."

"But there are empty cabins. He's of the clergy, and he's willing to pay."

"Those cabins are for the tenant farmers, not that we have many this time of the year. And besides, hanging out a shingle offering food and lodging is a lot of work. There's just not enough hands or food here to feed and take care of travelers." Martha jerked her chin toward the door. "You can tell the gentleman that the answer is no."

"Yes, ma'am."

"Martha, let's not be too hasty." Isabella stood, refilled her cup. "I don't see why Kiera can't offer this gentleman and his wife lodging for the night. As a matter of fact, I think it's an excellent idea. They can stay in the cabin closest to the well."

Kiera clasped her hands together. "Thank you, ma'am."

"I would help you with the cleaning—"

"No," Martha snapped. Kiera glanced toward the cook just in time to see the blood drain from the woman's face. "I forbid it. You're not to do any heavy lifting, not for another month, at least. Promise me?"

"Martha, between you, Papa, and Connor—"

"Promise me, Isabella?" Tears gathered in the stalwart woman's eyes.

"Oh, Martha, don't cry." Isabella stood, took the woman in her arms, and hugged her. "There, there, dear. I promise to do exactly as you say."

"I'll hold you to that promise, child." Martha sniffed, swiping at her cheeks with her apron. "Your body needs time to heal proper before—"

Isabella rested a hand on her flat stomach and smiled, but the tilt of her lips didn't quite reach her eyes. "Well, there you have it, Kiera. I'm afraid you're on your own."

"Amelia and Megan can help."

"Of course. That's an excellent idea." Isabella nodded.

A puff of dust flew out the open doorway of the ramshackle cabin, which had been empty yesterday, and Quinn jumped out of the way.

The door hung askew, the top hinge broken, but somebody was inside, sweeping up a storm and humming what sounded like an Irish lullaby.

Kiera, maybe?

He eased up to the door, peered inside.

It was Kiera all right. At least he was fairly certain it was through the thick cloud of dust that swirled in the small space. She wielded a broom as if the very devil were after her, swatting at cobwebs, knocking down wasp nests, just generally making a mess.

"What are ya doing, lass?"

She whirled, her skirts billowing out, creating another

dust storm. In spite of the dirt streaking her face, her blue eyes sparkled. She made a swipe with the broom. "What does it look like I'm doing? I'm cleaning."

"Cleaning? Whatever for?" He leaned against the doorpost—gently. He wouldn't want the structure to fall down if he put too much pressure on it. "Has me dear, sweet brother turned ya out on yer ear?"

He attempted to dodge as she swept dirt over his boots. Smirking, she leaned on the broom and blew a wisp of blonde hair off her brow. "If you must know, I'm cleaning this cabin for a guest."

"A guest?" Quinn raised an eyebrow. Surely Connor wouldn't put a guest in one of the derelict cabins. "Are ya jesting me?"

She frowned, went to the fireplace, and swept off the hearth. "Why would I jest? As you can see, I'm cleaning. You don't think I'd be doing such just for the fun of it, do you?"

"I suppose no'." He frowned. "If Connor and Isabella need room in the house t' entertain guests, the boys and I can vacate our rooms."

"You misunderstand. It's not that kind of guest. It's for Reverend and Mrs. Summers. They're traveling with the group camped by the well."

"And ya took it upon yerself t' provide lodging for 'em?"

"Do you think I'm daft?" She lifted her chin. "I made sure it was all right with Isabella and Martha."

"I see." He eyed the fireplace. "Did ya check t' make sure the chimney isna clogged?"

"Not yet." She studied the stone fireplace. "It should be fine, shouldn't it? Surely it hasn't been that long since these cabins were inhabited."

"Still, I'll check it. Ya'd hate to smoke out a paying guest, now, wouldn't ya?" Quinn nodded toward the rickety door. "And I'll fix the door. Ya can hardly offer them accommodations without a proper door."

A wide smile blossomed on her face. "Thank you, Quinn. I didn't know what I was going to do about the door. But this cabin was the best of the lot. I'd planned to just hang a blanket for the night, but if you could fix the door, that would be lovely."

"First things first." He knelt down and peered up the chimney.

As he built the fire, Kiera finished sweeping. Then she stood in the middle of the small cabin, the gaps in the chinking letting in the cold. She pulled her wrap closer. "It's so drafty. And there's no bedding. No washbasin. No table. No chairs." She faced him as the fire took hold. "What if it's unacceptable?"

Quinn rocked back on his heels, then stood, turned her toward the door, and pointed. "Look. They're camped out in the open in the cold with the threat o' more rain t' come. This cabin might not have much t' recommend it, but it's a sight better than where they are right now. They'll be grateful, I'm sure."

"You're right. I guess I was thinking about the nice soft bed I have to sleep on, how good Connor and Isabella have been to me, and I realize that I should be the one sleeping out here."

"Now why would ya think that, lass?"

"I don't deserve their help, their generosity." She turned away. "My sister—"

"You had nothing t' do with what yer sister did t' me brother." Quinn tipped her chin up with his forefinger, forcing her to meet his gaze. "Just like ya had nothing t' do with what she did t' ya."

"But—"

"No buts." Quinn silenced her words with the gentle pressure of his thumb against her lips. "You've done nothing wrong, and if my brother canna see that, he's a bigger fool than I thought he was."

The frown pulling her eyebrows together eased, and the gentle movement of her lips turning to a smile beneath his thumb sent a shiver from the tips of his fingers to the soles of his feet. He slid his thumb across her lips, feeling their softness. Her blue eyes, soft in the fading light, held his.

Quinn sucked in a breath of the cool night air, his gaze shifting across her face. Her eyes, her cheeks, the tilt of her nose, then back to her lips. Without thought or intention, he slid his hand along her jaw, cupped the back of her head.

Her eyelids swooped down, covered the brightness of her eyes, and she inched back, the movement instantly breaking the spell that had woven itself around them. They stood, silent and still for the space of a heartbeat.

She moved away to stand beside the fireplace. Then she

turned back, the softness in her blue eyes gone, to be replaced by a hardness that glittered in the firelight.

"Mr. O'Shea, if—if you're looking for favors for your assistance this night, then you should look elsewhere. I'm—I'm not my sister."

Quinn frowned, then dipped his head. "No favors requested or required, lass."

Chapter 9

KIERA LOOKED AT THE COINS IN HER HAND, amazed at the reverend's generosity.

She waved the travelers off, then lifted her skirts and ran toward the kitchen. Martha looked up when she entered.

"Martha, look." She held out the coins. "Reverend Summers paid me for the room last night."

Martha chuckled. "Well, don't you look like the cat that swallowed the cream."

Kiera clutched the few coins to her bodice and whirled. "It's the first money I've ever made, and it feels glorious."

"What feels glorious?"

She spun to find Isabella standing in the doorway. With a

delighted grin, Kiera crossed the room, reached for Isabella's hand, and deposited the coins in her palm with a flourish. "The reverend paid for his lodgings. Look."

"He was pleased with the accommodations. You should be proud." Isabella held the coins out. "But this isn't my money. You should keep it. You earned it."

Kiera shook her head and backed away. "No, ma'am. The cabin is yours. Well, Master Con—" At Isabella's raised brow, she amended, "Your husband's. The coins belong to Breeze Hill."

"But you did all the work."

"Quinn helped. He insisted on starting the fire to make sure the chimney wasn't clogged, and he fixed the door. One of the hinges had broken."

"He did?" Isabella's lips twitched.

"Yes, ma'am." She prattled on and on, too excited about last night's venture to keep it to herself. "Of course there were no beds, no washbasin, or anything to offer much comfort, but Quinn said that Mr. Summers and his wife would be grateful to be out of the rain. Which they were. Grateful, that is."

Isabella exchanged a glance with Martha. "Sounds like Quinn was a huge part of making the Summerses as comfortable as possible."

Kiera glanced between Martha and Isabella. "Is something wrong? Have I overstepped in some way?"

Maybe she shouldn't have allowed Quinn to help, but he hadn't given her much choice. He'd just shown up while she was cleaning, and one thing led to another. Her face flamed. Until he'd almost kissed her.

After that, she'd steered clear of him, even while he was repairing the door. He was Connor's brother, after all, and there was bad blood between Connor and Charlotte—

"Not at all. I'm glad he helped." Isabella moved toward the fireplace, reaching for a skillet. Martha shooed her away.

"Miss Isabella, you sit right down now, and I'll fix you some breakfast. Eggs? Ham?"

"Thank you, Martha, but I'm perfectly capable of scrambling an egg."

Martha went about her business as if she hadn't heard. Isabella sighed, placed the coins on the table, then sat down, tapping them with her fingers. "Kiera, you've only been here a few days and you've already shown that you're willing and able to work. I've noticed how you've been helping Martha in the kitchen, and then offering lodging to the reverend."

"Yes, ma'am." Kiera twisted her hands in her apron, wondering where Isabella was going with the conversation.

Isabella stacked the coins, the jingle pleasing to the ear. "After I went to bed last night, I got to thinking. Breeze Hill was a thriving plantation once, but the fire that devastated our crops in the fall of 1790 and almost killed my father very nearly crippled us." She glanced up. "I'm not sure how much you know of what all happened during that time, but my brother was killed, and—" she took a deep breath—"and let's just say it was a difficult time for all of us . . . emotionally, physically, and financially."

"Until Master Connor came and put everything to rights again."

Isabella shook her head. "Now, Martha. I'm trying to get Kiera to stop calling Connor master, and there you are doing the very thing I'm telling her not to."

"Yes, mistress."

If yesterday's exchange between them hadn't been proof enough, Martha's chuckle and Isabella's chiding look toward the cook clued Kiera in on the warm affection beneath their banter.

Isabella turned back to Kiera, eyes twinkling. "And besides, Connor didn't put everything to rights on his own. I'd like to think I had something to do with it. I did, after all, buy my husband off the auction block as an indentured servant."

Kiera gasped. "Truly?"

"Truly." Isabella chuckled. "Needless to say, he wasn't at all happy with the arrangement."

Kiera remembered to close her mouth. She couldn't imagine Connor O'Shea being indentured to anybody, especially not to Isabella. She eyed the beauty in front of her, the slight smile that played across Isabella's face telling its own tale. Whatever had happened between Isabella and Connor had turned out for the best, regardless of the fact that they'd started out as mistress and servant.

"Well, enough about that. I'm sure you'll hear the whole tale by and by." Isabella slid her palm across the coins, fanning them out. "Forgive me for such a personal question, but can you cipher? Manage household accounts? That sort of thing?"

"Yes." Kiera chose not to take offense at the suggestion that she might be illiterate. "I managed my father's accounts when his health failed, then for my brother-in-law until he sold Father's holdings in Ireland."

She didn't share that George required an exact accounting— to the farthing—of every expense. And he wasn't very forgiving of any lapse in judgment. She'd learned to weigh each decision carefully.

"That settles it then." Isabella smiled. "I talked to my father this morning, and we've decided that you would be an excellent asset to Breeze Hill, if you're agreeable."

"An asset?" Kiera tried to keep her confusion from showing.

"You took the initiative to ask about lodging for Reverend Summers. There are several empty cabins, and I'm sure you could scrape up some bedding for a few of them. As the weather grows warmer, most travelers will prefer to sleep outside, so you'd need to be prepared for that, but on these cold, rainy nights, I suspect you'll find many who'd want lodging and a hot meal."

"Lodging and a meal?"

"Of course. Any stand worth its salt provides a meal for its patrons." Isabella slid one of the coins back and forth with her index finger. "What do you think?"

Open a stand here at Breeze Hill? The thought terrified and excited her. To be able to provide a living for herself and her sisters, to make her own way in this new world that she'd been thrust into. But . . .

"What about Le Bonne?"

"We're a day's ride from Natchez. I daresay the tavern owner has forgotten you already."

Kiera prayed she was right. She frowned. "You said you talked to your father about this. Begging your pardon, but your husband doesn't seem happy to have us here."

"Leave Connor to me. Do you think you can do it?"

"Yes." Kiera nodded. "Yes. I can do it."

"Perfect." Isabella pushed the coins toward her. "Here's the first of your money to get you started. And I think I can locate a ledger for you to keep records."

Tentatively, Kiera reached for the coins. As she held them in her hands, still warm from Isabella's touch, she realized these small pieces of silver might be the start to a future where she and her sisters were beholden to no man—not her brother-in-law, Pierre Le Bonne, or even Connor O'Shea, who, despite his dislike and distrust of her, hadn't thrown her out. Yet.

Impulsively she rounded the table and hugged Isabella. "Thank you."

"Quinn, Kiera needs ya."

Patrick grabbed Quinn's arm and pulled him toward one of the cabins.

"What for, lad?"

In spite of the fact that he'd avoided Kiera ever since he'd almost kissed her in the cabin, he let Patrick lead him like a lamb to the slaughter.

"You'll see."

When they got to their destination, Quinn was relieved— or maybe disappointed—to find an empty cabin.

"There's nobody here."

"I never said there was." Patrick pointed toward the fireplace. "Look, the rod that holds the pot over the fire is broken. I told her ya could fix it."

Quinn arched a brow. "Ya did, did ya?"

"O' course. Ye're a blacksmith."

"O' course." Quinn squatted in front of the fireplace, frowning. Kiera was going to need more than a new rod if she was going to cook meals in this fireplace. One of the firedogs was broken. If it wasn't fixed, the firewood would rest on the stone foundation, restricting air flow and increasing smoke.

He squinted at Patrick. "Who said she was going t' be cooking in here?"

Patrick gave him a look that questioned if he'd been living under the Blarney stone. "So she can cook for travelers, like they do at Mount Locust. You can fix it, can't ya?"

"I suppose." Quinn shook his head. Kiera had certainly moved fast with her plans. "But I'll need someone t' pump the bellows. Think you can handle that?"

Patrick puffed out his chest. "O' course I can."

"Well, come on then. Let's see if we can fix this." Quinn

ruffled the boy's hair. He took a poker, pried the rod out, and then hooked the firedog and hefted it out of the fireplace.

Back in the smithy, he sent Patrick to draw a bucket of water. While he was gone, Quinn searched for coal. Not finding any, he eyed the stack of kindling.

He'd never burned lightered pine or charcoal in a smithy, but Seamus had talked about it. He decided to give it a go. He shaved off slivers of kindling, and soon had a nice fire going.

As the fire took hold, he sorted through the tools he'd need and donned the stiff leather apron.

It took longer to get a decent fire built up in the forge and teach Patrick how to man the bellows to keep the fire good and hot than it did to straighten out the rod. But they got it done. Next, he repaired the firedog and laid it to the side. While he had the fire going and Patrick to help, he repaired a kettle that needed nothing more than a new handle, and formed some S-shaped hooks to suspend pots. One last swing of the hammer should do it.

"Well, I'm certainly glad to see someone running this forge again."

Quinn stopped midswing, turning toward Isabella's father. "Master Bartholomew."

The man waved a hand and sat on a nearby stump. "Don't let me stop you. Your iron will get cold."

Patrick stared wide-eyed at the frail man with the scarred face.

"Keep pumping, boy."

Patrick did as he was told. It made Quinn nervous for Mr. Bartholomew to watch him work, but there was nothing for it. He finished the hook and plunged it into the slack tub. It sizzled, the iron cooling fast.

Mr. Bartholomew stood, shuffled over, and inspected the firedog. "Nice work, O'Shea."

"Thank you, sir."

"Connor tells me you were a blacksmith back in Ireland."

"I was. For a time. I have a lot t' learn, though."

"We never stop learning." Mr. Bartholomew rocked back on his heels. "We could use you here working the forge instead of out in the woods with Connor and the others. What do you think?"

"We discussed it."

"But?"

Quinn shrugged. "Something came up, and we didn't get back to it."

"Hmm." Mr. Bartholomew motioned toward the glowing coals. "I'd say that since you have a fire started and plenty of lightered pine at your disposal, now would be the perfect time to—uh—get back to it, wouldn't you?"

"If you think that's best, sir."

"I do. The forge has been shut down way too long."

Quinn nodded. Since he was here, there was nothing to keep him from working in the smithy. It was a job that needed doing, and he had the skills to do it.

Kiera passed by, a bucket of water in her hands. Spotting Mr. Bartholomew, she curtsied. "Good day, sir."

"Good day to you, too, miss." Mr. Bartholomew called her back. "Say, missy, hold up there."

Kiera turned, her blue eyes going wide. "Me, sir?"

"Yes, you." He motioned to the apron that Quinn had on. "Could you run up to the kitchen and ask Martha for some neatsfoot oil?"

"Yes, sir." With one last glance at Mr. Bartholomew, Kiera hurried off.

"I'd better be getting back. Good day to you, O'Shea. Hopefully the neatsfoot will make that leather apron more supple. It hasn't been used in well over a year." Mr. Bartholomew pushed himself up with his sturdy walking stick. He cast an eye on Patrick, then motioned toward the long, sloping hill that led to the house. "Would you mind helping an old man up that hill, boy? I wouldn't want to fall and roll back down, because you'd surely laugh, wouldn't you?"

Patrick stared, round-eyed. "No, sir. I mean, yes, sir. I mean—"

"Come along then." Mr. Bartholomew motioned him forward, placing one hand on his shoulder.

Kiera returned with the jar of oil in hand. "Here you go, sir."

"Oh, it's not for me. It's for him." Mr. Bartholomew motioned to Quinn. "Come along, Patrick."

"Were ya injured in the war, Mr. Bartholomew?"

"No, but I was a soldier."

"Really?"

The two shuffled off, Mr. Bartholomew keeping Patrick

entertained with a tall tale about being in the militia. Quinn held out his hand and she handed over the oil. He removed the heavy leather apron he'd donned to keep sparks from burning his clothes and his skin. A piece of hot metal down one's shirt was a little taste of hell on earth.

He rubbed the oil on the apron, then kneaded the leather, working the oil in. Slowly the leather became less brittle. There wasn't much he could do for the holes burned into it after years of use.

Kiera picked up the discarded gloves, the thick leather huge in her small hands. "These look like they could use a bit of that oil."

She reached for the oil, but Quinn shook his head. "No need. I rarely wear them."

"Why?"

"I canna feel the steel with gloves on."

She looked pointedly at the scars on his hands and forearms.

"If it makes ya feel better, I wore them earlier while working on something that got too hot t' handle."

"Well, you'll need them supple when you do." She dipped a cloth into the solution and started rubbing the oil over the gloves, the tips of her fingers running along the slick leather where countless hands had gripped hot metal. Quinn swallowed, the sight of her fingers on the gloves that he'd worn only moments before doing funny things to his insides.

She frowned, fingering the thin, slick leather across the palm. "These are almost worn through."

He jerked his attention away from her fingers and the

gloves, focused on her face, which only made the whoosh inside worse. For a brief moment, he felt like he was back on the *Lady Gallant* in the middle of the raging storm.

"They're sufficient."

Before he could stop her, she reached out and took his left hand, turning it palm up, revealing the red welt he'd inflicted on himself earlier. She ran the tips of her fingers over his palm, crisscrossed with scars and burns.

"Sufficient?" Arching a brow, she reached for the neatsfoot oil and rubbed a generous amount into his palm. "I think not, Quinn O'Shea."

Quinn sucked in a breath, the minor burn nothing compared to the trail of fire left by her touch.

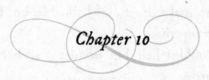

Chapter 10

THE EVENING MEAL SIMMERING OVER THE FIRE, Martha shooed Kiera out of the house kitchen. Kiera donned her cloak and ran through the rain toward the cabins she'd come to think of as her own.

During the last week, she'd spent every spare moment cleaning and repairing three of the cabins, designating the first one as a cookhouse since it was the largest and the closest to the well.

Even Martha, in spite of her hesitation at first, had scrounged up a rickety sideboard, a leaky washtub that was serviceable for the time being, and a smattering of pots and kettles.

Megan, Lizzy, and Patrick had helped chink the logs with mud and dried straw, and Kiera had taken the time to build fires in each cabin to make sure the chimneys were free and clear. The children stocked each cabin with dry firewood in anticipation of cold, wet days like today. There was still plenty to do to make the cabins habitable, but things were slowly coming together.

Still, she couldn't help but wonder if all her hard work was for naught.

Not one single traveler had stopped at Breeze Hill in the last week.

Determined not to give up, though, she'd decided to scrub the floor in the cookhouse, just in case.

As she neared the cabins, she glanced toward the smithy, where the ring of Quinn's hammer echoed across the clearing. He'd taken up residence in the blacksmith shop, hammering away most of the day instead of going into the woods with the rest of the men.

But in spite of his close proximity, he'd kept his distance all the while she'd been busy cleaning out the cabins. Her face flamed. Well, probably because she'd made a fool of herself assuming he might want favors from her when he just wanted to help. No wonder he'd avoided her all week.

She entered the cabin and headed toward the fireplace, stopping dead in her tracks. The rod had been fixed and two shiny new S-hooks were suspended from it. Even the firedogs stood straight and proud, no longer needing to be propped up.

Now she felt even worse for accusing Quinn of less than honorable intentions. There was nothing for it. She must thank him for his kindness, and there was no time like the present. She walked toward the door, then stopped as she saw him headed down the lane toward the sawmill, pushing a wheelbarrow full of repaired chains, axes, adzes, and other tools.

Even as she watched, he rounded the bend out of sight. Eyeing the empty smithy, she remembered the worn-out gloves and the stiff apron. An idea began to take root, and she glanced in the direction he'd gone. He was nowhere to be seen.

She hurried to the smithy and grabbed the gloves and the apron before she could change her mind. She'd barely made it back to the cookhouse and found a place to stash the items when Megan and Lizzy came tearing inside, their hair damp from rain and mud spatters along their hems. Both girls sucked in big gulps of air.

"Goodness, what is wrong with you two?"

"Travelers. A whole passel of 'em coming down the lane," Megan blurted out as soon as she caught her breath. "They want food and lodging. Well, three of them do."

Kiera's heart leapt. "How—how do you know?"

"We asked 'em." Lizzy grinned.

"Oh, Lizzy, you didn't."

Lizzy looked at her as if she'd gone daft. "O' course we did, Miss Kiera. How else would we know if they could pay for food and lodgin'?"

"How else indeed?" Kiera glanced toward the door. "Three men, you say?"

The girls nodded. Megan took her by the hand. "Come on, Kiera. Come see."

"All right. All right." She wiped her hands on her apron and allowed Megan to lead her outside. Eight, no, ten wagons congregated in the grove of trees on the other side of the well, the drivers looking cold, wet, and miserable.

Two men left the group and headed toward the cookhouse, shoulders hunched against the rain. Only two? The girls had said there were three. Maybe the third would be along shortly.

"Good day, sirs." She folded her hands, hoping she looked like a seasoned innkeeper. "Are you looking for lodging?"

"Yes, ma'am. Franklin Hamilton at your service." Mr. Hamilton removed his hat and bowed. He gestured toward the other man, who mimicked his action, removing his hat and showing deference. Raindrops splattered on their exposed heads. "My companion, Mr. Reeves. We were very pleased to find that there was lodging to be had here at Breeze Hill."

"It's not much, I'm afraid."

"Anything out of this weather would do. Your hospitality is most appreciated."

She hesitated, unsure if she should invite the men inside, but she could hardly expect them to stand outside in the rain. Not if they were going to pay for lodging for the night. And besides, the two girls stood there, grinning from ear to ear as if they were solely responsible for bringing the lodgers to her. And in a way, she supposed they were. She moved aside. "Please, come inside."

They looked around at the cabin, and she realized how cold and barren it must seem in their eyes. There wasn't even a fire in the fireplace. Somehow she had to stall them. "If you'd like to refresh yourself in the next cabin over, dinner will be served in an hour."

"Thank you, ma'am."

Kiera, Lizzy, and Megan peeked out the door, watching as the two men trudged through the rain to the cabin. The two girls giggled, and Kiera had the urge to join them. She had paying customers.

"Look. There's Quinn." Lizzy pointed, and Kiera spotted him returning from his errand, the wheelbarrow loaded with more items that needed repairing. Lizzy grabbed Megan's hand. "Come on, Megan, let's go tell him."

They took off down the lane. When they were gone, Kiera turned around, then stared at the cold fireplace. What could she serve that would be ready within the hour? She didn't even have anything in this cabin to make a decent meal—

The door banged open and Quinn shouldered his way inside, arms full of firewood. The girls crowded in behind him, arms also full.

"What am I going to cook? This is all so sudden."

"Sudden?" He dumped the firewood in the wood box and started laying a fire. "I thought this was what ya've been working on for the last week."

"It was." She twisted her apron in her hands. "It is. But I can't just cook a meal on the off chance that I'll have boarders on any given night."

"Ya do no' have any provisions?" One eyebrow shot upward. "I thought Isabella said ya could do this. She didna provide staples?"

"She gave her permission, but I can't use food from Breeze Hill stores. It wouldn't be right."

"Why no'? Those men paid their fee, didn't they? Feed them, and then ya can settle up with the household accounts in the morning."

"I—" She felt her face flame. "I didn't ask for any money. Yet."

"They didna pay?"

She shook her head, feeling foolish. Quinn was right. She should have asked for payment tonight before she promised them a meal and told them where to sleep. The rain fell harder outside and now she'd have to run all over grabbing foodstuffs to cook a meal that she'd promised would be ready in an hour.

What had she been thinking?

The door swung open and another man entered. Rainwater sluiced off his greasy-looking clothes and puddled on the floor. Kiera's skin crawled at the way he ogled her. "You the wench what's offering food and lodgin'?"

Kiera nodded. "Yes—"

"We are." Quinn stepped in front of her. "If ye're o' a mind t' spend the night out o' the rain, the sleeping quarters are in the cabin next door. Yer repast will be ready in an hour. Served here."

The man's eyes slid from Quinn to Kiera. "I reckon I'll take you up on the offer. I don't have a hankering to spend the night out in that mess."

He turned to go, but Quinn stepped forward, hand held out. "Yer payment, sir."

The man scowled but handed over his money.

He slipped outside, and Kiera grabbed her cloak. "I'd better hurry. I don't have a minute to lose. Ham and cornmeal mush should be decent fare for a quick meal, shouldn't it?"

"I'd eat it and be glad for it."

"Megan, you and Lizzy run over to the house and ask Martha for some cornmeal and—and salt." She headed for the door. "I'll get a ham."

Quinn grabbed her wrist, pulling her to a stop. "I'll get the ham while ya tend the fire."

"Thank you, Quinn. I—" Gratitude filled her heart. "I don't know what I'd do without you."

He opened her fist, tucked the coins inside, then chuckled. "Ye'd be worse than a chicken running around with her head cut off."

"'Tis true."

With a wink, he went in search of ham for the meal. While he was gone, Megan and Lizzy returned, followed by Patrick. All three were laden with staples from Martha's kitchen, abundantly more than she'd asked for. Kiera cleared a small side table. "Put it all here."

Determined to keep track of every staple she'd purloined—no, not stolen, just borrowed—from Breeze Hill's stores, Kiera made careful note of everything to record in her ledger later. Martha had outdone herself. Not only had she sent everything needed to make mush, she'd included butter and molasses and drink for the men.

Quinn returned with a ham, plopped it on the side table, and grabbed a poker, urging the fire to take hold. The fire sputtered and spit. Without so much as a by-your-leave, he grabbed two pails and headed out the door. Moments later, he returned, shouldering the cabin door open once more. "Stand back, lass. These have hot coals in 'em."

"From the smithy?"

"Aye. We do no' have time for your fire t' get hot enough."

He emptied the coals out of one, then scraped them into a pile. Dusting his hands, he stood. "There ya go."

"Thank you." Kiera smiled. "I wouldn't have thought to grab coals from the smithy."

"And do no' be thinkin' ya should." He glowered at the three youngsters. "And none o' the rest o' ya either. Understood?"

"Yes, sir."

"Good, then." He removed his coat and rolled up his sleeves, picked up a knife and reached for the ham. "Do ya have plates, cups, something for them to drink?"

"Martha sent a keg of ale." Kiera shook her head. "But no utensils—"

"The men should have their own chargers and spoons,

but, Megan, go ask Martha for some just in case. Patrick, fetch a bucket of water. We'll water the ale down a wee bit."

The children shot out the door to do his bidding.

"I've made a mess of everything. I was so focused on lodging that I completely forgot to plan for meals. Martha said there were few travelers this time of year, and I thought I'd have more time to prepare." Feeling overwhelmed, Kiera plopped down on a chair, the mush mixture clasped against her. "This whole venture is going to be a dismal failure."

Quinn dropped the knife and moved to crouch in front of her, his hands braced on either side of her against the seat, his muscled forearms glistening in the firelight. "It's no' a failure, lass. No' yet. In the morning, when the men who've paid their coin for food and lodging shake their fists at ya and say that they'll tell everyone how terrible yer service was, then you can call yerself a failure."

"They'd do that?" Kiera whispered.

"Aye." He winked, and she knew he was teasing. "But not if ya fill 'em full o' ham and mush sweetened with molasses, and they sleep warm and dry tonight. Then they'll tell a different tale altogether. Now, ya'd better get started on that mush. Looks like I'm stuck frying ham until Megan and Lizzy return."

He reached for the knife and resumed slicing ham, whistling a jaunty tune from the homeland. Blinking back the sting of happy tears, Kiera turned toward the fireplace.

How had she ever gotten along without Quinn O'Shea?

Early the next morning before daybreak, Quinn built up the fire in the forge. He told himself it was because there were so many broken, bent, rusted, and worn tools lying around the plantation that needed fixing.

But the truth was he wanted to keep an eye on Kiera until the caravan left. It had rained most of the night and he'd suspected more of the travelers had decided to seek shelter inside the cabins. And he didn't intend to let them take advantage of Kiera by cheating her out of her fee.

He stepped to the edge of the smithy and saw that the travelers who'd chosen to endure the elements were beginning to stir. Across the clearing, the door of the cabin opened and a man stepped outside and stretched. Quinn didn't recognize him from the night before.

He headed that way, nodded at the early riser, and stepped inside. Sure enough, there were eight men, including the one outside.

"Good morning, gentlemen. I hope ya slept well."

"Tolerable." Two of the men exchanged looks.

"Good t' hear it. Looks like yer party is getting ready t' depart. I'll make sure Miss Young has breakfast ready so ya can grab a bite to eat and settle up with her before ya leave." He made eye contact with each man in turn. Even though he could hardly make out the inhabitants' features in the darkened interior, he wanted each man to know he'd seen them. "I'm sure she'll deduct last night's meal off for anyone who didna eat."

He backed out of the cabin and came face-to-face with Kiera, her brows lowered in a frown. "May I have a word with you?"

"O' course."

As soon as they were out of earshot of the cabin, she turned. "What are you doing?"

Quinn shrugged. "Just making sure none o' those men cheat ya, lass."

"I can handle it."

"Can ya now?" He crossed his arms over his chest. "And just how were you going t' know how many men had snuck into the cabin in the middle o' the night?"

"I—" She lifted her chin. "I could tell when they came outside."

"Ye're not always going t' be around when they get ready t' leave."

She sighed. "Quinn, I appreciate your help, but I've got to do this myself."

He opened his mouth to argue but stopped when one by one the men exited the cabin. Mr. Hamilton dipped his head. "Morning, miss. Sir."

Kiera bobbed slightly. "Good day, Mr. Hamilton."

As the lodgers made their way toward the cookhouse, Kiera turned back to Quinn. "See. There are some gentlemen traveling the trace. They're not all out to cheat me."

"Sometimes it's the gentlemen ya have t' watch out for, lass." Turning on his heel, he went back to the smithy.

Once inside, he searched for the leather apron, but it was nowhere to be found. Patrick had taken to wearing the moldy piece of leather while trying his hand at pounding out small strips of iron. No telling what the boy had done with it.

Oh, well, the stiff, unwieldy apron was almost more trouble than it was worth. Growling, he picked up his hammer and took his frustration out by beating metal into submission.

"Quinn, can I have a word with you?" Connor strode into the smithy. "I've decided t' take three loads of lumber to Natchez. And I'd like you to go along."

"Why me?"

"Sometimes the ships bring pig iron from Pennsylvania and Maine. And if not, there's an ironmonger in Natchez. I need all the scrap iron, broken wheels, and wagon parts I can get. As a blacksmith, you have more knowledge of what's needed, and I'd like your input."

"All right." Quinn shoved a peeler into the slack tub, the cold water cooling the metal quickly. He didn't know how much help he'd be, but a trip to Natchez might be just what he needed.

Chapter 11

As Kiera's lodgers sat down to break their fast, Connor stepped through the cabin doorway. It was all she could do not to let the surprise show on her face.

She'd hardly seen Quinn's brother in the two weeks she'd been at Breeze Hill. She curtsied, feeling foolish, but the man scared her spitless. "Master O'Shea."

"Miss Young." He scowled, and she cringed. Isabella had told her time and again not to call her husband master, but she couldn't help herself. He had the power to send her and her sisters away, and with good reason. She stood mute beside the fireplace.

He turned his back on her and approached the table full of men. "Mr. Hamilton, may I have a word with you?"

"O'Shea." The kindly gentleman who'd been the first to take up Lizzy's offer of lodging for the night jumped to his feet. He pumped Connor's hand in greeting. "I say, sir, opening a stand here at Breeze Hill is a splendid idea. Simply splendid. Some days—like in yesterday's downpour—it's impossible to press on to other accommodations. Knowing I can stop here instead is truly a godsend."

"I can't take the credit, sir. This is all Miss Young's doing." Connor nodded toward her.

Kiera blushed and turned back to the fireplace. Connor returned his attention to Mr. Hamilton, clearly having dismissed her just as suddenly as he'd acknowledged her presence. "Would it be possible for my wagons t' travel along with you toward Natchez?"

"Certainly, but—" Hamilton paused, pulling at his earlobe—"I thought after that nasty business with Nolan Braxton, the highwaymen were no longer a threat, and we could travel without fear of being accosted. As a matter of fact, that's the only reason I decided to take the road instead of traveling overland to the river and taking the time to construct flatboats. We'd been told it was safe."

"While the threat isn't as dire as it was last fall, many of us in the area expect the highwaymen to come out in droves as summer approaches. As long as there are travelers along the trace, we'll have those who want to relieve them of their coin. I'm not willing to take the chance."

"This is an unexpected development." Mr. Hamilton frowned. "To tell you the truth, your company will be most welcome. We've had half a dozen riders join our party along the way. I wasn't overly concerned as I'm transporting the last of my cotton to market and doubt anyone would rob us knowing we have not sold our wares. The trip back is certainly a worry, of course." He rubbed a hand down his face. "Can your men be ready to travel within the hour?"

"We'll be ready." Connor nodded, turned on his heel, and departed.

Mr. Hamilton deposited his fee in Kiera's palm. "Thank you for the lodging, miss. It was greatly appreciated."

As the rest of the men filed out the door behind Mr. Hamilton, they pressed coins into her palm, each expressing his appreciation. Kiera clasped the coins tight, elated with the success of her venture.

Eight lodgers the first night. It was . . . simply astounding.

She fingered the money in her pocket. She needed supplies, and Connor was sending wagons to Natchez. But did she dare ask him to purchase supplies for her? The very thought made her knees quake.

Martha would know what to do. Grabbing her ledger, she hurried toward the kitchen.

The cook glanced up. "Goodness, girl, what's got you in such a tizzy?"

"Master O'Shea—I mean, Connor—is sending some of the men to Natchez to deliver lumber." She pulled the coins out of her pocket. "I thought I could get some staples."

Martha peered at the coins, shaking her head. "Would you look at that? Who would've thought men would pay that much for a bit of ham and a pallet for the night." She clucked her tongue. "Back in my day, I would've slept on the ground before I'd part with hard-earned money for a place to lay my head."

"There's not much time to lose, Martha. Where's Isabella? I need to give her my list."

Martha's lips twitched. "Why can't you just give it to Master O'Shea?"

Kiera's face flamed.

Martha laughed. "That's all right, girl. He's not nearly as scary as you think he is. But don't you worry." She moved across the room, opened a crock, and fished out a slip of paper. "Let me see your list."

Kiera opened her ledger, and they compared notes.

Martha scratched out some numbers and rewrote them. She handed Kiera the revised list. "Now, you take this list to Mews, and he'll see that we both get the staples we need. Tell him Martha sent you."

"Yes, ma'am." At the door, she whirled. "Oh, should I give him the money?"

"You keep it for now. Mews will use proceeds from the sale of the lumber to buy what we need. And then you can settle up with Miss Isabella as needed."

"Yes, ma'am."

The yard was full of horses, men, and wagons, but it wasn't hard to distinguish the wagons that belonged to Breeze Hill as they were loaded down with lumber.

Kiera searched for Mr. Mews, knowing she didn't have

much time. Finally she spotted him close to the end of the line, climbing onto a wagon seat. Quinn stood next to the wagon, fiddling with the harnesses.

"Mr. Mews, wait."

Both men glanced up. "What is it, lass?"

"Miss Martha wanted me to give you this list."

"That woman. I can't ever get off to Natchez without her wanting something or t'other." He reached down. "Hand it over."

"Thank you, Mr. Mews."

"There. That should do it." Quinn stepped away from the harnesses. Mews clucked to the team and drove off, joining the line of wagons.

Quinn reached for a pack, then turned back to Kiera. "Will ya keep an eye on Patrick for me?"

"Yes, but—" Kiera had a moment of panic. "You're going too?"

A smile quirked up one side of his mouth. "Will ya miss me, lass?"

"No." A swoosh of heat flushed her cheeks, and Kiera lifted her hand to shade her eyes, hoping he didn't notice her reddened cheeks. She shrugged. "I was just surprised, that's all. I expected you'd stay here and work in the smithy."

"That's why I'm going along. Connor wants t' buy iron for the smithy and needs my advice."

"Oh. I see." The call came down the line for the wagon train to move out. Kiera stepped back. "Godspeed, Quinn."

"Godspeed, lass." He jogged away, hoisted himself up beside Connor.

Kiera watched until the wagons disappeared around the bend and out of sight. She'd said she wouldn't miss Quinn, but that wasn't exactly true.

She missed him already.

"Take this, compliments of Mr. Bartholomew."

Connor held out a pistol and a bag of shot. Quinn took the weapon, tucked it into his waistband, and slung the bag around his neck and under his arm.

"Are ya expecting trouble?"

"We should always expect trouble on the trace."

Two hours later, after not meeting one soul on the long, lonely road, Quinn relaxed his guard. He had yet to understand the precautions the locals exercised when traveling to and from Natchez, but if they believed the highwaymen were a threat, who was he to discredit their unease?

He eyed the long line of wagons snaking along the dark, forested lane. "So why do ya no' float the lumber down the river? Seems like that would be easier and safer since we're beset with thieves on every side."

Connor tossed him a look and slapped the reins against the horses' withers. "Have you seen a river anywhere around here?"

Quinn frowned. "Come t' think o' it, I havena. But I thought the trace ran along the Mississippi River—"

"Nay. Once you leave Natchez, the trail veers off t' the northeast. Breeze Hill is maybe ten, fifteen miles east o' the river, and there's nothing but wilderness and swamps between the two. It would be foolish t' haul the lumber that far just to float downriver when it's only a day's ride down the trace."

"Makes sense." Quinn jostled along for another five minutes, thinking about what Connor had said. "Maybe if you harvest the trees closer t' the river, you could float them downriver. That should be easy enough."

Connor nodded, brow furrowed. "Perhaps. Wainwright owns that tract of land. It's something t' consider if he'd be willing."

Quinn and Connor continued to discuss the merits of harvesting trees along the river's edge as they traveled along. It certainly made the trip go faster.

After a long and uneventful day of travel, the wagons pulled into a small meadow dotted with oaks next to Wainwright House. They'd hardly come to a complete stop when Thomas Wainwright came out to greet them. Quinn jumped down from the wagon just as the elder Wainwright shook Connor's hand.

Wainwright eyed the heavily laden wagons. "Another load of lumber for Wicker, eh?"

"If he wants it." Connor grinned. "If not, there's plenty who do."

"Aye. You're right about that." Wainwright inspected one of the boards. "The British are paying top dollar for indigo, tobacco, cotton, everything we can produce. And the plantation owners are all trying to outdo each other by building grand homes here in Natchez to parade their wealth."

"And what about you? Do you plan to build a larger home here in Natchez?"

"No need. Wainwright House is big enough for our needs as we enjoy spending most of our time out in the country. Which reminds me. How long will you be here? I'd like to ride back with you as far as Breeze Hill."

"Two or three days at most."

"Good. That will give me time to get my affairs in order." Wainwright nodded at Quinn. "It's good to see you again, Quinn. I trust your trip to Breeze Hill was without incident?"

"Yes, we made it fine." Quinn glanced at Connor before continuing. "Have you learned anything new about Miss Young and her sisters' plight?"

"Nothing." Wainwright shrugged. "Of course there hasn't been enough time to hear back from my contact in London. I'm hesitant to approach Monsieur Le Bonne until I hear what the girls' brother-in-law has to say on the matter."

Connor scowled. "Who is this Le Bonne?"

"He's a vagabond and a cutthroat and a scoundrel of the worst order. You'd recognize him if you saw him. He has a jagged scar running from here to here." Wainwright ran the tip of his finger from the corner of his eye to his chin. "He showed up a few months ago, purchased the Blue Heron, and quickly became the kingpin in Natchez Under-the-Hill. He's not a man easily forgotten."

"What about Marchette's death?" Quinn frowned. "Is there nothing t' be done?"

"Nothing, I'm afraid. There were no witnesses, and if there were, I'm not sure they'd talk. I sent a letter of condolence to his family, along with his personal effects."

Quinn clenched his fist. "If Le Bonne discovers where Kiera and her sisters are, he could demand their return, couldna he?"

"He could." Wainwright sighed. "It's one thing for a grown woman to enter such an agreement of her own free will, but to force children into that kind of life is . . . well, it's simply barbaric."

"Wainwright, surely you're aware that this kind o' thing is common, especially with female indentures." Connor folded his arms, his stance denoting his disgust.

"That may be, but that doesn't mean I agree with it or that the law condones it."

"The law turns a blind eye t' a lot o' things," Connor growled. "Especially the goings-on under the hill."

Pierre stood in the shadows on the balcony overlooking the tavern floor. The place was busy tonight. Ale flowed quick and fast like the Mississippi at flood stage.

On the tavern floor, one of his barmaids was doing her best to entice a patron upstairs. Another plied three men with drink. Assuredly the three would all leave with empty coin purses, the way they held out their cups for more each time she came around.

"That's mine. Give it back."

"I saw it first."

Pierre shifted his attention, saw two of his barmaids standing on the landing. He watched as Penelope reached out and grabbed Lise by the hair.

"It's mine, you wench. Give it back."

The two wrestled over a satin skirt, the golden embroidery shimmering in the candlelight. Beyond the means of either of the worn-out wenches, the prized garment undoubtedly came from one of the trunks left behind by Kiera Young and her sisters.

Pierre snapped his fingers. The barmaids turned, saw him, and froze in shocked silence. Without blinking, he let his stare wander from one to the other, then back again. They were both so frightened they didn't dare utter a sound.

He moved out of the shadows. "*Mes chères*, our recent . . . guests . . . left two trunks full of beautiful clothes, did they not?"

"Yes—yes, sir." Penelope, the more brazen of the two, managed to squeak out an answer.

"Then I suggest the two of you share the bounty without quarreling." He glanced at the tavern floor, then skewered them both with a look. "Tomorrow morning when the tavern is closed. Do I make myself clear?"

"Yes, sir."

Leaving the garment where it lay, the girls scurried down the stairs, clearly thankful to escape with nothing more than a scolding. But Pierre had more on his mind tonight than a couple of brawling barmaids.

Stooping, he picked up the discarded skirt, the silky material flowing like liquid through his fingers. Just like Kiera and her sisters had slipped away without a trace.

He crushed the material in his hands.

Looking over the railing, he spotted Claude near the door. He beckoned, and instantly the man made his way across the room and up the stairs.

"Monsieur?"

"Any sign of those three girls?"

"Non."

"Very well. You may go." Pierre waved Claude away, the tips of his fingers rubbing the scar that ran down the side of his face. Many thought he'd gotten the scar from a knife fight, and he'd chosen not to enlighten them. A knife fight was much more interesting than the measly tornado that had ripped Braxton Hall apart.

But along with the scar, Pierre had managed to end Nolan Braxton's life and haul away almost a year's worth of coin stolen in raids along the Natchez Trace. So his injuries hadn't been in vain.

He'd used the proceeds to buy the Blue Heron and lie low for a while.

After Claude left, Pierre retreated to his private quarters. Loosening his collar, he pondered why the well-dressed stranger had involved himself in Pierre's business. Why did he even care about the three girls? They were nobodies. They didn't have anything of value and were just half-Irish wenches that Manderly and his wife wanted off their hands.

Pierre clipped the end off a cigar, lit it, and pondered the situation.

Which brought him to the Irishman and the scrappy youngsters from the wharf. Where had they gotten off to? Were they someone's indentured servants? Freemen? Pierre had the feeling he'd seen the elder one before. There was something familiar about him. But he couldn't put his finger on it. Did they also have something to do with the girls' sudden disappearance?

He would bet the Blue Heron and all he owned that they did.

He drummed his fingers on the tabletop. Somehow he had to find out who the Irishman was and where he'd gone.

If he didn't miss his guess, finding one would lead him to the other.

After two days of clear skies, the clouds rolled in once again as Quinn and Connor headed toward the wharf to look for iron.

Their first stop was at Bloomfield's office.

Bloomfield shook his head. "There's little iron to be found. And what does arrive is quickly purchased by the Spanish garrison or the builders here in the city."

"What about the ironmonger? Would he have anything?"

"Perhaps. Just follow the road that curves along the river and you can't miss his shop."

On the way to their destination, they spotted an over-turned wagon in the middle of the road; another wagon had a broken wheel and at least one horse was down.

"We won't be able to get through there for a while."

Connor motioned to the left. "Turn here. There's another road that curves to the right and will lead us back to the river road."

Quinn did as Connor suggested, drove up the long, wind-ing road, then took the fork to the right, heading downhill toward the river, the winding lane growing narrower by the moment. As they neared the riverbank, they passed shacks one after another that were little more than pigsties. Some were just boards nailed together—lumber from abandoned flatboats. Hollow-eyed women watched them from between the slats, some offering catcalls and invitations, while others just stared as in a stupor.

The clouds opened up and dumped buckets of rain on them, making Quinn wish they hadn't embarked on this fool's errand.

Boys, haggard and dirty, played in the streets, moving out of the way long enough to allow the wagon to pass, then fall-ing back in, hardly deterred by the rain. Some of these boys were probably the same ones he'd seen on the wharf the day he arrived, picking the pockets of unwary travelers who'd just disembarked.

A young woman huddled in a doorway, long, stringy hair matted against her scalp. She was barefoot and barely had on enough clothes to keep a cat warm, let alone a human.

Her blue-eyed gaze, dull and lifeless, rose, meeting his as the wagon neared.

Eyes that reminded him of Kiera.

For a moment, he saw the bleakness that stretched before this young girl, the hand she'd been dealt, either through choice or circumstance. Regardless, hers was a painful glance that cut to the quick.

Would this have been Kiera, Amelia, or Megan had he and Wainwright not been able to spirit them away from Le Bonne's clutches? Or even Patrick, like the boys he'd just passed, playing in the streets, waiting for the next ship to arrive so they could converge on the wharf like rats and pick the pockets of unsuspecting travelers one by one? Would one of those boys have been Patrick if something had happened to Quinn in the mines? His little brother in debtors' prison or shipped off to the colonies to fend for himself, sold as a servant, treated like a dog?

Compassion smote him.

He handed the reins to Connor, pulled off his coat, and tossed it to the girl as the wagon passed. It fell short, in the mud at her feet. Quinn looked back, watching as she slowly reached out, picked up the coat, and shivering against the cold, pulled it over her shoulders.

Then her gaze rose, blue eyes watching until the wagon rounded the bend and they passed out of sight.

Connor never said a word, and Quinn didn't know what he would have said if his brother had questioned why he'd given the girl his coat. Honestly, he didn't know himself.

But he did know one thing.

Whatever happened, God had used Connor's banishment to the colonies for good.

And Quinn would be forever grateful for that.

Chapter 12

CLUTCHING THE LEATHER APRON AND GLOVES against her, Kiera slipped inside the smithy, the smell of long-dead fires and molten iron still pungent. The men would be back soon, and she needed to return Quinn's apron and the gloves.

She'd salvaged a supple piece of leather off an old powder bag to cushion the palms of the gloves. It had taken all her skill to fit the leather snugly in place, and she had the pricked fingers to show for it. But at least Quinn's hands would be protected from the red-hot metal he worked with day in and day out. She'd patched the worst of the holes, but the apron was still old, stiff, and moth-eaten. She left the gloves on his worktable, then hung the apron on its peg.

Turning away, she spotted a row of hammers lined up neatly on a shelf. One hammer lay on the anvil, the handle polished from constant use. She ran a finger along the wood, smooth and cool to her touch. Had Quinn used this hammer before he left? Had his strong fingers gripped the wood as he pounded iron to his will?

She shivered as she recalled the touch of his fingers against her skin. How could one man's hands be so strong, so powerful, yet so gentle? She jerked her hand back when she heard a shout, then rushed to the door. Had the men returned already? While she hadn't done anything wrong, she wouldn't want to be caught snooping in Quinn's workshop.

She stepped outside, at first relieved that it wasn't Quinn, but her relief turned to suspicion at the battered strangers shuffling down the main road toward the well. Connor and Quinn were still away, and the remaining crew of lumbermen were harvesting trees far away from the main house. Mr. Bartholomew would be no match for these men should they be bent on mischief.

Spotting Amelia staring at the men from the cookhouse doorway, she hurried that way, putting herself between her sister and possible harm.

As the two men neared, it was evident one was hardly more than a boy and badly injured. When they reached the well, the boy slumped down. Leaving him leaning against the sturdy well, the older man hurried forward.

"Amelia, fetch Mr. Horne." For once, her sister obeyed without question. *Please, Lord, let the man be close to hand.*

"Reginald Wheaton Caruthers, at your service." In spite of his disheveled appearance, his torn and stained coat, he still carried himself like a gentleman. But she wasn't convinced he was trustworthy. Her brother-in-law could carry off the act of an honorable gentleman just as effectively, and he'd proven he was anything but.

"May I be of service, sir?"

"Forgive me, mistress, but my son's been shot."

"Shot?" Alarmed, Kiera jerked her gaze to the young man.

"We were attacked on the road north of here. Do you offer food and lodging, a place I can tend his wounds?" Mr. Caruthers twisted his hat in his hands, his attention straying to his son. "I'm afraid I have little to offer in payment. All our possessions were stolen, including our provisions, coin, and horses." The boy groaned and Mr. Caruthers whirled, took two steps toward his son. "Weston?"

"Father—" Grimacing, the young man gripped his leg, then pitched forward into the dirt.

Mr. Caruthers turned back to Kiera, pleading in his expression.

Compassion overrode her fear, and Kiera pointed to one of the cabins. "Take him there. There's wood for a fire. I'll fetch water and some clean linen to dress his wounds."

"Thank you, miss." Mr. Caruthers helped his son to his feet, half-dragging, half-carrying him the rest of the way.

As they disappeared inside, Isabella came hurrying toward her. "Amelia said someone's been injured?"

"A Mr. Caruthers and his son. The boy's been shot." Kiera

pressed a hand to her stomach, the gravity of the situation sinking in. "I couldn't turn them away."

"Of course you couldn't." Isabella patted her arm.

"Thank you. I was afraid I'd done the wrong thing. They don't look like highwaymen."

Isabella sighed. "It's a hard thing to know who's trustworthy and who's not. All we can do is give people the benefit of the doubt until they prove otherwise."

Mr. Horne came running, followed closely by Amelia. "Where's the boy?"

"There." Kiera pointed toward the cabin. "We'll bring water and something for bandages."

"I'll get the water." Amelia rushed toward the cookhouse.

Isabella turned away. "I'll find Martha. She has some experience with injuries."

Kiera hurried into the cookhouse, found Amelia pouring hot water into a bucket, then adding a bit of cold to temper it. She stood back as her sister lifted the bucket, slipped out the door, and started toward the cabin. Amelia wasn't one to offer assistance in any fashion whatsoever. As a matter of fact, she was rarely to be found when work was involved.

Staring after her, Kiera shook her head. What had gotten into her sister?

The rest of their party, including Mews and Wainwright and a dozen others who'd joined forces to make the journey northward, fell behind.

"What's yer hurry, man?" Quinn gritted his teeth and held on as the wagon jostled along the rutted road toward Breeze Hill. The meager pile of iron they'd managed to purchase from the ironmonger skittered across the wagon bed. Connor's plan to stock up on iron to keep Quinn busy in the smithy had come to naught.

"Whoa." Connor pulled on the reins, urging the horses to a slower pace. "No hurry. Just anxious to be home. I don't like leaving Isabella, especially not since . . ." He paused, jaw clenched, a look of pain creasing his brow. "Not since she lost the babe."

Quinn threw him a glance. There'd been a babe? He hadn't known, but then again, it wasn't the kind of thing men talked about. Now Connor's crazed reaction the day the horse had gotten tangled in the traces made sense. "I'm sorry. I didn't know."

"It happened in December. She'd just told me, then . . ." He shrugged, his broad shoulders jostling against Quinn's.

There was nothing else to say, and they rode in silence for a while. Before long, Connor urged the horses to pick up their pace again, and Quinn didn't complain about the rough ride.

He thought of Breeze Hill up ahead, his brother's anxious desire to get home, to see his wife. A sudden longing for the old country and even the cold and drafty shack they'd called home for his twenty-six years welled up within him, the closest thing to the feeling of home that Quinn could muster.

"Connor?"

"Hmm?"

"How long before ya stopped missing Ireland? Missing the old home place?"

His brother sighed. "I missed it every day until I found Isabella. She's my home now."

Quinn scowled. "How can a woman be home?"

Connor chuckled. "You'll know when you find a woman you can't live without."

While Mr. Caruthers and his son weren't the paying guests she'd hoped for, Kiera had a pot of stew simmering in the fireplace when she heard the sound of wagons coming down the lane. She frowned. More travelers?

She wiped her hands and went to the door. Megan, Lizzy, and Patrick came running, and within minutes, the children had secured four more lodgers for the night.

Thinking quickly, Kiera sent Megan to the storehouse for more potatoes to stretch the stew to feed the extra men. Less than an hour later, when they filed in, Kiera scrambled to get everything on the table.

Amelia stepped inside, followed by Mr. Caruthers. The man looked ready to fall flat on his face. Kiera motioned to the table. "Please, Mr. Caruthers, have a seat. How's your son?"

"He'll live, the Lord be praised."

"I'm so glad to hear it." Awkwardly, she patted his shoulder. "You must be famished."

"Thank you, miss, but if you would be so kind, I'd rather take something to my son. Just some broth—"

"More stew, wench." An unkempt man with a nasally wheeze and a bulbous nose that had been shattered at one time held out his bowl, not caring that he'd interrupted.

"Yes, sir." Biting back her irritation, Kiera took the bowl, ladled a third helping of stew in, and handed it back.

"I'll take Weston something while you eat, sir." Amelia sidled past Mr. Caruthers.

"Thank you, miss." Mr. Caruthers smiled kindly at her. "A bit of stew does sound wonderful. We haven't eaten since late yesterday."

Kiera placed a bowl of stew before him, then joined Amelia at the hearth. "Amelia, it's unseemly for you to spend time in the men's sleeping quarters with—with that boy."

"His name is Weston, and he's injured." Amelia's cheeks pinkened, and she grabbed a slab of corn bread and shot out the back door before Kiera could stop her.

"Amelia," Kiera hissed, starting after her sister. Before she'd taken two steps, the same uncouth man banged his tin cup on the table, demanding ale and another bowl of stew. Kiera should have charged double for this one. He was filthy and ragged, had consumed more than his fair share of ale as well as a fourth bowl of stew. As she leaned over the table to fill his cup, he stared at her. "Have I seen you somewhere before, wench?"

"I—I don't think so."

"I think I have." He nodded, chuckling. "It'll come to me. It always does."

Kiera jerked away as she felt the brush of his hand along her thigh. Of course, the touch was far removed given that she wore several layers of skirts, but it was enough to send her scurrying across the room toward the fireplace.

Hands shaking, she grabbed a knife and started slicing bread, wondering what she'd gotten herself into. Would the other men at the table defend her against this vile man should it come to that? Would Mr. Caruthers? He'd done nothing to make her think otherwise, but he was a stranger, after all.

Her hands paused in their task as she heard the jingle of harnesses, then the creak of wagons coming down the road. More travelers? Surely not this late in the day. Drying her hands on her apron, she peered out the door.

Relief filled her when she realized it wasn't strangers, but Breeze Hill's own men. She searched for Quinn. Even in the fading light, she spotted him riding on the foremost wagon with Connor.

Patrick came running to meet them. "Did you get robbed on the way home?"

"Robbed?" Quinn pulled back on the reins. "Why would ya ask such a question, lad?"

Patrick pointed toward the cabin. "Mr. Caruthers's son was shot, and highwaymen stole everything they had."

"Shot, you say?"

Patrick nodded.

Connor, followed by Quinn, jumped to the ground and

hurried toward the cabin where Weston Caruthers lay. Kiera stepped back inside, only to meet the hooded stare of the man who'd tried to take liberties with her.

"*Fröken?*"

Kiera turned toward the hulking frame in the doorway, came face-to-face with one of Connor's lumbermen, the Swede. "Mr. Björn, can I help you?"

He grinned, looking pleased she'd remembered his name. Hat in hand, he motioned toward the stewpot. "That smells good, *fröken*. Not like the *skulor* Lafitte cooks."

Kiera didn't have to know what *skulor* meant to understand his distaste of the Frenchman's cooking. "Would you like some?"

"*Ja.*" He quickly found a place at the table.

Kiera was glad of the big Swede's presence.

As the meal wound down to its end, the vile man who'd already accosted her once banged his tankard on the table, then pointed at her. "I know where I've seen you. I saw you in Natchez. Now ain't that so?"

Kiera's heart started a slow, painful pounding against her rib cage. "I don't know what you mean, sir."

She'd been only one place in Natchez. *Oh, please, Lord, no.* Her cheeks burned at the memory of standing on that dais with all those men around, at the thought of what would have happened if poor Mr. Marchette hadn't tossed those coins on the platform when he did.

"Oh, I think you do." He cackled, the sound cruel and gut-churning. "You're—"

"Mistaken."

Kiera whipped around. Quinn stood in the open doorway, a wicked-looking knife in his hand. Silence descended over the cookhouse.

Quinn stepped inside, blue eyes glittering like jewels in the light from the fireplace. At the table, he propped one boot on the bench seat, his forearm resting on his knee, the knife blade winking in the dim light. He studied the bowl of crab apples in the center of the table, stabbed one with his knife, started peeling it.

"I meant no harm, guv'nor." The stranger rested both hands on the table in plain sight. "I thought I recognized the wench—"

"And now?"

The man's gaze darted from Quinn, to Kiera, then to the others around the table, watching. "I can see that it's not the same gel. Beggin' your pardon, miss." He stood, bolted for the door, stumbling over his own feet.

Kiera stared at Quinn, fear slithering down her spine.

Chapter 13

QUINN RESUMED PEELING THE APPLE as if nothing had happened. Kiera turned back to the fireplace. Without another word, she filled a bowl with stew and placed it on the table.

Only he knew how shaken she was by the encounter.

Quinn sat and ate, and the conversation around the table resumed. One by one, the travelers finished their meal and took their leave until only he and Kiera were left.

The hiss and pop of fire eating at the logs filled the silence between them, broken only by Kiera rinsing dishes and placing them on the sideboard to dry.

Finally she stopped filling the silence with busyness and turned to face him, worry stamped on her features. "Do you think he believed you?"

"No."

"I never dreamed that anyone from the tavern that night would stop here at Breeze Hill. What if he tells Le Bonne where we are? What will we do? The girls—"

"Ye're safe here."

"Safe? How can we be safe? My brother-in-law *sold* us to pay off a debt. We have no rights. We're runaways." She wrapped her arms around her waist, blue eyes glistening with tears. "We'll leave. We'll go somewhere—"

"Where will ya go, lass? Back to Natchez?" He tipped his spoon toward the fireplace. "That'd be like throwing yerself in the fire there."

"If Le Bonne finds out where we are, he'll have the magistrates take us by force." She dashed at the tears on her cheeks. "It's his right."

"I do no' think me brother will let that happen. Not after talking t' Mr. Wainwright."

"You saw Mr. Wainwright?" She speared him with a look as she sank down into one of the chairs across from him. "What—what did he say?"

Quinn shrugged. "He confirmed what we'd both told Connor. Told him o' Le Bonne's nefarious dealin's."

"Did hearing such from someone he respects change his opinion of me?" Her lip curled. "Charlotte's half sister."

"In spite o' his failings, Connor is a good man."

"I know. If he weren't, he'd have sent us packing that first day." Kiera sighed. "Everything about the day we landed in Natchez, that night, and the next is a blur."

"And a good thing it is, if ya ask me." Quinn scowled, wishing he could block out the events so easily.

"Why'd you do it?" She picked up the half-peeled apple and his knife and started peeling.

"Do what?" He motioned toward the knife with his spoon. "Watch yerself with that knife. Sharp it is."

The glance she tossed his way said she knew how to handle a knife in the kitchen. "You didn't answer my question."

"I do no' know." Quinn took a bite of stew, chewed. "Ya didn't belong in the Blue Heron, and neither did yer wee sisters."

"But you didn't even know me . . . us."

"I knew enough."

A becoming blush stole over her cheeks. He could tell what he'd said pleased her. But he doubted she'd like what he was about to say next.

He leaned forward, resting both forearms on the table. "But do ya think ya should continue providing food and lodging for strangers?"

Her busy hands stilled, and she looked up, her pale brows arching upward. "Pardon?"

"It's only going t' expose ya t' more people knowing where you and yer sisters are." He motioned toward the door. "Like tonight."

"You're right, of course, but I can't just quit. Isabella is depending on me." She plucked another apple from the bowl and started peeling.

"Kiera—"

"Please, Quinn, don't ask me to give this up." Her gaze searched his. "For the first time, I have some control in what I do with my life. If—if I can make this venture prosperous, then who knows where it might lead. Maybe . . . maybe I can even save enough to buy our freedom from Le Bonne."

"He doesn't own ya and yer sisters, Kiera."

"According to the law, he does." She peeled the apple in jerky movements.

"Hand me that," Quinn ordered, holding out his hand. "Ya be getting on me nerves."

She reversed the knife with a quick flick of her wrist and handed it over. Plucking an apple from the basket, she held it out, a cheeky grin on her face. "You might as well put it to good use."

Quinn took the apple. "Not what I had in mind, lass."

"You asked for it."

Kiera stood, grabbed another knife from the table beside the fireplace, sat back down, and started peeling. "All I know is that I feel useful here, and like you said, we have nowhere else to go. I'll just pray that something good will come of what my sister and her husband did to us."

"How can something good come out o' anything yer sister does?"

Kiera carefully cut away a rotten spot in the apple, letting the putrid brown meat fall to the table. Maybe her sister had done her a favor. By allowing George to send them to the colonies, had she unintentionally provided a better future for all of them?

A future that might include Quinn O'Shea?

Her heart thumped against her rib cage, then settled into a slow, painful rhythm. Where had such a thought come from? She wasn't looking to tie herself to any man. So far they'd been nothing but trouble for her and her sisters. Except for Mr. Wainwright, Mr. Marchette, and if she was completely honest, Quinn. They'd been honorable, and they'd rescued her from Le Bonne. But—

"Meanin' no disrespect, but she's the reason me brother fled Ireland, leaving the rest o' us t' fend for ourselves." Quinn scowled, his attention on the apple in his hand. "I spent all these years hating him for something he didna really have any control over."

Kiera dropped her gaze to his large hands, scarred from working the forge, but dexterously working the knife and the small fruit with ease. How could such an innocent job of peeling apples make her so aware of another person? She jerked her attention back to the task of peeling her own apple before she proved him right and cut herself.

"You hated him for leaving you behind? What if he'd sold you, Rory, and Patrick to pay off a debt? That would be something you could hate him for."

"Maybe *hate* is too strong a word for what I felt. But if he'd listened to me *da* and worked in the mines instead o' chasing off after yer sister, then—" he shrugged, the frown softening, turning wistful—"things would be different."

"Different? How?"

The apples were all gone, and he put his knife away, leaned his arms on the table, and stared at her, but somehow she got the impression he was looking into the past, not at her. His lips curved into a small, crooked smile, and he shook his head. "I do no' know. Mayhap we'd still be in Ireland. Connor would be married t' some Irish lass much like yerself—"

"I don't think Isabella would appreciate that."

"True." He chuckled. "So mayhap something good has come from all o' this."

Kiera sucked in a breath, marveling that he'd voice what she'd thought only moments before. His gaze caught and held hers for a moment, until Kiera looked down at the apple peelings scattered on the table, the haphazard swirls and curls as twisted as her midsection.

"And where would you be?" she managed to blurt out, pleased when the question didn't come out as garbled as the rest of her.

She risked a glance at him. He sat back, hooked an arm around the back of the chair. Her stomach roiled afresh at the slow wink he gave her. "I'd be off somewhere in the tropics eating fresh fruit instead o' peeling dried apples on the backside o' Natchez. Or maybe I'd be sailing the Orient or even down in South America."

"But not back in Ireland?"

He sobered, gave her a sad smile. "Ah, lass, ya do no' have the least inkling what it's like t' have nothing, no' even the roof over yer head, do ya?"

Kiera shrugged and pushed the apple peelings into a neat little pile. "We were far from rich—"

"Ah, but ya had a roof over your head, peat for the fire, and food aplenty, didn't ya? If the mines closed, we went hungry. Many a widow was cast out t' beg in the streets when her man died o' the lung sickness. And nobody cared."

"Sounds to me like you should be thanking Charlotte and Connor instead of blaming them."

"Are ya daft, lass?"

"If Charlotte hadn't done what she did, Connor wouldn't have come to America. He wouldn't have met Isabella, and the governor wouldn't have sent for you and your brothers."

He gaped at her, then nodded. "'Tis true in a twisted fashion. I'll grant ya that."

"See? All's well that ends well."

"I suppose." He chuckled. "From the time I received notice that the governor was going t' pay passage for all o' us at once, all I could think about was getting Rory and Patrick safely t' the colonies so I could pack me things and see the world." Quinn stood, leaned against the table, eyes twinkling. "And what did I do? I wasna off the boat good and proper before I saddled meself with three lasses that needed more care than me brothers ever did."

"Saddled?" Kiera stood, grabbed a bowl, and scraped the apple peelings into it, the tender feelings she'd had only moments ago gone in a flash. "I'll have you know, Quinn O'Shea, that you aren't saddled with me or my sisters. You're welcome to leave any time you wish. It won't put my nose out of joint."

Quinn leaned over and tapped her nose. "And such a pretty nose it is."

"Stop that." The bowl tucked under her left arm, Kiera batted his hand away with her right. The bowl slipped; apple peelings slid toward the floor. Laughing, he grabbed for the bowl, his hand closing over hers, his fingers wrapping around her wrist.

She froze, and time stood still as well.

The sweet smell of apples wafted around them, dust motes danced on the air, and somewhere in the distance, she heard the sound of Mews's fiddle as he played a haunting melody before turning in for the night.

All amusement fled Quinn's face, leaving his blue eyes glittering in the firelight, so serious her heart pounded with fear—not fear of Quinn, because she could never be afraid of him—but fear of the things he made her feel.

His gaze swept over her face. Without releasing his hold on her wrist, he lowered his head, his eyes sliding closed. In the fraction of a second before his lips touched hers, Kiera realized that she should move away, that he didn't hold her captive, save for his fingers wrapped lightly around her wrist, but even that was nothing compared to the invisible tether that bound them together.

But she didn't pull away. She couldn't.

Because she wanted his kiss. She wanted—

His lips touched hers, soft yet firm, cool yet sweetly

warm. He shifted, the movement turning her more fully toward him, his free hand splayed against her side, then sliding around her waist, and she shivered at the skim of his thumb along her rib cage.

All thought fled save the feel of his lips against hers, the sweet nectar of his kiss, the gentle way he held her, as if giving her permission to break away at any time. And that very thing was what made her arch into his kiss.

The wooden bowl slipped, fell to the floor. Kiera jumped, the clatter breaking the spell of Quinn's sweet kiss. He pulled away, his eyes, dark pools of deep-blue still waters, searching hers. Slowly he lowered his gaze to where he still held her, his fingers wrapped not uncomfortably around her wrist. His thumb slid across her pulse; then he let go and stepped back.

"I didn't mean t' take liberties, lass. Please forgive me."

He turned, strode to the door, and was gone before she could answer.

Weak-kneed, Kiera sank into one of the chairs and stared at the apple peelings scattered across the floor.

Scattered as surely as her feelings about Quinn O'Shea and the kiss they'd just shared.

Chapter 14

LONG BEFORE DAYBREAK THE NEXT DAY, Quinn spotted Kiera and Amelia coming down the hill from the main house.

Amelia?

Since when did Kiera's younger sister rise before dawn? The girl wasn't known for being industrious. Of course the same could be said for his brother Rory. He'd prodded the lad awake over an hour ago, told him he needed help in the smithy, but the boy still hadn't put in an appearance.

But Quinn would have the last word on the matter. Once Rory showed his face, he'd keep him working nonstop till suppertime if that's what it took. Quinn had been working in the mines for six years by the time he was Rory's age. He'd been too soft on the boy, for sure.

His gaze lingered on Kiera, and his thoughts ricocheted back to last night's kiss. He hadn't meant to kiss her. But she'd looked so sweet, so tempting. One minute they were peeling apples; the next, he'd stepped over a boundary he'd never planned on crossing.

When he'd left Ireland, his goal was to deliver his younger brothers to Connor, then take off for parts unknown. Rory was old enough to not care overmuch if he never saw Quinn again, and Patrick was assimilating to life at Breeze Hill like a fish to water. He'd made new friends here and had the run of the plantation. And when he wasn't running around with those tomboys Lizzy Mews and Megan Young, he followed Connor like a besotted puppy.

Quinn didn't doubt that Patrick would accept his leaving as part of the natural way of things, and in spite of his own reservations about Connor, his older brother was firmly settled, had a wife and a livelihood to provide for Patrick until the boy was old enough to make his own way in the world.

Yes, his brothers were safely settled at Breeze Hill, but what about Kiera and her sisters? He'd told Kiera that Connor wouldn't let Le Bonne take her away, but how could he be sure that Le Bonne wouldn't use the law to force them to return to him?

He'd stay until their plight was settled; then he could leave with a clear conscience. He turned back to his work, trying to drive thoughts of Kiera from his mind.

Just about the time he thought he was going to have to go drag Rory out of bed, Connor rounded the edge of the building, lugging a length of chain along behind him. "Do you think you could fix this? Broke first thing this morning, and I don't have any t' replace it."

Quinn jerked his chin toward the forge. "If ya can man the bellows."

Connor moved to the pump handles. "Where's Rory?"

"He'll be here shortly." At least Quinn hoped he would. "Slowly now."

As the sound of his hammer rang across the clearing, the travelers began to stir, some preparing food to break their fast, some hitching up their wagons, greasing wheels, while others strode across the way to Kiera's cookhouse.

A short time later, Mr. Caruthers and another gentleman left the cookhouse and headed toward the smithy. "Ah, Mr. O'Shea, may I have a word with you?"

"O' course." Connor stopped pumping the bellows.

He motioned to his companion. "This is Neville Granger."

"Mr. Granger."

"Considering my unfortunate experience on the trail yesterday, Mr. Granger has agreed to allow me to accompany his party to Natchez."

"And your son? How is he this morning?" Connor asked.

"Stiff and sore. Thankfully, the musket ball passed through his thigh and didn't hit the bone. We stopped the bleeding with your man Horne's help, but Weston doesn't need to travel for a few days. Would it be possible for him to stay here until I return from Natchez?"

"He's welcome to stay as long as he needs to."

"I shouldn't have brought him with me on this trip." Mr. Caruthers eyed the cabin where his son lay, then turned back. "If something happens to him, too, I don't know if my wife could survive a second shock."

Quinn and Connor exchanged confused glances.

"My apologies." Mr. Caruthers smiled, looking tired. He pulled out a miniature portrait of a young man wearing a royal-blue overcoat trimmed in black velvet. Brown-haired and clean-shaven, he greatly resembled the youth lying on the pallet in the dirt-floor cabin a stone's throw away. "My oldest son, Reginald Wheaton Caruthers III, disappeared in Natchez two months ago."

"In Natchez proper? Or on the trace? As you found out firsthand, the trace itself is known to be quite dangerous for travelers."

"Word came that he was last seen in Natchez. He'd wanted to take on more responsibility, and much to my wife's dismay, I allowed him to accompany a flotilla of flatboats carrying cotton downriver. He sold the cotton at a nice profit and promptly disappeared. After a few days without word, my agent, Mr. Bloomfield, sent a letter that he never returned to pick up the money for the sale of the cotton."

"I'm familiar with Bloomfield." Connor nodded. "He's done me a good turn or two."

"Yes. He's a good man. Very trustworthy. But as you can see, that's why I'm on the way to Natchez. I want to find out what happened to Reggie. I'm afraid my wife will not rest until she knows." Caruthers cleared his throat. "I regret that I must throw myself and my younger son upon your mercy."

They all turned as Amelia exited the cookhouse, a cloth-covered tray in hand. She paused as she neared them, her face aflame. She mumbled a greeting, then skirted around them and hurried on to her destination.

Connor chuckled. "Have no fear, sir. It seems that your younger son will be well cared for in your absence."

Amelia fussed with her dress. "I hate this dress, Kiera."

Sighing, Kiera crossed the room to her sister. She'd looked forward to Sunday services all week. Everyone on the plantation had the day off, and they turned out in their best for outdoor services in the courtyard.

The day of worship provided a welcome break from the monotony of daily life.

"I'm sorry, Amelia, but there wasn't time to grab anything else."

The dress, a hand-me-down from Kiera, was a bit too loose in the waist, but it couldn't be helped. She picked up a white lace fichu, draped it around her sister's shoulders, cinched in her waist with a dark-blue satin sash, and stood back to admire her handiwork. "There. How does that look?"

Amelia preened in front of the mirror, smoothing the skirt over her narrow hips. "It'll do, I suppose."

Kiera shook her head. It didn't matter what Amelia looked like today. It was chilly enough that she'd have on a cloak the entire time, but still, keeping Amelia happy was easier than listening to her whine and complain.

"Hurry up, Megan; it's time to go. I hear Mr. Mews tuning his fiddle."

"Ready." Megan came running from the bedroom she shared with Amelia. Her mass of curls looked like a rat's nest. "I'm going to find Lizzy. She said she'd save me a spot beside her."

Kiera grabbed the child as she shot past. "Not so fast, missy."

"Kiera!" Megan squirmed. "They're starting."

"Hold still. This will only take a minute."

As quickly as she could, Kiera brushed the tangles from her sister's hair, then braided it as Megan squirmed. Tossing a mobcap over the unruly mess, she hugged her little sister. "There. Much better. Keep that cap on—"

"I will." After a quick hug, Megan rushed toward the courtyard. Kiera and Amelia followed at a more sedate pace.

Almost everyone had turned out for the service, from the family to the lumber crews. Mr. Bartholomew sat on the veranda outside his suite of rooms in a sunny spot that blocked the wind but offered warmth from the midday sun. Martha bustled toward him, a heavy quilt draped over her arm. Connor stood nearby talking to—

Kiera smiled when she recognized Mr. Wainwright and a younger man who carried himself in such a way that the two must be related.

Isabella sat in a rocking chair holding a baby wrapped in

a thick shawl, a small-boned blonde Kiera didn't know lean-ing over her and the child. Their laughter rang out across the courtyard.

The men congregated in groups, a few lounging on the veranda steps. Mr. Horne and his large family stood in front of the entire group, Mews seated nearby with his fiddle.

"There's Weston." Amelia smiled. Sure enough, Weston Caruthers limped up the path, Rory at his side. "He said he thought he felt well enough to attend."

"I see. And when did you see young Mr. Caruthers?"

A pink glow suffused Amelia's face, and she flounced away, ignoring Kiera's question.

Kiera let her go, lifted her skirts, and headed toward where the others were congregated on the porch. As she neared the stairs, movement along the upper veranda caught her attention.

Quinn.

His hair was still damp from his morning ablutions, and he was busy buttoning a dark-blue vest over his flat stomach. Frowning at the top two buttons that refused to meet over his broad chest, he gave up the task of trying to fasten them.

He looked up, his eyes meeting hers as he reached the top of the staircase. He paused, then took the stairs to the first-floor veranda. His gaze skimmed over the simple day dress she wore, then swept upward to her face, the appreciation in his expression obvious. "Good day to ya, Mistress Young."

Heat rushed to her face at the near caress. "Master O'Shea."

Quinn offered his arm. "Shall we?"

"Thank you." Kiera swallowed, placed her hand in the crook of his arm, and allowed him to escort her along the veranda to where the others waited.

Isabella motioned her over, dark eyes dancing with happiness. "Kiera, I'd like you to meet my sister-in-law, Leah Bartholomew Wainwright. Leah, Kiera Young, late from Kilkenny, Leinster Province, Ireland."

Kiera curtsied. "Madam."

Connor snapped his fingers at Patrick, who sat in one of the rockers. "Up, lad. Give the lady your seat."

Patrick shot out of the chair. Kiera thanked him and settled in next to Leah.

Leah leaned toward her. "So you're from the same area that Connor and his brothers are from?"

"Yes." Kiera nodded.

"That's interesting." Leah smiled. "It really is a small world, isn't it?"

"Smaller than you'd think, dear." Isabella chuckled, then angled the baby where Kiera could see. "And this darling young man is my nephew, little Jon."

"He's adorable. So handsome." Kiera dutifully admired the chubby baby, snug and warm in his aunt's arms, fast asleep. She glanced at Isabella's pale-skinned, blonde sister-in-law and her equally fair husband. With his dark lashes and a head full of dark hair, the baby looked nothing like either of his parents. "He has your coloring."

Isabella kissed the baby's forehead. "And his father's—my late brother, Jonathan."

"Jonathan was killed before little Jon was born." Pain flitted across Leah's face.

"My—my condolences, ma'am." The words were inadequate, but they were all Kiera had to offer.

Isabella reached out and took Leah's hand. "He'd be glad to know that you're happy with William, dear."

"Yes. I know." Leah's gaze rested on her husband, the sadness melting away to be replaced by tenderness.

Everyone grew silent as Mrs. Horne and her daughters started singing, and Mr. Mews joined in with his fiddle. After three songs, they all sat in enraptured silence as Mr. Horne stomped and shouted and berated them with a sermon filled with fire and brimstone. It was unlike anything Kiera had ever heard, but Mr. Horne was so passionate, so intent that Kiera couldn't help but be moved by his oratory. When the service ended, she wasn't sure if she was glad or sad.

After the service, the men scattered. Sunday was a day of rest, and they were happy to have the day off.

Isabella stood, the sleeping baby's head lolling on her shoulder. "Kiera, would you and your sisters join us for lunch?"

"Thank you, but I have a pot of stew simmering at the cabin. Monsieur Lafitte isn't feeling well today, so I volunteered to prepare something for the men down at the lumber camp."

Isabella arched a brow. "And what ails Monsieur Lafitte?"

Kiera lowered her gaze. "I'm sure I don't know."

"It's common knowledge that the cook takes every

opportunity to imbibe overmuch in ale, and especially on Saturday night." Isabella pulled the blanket up, covering the baby's head. "Don't let Monsieur Lafitte take advantage of your good nature. It's his responsibility to feed the sawmill crew, not yours."

"Yes, ma'am." Kiera turned to Leah. "It was a pleasure to meet you, Mistress Wainwright."

"Please, just Leah." She reached out and hugged Kiera good-bye. "There are too few of us ladies in this area, and as Isabella has always told me, we don't stand on ceremony at Breeze Hill."

"Leah, then." Kiera smiled. "Good day."

Quinn watched as Kiera walked toward the cookhouse.

Connor stepped forward, arms folded across his chest. "Did I hear Miss Young say she was cooking for the loggers today?"

Isabella nodded. "You did."

"What's wrong with Lafitte?"

"You have to ask?"

"That tears it." Scowling, Connor brushed past his wife. "I'm going t' put an end t' this right now. I told him if he came in drunk one more time, he was done. And besides, he can't cook worth spit anyway."

"Connor, surely it can wait." Isabella motioned to the Wainwrights. "We have guests."

Quinn's brother stopped dead in his tracks, blew out a

deep breath, and turned. William Wainwright grinned at him, his wife on his arm.

"My apologies. I lost my head." Connor wagged a finger in Isabella's direction. "But mark my words, Wife, Lafitte will be gone before the day is out."

"Whatever you say, Husband." Isabella placed her arm in his and allowed him to lead her to the dining room. "Quinn, please join us. It is Sunday, after all."

Quinn much preferred eating in the kitchen alone or with the boys or down at the cookhouse with Kiera to the fancy dining room in the main house, but he could hardly refuse his sister-in-law's request in front of her guests. "Yes, ma'am."

The Wainwrights took their leave soon after the noon meal. As they were waved off from the front porch, Connor headed for the steps.

Isabella called out after him, "Are you really going to fire Lafitte?"

"I said I would."

"I know, but I hoped you'd calmed down enough to see reason."

"Reason?" Connor snorted. "The man causes more trouble than he's worth."

"Well, who's going to cook for the men if you send him away?"

"I'll cross that bridge when I come to it." He took off across the withered winter grass toward the cookhouse.

"Go with him, Quinn. No telling what he'll say—or do— if he loses his temper."

"Yes, ma'am." Quinn bowed. "Thank ya for dinner, ma'am."

As soon as he stepped off the porch, he saw Kiera standing on the stoop at the cookhouse, the men gathered in a semi-circle outside, looking nervous, some with fists clenched at their sides. All were facing the open door of the cabin where Kiera stood, her focus on someone at the front of the crowd. A rumble of dissent reached him.

"Leave the girl alone, Lafitte," Björn's voice rang out. "She has done nothing wrong."

"Yeah, go sleep it off, Lafitte."

Quinn caught up with Connor and, pushing through the circle of men, saw the cook weaving unsteadily on his feet. He was filthy, smelled of stale ale, and looked like he'd rolled in a pigsty.

He stabbed a finger at Kiera. "You . . . you will not take my job."

"Monsieur Lafitte, I don't want your job. I just—"

"*Non!* I will not stand for it." He moved forward, shaking a fist in Kiera's face. She gasped and stepped back.

Quinn grabbed the man, spun him around, and punched him in the face. The Frenchman reeled, arms flailing. He fell, lay on his back, out cold. Kiera had one hand pressed against her bodice, the other hugging her waist. She stared at Lafitte, then lifted her stricken gaze to Quinn. "I only wanted to help."

Connor stalked inside the cabin, returned with a bucket of water, and dumped it on the cook's head. Coughing and sputtering, the man rolled over. Connor grabbed him by the shirtfront and hauled him to his feet. "Get your things and get out. Your services are no longer needed."

With one last glance in Kiera's direction, Lafitte staggered away, down the lane to the cabin where he lived.

All was quiet for the space of a heartbeat before the men all started talking at once.

"Good riddance, I say. I was tired of eating swill prepared by that pig."

"Same here."

"If you hadn't come along when you did, Quinn, me boy, I would have decked 'im myself."

"Who's going to cook for us now, eh, Mr. Connor?"

They all turned to Connor. Eyebrows lowered in frustration, he stood, his hands propped on his hips. He eyed the group. "Any cooks among ye?"

One by one, the men shook their heads.

"Ain't none o' us got time t' make three meals a day and work in the woods from daylight to dark."

"I ain't no cook. I'm a sawyer."

"Don't look at me." Mews held his hands aloft. "Martha's been feeding me and mine for years."

"What about Miss Young here? She could do it."

Ten pairs of eyes shifted toward Kiera. Quinn inserted himself between her and the men. "I do no' think that's a good idea."

Kiera poked him in the side. "Why not?"

"It's a lot of work to fix three meals a day for a crew this size."

Ignoring him, she appealed to Connor, who had the final say, regardless. "I can do it. I know I can."

Quinn crossed his arms, willing his brother to say no. Connor sighed, looked down the lane toward the distant row of cabins where the lumbermen lived, then turned back to Kiera. "All right. But you'll do it here." He motioned toward the cookhouse. "We'll add a lean-to on the front and some tables so that you can feed all the men quickly. And this is temporary, Miss Young, so don't get settled in too much."

Kiera sucked in a breath. "Thank you."

And with that, Connor stalked away.

The men whooped, slapping each other on the back. "We're gonna eat good from now on."

"Thank ya, Mistress Young."

Each of the men doffed his hat and wandered away.

Kiera whirled in a circle, then stopped in front of Quinn, astonishment wreathing her face. "I can't believe Con—your brother agreed to this."

"I do no' like it." Arms crossed, he glowered at her.

Mimicking his stance, she arched a delicate brow. "Quinn O'Shea, I'm beginning to think that you like me less than your brother does."

"That's no' true." He shrugged. "It's just that those men are rough-and-tumble loggers. I'm afraid—"

"There's no need to be afraid. If anything happens, you'll be right there at the smithy."

"I will no' always be here t' protect ya, lass."

All trace of playfulness disappeared. "I know. You plan to leave as soon as you can."

"Aye, that's me plan."

But striking out on his own no longer felt like the adventure he'd always longed for. It had begun to feel like an unwanted chore thrust upon him.

Chapter 15

KIERA PACED THE SMALL CABIN, eyeing the ledger on the table. She'd practically begged Quinn's brother to let her cook for ten men on a daily basis, in addition to cooking for any travelers who stopped at Breeze Hill.

What had she been thinking?

Making a decision, she grabbed her light wrap and the ledger and hurried toward the house. She knocked on Connor and Isabella's sitting room door.

When Isabella bade her enter, she blurted out, "I don't think I can do this."

"Do what?"

"Connor fired Monsieur Lafitte, and now there's no one

to cook for the loggers. Except me. And Connor agreed to let me try it."

Isabella smiled. "That's a good thing, don't you think?"

"Pardon?"

Isabella rose, moved to her desk in the corner, and pulled out the household accounts. She returned to her seat, patted the place next to her. "Come. Sit."

Kiera obeyed, her gaze darting toward the door that led to the bedchamber. "Is your husband here?"

"No. He's down at the sawmill with Quinn." Isabella opened the ledger and inspected Kiera's entries. "You're safe."

Kiera pointed to a couple of blank entries. "I need to deduct for the ham and vegetables that we got from the storehouse."

"All in good time." Isabella turned the pages. "I'm just so glad to see that your idea is blessing others."

"Quinn doesn't see it as a blessing. He wants me to stop offering food and lodging to travelers."

"You're doing a wonderful job, and your ledger shows that you know what you're doing."

"It's not that. He thinks it's dangerous, that I'm just setting myself up for Le Bonne to find us and demand that we return to Natchez." She shuddered as thoughts of the nasal-twanged stranger tumbled through her head. "And . . . and some of the men seem to think that a woman alone is fair game to—to—"

"Someone accosted you?" Isabella's eyebrows dipped in anger. "Was it one of Connor's men?"

"No. It was just someone passing through. But Quinn was there. He—he put a stop to it."

"Thank goodness for that."

"But the man was sure he'd seen me in Natchez. Other than the docks, there's only one place in Natchez he could have seen me." Shame heated her face.

"Mr. Wainwright is going to get that mess straightened out, and you won't have to worry about Le Bonne anymore." Isabella tapped her household accounts. "But in the meantime, take a look at this. Here are the amounts of food Lafitte pulled from the stores the last two days alone. And to tell you the truth, I suspect he pilfered more than he prepared. The men were always complaining about the poor fare."

Kiera looked at the numbers. "Oh, my. That is a lot of food just for ten men."

"Exactly." Isabella took her hands. "You can do this, Kiera. And what's even better is that you'll already be cooking breakfast and supper and if there are travelers, you can easily stretch the meal without a lot of trouble."

Kiera nodded. "That's what I did the other night. I had a pot of stew on when another group of travelers arrived. So I just added potatoes to the pot." Kiera glanced at the ledger. "What about the noon meal?"

"They take pails with them and eat in the woods or down at the sawmill. So anything that will keep until noon will do. Johnnycakes, fried ham, pemmican."

"Cheese? Bread? Boiled eggs? Souse?"

"Yes." Isabella gathered the ledgers and stood. "We need

to figure out how much food you'll require for the next few days. There are ten men who will be standing at your door in a few hours. And I know just the person to help us: Martha."

Reginald Caruthers knocked on James Bloomfield's door before pushing it open.

The lawyer looked up, stood, and moved across the room, taking his hand in a hearty shake. "Reginald. So good to see you."

"Likewise, James. Likewise."

Concern overshadowed Bloomfield's ready greeting. "Any word from your son since we last communicated?"

"None."

"How unfortunate. I'm sorry." Bloomfield waved a hand toward a chair. "I have your payment for the cotton. I've kept it safe for you, but not here. I wouldn't dare leave that much coin unattended and ripe for the taking."

"Thank you. I knew I could count on you, sir. But that's not the only reason I'm here." Reginald perched on the edge of a chair, too keyed up to relax. He searched his agent's face. "I need you to tell me everything you can about the last time Reggie was here."

Bloomfield moved back around his desk and sat, his hands folded across his ample stomach. "There's not much to tell, I'm afraid. Reggie and his crew delivered the bales of cotton on November—" he thumbed through his manifests—"December 15. They left the cotton here to be weighed and went to find lodging and a pint of ale. They never returned."

Reginald stroked his chin. "He didn't leave anyone behind to guard the cotton?"

Bloomfield bristled. "Are you accusing me—?"

"No. Forgive me." Reginald held up a hand. "I'm grasping at straws. Four men don't disappear like that unless there's foul play."

"And a ship that needs sailors."

"Conscription?"

Bloomfield shrugged. "I've heard rumors."

"Here? In Natchez?" Reginald's heart thudded against his chest. Good heavens. He'd sent his son into a nest of vipers. "Do you have a name? Who's the boarding master behind such atrocities?"

Bloomfield stood, moved to the door, and looked out, first to the left, then to the right. He turned, keeping his voice low. "Mind you, it's just rumors, but too many men have disappeared over the last six months. It can't be coincidence."

"The name," Reginald ground out.

"Pierre Le Bonne."

"Where can I find this Pierre Le Bonne?"

"He owns a tavern called the Blue Heron. But, Reginald, going off half-cocked isn't going to solve anything. Le Bonne is a dangerous man. And there's no way to prove he's conscripted anyone against their will. It would be better to go home to your wife and your family and pray for your son's safe return instead of trying to deal with the likes of Pierre Le Bonne. The things he's done would curdle your blood."

"Be that as it may, I'll get to the bottom of Reggie's disappearance or die trying."

Bloomfield looked troubled. "You might get your wish, my friend."

"I don't think it'll come to that. I must take my leave." Reginald stood. He needed to find lodging and locate this Pierre Le Bonne before nightfall. "I say, Bloomfield, does the Blue Heron offer lodging?"

"I'm sure it does, but it's not exactly the kind of place you'd want to stay, my friend."

"It might be exactly the place to stay if I want to find my son." Reginald paused, his hand on the door latch. "If anything should happen to me, would you get word to Breeze Hill Plantation? My younger son is there recuperating from a gunshot wound."

"Gunshot? My word, Reginald. All the more reason you should head home immediately and hire managers to attend your business."

"I tried that." Reginald shook his head. "And the last one ran off with my money."

"Well, it seems you are between the devil and the deep blue sea. So you stopped by Breeze Hill on the way here? Did you meet Quinn O'Shea?"

Reginald nodded. "I met two men by the name of O'Shea. Brothers, I believe."

"Connor is the owner, or rather he's married to Mr.

Bartholomew's daughter and is acting manager until her nephew is old enough to inherit. It's all quite confusing, but not to worry." He rubbed his chin. "Interesting that you stopped at Breeze Hill. O'Shea's brothers came in on the same ship that delivered Le Bonne's bride. There was some altercation on the docks about it, but then the young lady and her sisters left with Le Bonne after all." Bloomfield shook his head as he escorted Reginald out the door. "Her brother-in-law sent her halfway around the world to marry Le Bonne. Or that's what he led her to believe. I'm afraid the truth is much less palatable."

"I need chains. Skid tongs. Axes and peelers. Wicker wants ten more loads of lumber as soon as possible."

Connor picked through the scrap, tossing broken shovels, hoes, adzes into a pile in the middle of the smithy.

"Steady now, Patrick." Quinn kept his attention on the job at hand even as his older brother ranted nearby. The whoosh of the bellows, the roar of the fire, and the ring of his hammer filled the smithy as Quinn pounded the ax head into shape.

His gaze landed on the glove on his left hand. The reinforced gloves and the apron had reappeared just as suddenly as they disappeared. The minute he'd picked up the gloves, seen the thick padding of leather carefully and securely stitched to the palms, he'd known who'd secreted them away.

Kiera.

Quietly, and without fanfare or the need for recognition, she'd taken the time to ease his discomfort. Just as he'd tried to make her job easier in the cookhouse.

He could feel the heat running up the short tongs from the ax head, but he was almost done. He plunged the iron in the cooling bath and eyed his handiwork.

It would do. A new handle, a good sharpening with the grinding wheel, and the ax would make a fine piece.

"Hardly more than enough t' make a candlestick." Connor's growl mingled with the clang of iron against iron as his small pile grew.

Quinn motioned for Patrick to stop pumping the bellows, then pulled off the gloves and tossed them on his workbench. Turning to the pile of scrap, he hunkered down. "I've scoured the place for scrap, even had Megan and Lizzy on the lookout. Short of beating the plowshares into logging tools, there's precious little to be had."

Connor shook his head. "We need the plowshares to break up the fields. Bloomfield promised to let me know of any iron coming into Natchez, but I need tools now. . . . Wait." Connor snapped his fingers. "Braxton Hall. There's bound t' be scrap iron there. Let's go."

"Braxton Hall?" Quinn followed Connor to the stables. "Why would we find scrap there?"

"You'll see." His brother led a horse out of a stall. "Saddle up."

They mounted and soon left Breeze Hill far behind. Quinn wondered what wild-goose chase Connor was taking him on. They both needed to be back at Breeze Hill trying to figure out how to meet the contracts Connor had signed with Wicker.

After a couple of miles, Connor turned onto a lane that showed no recent travel. An hour later, they came upon a section of trees that had been sheared off about three feet from the ground, leaving limbs and debris scattered everywhere. A narrow path had been cleared so that they could get through and continue on, but otherwise the destruction continued for half a mile or more.

"What happened here?"

"Tornado spawned by a hurricane last fall."

Quinn glanced over his shoulder at the destruction. "Good thing it didna hit Breeze Hill and that ya were no' in its path."

"We were in its path. At least Isabella, William Wainwright, and I were."

Quinn raised a brow.

They rounded a bend, pulled to a stop, and eyed the valley spread out before them. Even in late February, the clumps of evergreens scattered among the fallow fields provided bits of color. The majestic glen was marred only by the ghostly remains of a plantation home situated on a slight rise a quarter mile away. Tall white pillars supporting wind and air, standing sentinels to walls that no longer existed. The entire thing seemed to have imploded upon itself like kindling tossed in the wood box willy-nilly.

"This is Braxton Hall?"

"What's left of it." Connor urged his mount down the gently sloping hillside along a lane lined on both sides with giant magnolias. "It's O'Shea land."

"How many acres?"

"A thousand."

Quinn whistled. "Ya jest."

"No, 'tis true." Connor grinned. "I have the deed, free and clear."

"Will ya rebuild?"

"Someday. I promised Isabella that I would see to Breeze Hill until little Jon is old enough to take over. As much as we'd like to think otherwise, her father can't take on the daily running of the place." Connor gave the valley a sweeping gesture. "It would be foolish to let the forest reclaim these fields, and I need a manager. I was hoping you might be that man."

"I—"

"And not just as a manager, but a partner. This land belongs to the O'Sheas. You, me, the lads."

"What o' William Wainwright? Where does he come in? He is the child's stepfather."

"With over five thousand acres, less than half that's been cleared, William has all he can handle with the Wainwright plantation." Connor shrugged. "And he'd never offend Mr. Bartholomew by presuming t' make decisions regarding Breeze Hill."

Quinn eyed the surrounding fields. Isabella's nephew was just a baby, not even a year old. It would be twenty years before the child took over the reins of the plantation he'd rightfully inherited from his father, Isabella's brother.

Twenty years.

Quinn swallowed, the thought of being tied down for another twenty years smothering him. Their mounts clomped down the lane, a gentle breeze stirring the large, waxy leaves on the magnolia trees. Even now some of the trees were beginning to bud.

He shook his head. "How can ya put yer own future on hold for so long? I do no' understand."

Connor chuckled, his gaze resting on the destruction at the end of the long row of trees. "Moments before the tornado struck, I was standing in the hallway fighting for my life. It was just by the grace of God that Isabella and I found shelter under the stairs and were spared. Nolan Braxton was an evil man, and he would have killed anyone who stood in his way—even an innocent babe. It was no hardship to promise to cultivate Breeze Hill until Jon was of age. William also agreed to the same stipulation to protect the child's inheritance. After what Isabella and Leah had been through, it was the least we could do to set them at ease. And then—" Connor waved a hand at the acreage surrounding them—"being granted this tract of land was above and beyond anything I ever dreamed of."

Quinn shifted in the saddle. His brother was a better man than he was. He'd put his own life on hold for his wife's nephew.

"So what do you think? Do you think you could be happy

here?" Connor nodded toward what looked to have been a grand home at one time. "We'll rebuild someday."

"I'll have t' think about it."

"You don't have to answer me right now. There's plenty of time before the ground has to be broken up for spring planting."

It didn't sound like any time at all.

Spotting the twisted wrought iron railing from the porch, he jumped at the chance to change the subject. "We came t' look at the iron."

"Yes, of course." He could hear the disappointment in his brother's voice, but thankfully, Connor didn't pursue the conversation.

They dismounted and poked around outside the barn, remarkably intact, then followed the path of debris left behind from the tornado.

A fancy carriage had wrapped itself around a tree, the undercarriage mangled, one wheel badly bent, but the other three seemingly intact.

The destruction was a blacksmith's dream. Wrought iron from the house, broken and shattered farm wagons, tools, pots and pans, even the doors from the barn, ripped and torn, but the hinges still intact. Quinn squatted, turned over a large cauldron that looked to have survived the tornado without a crack.

"What do you think?" Connor crouched beside him, hefting a twisted piece of iron in his hand. "Can you work with this?"

"Yea. Lots t' work with here." The mangled iron didn't look like much on the surface, but Quinn could see the tools, hooks, tongs, chain links, and nails that could come out of every piece that had been twisted, broken, and destroyed.

He wished he could visualize his future as easily.

Chapter 16

QUINN DROVE DOWN THE LANE, Patrick, Megan, and Lizzy squished on the seat beside him, the wagon bed full of scrap iron.

Isabella stood in the middle of the road in front of the cookhouse, a sketch pad and a piece of charcoal in her hands. She moved out of the way and let them pass.

Before the wagon came to a stop good and proper, Patrick hopped off, followed quickly by the two girls.

"Race ya to the kitchen for some of Martha's tea cakes."

Quinn let them go. They'd put in a hard day's work and deserved a treat. He'd corral them later to unload the wagon. He set the brake and jumped down.

Isabella motioned him over and held out the paper. "I've been thinking about Connor's idea of building a lean-to on this cabin. Instead, I was thinking it might be better to move one of the cabins and combine the two to make a larger space."

"That's a lot of work." Quinn studied the drawing, then pointed at the cabins. "What if you didn't move them at all, but built a dogtrot or another room connecting them?"

"Hmm, that might work." Isabella sketched another drawing. "Like this?"

"Yes." Quinn tapped the drawing. "And add a door for the men to go in and out."

"I like it." Isabella smiled. "The men could eat in the center room and Kiera could use one fireplace for meats and stews and the other for baking."

"Do ya think Connor will want t' put that much work into enlarging the cabins? He told Kiera this was temporary."

"If it keeps the men happy and fed, I don't see why not. And it will definitely cost less to cook one meal instead of two if travelers do stop by. There's really no reason for him to say no."

"No reason to say no to what?"

Isabella whirled, spotted Connor coming around the bend. She waved the drawing under his nose. "To my plans for the new cookhouse."

Connor's brows slashed downward in a frown, but he didn't dispute his wife's ideas as she drew him away to show him her plans.

Breakfast was chaos as usual with the men needing to eat in a hurry and get to the mill by daybreak.

After almost a week of cooking for the sawmill crew, Kiera wanted to scream. Ten hungry men crowded inside the small cabin, all jostling for a place at a table that could hold eight in a pinch. The fireplace was too small to cook enough for all of them at once, so she'd been serving corn mush for a week. It was the easiest thing to cook that made enough for everyone and filled their stomachs.

The only saving grace was that there hadn't been any travelers since she'd started cooking for the sawmill crew. She wasn't sure if her sanity would have survived if there had been.

Someone darkened the door, and she groaned. Where would she put another human being? She could barely move around enough to feed everyone inside as it was.

She turned, a bowl of mush in her hand, then froze at the sight of Connor in the door, raking the chaos inside with a glare. Without a word, he turned and left. She didn't have time to wonder at his sudden appearance or equally abrupt departure.

Mr. Björn looked up. "Is that mine?"

"Yes, Mr. Björn."

"*Tack*." Grinning, the big man took the bowl, plopped in a healthy dollop of butter and syrup, stirred, and kept eating.

By the time the men finished their breakfast, thanked her,

and left, Kiera was worn to the point of exhaustion. And the cabin looked like a hurricane had blown through. Was this why Connor had left so suddenly? When he'd seen the mess, had he realized she was in over her head?

Amelia came rushing in the door of the cabin, looking fresh as a daisy, every hair in place, her dress—

"What are you wearing?"

Amelia twirled. "Isn't it lovely? Isabella gave it to me. She said it was too small for her, and with a few tucks here and there, it fit perfectly."

"It is lovely, and if you don't want to soil it, I'd suggest you go take it off this instant and change into something more appropriate for cooking and cleaning."

"Kiera, why do you have to be so mean?" Amelia glared at her, then eyed the empty pot of mush. "There's nothing left. What am I going to feed Weston?"

Kiera gritted her teeth. The Caruthers boy hadn't lifted a finger to do anything since he'd been here. Granted, he had been shot, but he was no longer bedridden, so she didn't feel the least bit sorry for him. "Well, if Weston wants to eat, he needs to get over here before it's all gone. And that goes for you, too, young lady. Now go change that dress and—"

Something banged against the cabin wall.

"What in the world?"

Wiping her hands, Kiera hurried outside and around the side of the building. Quinn stood there, along with all the men and a wagon loaded down with lumber from the sawmill. Connor was pacing off the distance between the cookhouse and the cabin next to it. Quinn leaned against the cabin, arms crossed, grinning at her.

"What—what's he doing?"

"We're going to connect the cabins and make a dining area here in the middle."

"A dining area?" She couldn't believe it. "Really?"

"Really." Quinn pulled her out of the way as the men hauled cornerstones and placed them between the cabins. "Ya should probably get inside and cover all the foodstuffs because we're going t' cut a door in the cabin, right there."

"A door?"

"Yes. A door. Now quit repeating everything I say and get out o' the way."

Kiera hurried inside to the same disaster she'd left. Amelia was nowhere to be found. Of course her sister would take the opportunity to abscond with what little food was left from breakfast while her back was turned. She'd likely not see her again until suppertime. She spotted Lizzy and Megan standing outside watching the men.

"Megan! Lizzy! Get in here. I need your help."

They ran toward the door, excitement on their faces. "What's going on?"

"The men are connecting this cabin and the next one over so that there's room for everybody to eat."

"Really?" Megan turned toward the door.

"Megan Young, come back here. There will be time enough to see what they're doing. After we clean up."

"Yes, ma'am." Megan trudged inside.

Kiera put the girls to washing dishes while she made up bread dough to rise. The noise outside was deafening, but the sound was music to her ears. She was as excited as the girls about the addition, but first things first.

Once the table was clear, she and Lizzy moved it to the opposite side of the cabin, away from the spot where the new door would be. Then she covered the dough with damp cheesecloth and inverted pans to keep dust and debris out.

"Can we go watch now?" Megan asked.

Kiera turned. The cabin was clean, the iron griddles, hooks, and kettles all washed and put away. "Yes. Let's."

She grabbed her wrap and joined the girls outside. Her mouth rounded in surprise. The men already had the connecting room framed up. Two men were putting down flooring, while four more constructed walls, and two others roofed the structure.

It was like a barn raising, but on a much smaller scale.

Even as she watched, Quinn and Connor cut a hole in the adjacent cabin so that she wouldn't have to go outside to enter the new space.

"Well, this is a sight to see." Isabella joined her, smiling as she watched the progress. "I came to bring Connor his breakfast, and this is what I find."

"Isn't it amazing?" Kiera hugged herself. "After breakfast, I expected the men to head to the woods, and then this happened."

Connor joined them, hands on hips. "Well, Wife, what do you think? Is it to your liking?"

"It's perfect. Just the way I imagined it."

Kiera gaped at Isabella. "This was your idea?"

"Yes. Well, connecting the two rooms was Quinn's. I've also decided that Mary, and her daughters if needed, should help in the expanded kitchen space. You can break up the cooking however you see fit, but with two fireplaces, you should be able to get the work done without pulling your hair out." She smiled at Connor. "We've seen how hard you've worked this past week, haven't we, Husband?"

"Aye. That we have," Connor murmured, his attention on the men. "Björn, did you measure that beam? It's weight-bearing, so has to fit just right."

"And the men are much happier with Kiera's cooking, aren't they, dear?" Arms crossed, Isabella arched a brow at her husband, then looked pointedly at Kiera.

Connor squinted at his wife as if he wondered how much of the conversation he'd missed, but he cleared his throat and glanced at Kiera. "They do seem happier. Thank you, Miss Young, for stepping in to fill Lafitte's shoes."

Kiera blinked, then looked away. "Thank you."

Mr. Horne called out to Connor from the top of the new structure. "You want we should go ahead and put the shingles on now?"

"No, that's enough for today. We'll add doors, shingles, and shutters later. You men pack up and head t' the woods. Daylight's a-wastin'."

Isabella grabbed Connor by the arm. "Now, Husband,

everyone has had breakfast except you. Come, I'll walk with you to the sawmill, and you can break your fast."

"Isabella, I told you—"

"I'm fine. And I promise to take my own sweet time on the way back." She held out the basket. "But you can carry the basket if you wish."

Connor took the basket, and the two of them walked away. The men gathered up their tools, deposited them in the wagon, and climbed in, some casting shy glances in Kiera's direction.

Kiera didn't know whether to hug them or what. She settled for a quick curtsy. "Thank you. Thank you all."

And with that she fled inside lest they see her cry.

Quinn leaned against the doorframe, the new-lumber smell surrounding him. Kiera stood in the center of the empty room, her head in her hands, shoulders shaking.

His heart ached at her sobs. In three strides, he crossed the space and took her by the shoulders. "Hush, lass." He tucked her head under his chin and wrapped his arms around her. "There's no need t' cry."

At his words, she cried harder. Why, he hadn't a clue. He stood there, his hand smoothing the thick blonde braid that felt like silk beneath his touch. Whatever had put her in such a dither? Was the new addition not to her liking? Had one of the men offended her?

His jaw hardened. He'd pound the man who hurt her into the ground.

When she quieted, he held her at arm's length, looking into her eyes, awash with tears and the color of the sky after the clouds lifted from a gentle summer rain. His gaze dipped below, to the tip of her turned-up nose, red from crying, then even farther to her parted lips—

Sucking in a breath, he jerked his attention back to the matter at hand. "Now, lass, what was all that blubbering about?"

Her lips trembled, and he thought she was going to start bawling again. But somehow she managed to hold it all together.

"It's so big." She glanced around the space. "Two fireplaces to cook with and both butt up against this room and will keep it warm. Instead of building a fire in some of the other cabins, travelers could bed down in here."

Quinn frowned. She did get the oddest notions. "Are ya sure ya'd want them in here when you'll be cooking in the very next room?"

"I hadn't thought of that, but Mary will be here from now on. And you're still close by. At the smithy."

He moved away. First his brother, then Isabella, and now Kiera all assumed he'd be staying at Breeze Hill indefinitely. But his plans hadn't changed. "I will no' always be here."

Frown lines knit her brow. "If you're still mad at Connor—"

"O' course I'm still mad at him. Sometimes I just want t' throttle him for what he did."

"What *he* did?" She chuckled. "You don't know my sister. She is a master manipulator. How old was Connor when he met Charlotte? Rory's age? Weston's and Amelia's? You see how easily swayed they are. All Weston has to do is crook his finger and Amelia comes running. I'm afraid he's not much different from Charlotte and is simply toying with my sister. I worry—"

She broke off, the blush on her cheeks telling him the direction her thoughts had taken. And one thing was for certain: Amelia was just immature enough to throw caution to the wind when it came to the Caruthers boy.

"Maybe Connor should send him away."

Kiera shook her head. "Connor promised his father that he could stay until Master Caruthers returns."

Quinn scowled. "Well, the least I can do is put the boy t' work. He'll be so tired at the end of the day that he will no' be able t' dally with your sister."

"Dally? I wouldn't say it's gone that far."

"Well, what would ya call it then? They're together every chance they get and Amelia makes it her job t' take care of him."

"She's young and impressionable—"

"Yer sister is playing with fire. Worse, she doesna have anybody who's willing t' put their foot down and tell her no."

"And just how do you propose I do that?" Kiera crossed her arms. "I've tried everything I possibly can to keep her on a tight rein, but it's useless. One minute she's here; the next she's gone."

"Well, somebody better put the fear o' God in her . . . before it's too late."

"Very well. Keep Weston busy if you think it will do any good."

Quinn thought back over the last week. He'd put the fear of an empty stomach into Rory. He figured he could do the same to Weston. "Oh, I think I can handle that."

Chapter 17

QUINN WAS AS GOOD AS HIS WORD. The next day, he corralled Weston Caruthers and put the boy to work in the smithy.

The boy's sullen attitude would have been amusing if it weren't so pathetic. Kiera hoped Amelia would see how immature and spoiled he was, but instead, her sister chose to defend Weston.

"You hate me!" Amelia screamed at Kiera for the third time. "And you hate Weston, too."

"Hold your tongue, young lady." Kiera attempted to keep her temper in check. "Nobody hates you or Weston. But the truth of the matter is that the two of you have been taking advantage of Connor and Isabella's generosity. You've been sneaking out at all hours of the day and night to see him. He hasn't even bothered to offer to do any work—"

"He was shot, Kiera."

"That hasn't stopped him from traipsing all over the plantation with you, now has it?"

"We—we stop and rest when he's tired." Amelia plopped her hands on her hips and glared at Kiera. "Besides, Weston is our guest. He shouldn't be asked to work."

"*Our* guest?" Kiera lifted a brow, and Amelia had the grace to blush. "Now, go get that bucket of water like I asked you to."

Amelia pouted. "When Weston's father comes back, I'm going with them. I'll be lady of the house, and nobody can make me do anything."

Kiera shook her head. "Amelia, you do get the strangest notions."

"Just wait. You'll see." But to Kiera's relief, her sister grabbed the bucket and, with a huff, flounced out the door.

Kiera blew out a breath of frustration and turned back to the fireplace, stirring the pot of stew. The sound of singing and the aroma of baking bread and apple pies wafted from the other room.

They'd discovered quite quickly that the smaller fireplace in the second cabin was ideal for baking. Quinn had beat out a piece of tin to make a portable door for the fireplace. The tin cover reflected the heat and held it in. Mary could bake six loaves at a time in the oven.

The chaos of last week was a distant memory. Smiling,

Kiera checked the greens simmering in another pot. Amelia pushed through the door, slapped across the floor, splashing water everywhere, but Kiera refused to let her sister's sour attitude quench her rosy outlook. "Caravan coming."

"Really?" Kiera moved to the door and saw a small group of travelers. "What a blessing that the men finished the new dining area before they arrived."

"Just more work for me."

"Instead of complaining, you should be thankful for the work, the roof over your head, and food to eat." Kiera slid a bowl of potatoes across the table. "Peel these and add them to the stew. After that, you can go freshen up. I know you'll want to look nice when you see Weston at supper."

Amelia glared at her but did as she was told without further complaint.

Kiera turned away, careful not to let her sister see the grin on her face. She'd learned a trick or two from Quinn about keeping her sister in line.

"Time for supper."

Quinn chuckled when Weston moved faster than he had all day. The youth had actually been a decent help when Amelia hadn't been coming around distracting him from the task at hand.

Quinn pushed the doors shut and eyed the small group of travelers that had made camp in the grove of trees beyond the well. Three men left the camp and walked across the road toward the cookhouse. They looked harmless enough—at least what he could tell of them in the fading light.

Down the lane, he heard the crew from the sawmill headed his way, lunch pails banging against their thighs, the drag of chains and the sound of banter between them. He spotted Patrick's small form among the men. Patrick had mastered the art of working the bellows and now had a hankering to be a sawyer. Who knew what he'd be doing tomorrow? He couldn't do much, but at least he wasn't afraid to do what he could. Quinn waited until the sawmill workers drew nigh the smithy, dropping broken tongs and lengths of chain as they passed.

"More work for ya, smithy."

"Thank ye kindly, boys." He doffed his hat; then he turned his attention toward his little brother, covered in dirt and sawdust. "What have ya been up to, lad?"

Patrick peered up at him, not much visible beneath the dirt and dust except his eyes. He blinked. "Digging sawdust out of the saw pits."

From the looks of him, he'd rolled in the stuff. Quinn collared him. "Come in here and let's get ya cleaned up."

"Aw, Quinn. I'm hungry."

"You're not going to sit down to Kiera's table until ya wash yer face and hands."

The others went on and Quinn helped Patrick wash up inside the smithy. After scrubbing his face and hands, Quinn brushed him off as best he could. Patrick ducked away. "Ya done yet?"

"I'm done. Go on with ya now."

Patrick rushed out of the smithy. Chuckling, Quinn finished washing up. As he left the smithy, he spotted Amelia at the well, Weston reaching for the bucket. But when they turned toward the cookhouse, Quinn realized it wasn't Weston, but a stranger.

At the door, he handed her the bucket. "Thank you, Mr. Beckett."

Then with a shy smile, she hurried inside. After a moment, the man called Beckett entered the dining area, and Quinn followed. Beckett sat with his companions and Quinn found a seat with Patrick, Weston, and Mr. Horne. Amelia came through refilling bowls. Beckett caught her eye and winked. Blushing, the girl hurried from the room.

Weston, focused on his meal, didn't notice the exchange. Which was what Quinn had wanted. Work him hard so that he'd appreciate a good meal, an early night, and a soft bed. His attention returned to the stranger named Beckett. It was probably a good thing Weston was so famished, what with the man flirting with Amelia.

Hopefully, they'd all get out of here before he noticed.

The next time the girl came in with bowls of bread pudding, she cut her gaze toward Weston. When he didn't even look up, she pouted, plopped a bowl down in front of him, and moved away.

She sashayed across the room, Beckett following her every move. This time Weston noticed. When she eased a bowl of the sweet dessert in front of Beckett, Weston dropped his fork, glaring at Beckett. He started to stand and Quinn grabbed his arm in a viselike grip. "Let it go, Weston. They'll be gone by daybreak."

"But—"

"I said let it be."

Weston jerked his arm free and stormed out. The others watched him go, but Quinn ignored their looks, finished his pudding, then reached for Weston's. If the boy wasn't going to eat it . . .

When the last of the strangers left, he stood, grabbed his hat, and turned toward the smithy.

As had become his habit of a night, Quinn swept the smithy, organized his tools, and laid out his work for the next day. Whistling as he worked, he glanced across the way toward the cookhouse every time he passed the open door. He usually finished his end-of-day chores about the same time the women were done cleaning the cookhouse. And even if he finished first, it was no hardship to linger until they were safely inside for the night.

As he reached for the shovel to bank the fire, he heard girlish giggles.

Frowning, he moved to the door of the smithy. Peering out into the darkness, he could see the lights still on in the cookhouse, where Kiera and the women were washing up.

The strangers had made camp in the trees on the other side of the clearing and had settled in for the night. So whom had he heard?

Another round of giggles came out of the darkness, and

he spotted the silhouette of a couple in the shadows at the edge of the trees. His jaw clenched. Amelia? And Weston? He stalked toward them.

Seemed Amelia was more like her older half sister than any of them knew. And Weston was an overgrown spoiled brat who needed a good switching, and Quinn was in the mood to give it to him.

But before he reached them, a shadowy form launched itself out of the shadows toward the couple.

"Get your hands off her!"

Weston?

Then who—?

Kiera's heart plummeted toward her toes when she heard Amelia scream. She rushed outside, spotted Mr. Horne and several of the other men running toward an abandoned cabin behind the smithy.

But there was no sign of her sister.

She pushed through the men just in time to see Weston charge at the man called Beckett. They both went down in a flurry of arms and legs, wrestling on the ground.

As they rolled across the alleyway, kicking, gouging, and grunting, the men fell back, giving them room. Quinn snagged Kiera around the waist and pulled her out of harm's way. She glanced up to see his jaw jutted out as he watched the fight. The iron band around her waist loosened, and he put her behind him, angling his body between her and the fight.

"Where's Amelia? I heard her scream."

He jerked his chin toward the door of the smithy. "There."

Kiera didn't stop to wonder about the tightness in his voice. Amelia saw her and ran toward her, tears streaming down her face.

Kiera cupped her face. "Are you all right? What happened?"

Amelia shook her head. "I don't know. They just started fighting—"

Quinn snorted, throwing a disgusted look at her sister. Beckett's fist slammed into Weston's cheek, and Amelia cringed. "Quinn, make them stop!"

"Not yet. A good thrashing is just what they both need." He glared at her. "And you, too, lass."

Amelia gasped, loosened her hold on Kiera, then turned and ran toward the smithy.

Kiera gaped at Quinn. "Quinn, please." She put a hand on his arm, her gaze pleading. "Weston is no match for that man and you know it."

Growling low in his throat, he shook off her hand and waded into the fight, grabbing Weston by the collar. Björn did the same with Beckett.

Quinn shoved Weston's hat toward him. "If I see ya out o' yer quarters before daylight, I'll beat ya myself. Is that clear?"

With a sullen glance in Beckett's direction, Weston grabbed his hat and stalked off.

"As for you, Mr. Beckett, I suggest you stay with your party for the rest of the night as well. Is that understood?"

Beckett glanced around at the circle of men, turned on

his heel, and headed back to the fire the visitors had built on the other side of the well. Kiera was glad to see him go. Relieved that the fight was over without more fists being thrown, Kiera hurried toward the smithy. She pushed open the heavy doors, blinking in the dim light cast by the banked fire from the forge. "Amelia?"

Her sister flung herself into her arms. "Oh, Kiera. Is it over?"

"It's over."

Amelia sniffled, then lifted her tearstained face to Kiera's. "Truly?"

"Yes, I think so. Quinn and Björn put a stop to it."

Amelia pulled away. "I need to go to him. See if he's all right—"

"Don't ya think ya've done enough damage for one night?" Quinn stood just inside the smithy, the firelight dancing across his face, giving his features a ferocious scowl. He advanced on them, his face blazing with fury. "I ought to turn ya over my knee and give ya a good wallop, missy. Do ya know what Beckett might have done to ya if Weston hadn't stopped him?"

Amelia shrank back against Kiera. "I don't know what you're talking about—"

"Ya know exactly what I'm talking about. This isna Ireland, Amelia, and you are no' Charlotte. Ya do no' have yer father's money, position, or prestige t' get ya out o' scrapes. Chasing after the Caruthers boy is bad enough, but pitting him against a man like Beckett could get him killed." Quinn paused, then just as suddenly, threw his hands up. Chest heaving, he raked a hand through his hair before directing his anger at Kiera. "She's yer sister. Maybe you can talk some sense in t' her."

"Amelia, what's he talking about?" Kiera grabbed her sister by the arm.

"I didn't do anything . . ." Her sister's eyes filled with tears, and with one desperate glance at Quinn, she wrenched free and rushed out of the smithy.

Kiera watched her go, then wrapped her arms around her waist, a cold chill cascading from the top of her head to the soles of her feet. Shivering, she moved closer to the forge. "What did she do?"

"She was with Beckett. That's why Weston hit him."

Dread clamped around Kiera's heart. Had Beckett compromised her sister? She tried to think how long Amelia had been gone from the kitchen. It couldn't have been long. They'd finished washing the supper dishes, and Amelia had left. Kiera had set bread to rising.

"Did he—?"

"Nothing happened." Quinn's voice seemed to be coming from far away. "But she wasna exactly discouraging him either."

A pain like none she'd ever experienced knifed through Kiera. She'd hoped and prayed that time, distance, and maturity would teach Amelia to be circumspect and prudent in her behavior. It seemed she'd been wrong.

It was one thing for Amelia to be infatuated with Weston,

causing Kiera no end of grief, but to sneak away and meet with Mr. Beckett—a stranger, no less—gave Kiera the urge to lose her dinner. Surely Amelia realized the danger she'd put herself in this night.

"Connor is going to be livid. He already thinks the worst of Charlotte, of me. Now Amelia is following in our sister's footsteps, playing with men's affections." Kiera blinked back the sting of tears. "We'll leave. I'll take Amelia somewhere—"

"Do no' be daft." Quinn turned her to face him. "Ya have no place t' go, lass."

He was right, and the thought of taking Amelia back to Natchez, risking ending up in Le Bonne's clutches, made her stomach sink. The tears spilled over. "What am I going to do with her? She's so young—"

"She's sixteen." Quinn wiped her tears with his thumbs, and she shivered at his touch. "Many girls are wed by that age. Maybe she and Weston—"

"He's just a boy." Kiera shook her head. "I doubt Mr. Caruthers would give his blessing to a penniless girl from Ireland with no dowry and no title."

"It could happen. Look at Connor and Isabella."

"Thank you for trying to make me feel better. But I'd best go." Smiling sadly, Kiera eased out of his hold and pulled her shawl closer. "I need to make sure Amelia makes it to the house without getting into more trouble."

"I'll walk you."

He held the door and then escorted her up the long, sloping hill toward the main house. Night had fallen, and the majority of the house stood in darkness, save a single light from Connor and Isabella's bedroom.

Worries over how Connor would react to Amelia's latest escapade slammed into her full force. They were here on sufrage, only because of Quinn's influence. And he'd made it plain that he would be leaving as soon as he could.

They reached the steps that led up to the second-story veranda and Quinn paused. Time to part ways as he took the stairs and she headed to the right.

"Do no' worry, Kiera. Everything will be fine." He leaned down and kissed her forehead, his lips lingering against her skin. She closed her eyes, but all too soon he pulled away, a lopsided smile tipping one corner of his mouth. "Good night."

"Good night, Quinn."

As Quinn mounted the stairs that led to the rooms he shared with his brothers, she shuddered, not so much from the chill in the air, but the heavy burden of her sisters that she shouldered alone.

Ever since Quinn had stepped into her life, she'd begun to count on him, but he wouldn't always be around to watch over her, pull her sister out of danger, or dry her tears.

If she felt this bereft now, how would she feel when he walked out of her life for good?

Chapter 18

"There were at least fifty turkeys in that flock." Mews spread his hands wide. "And that tom was this big."

The men around the breakfast table almost fell out laughing at Mews's pronouncement over breakfast.

Quinn's gaze met Kiera's across the top of Mews's head. Her eyes twinkled and a wide smile spread across her face at the men's antics over Mews's tall tales.

Suddenly he was transported back to Saturday night after the fight, Kiera's worry over her sister, then escorting her to the main house. He'd wanted to take her in his arms, to kiss her again, but he'd settled for a chaste kiss to her forehead. He'd told himself that the fight and her need to check on her sister had held him back, but the truth was that he was afraid.

Afraid of where his feelings for Kiera were going to take him. Afraid of what his future held. It wasn't fair to either of them for him to explore this passion that flared every time she was near when he had full intentions to walk away from Breeze Hill and never return.

But when Kiera looked at him, her blue eyes flashing with laughter, her face wreathed with a smile, it was hard to remember his reasons for wanting to be free from responsibility, free from all ties that held him to one place.

She glided across the floor toward the kitchen, and it was like a cloud descended over the room when she was gone. He sighed, looked at his plate, and wondered at the way she drew him.

"I ain't never seen a tom turkey that big."

"You should catch him and teach him to ride, then."

Mews's face turned red, and he blustered, "I'm telling you—"

"Where did you see this flock of turkeys?" Björn asked, his thick accent garbled even more by a mouth full of ham.

Kiera returned with a pan of biscuits and made her way around the table. Mews glared at the beefy sawyer, reached for a biscuit, tore it in half, and sopped it in gravy. After popping a morsel in his mouth, he shook his finger at Björn. "I ain't going to tell you. Since they don't exist and all."

Björn scowled. "Instead of telling how big of a flock, you should take your gun tomorrow and shoot a turkey.

Slow-roasted turkey sounds good." He glanced up, his broad face turning splotchy with embarrassment. "Please forgive, miss. I did not mean that what you are already preparing is not to my liking."

Kiera smiled. "No need to apologize, Mr. Björn. A slow-roasted turkey does sound wonderful after a winter of salt pork."

"Ja." He smiled, pleased to stay in Kiera's good graces.

Mews slapped his hand on the table. "Then you shall have your turkey, Miss Kiera."

"Thank you, Mr. Mews. Although I'm not sure if I'll be able to roast it properly without a spit, but I'll do my best."

"Good day t' ye, men." Connor's voice broke in on the revelry. Quinn glanced up to see his brother standing in the doorway. He turned toward Kiera. "Miss Young, if these clodhoppers can't seem to finish eating in a timely manner, I suggest you cut your breakfast fare in half from now on."

"Yes—yes, sir."

Connor turned on his heel and left just as suddenly as he'd appeared. The men stuffed the rest of their breakfast in their mouths, grabbed their lunch pails, still jostling each other and ribbing Mews about his flock of wild turkeys on the way out.

Kiera stared at the door. "Well, of all the nerve—"

"He didn't mean it." Quinn chuckled.

She cut her gaze to his. "How could you tell?"

"If the men thought he was serious, they would have left quietly withou' much hullabaloo."

"That makes no sense."

"That's just the way it is, lass." He shrugged.

"Men." She shook her head, started clearing the table. "Where's Weston?"

"Down at the smithy. Said he wasna hungry."

"Weston not hungry? I find that hard to believe."

"I do no' think he wanted t' face the men after causing such a ruckus Saturday night."

"Is he—" a frown of concern marred her brow—"is he all right?"

"The lad's fine. A few bruises, but he's mostly just sulking."

She motioned toward the leftover ham and biscuits. "Well, take him something to eat. Regardless of how ridiculous it was to pick a fight with that man, he needs to eat."

Quinn glanced at her. "Ya do no' think he should have defended yer sister's honor?"

"From what you said, Amelia's honor didn't need defending."

"But Weston didna know that."

Her lips thinned. "Well, it's high time he learned."

One of the Horne girls came in, glanced shyly at him, and started gathering dishes.

"Speaking of Amelia, where is she?"

"Sleeping in. With Mary and her girls helping out, I don't need her as much. I told her if she'd help with the evening meal without complaint, I wouldn't make her get up before daylight to help cook."

"But ye're getting up before daylight and cooking the evening meal as well. That doesn't leave much rest for you."

"The middle of the day isn't that busy." She shrugged. "I can rest then."

She grabbed his plate and swept through the opening that led into the kitchen. Quinn stood, snagged a piece of ham from the table, and followed. He leaned against the door-frame, watching her.

"But do ya?"

"Do I what?"

"Rest. During the day."

Her cheeks pinkened, and she picked up a bucket. "Sometimes."

Which meant never. Just as he'd suspected, she was working from sunup till sundown and then some, determined not to be a burden to anyone.

She sailed out the door, calling over her shoulder, "Don't forget to take Weston something to eat."

When she was gone, he stuffed the bit of ham in his mouth, wiped his hands, and plucked a length of straw from a broom in the corner. Then he hunkered down in front of the fireplace and used the straw to measure for a spit.

Five minutes later, he heard Kiera coming back to the cabin, her humming sounding cheery and happy. She stepped inside, the bucket of water held at arm's length to keep from sloshing it on her skirts. "What are you doing?"

He tucked the broom straw in his shirt and snagged a piece of cheesecloth off the side table. "Just getting something t' wrap Weston's breakfast in."

Once back at the smithy, he found the boy dozing by the

fire. He tossed the cheesecloth bundle on top of him, then started gathering his tools to make Kiera's spit.

Weston groaned and sat up. "What's this?"

"Breakfast."

The boy threw him a look, looking lopsided with one eye swollen shut. "Thanks."

Quinn shrugged. "Do no' thank me. Kiera sent it. If it was left up to me, you would've gone hungry."

But Weston wasn't paying him much attention. He was too busy wolfing down his breakfast. As soon as the boy finished, Quinn put him to work.

As the morning wore on, he could hear the faint sounds of singing from nearby. Kiera, Mary, and her daughters were busy breaking up ground for a garden plot.

The fresh scent of spring wafted through the smithy, blowing the dull odor of smoke and sulfur away. He had no doubt they'd experience another cold snap or two, but the grass had already started to turn green and the trees were budding. Birds sang in the trees, chirping and chattering in a hundred different bird languages, but somehow all still in perfect harmony.

As he worked, he found himself humming along with the women, the ring of his hammer keeping time with their catchy tune. His heart swelled with a feeling of coming home. In that instant, the grip of steel in his left hand, the hammer in his right striking metal, he had no desire to leave, to rush away to places unknown.

Would it be so bad to put down roots here, to help his brother rebuild Braxton Hall into a flourishing plantation?

He'd never dreamed of doing such. There'd been no reason to even think that a penniless, rootless, landless lad from the old country would ever have such an opportunity. He'd be foolish to throw it away on the dreams of his youth.

Wouldn't he?

The singing stopped, and the women started talking, their voices too low and too far away for him to begin to guess what they were talking about. Still it was easy for him to separate Mary's deep-throated chuckle, laced with her native tongue, from Kiera's dulcet tones.

Her laughter rang out and his heart quickened.

Did his newfound desire for hearth and home hinge more on the promise of land or a certain blue-eyed blonde lass from the old country?

Reginald sat in the shadows of the Blue Heron sipping stale ale and listening to the talk among the patrons. This was his seventh night to frequent the tavern, and he had yet to see the man named Le Bonne.

He ignored the men drowning their sorrows in drink and the women who encouraged them to empty their pockets of every last coin before the night was done.

He'd witnessed three fistfights, a knifing, and endless displays of women in indecent dress stalking the crowd for easy prey. After they'd found that he wasn't interested in their favors but only sought information, the tavern wenches had left him alone.

Maybe Bloomfield was right. He'd learned nothing since arriving in Natchez. Nothing at all. Should he return to Breeze Hill, collect Weston, and head north toward home?

Sick at heart at the thought of admitting defeat, he guzzled down another gulp of ale. He'd promised his wife that he would return with Reggie. How could he bear to tell his darling, sweet wife that their eldest son was lost to them—possibly forever? He feared she might not survive the shock—

The hard slap of a palm against the top of the next table interrupted his half-drunken musings. "She was here, I'm telling you. I saw her right there on that dais not a month ago."

Much to his disgust, Reginald recognized the voice from the long trip into Natchez with Granger's party. Stricklund? Stanhope? Stoddard? That was it. Stoddard. It was hard to remember the man's name, but his nasally voice, battered nose, and stomach-churning odor were not so easily forgotten.

He glanced up, spotted the man at the next table, and at the same time caught a whiff of something foul. Yes, it was Stoddard all right. Reginald slouched over his drink, hiding beneath the brim of his hat, not wishing to be recognized by the lout.

"Aw, go on wi' ye. I've seen 'em all, and there ain't no Irish gals here, let alone pretty ones. Or even young ones, for that matter."

"That's what I said, you blockhead."

Reginald leaned closer, trying to distinguish Stoddard's words through the wheeze caused by his broken nose.

"She was here, but she ain't now. She's running a stand out at that plantation on the trace. Wind in the Trees or sumpin' like that."

"Breeze Hill?"

"Yeah, that's it. Breeze Hill. She acted like it wasn't her, but I never forget a pretty face. It was her all right. And she treated me like I was dirt."

"Ye are dirt."

Stoddard laughed, too drunk to take offense at the insult. "I wonder if Le Bonne would pay for the information?"

"Ye'd best not mess with Le Bonne. He'd cut your heart out soon as look at ye."

Reginald sat back. Stoddard had to be talking about Kiera Young, the pretty young Irish miss who'd provided food and lodging for him and Weston at Breeze Hill. Could she be the same girl Bloomfield had mentioned? The one sent to the colonies to marry Le Bonne?

Then how had she ended up at Breeze Hill?

The spit turned like a dream.

Kiera reached for the handle and gave it another turn, marveling at the ease of it. It couldn't be more perfect, situated in the updraft with a drip pan underneath to catch all the juices for basting and making gravy.

Her mouth practically watered thinking of all the savory delicacies to be produced with such a contrivance.

She didn't have to ask who'd fashioned the spit and installed it in the fireplace in the dead of night while everyone else was sleeping.

There was only one man who had the skills and only one man who cared enough to do it.

Quinn had thanked her for repairing the gloves and the apron, not in words, but in deed. For surely he'd found both by now and realized they'd been repaired. Her lips tugged upward at their silly little game of doing favors for each other without uttering a single thank-you. Heart light, she turned the spit again, planning to do something special for him.

Soon.

If Mr. Mews supplied the turkeys he'd promised, Quinn and the others would have the slow-roasted meat they'd salivated over. Tucking her pleasure away, she bustled about preparing breakfast. The men would be arriving soon, and she didn't want to make them late, especially after Connor's remark earlier in the week.

She heard Mary in the other cabin, and soon the aroma of baking bread wafted through the cookhouse. They had breakfast on the table before the men arrived and had them out the door before Connor could come looking for them.

All in all, a successful morning.

On his way out, Mews stuck his head in the door. "I'm going to shoot a turkey today for sure, miss. You can count on it."

"I will." Kiera smiled. "Thank you, Mr. Mews."

The first rooster of the day crowed when he walked away, whistling. Kiera turned to the mess that the men left every day. She could hear Mary singing in the next room, and she joined in as she did every morning. When all the pots and pans were washed and put away, and the plates and cups stacked and ready for the evening meal, Kiera swept the floor, leaving the door wide-open, letting the early morning sunlight filter in.

She spotted a woman walking down the lane, her broad face framed by straight black hair.

"Mary, someone's coming."

Mary joined her at the door. "My cousin Fala."

The woman, a reed basket over her arm, stopped a few feet shy of the steps, held out two rabbit pelts, and jabbered something in a language Kiera didn't understand. Mary replied in the same melodious language.

Mary turned to Kiera. "She wants to trade."

"Trade?" Kiera's brow furrowed. "For what? I don't have anything to trade."

Mary spouted off a string of garbled words, then turned back to Kiera. "Salt. She wants salt."

Fala offered the rabbit pelts again.

Kiera chewed her bottom lip. "Tell her I don't need the pelts, but if she can bring fresh meat, I will trade."

More talk flowed between the two before Fala folded her arms and shook her head.

Kiera glanced toward Mary. "What did she say?"

Mary shrugged. "She cannot bring meat. Her family needs all the meat they can get."

"Did she forage for those?" Kiera motioned toward the

basket of greens at her feet. "Can she show me what's growing right now? Things like herbs, mushrooms, wild greens, and berries. And I need a tanned hide. Something large, like deerskin, not rabbits."

Mary relayed Kiera's words, and Fala gave a short, quick answer. "She said she will show you what to look for."

Fala reached into her basket and drew out several small packets wrapped in cornhusks. As she handed them over to Mary, she patted each packet, naming off each seed in her native tongue. Mary repeated the words in English. "Corn. Squash. Beans. And pumpkin."

"Seeds for our garden? Wonderful." Kiera smiled and patted Fala's arm to show her gratitude. "Wait here."

She hurried into the cookhouse, found a small leather pouch, and filled it with salt. On the stoop, she held it out. "I'm sorry; it's not much."

Fala took the pouch, tucked it into her basket, said a few words, then turned and walked away.

"What did she say?"

Mary shrugged. "Fala will come back tomorrow to show you where to find the greens."

Chapter 19

ALMOST A WEEK LATER, FALA RETURNED. By that time, Kiera had realized that *tomorrow* didn't necessarily mean the very next day to Mary and Fala's people.

Baskets in hand, Kiera and Mary followed Fala, watching closely as the woman pointed out each plant. She motioned to a tangle of thorny vines twined in and around a split-rail fence, jabbering in her native tongue.

Kiera peered at the bushes, then hurried to catch up. "Were those blackberries?"

"Yes. Ripe in summer. June. July."

Kiera's mouth watered at the thought of blackberry cobbler, jams, and jellies. "Truly? Back in Ireland, it would be autumn before we would have blackberries."

As they walked, she made note of every large patch of brambles she saw. The trail led them to the edge of a meadow, last fall's dried grasses starting to wilt into the earth. But sprigs of pale green peeked through here and there, a sign that spring was well on the way.

Fala skirted the edge of the meadow, pointing at the leafy greens tucked out of the wind along the ridges and hollows. She reached down and snapped off a leaf as wide as her palm, rubbed it between her fingers, and held it up. She mumbled one word, smiling as she held the leaf out to Kiera.

Mary translated. "Mustard greens."

Kiera took the leaf, fingered the course fibers on it, and frowned. "Are you sure this is good to eat? What happens to these little hairs?"

Mary repeated her question to Fala, and the cousins shared a laugh.

Fala jabbered away, then held up one hand, the tips of her fingers held together. She spread her fingers. *"Poof."*

"The prickly hairs disappear when the greens are cooked?"

Mary translated, and Fala nodded her approval.

Kiera smiled, mimicked Fala's motions. "Go *poof.*"

The three women filled their baskets with the greens as Mary explained how to rinse and cook them. "A ham bone, vinegar, salt. Corn bread. Good."

An hour later, they headed toward home, baskets full.

Kiera looked up when she heard a shout. Quinn was jogging toward them, a flintlock in his hands, a pistol tucked in his waistband. The presence of the firearms shot a bolt of alarm through her. Quinn kept the weapons hanging over the door in the smithy. Had something happened to Megan? Amelia? "What's wrong?"

He stopped a few feet away, breathing heavily. His blue gaze, bright with worry, took in the overflowing baskets, Mary and Fala, then settled on Kiera.

"A group of Indians came t' the smithy. They kept jabbering something at me, but I couldna understand them. After they left, I couldna find ya." He motioned to Fala. "Who's this?"

"This is Mary's cousin Fala."

"Ya should've told me where ya were going."

Somehow the knowledge that he'd been worried put a warm glow in a tiny corner of her heart. She fell into step beside him, and Mary and Fala hung back, walking several feet behind them. "I really am sorry. I didn't mean to worry you."

"Though Connor assures me the Natchez are peaceful, there are rumors that there are renegades who run with the highwaymen." He frowned. "I still do no' know what they wanted. They were more than a wee bit agitated."

"Perhaps they were looking for Fala."

Quinn nodded. "Perhaps."

Suddenly he reached out and took her by the arm, pulling her to a stop, focused on something down the path. Kiera spotted the Indians stalking toward them. "Is that them?"

"Aye." Quinn stepped in front of her, and for that she was grateful. With shaved heads except for one ridge of hair,

they looked quite fierce. They wore a hodgepodge of clothing, from English breeches and soft cotton shirts to fringed
leggings and little else. One had on a ruffled shirt that might
have been white at one time but had long since turned a
dingy brown that blended with the rest of his attire. All the
men had some kind of weapon, from spears and wicked-
looking clubs to tomahawks.

They stopped several yards away. Ruffles looked at Quinn;
then his attention shifted, landed on Kiera, and his lips flat-
tened in a straight line, a furrow between his brows. She
sucked in a breath, trying not to let her fear show. Passing
her over, he turned to Fala and said a few words, his voice
low and harsh.

"Fala's husband," Mary whispered. "He's upset that she
didn't tell him where she was going."

"Have her tell him about the salt."

Mary spoke quickly to Fala and her cousin pulled the
pouch of salt from her basket and showed it to her husband,
pointing at Kiera.

Flat black eyes in a wide square face captured and held
Kiera's. She held her breath until with a grunt, the Indian
took Fala by the arm, and the entire party melted into the
woods.

Kiera remembered to breathe.

Quinn motioned Kiera and Mary to follow him. "Let's go
before they change their minds."

"Change their minds about what?" Kiera fell into step
beside Quinn. As was her custom, Mary walked a few steps

behind. "They were just worried about Fala, just like you were worried about me."

"Ya canna know that." He urged her forward along the path. "What were ya doing out here?"

"Fala came by last week. She wanted to trade two rabbit pelts for salt, but I said no. I asked for meat, but she didn't have any. Instead, she showed us where to find mustard greens, wild onions, mushrooms, and berries."

"Mushrooms?" Quinn scowled at the basket. "She's liable t' poison the lot of us."

Kiera shook her head. "No, she was very careful to point out the ones that are edible. And Mary knows what to look for as well."

"And you? Do you know what's edible and what's not?"

She lifted her chin. He had little faith in her. "I was fairly knowledgeable about the edible plants back home in Ireland. I daresay I can learn the difference here in the colonies quickly enough."

"Well, the next time ya want t' learn, do me the kindness o' letting me know where ye're going." He ran a hand through his hair, and it stood on end, making him look even wilder than he had when she'd seen him barreling down on them. "I didna know if those Indians had made off with ya or if Le Bonne had found ya or what."

"I was fine. Mary was with me, and so was Fala. There was no need to worry."

"Women." With an annoyed glare in her direction, he stalked down the path, and Kiera struggled to keep pace, torn between relishing the fact that he'd been worried about her and telling him that she could take care of herself.

Thirty yards down the trail, Quinn glanced back, saw Kiera and Mary falling behind. He took a deep breath, slowed, and let them catch up. He matched his pace to Kiera's. "Sorry for being such an *eejit*."

"All is forgiven." Her lips twitched. "It's nice to know someone was worried for our welfare."

He shook his head. What had she been thinking, to just traipse off into the woods with two squaws without telling anyone? Granted, Mary Horne was a familiar face, but the other one? None of them knew anything about the Natchez woman named Fala.

When those men had shown up, repeating the same thing over and over and becoming increasingly agitated, Quinn hadn't known what they wanted or how to get rid of them. So he'd just stood there with a flintlock in hand. Not that it would have done much good against the six muscular braves. After they'd left, he'd rushed to check on Kiera and Mary.

And his heart had almost stopped when he'd found them gone.

He glanced at Kiera, knowing that if the Indians were bent on mischief, her pale skin and blonde hair would be hard to resist. Remembering how the warriors had stared at her, he felt his stomach clench anew.

Even Le Bonne had recognized the prize that had been

thrown into his lap that day on the wharf. Men would pay handsomely to claim her, even if for a short time.

His heart thudded against his rib cage like someone pumping the bellows until the fire was raging hot, hot enough to melt cold steel so that it could be shaped, pounded, and molded into something fresh and new.

Much like he felt right now.

Slowly his desire to abdicate responsibility for his brothers, Kiera, and her sisters to someone else was melting away, and he was like molten steel in her hands, ready and willing to be shaped into the kind of man that would stand by her side.

The moment they arrived at the cookhouse, Quinn gave a stiff bow and, without another word, left them and stalked away toward the smithy.

Frowning, Kiera lifted her skirts and went inside, Mary close on her heels. Quinn had grown more silent and withdrawn with every step toward home. He'd truly been worried over her safety.

But they'd only ventured a mile or so from the plantation. Surely they were as safe as the men and women who worked the fields and the loggers who entered the forests each day. Even the children had the run of the woods and the creek that meandered through the plantation.

On one hand, his sweet protectiveness endeared him to her, but on the other hand, it made her uneasy.

But why?

She plopped the basket down on the table. Removing the greens, she fingered the leather that Fala had brought her. It was almost too soft to make into a blacksmith's apron as she'd planned, but Quinn needed the protection against the sparks. Frustrated with her mixed-up emotions, she pushed the deerskin to the side, picked up a bucket, and headed toward the well. As she drew water, the reason for her unease hit her.

Quinn made her feel cherished. He made her want to depend on him. And she didn't want to be dependent on any man ever again. Her father hadn't seen fit to provide for her and her sisters in spite of knowing what kind of man her brother-in-law was. And while nothing should have surprised her about George's intentions, the depth of his hatred—or was it Charlotte's?—that led him to sell her and her sisters to pay off a debt had shocked her to the core. Then there was Pierre Le Bonne. She couldn't even bring herself to think about what would have been in store for her and her sisters at the Frenchman's hands.

But Quinn had rescued her, defended her, and protected her. He'd recognized her worth as a person, not as property to pass from hand to hand without thought or care. Actions that made her think of a future that might include him.

And there was the rub.

He'd made no bones about leaving, taking off for the big adventure that he'd been denied in his youth. As much as she might want to, she couldn't tie her hopes and dreams to a man with journeying in his soul.

But did it really matter whether Quinn decided to go or to stay? Her days at Breeze Hill were numbered.

Charlotte had seen to that.

Chapter 20

Connor sat at the desk in the sitting room, quill poised over the ledgers. He scowled at the numbers, tossed the quill on the desk, and ran both hands through his hair. He closed his eyes as Isabella's soft hands landed on his shoulders and started kneading the tense muscles.

"It's not that bad, is it?"

"Compared to what?"

She leaned over his shoulder and turned the ledger so she could read his entries. "Compared to where Breeze Hill was a year ago, I'd say we're doing quite well."

"But is it well enough? Wicker wants more lumber. I'd planned to cut back on production and use half the men for spring planting. Now—" he blew out a breath—"now I need more loggers, more wagons, more tools, and more day laborers for the fields, but . . ."

"But what?" Isabella arched a brow.

"After the last two years of one catastrophe on the heels of another, nobody's willing to work."

"They're afraid they won't get paid." It was a statement, not a question.

"Yes." Connor sighed. "And I'd hoped Quinn would agree to manage Braxton Hall—"

"Don't call it that." Isabella cringed. "I'd rather not ever hear the name Braxton Hall again."

Connor turned to look at her. "Sorry, lass. 'Tis a hard habit t' break."

"I know. We must come up with a new plantation name."

"What's the point?" He pulled Isabella into his lap, and she wrapped one arm around his neck. "Without day laborers, the land is going to lie fallow."

Isabella reached for the quill and started doodling on the edge of his ledger. "Are you regretting your promise to make Breeze Hill a working plantation until Jon is old enough to take over? Twenty years is a long time."

"No, I don't regret making such a promise." Her doodles turned to a border of magnolia blossoms. He chuckled. "Is that what you see when you think of . . . that place?"

She tilted her head, a smile on her face as she eyed the flowers. "Yes. In the springtime, the magnolia blossoms are so beautiful, the trees marching down the valley toward the house perched on the hill, the setting sun reflecting off the white columns. Or at least it used to be beautiful before—"

"It will be again. We'll rebuild."

She dipped the quill into his inkwell, then continued to draw, adding majestic columns behind and beyond the magnolia blossoms. "What do you see when you think of it?"

"I never think of the house, the one the tornado ripped away. Like you, I think of the valley. Long and narrow as it is, it reminds me o' home. Our house back in Ireland was little more than a hovel, but it was a good mile upwind of the mines, and the air was pure and clean. When ya topped the ridge, ya could see clear across the glen to a little rise where our home sat. As a lad, after a long night in the mines, I'd stand atop that ridge, see the smoke from the peat fire, and know that *Mam* would have hot porridge waiting for me when I walked through the door."

They sat, both lost in the memories of their childhoods, the silence broken only by the peaceful scratch of the quill against the ledger. Connor could picture the magnolia blooms, smell their sweet fragrance, and feel the wind blowing up from the glen, whether it was from the old home place or the new one, he couldn't tell. But—

"Magnolia Glen," he whispered. "Does the name suit you, Wife?"

Isabella paused, turned her dark eyes on him; a soft smile graced her face. She cupped his jaw, and he shivered at her touch.

"It suits, Husband. It suits me well."

Natchez Under-the-Hill was abuzz with news of a ship that had been lost at sea. Reginald stood off to one side, watching as men, women, and children converged on the wharf.

The families of the men from the doomed ship stood in small groups, anxiously waiting as one after another of the survivors departed from the *Vision Quest*. He overheard a nearby conversation.

"What happened?"

"The clipper *Lillian* was hit by a storm two weeks out from New Orleans. It was sheer luck that the *Vision Quest* spotted the sinking ship and was able to rescue as many survivors as she did."

One by one, the women left the clusters, rushed to the gangway, and clutched their men. Some were sons, fathers, and husbands. Some had no family to welcome them, but even they were greeted with open arms and escorted to one of the many taverns along the wharf with the promise of ale to celebrate their safe return.

By and by, the ship emptied and there were no more sailors to step onto the gangway and make their way to land. Reginald's chest twisted with sympathy as a half-dozen or so women stood in shocked silence when they realized that they were the ones left, they were the ones whose men had been lost when the ship went down.

One woman fell to her knees, clutched her children to her bosom, and wept, while another, dressed in little more than rags, bent double and deposited her meager breakfast onto the cobblestones at her feet. Four small children huddled near, looking bewildered by their mother's display.

As the crowd dispersed, some to their homes in thankfulness that their loved one had been spared, others to wallow in their despair, Reginald turned away.

"No pay?" a shrill voice arched across the wharf. The woman, the same one who'd become ill at the realization that her husband wasn't coming home, clung to the door of an enclosed carriage. "My Samuel is dead. How will my children and I survive without him? You signed him to this voyage. You owe me—"

"Do you have a copy of your husband's contract?"

She shook her head. "No, *monsieur*, but—"

The same hulking giant who guarded the entrance to the Blue Heron night after night held the reins of a matched pair of bays. Reginald's heart lurched. Might the Frenchman inside be the elusive Monsieur Le Bonne? Reginald made his way toward the carriage, hoping to get a glimpse of the man.

"Then I'm afraid I don't owe you anything, *madame*. If you don't have a copy of your husband's contract, there's no proof that he was even on the *Lillian*."

"You can't do this. I'll work. I'll do anything. Please."

"*Madame*, you have nothing to offer anyone who frequents any of my establishments."

The man's gaze met and held Reginald's, the flat black eyes emotionless. Without a nod or any indication he'd even seen Reginald, he tapped his cane on the roof of the carriage. "Drive on, Claude."

And with the woman still clinging to the door, begging for mercy, the coachman slapped the reins against the horses and the carriage lumbered off, scattering pedestrians right and left, leaving the woman sprawled in the street, her pleas going unheeded.

The moment Claude wrenched open the door of the carriage in front of the Blue Heron, Pierre addressed him.

"Who was that man?"

Claude's brow furrowed. "What man, *monsieur*?"

Pierre sighed. Did Claude pay attention to nothing? "The man at the docks, the one who approached the carriage."

The look in the man's eyes had told Pierre that he hadn't drawn near the carriage out of curiosity. There'd been something more, something deep and dark and feral in that singular glance.

Claude's wide features cleared, and he smiled. "Oh, *monsieur*, that is Reginald Caruthers, a plantation owner from a hamlet several days north of here."

"Caruthers?" The name sounded familiar.

"Yes, *monsieur*. He's searching for his son, a young man who disappeared two months ago."

"I see." Pierre leveled his gaze on Claude. "And you saw no need to bring this to my attention?"

Confusion clouded Claude's features. "I'm sorry, *monsieur*. I didn't think—"

"Never mind." Pierre sat back in the carriage. "I've changed my mind. Take me back to the docks, to the *Pathos Unrequited*."

"*Oui, monsieur.*"

Claude clambered up to the driver's seat and drove away. As the carriage swayed along the cobblestone streets, Pierre thought on the desperate father searching for his son.

He wasn't the first, and he wouldn't be the last.

At the docks, he exited the carriage, strode down the gangway.

The captain met him, hat in hand. "Monsieur Le Bonne. To what do I owe this visit?"

Pierre eyed the ship, old, battered, listing to one side. "The repairs?"

"We are making progress." The captain mangled his hat. "But the men, they are restless."

"I see. Tell them to come by the Blue Heron tonight. I'll extend credit to every man who stays on board and gets this ship ready to set sail within the month."

"Thank you, *monsieur*."

Pierre strode past him and headed toward his stateroom. If it could be called that. He was expanding his holdings with the *Pathos Unrequited*. As soon as the vessel was made seaworthy again, he planned to send her out. She'd haul cotton, corn, tobacco to Europe and bring back slaves, indentures, or anything else that was paying cargo.

He stood on the deck watching the captain share the news of unlimited credit at the Blue Heron with the construction crew on board.

The poor saps had no clue that they were digging themselves into deeper and deeper debt. By the time the *Pathos Unrequited* set sail, they'd be so deep in debt to him, they'd agree to anything.

Even signing on the *Pathos Unrequited*'s maiden voyage if he demanded it.

On the eleventh day of stalking the woods every morning, Mr. Mews bagged two massive turkeys. You would have thought he'd poached deer from the king of England's own private herd, he was so proud.

As the afternoon waned, Kiera smiled, remembering when he'd waltzed into the cookhouse as the rest of the men were polishing off breakfast. You could have heard a pin drop when he plopped those birds on the table.

Suddenly, instead of poking fun at him as they'd been doing for the last week, the men all wanted to know where he'd found the flock of turkeys, but Mews refused to say and asked Kiera if she'd roast the turkeys for supper.

And of course she said she would.

As the aroma of roasting meat filled the cookhouse and made her mouth water, she bent down and spooned the juices out of the pan and drizzled them over the roasting birds. Her shoulder jostled Megan, who was busy turning the spit, slow and steady. "Smells good, doesn't it?"

"Yes, but I'm tired."

"You were in an all-fired hurry to turn the spit earlier today. Seems like you and Lizzy practically came to blows over who got the privilege."

"That was earlier." Megan sighed. "My arm hurts. Isn't it Lizzy's turn? Or even Amelia's?"

"I sent Lizzy to dig some beets, and Amelia is helping Martha. Besides, the men will be here soon and you can stop then."

"I hope there's some left for me after all this hard work."

"Megan Young, have I ever let you go hungry?"

Her sister wrinkled her brow. "No, but you haven't ever had roasted turkey and ten men to feed either."

"True. But rest assured, dear heart, I'll make sure you and Lizzy have a taste for all your efforts." Kiera kissed her sister on the forehead, then grabbed a bucket. "I'll be right back."

Twilight was fast approaching, and she still had to boil the potatoes and snap beans. But first, water for the potatoes and beans. She headed toward the well, bucket bumping against her swishing skirts. She'd just drawn water when she spotted movement through the trees along the road. The three travelers looked tired and dusty as if they'd traveled a long distance this day.

"Good evening, gentlemen." Kiera bobbed a greeting. "Will you be needing a meal or lodging tonight?"

They glanced at each other, then back at her. Two of them

leaned on their saddle horns, but one dismounted and moved toward her. The look he gave her made her skin crawl. "Well, since when does Breeze Hill offer lodging and all wrapped up in such a pretty package?"

Kiera backed up a step, realizing she was alone here with these men. Quinn had warned her of this very thing, and after the incident with the man who remembered her from the Blue Heron, she should have taken more precautions. "As of a few weeks ago. Meals and lodging. Over there." She pointed toward the cabins and the newly constructed dining area. "I must go finish preparing the meal. The men will be here soon for supper."

She turned away, picked up the bucket, but before she could take two steps, the man moved to her side, grabbed for the bucket. "Allow me."

"No thank you. I can manage."

He caught her around her waist and pulled her close, running the tips of his fingers down her cheek. "Lodging, eh? Does that include your company, wench?"

When his hand slipped below her jaw to the hollow of her throat, Kiera swung the bucket at him. It connected with his knee with a solid thwack, and he jerked away, eyes glittering.

His companions laughed. "Looks like you've got a wild one on your hands, Simpson. What are you going to do with her?"

With a firm grip on her, he wrenched the bucket out of her hand and tossed it aside. "You'll pay for that, wench."

"Let me go!" Kiera struggled against his hold.

"I don't think so. You're the one what offered lodging for the night. I'm just taking you up on the offer."

He wrapped both arms around her, lifting her off the ground. He nuzzled her neck, and his companions snickered and egged him on. Sickened, Kiera fought, scratching and clawing, kicking.

"Let the lass go."

Kiera went limp with relief at the sound of Quinn's voice.

Her assailant pushed her away so suddenly that she stumbled and would have fallen if Quinn hadn't caught her and propelled her toward the cookhouse.

"Go inside," he ordered, his voice as hard as the steel he worked with on a daily basis.

Kiera stumbled back, needing to do as Quinn said but unable to leave him to face the three men alone.

The man who'd assaulted her raised his hands, grinning. "I was only taking the wench up on her offer."

"What offer might that be?" Quinn grated.

"An offer of food, lodging, and—" he smirked, throwing a glance at Kiera—"companionship."

Chapter 21

RAGE FLASHED OVER QUINN SO FAST he didn't even know where it came from. With a primal growl, he swung, his fist connecting with the man's jaw.

And then there was no turning back.

The man threw a punch, the blow glancing off the side of Quinn's head. He reeled backward, gained his footing, then circled. The man was taller than Quinn by a head, but working in the forge gave Quinn an advantage of upper body strength the other man lacked.

Quinn hit him again, first with his left hand, followed quickly with his right. His opponent ducked, then came up into a crouch, and Quinn caught the glint of a knife in the fading light. His adversary lunged, and Quinn jumped back, feeling the burn as the knife ripped through his shirt and swiped across his rib cage.

Taking advantage of the moment, Quinn tackled his opponent and wrestled him to the ground, focused on getting his hand on that knife.

They rolled up against the rough stone that bordered the well, and Quinn slammed his opponent's arm against the stones, breaking his hold on the blade.

The bigger man broke free, scrabbled for the knife, then crouched, wielding it with precision. He grinned, and Quinn circled, waiting. He might not be as fortunate as he was the first time. Quinn heard shouts and knew that help was on the way. But would his brother and the others get here in time?

The boom of a musket shattered the silence and Quinn ducked, unsure where it had come from. His adversary's companions shouted a warning, then kicked their mounts forward. Quinn tried to dodge the oncoming horses but caught a glancing blow, spun, and slammed into the side of the well, pain lancing his ribs before he rolled off the stones and landed in the dirt.

The next few seconds were a blur as his opponent swung into the saddle and all three men raced down the lane toward the trace, the ground shaking under the pounding of their horses' hooves. Quinn struggled to stand, even as Kiera ran to his side. She slipped under his arm, her arm around his waist. Long, slender fingers touched his blood-soaked shirt, her touch burning almost as much as the open wound across his rib cage.

"You're hurt." Tears tracked down her face, and worry pulled at her brows.

"I'm fine."

Weston ran toward him, the flintlock in his hands. Quinn clenched his teeth against the pain. "Did you shoot that thing? That was a fool thing to do. You could've hit Kiera."

"Sorry, Miss Kiera, I didn't mean to scare you." Weston glared at Quinn. "And I didn't shoot to kill, just to give warning to those scoundrels that help was on the way."

Quinn grunted.

The next thing he knew, he was surrounded, the men from the sawmill with pistols drawn. Somebody came running with a lantern.

"What happened?" Connor bellowed.

"Three men." Quinn snugged Kiera closer, fury rising again at the crude insinuation the stranger had leveled at her. "They—"

"They wanted food and lodging but refused to pay. One of them—" Kiera looked up at Quinn, her gaze pleading—"one of them jumped Quinn when he told them to leave."

The light from the lantern cast shadows over Kiera's face, and Quinn nodded. "Aye, that's what happened."

Connor glanced from Quinn to Kiera and back again. "Are you all right?"

Quinn stood straight, his arm pressed against the knife

wound. "I'm fine. Banged up me ribs when I fell against the well."

"Should we give chase, Master Connor?"

Several of the men voiced their desire to go after the blackguards.

Connor shook his head. "No. They're long gone and shan't return, I think."

When Quinn didn't show up for supper, Kiera went in search of him.

Carrying a basket filled with strips of cloth and some salve, she slipped inside the smithy. Pausing inside the door, she blinked, letting her eyes adjust to the light.

Quinn had yet to bank the fire, and it cast a pleasing glow in the enclosed space. A lantern hung from an overhead beam, casting a halo of light in the center of the shop.

She froze, feeling heat rush to her face when she spotted Quinn standing beneath the lantern, his shirt bunched in his left hand as he dabbed at the blood on his side. He turned, saw her, and arched a brow.

"Here. Let me." Kiera dropped the basket of linen on a nearby table and took the cloth from him. Wrinkling her nose, she tossed the filthy rag on the table and grabbed a clean one from her basket.

She dipped the cloth in the bucket of water, wrung it out, and dabbed at the jagged cut that ran along his lower ribs and around his side. She grimaced as she tried to stanch the rivulet of blood that soaked his waistband.

"How bad is it?" He twisted to look, making the wound gap open.

"Be still. You're blessed that the tip of the knife glanced off your ribs." Tears stung her eyes. "If it had been an inch lower—"

"Do no' think o' what might have been." Quinn growled, the shirt slipping down. "It wasna an inch lower, so no need t' dwell on it."

"I'm sorry. Just—just hold up your shirt and let me finish." She pushed the shirt up, her fingers colliding with the warmth of his.

She winced afresh at the sight of his torn, bloody flesh. What if things had turned out differently tonight? What if Quinn now lay on the ground, his body lifeless and growing cold? She shuddered.

Dear Lord, thank You for Your providence, for sparing Quinn's life. I could never forgive myself if another man died because . . . because of me.

Remorse hollowed Kiera's insides. Forcing herself to remain calm, she washed off the blood. "I guess you're wondering why I didn't let you tell Connor what happened."

Inches away, his hooded gaze caught and held hers. "I figured ya had yer reasons, lass."

"I realized that—that I'd put myself in a dangerous position, and I was afraid he'd be angry." She shrugged, trying to concentrate on the job at hand. She glanced up. "You can say that you told me so if you wish."

"I will no'." One side of his mouth kicked up. "Being right in this case doesna make me feel any better."

"Thank you, all the same." She smiled. "Seems you're always having t' rescue me."

"My damsel in distress."

He winced, and she jerked the cloth away, flinching along with him. "I'm sorry."

Gently she touched the cloth to his torn side again. When she'd cleaned the area as best she could, she dipped her fingers in the salve and smoothed it along his rib cage, blushing anew at the ripple of taut skin, muscle, and sinew beneath her fingertips.

She reached for a length of cloth to bind his wound, finding it hard to ignore the expanse of male chest and flat stomach. She glanced up, saw his bright-blue eyes watching her.

Heart pounding, she stepped away, putting a little space between them. With her left hand skimming along the bandage to keep it in place, she circled, wrapping the gauze once, twice, a third time. The only saving grace was the layers of bandage that kept her from touching his skin outright. Relieved when she finally ran out of bandage, she motioned toward the binding. "Hold this, please."

He splayed his hand against the cotton with one hand while still gripping his bunched shirt with the other. Kiera tore the ends and knotted them, pulling them tight against his ribs. Quinn emitted a groan, and her gaze shot to his face. "I'm sorry. I know it hurts."

"Just do what ya need t' do," he gritted out.

She bit her lip and finished tying the knots, sneaking glances at his face. Sweat glistening on his brow, jaw clenched tight as the vise on his worktable, and eyes closed, he was the epitome of strength fighting pain. If both hands hadn't been tied up with the bandages, she would have reached out and smoothed the furrow between his eyes, kissed away the tight clamp of his lips, eased his pain—

She sucked in a breath.

What was she thinking?

With one last tug, she secured the bandage and stepped back, finally remembering to breathe. "All done." Her voice came out as a breathless squeak.

Hands shaking, she put the lid on the jar of salve, wrapped it carefully, then packed the remaining linens away. Out of the corner of her eye, she saw Quinn step deeper into the shadows, lift the bloody shirt over his head, and toss it aside. Taking a clean shirt off a peg, he slipped it on, the soft material stretching over his muscular chest and flowing free from his lean torso.

Kiera didn't know whether to stand still or to flee. Other than the kiss to her forehead to reassure her after Amelia had gone off with Beckett, Quinn had steered clear of her since the kiss they'd shared weeks ago.

Maybe he didn't—

"Thank you for your ministrations," his voice rumbled

from the shadows. Then he turned, jerking his head toward the door. "You'd better go. They'll be looking for you."

Face flaming, she grabbed the basket and headed toward the door. She hurried toward the cookhouse, trying to squelch the knot in her chest that said she'd fallen in love with a man who'd simply done the honorable thing and helped a damsel in distress.

Quinn watched Kiera go.

His ribs felt like somebody had raked hot coals across them, then for good measure laid a hot poker to the exposed flesh.

But the pain was nothing compared to the exquisite torture of Kiera's soft hands applying the salve to his rib cage, then the brush of her fingertips as she'd wound the bandage around his chest.

Even now, his breath hitched. It had been all he could do not to wrap her in his embrace and kiss her lips, pink and pale as the fresh blush of apple blossoms in the spring.

But he'd held himself in check. She'd just been accosted by a stranger and was as skittish as a newborn colt. Even an *eejit* like himself had sense enough to know she wouldn't welcome his kiss, not tonight.

Maybe not ever.

He stood just inside the smithy and eyed the faint light spilling out of the open doorway of the cookhouse. The easy banter from the sawmill crew wafted by on the breeze as they enjoyed the special treat Mews had provided. But he couldn't bring himself to go and join them. Not if it meant Kiera would be hovering over his shoulder, passing out roasted turkey, refilling his cup with ale, close enough to touch once again.

Not when his future lay elsewhere.

He turned back to the blacksmith shop, took in the improvements he'd made, the neat rows of tongs suspended from pegs, hammers organized by size and purpose. The anvil he'd found in the corner now sat bolted to a heavy square block that Connor had cut from a massive oak tree.

Plows repaired and blades sharpened, with fresh hickory handles, stood ready and waiting for Mews to collect so he could start the spring plowing. A dozen hoes hung from the rafters, green-cut handles curing so that the heads wouldn't slip.

They'd even hauled the carriage from Braxton's after deciding it was worth saving. Piece by piece, he and Connor were repairing the fancy rig, each of them contributing their own skills to the project. The carriage would be a thing of beauty when they were done. Quinn hadn't expected to enjoy working with his brother as much as he did.

But was it enough?

Was a brotherly kinship of working with metal and wood enough to overcome the past? Could he be happy here? And what of Kiera and her sisters? Once the business with Le Bonne was cleared up, would they remain at Breeze Hill? And more importantly, would Connor allow them to?

Quinn growled low in his throat, then thrust a hand through his hair, the sudden movement causing a shaft of pain to shoot through his injured midsection.

All his carefully laid plans to see his younger brothers settled with Connor before taking off for parts unknown were coming unraveled at the seams, and he didn't know which way was up anymore.

Stay here and be at his brother's beck and call just as he'd been for the last nine years or so? Maybe Connor hadn't been in Ireland giving orders all that time, but he might as well have been. Because Quinn couldn't leave. He'd been honor bound to raise his brothers.

There had been no one else.

And the weight of seeing after the little ones after *Mam* and *Da* died had almost been more than he could bear. He'd been so young, but he'd promised *Da* that he'd keep the boys together. He and Caleb both had promised, but then Caleb had left, breaking that promise and leaving Quinn to battle with Rory's indolence and Patrick's intractable ways.

Breeze Hill and its trappings represented all the things he wanted no part of: responsibilities, earthly possessions to tie him down, family, permanence.

But he was afraid if he didn't make plans to leave—and soon—a certain blonde, blue-eyed lass who represented everything he'd never wanted would be his undoing.

Chapter 22

BRIGHT AND EARLY ON SUNDAY MORNING, Patrick jumped
on Quinn's bed, the boy's knee slamming into his sore ribs.

Quinn rolled into a ball, clutched his ribs, and fought the
dark vortex of pain that almost sucked him under.

"Quinn! Get up. It'll be time t' go soon, and Connor
needs your help with the wagons."

"Go where?" Quinn groaned. "What wagons?"

"Don't ya know nothing? We're going t' Braxton Hall—
except I'm not supposed t' call it that anymore—for a dedication service today. Miss Isabella told us last night at supper."

Ah, that explained it. He hadn't joined the men for supper
but had grabbed a piece of bread, a sliver of roasted turkey,
and a hunk of cheese after everyone else had gone.

"Hurry up." Patrick crawled across Quinn's legs, elbows and knees gouging him from head to toe. "Connor's taking everyone in the farm wagons, and we're going t' have a picnic after the service."

"I think I'll just stay here today." Quinn flexed his jaw, then winced at the pain. He wouldn't mind a day all by himself.

"You *can't*. It's a special occasion. Everybody's going."

"All right. All right. Now get off me."

Two hours later, the party arrived at the ruins of Braxton Hall. A sense of excitement ran through the women and children as they pulled quilts and blankets from the wagons, baskets of food and kegs of ale.

Mr. Horne stood with his back to the chaos, facing the massive white columns that had once shored up the roof of the plantation home.

The preacher strode up the steps to the marble entryway, swept clean of debris. Facing them, he rocked back on his heels, lifted his face toward the sky, and smiled. He made an imposing figure, even in his worn black suit. Not that he wasn't respectable—and respected—all week, but there was just something special about him when he took the pulpit to share a message from God's Word.

He stood beneath the towering columns, waiting patiently until everyone gathered around, facing what was once the entryway to a grand plantation home. Then he flipped open his Bible.

"Today's Scripture comes from Psalm 89:34. 'My covenant will I not break, nor alter the thing that is gone out of my lips.'"

Quinn leaned against an oak that had survived the tornado, listening. Pacing what remained of the porch, Mr. Horne pivoted, sweeping the enraptured group with a piercing glance.

"Not seven months ago, Master Connor and Mistress Isabella huddled beneath that staircase—" he stabbed a long, bony finger toward a portion of a back wall and a half-collapsed set of stairs—"as Braxton Hall disintegrated around them during a raging tornado. Beneath that staircase, they made a promise to each other and to God, to dedicate their lives to the care of Breeze Hill for Isabella's nephew's sake, knowing that at the end of twenty years Breeze Hill would belong to that child, and they'd be left with nothing except whatever tribute Jonathan William Bartholomew decided to bestow upon his aunt and uncle."

Quinn straightened. The covenant Connor and Isabella had willingly made for little Jon was strikingly similar to what he'd promised his father on his deathbed. At the time, he'd expected nothing in return from any of his brothers other than that they grow up to be healthy, God-fearing men.

"They made a commitment to each other that day, even though it was several weeks later that I made it official." Mr. Horne smiled, the humorous sawyer Quinn saw on a daily basis peeking through the intense seriousness of the preacher.

"They were determined to follow through on their promise to the heir of Breeze Hill." He turned the pages of his Bible and then read again. "'And Jesus said unto him, No man, having put his hand to the plough, and looking back, is fit for the kingdom of God.'

"Connor put his hand to the plow, putting little Jon's future before his own. But the very next day, God rewarded his sacrifice threefold—" Mr. Horne spread his arms wide, his Bible clutched in one hand—"when Governor Gayoso granted him this land."

Quinn glanced at Connor and was amused to see the scowl on his face. It was obvious he was not happy with Mr. Horne's flowery discourse.

"Today we're here to wipe the slate clean and rename and rededicate this property formerly known as Braxton Hall. From this day forward, this land will be known as Magnolia Glen. Mistress Isabella chose *magnolia* as a tribute to the magnolia trees that border the lane leading to the planta-tion home, and Master Connor chose *glen* in honor of the vale he lived in as a boy back in Ireland. God chose to give Connor and Isabella a new future, blessing their promise to a child who wasn't even a day old at the time. May the acreage of Magnolia Glen help Connor and Isabella always remember the promises they made to little Jon, to God, and to each other."

Before dawn on Monday morning, Kiera slipped into the smithy, grabbed Quinn's bloody shirt, and hurried back to the cookhouse. She stuffed the shirt in a bucket of cold water, letting it soak.

She groaned when she turned to the fireplace. Amelia hadn't banked the fire good and proper and the embers had grown cold and lifeless. By the time she had the fire going and johnnycakes sizzling on the griddle, the sun was peeking over the horizon, and the men were fit to be tied. Connor expected them to be ready and waiting come sunup, and they chafed at the delay. She rushed from the kitchen and slid a platter of johnnycakes to the center of the table. As one, they grabbed for the hotcakes, filling their plates.

"Pass the molasses."

"Where's the butter?"

"Oh, I forgot." Kiera dashed to the pie safe and grabbed the crock. She plopped it down on the table, then—

"I smell something burning, missy."

"Oh no." Kiera flew back to the other room to flip the last batch of pancakes. The fire hadn't had time to burn down to coals, and the griddle was hotter than usual.

"Where's that molasses, girl?"

"Be right there." She gritted her teeth.

She hefted a keg of molasses, the platter of half-burned flapjacks, and hurried back to the table.

Mary walked in, ignored the chaos, and went straight to the lunch pails lined up on the sideboard. She dropped a piece of corn bread into each man's lunch pail, then bustled into the kitchen to gather leftovers for each man's lunch. The men finished eating, grabbed their pails, and rushed out, most of them not even bothering to thank Kiera for their breakfast. But she couldn't blame them. The meal had been far from her best. The eggs were runny, the ham stringy, and the pancakes almost burned to a crisp.

But she and Mary had managed to feed them one more time.

Mary shooed her two oldest daughters out of the kitchen. "Make haste. It is wash day, and we have much to do. Go help Miss Martha and Susan draw *kun*—aiyee—water for the big pots." She flapped her hands at the girls. "Hurry. Your father has no clean clothes left to do his work."

"Yes, Mama."

The girls left, and Kiera and Mary cleared the table, set the turkey bones to simmering over the fire for bone stock, then made their way toward the grove of trees in the backyard. Kiera carried a bundle of kitchen towels from the cookhouse, Quinn's shirt, and laundry for herself and her sisters. The other women had already gathered, all bringing their own laundry from the respective households.

Even Amelia pitched in to help without complaint. Soon they had water boiling in half a dozen kettles, and Kiera found herself beside Isabella.

Kiera gaped at Isabella when she started scrubbing a pair of Connor's leggings.

Isabella arched a brow. "What's the matter?"

"It's just that—" Kiera scrubbed Megan's soiled pinafore, her gaze roaming over the women laboring over the wash—"you're the mistress of the house, but you still wash clothes, help Martha in the kitchen, cook and clean."

"Did you not do the same back in Ireland?" Isabella asked.

"Yes, but I wasn't the lady of the house. My—my half sister was. She was . . ." Kiera felt her face heating all over again.

"You don't have to tell me anything about Charlotte. Connor has told me all about her, and if you don't mind my saying so, I'm glad that you are nothing like her."

"I'm sorry for what Charlotte did to your husband."

"Everything works together for good." Isabella shrugged. "I don't hate your sister. Because of her, I have Connor. How can I hate her for sending him to me?"

Kiera looked away, squeezed the water out of the garment, and placed it in a tub. Would there come a day that she could forgive Charlotte so easily?

"What, I've shocked you?"

"No. Yes." She hesitated. "And what of Connor? Has he forgiven her?" Kiera had her doubts, especially given how he'd only allowed them to stay when Quinn insisted. If it hadn't been for Quinn and the danger Pierre Le Bonne presented to them, Connor would have sent them packing the day they arrived.

"I don't know. I pray he has. Would he be able to accept her presence here at Breeze Hill? I doubt it. To tell you the truth, I would be hard-pressed to let her stay here myself." Isabella's eyes twinkled. "Perhaps we could offer her lodging in one of the cabins."

Kiera giggled, the very thought of her sister deigning to spend the night in a dirt-floor cabin with little to no bedding, save her own bedroll that she'd packed on the back of a horse, filled her with such incredulity that she couldn't help but laugh.

Isabella grew sober. "What Charlotte did to Connor is nothing compared to what she did to you and your sisters—her own flesh and blood. Do you think she knew what awaited you once you reached Natchez?"

Kiera scrubbed Quinn's shirt, watching the water turn rusty brown as the blood washed out. Blood he'd shed for her. "I don't know. Unfortunately Charlotte rarely thinks of anyone besides herself, but I'd like to think she wouldn't be so cruel."

"As Mr. Horne said yesterday, I'd advise you to put your hand to the plow and never look back. You're not likely to ever hear from your sister again, and from where I stand, that's not a bad thing." She motioned to the shirt. "Is that the shirt Quinn was wearing the other night?"

"Yes." Kiera touched the jagged tear in the garment. "I'm afraid it's ruined."

"Nonsense. A little darning and it'll be good as new." Isabella eyed the stains. "Well, at least good enough for a work shirt. I can't believe those men caused such a ruckus over being asked to pay for lodging. You must have been scared out of your wits."

"Yes, I was." Kiera bowed her head, pretending to be engrossed in the stains on Quinn's shirt.

"Kiera?"

She glanced up, caught Isabella watching her carefully.

"Is there something you're not telling me?"

She cleared her throat, her worry over Quinn prompting her to confide in Isabella. "One of the men thought—he thought that lodging meant more than I intended, and he . . ."

"He forced himself on you?" Isabella's eyes narrowed to slits.

"No, nothing like that. Quinn stopped him . . ."

"So that's what the fight was about." Isabella shook her head. "I knew there was more to the story than what Connor told me."

"Yes." Kiera lifted the shirt, fingered the jagged rip, remembering her terror. "The man had a knife. He could have killed Quinn."

"He stabbed him? I thought he seemed a little too stiff yesterday, but I just chalked it up to being stove up from the fight." Isabella's brow wrinkled. "Does Connor know?"

"I—I don't know." In her haste to see that Quinn was all right, it hadn't occurred to her that neither Connor nor any of the other men had come to Quinn's aid. It had been dark, and when she'd downplayed the entire incident, Quinn had gone along with her. "I don't think so."

"You were afraid Connor would blame you, so you didn't tell him the truth."

"Yes," Kiera whispered, her eyes filling with tears. "It was awful. I keep replaying it over and over in my mind. He could have died because of me."

"Kiera, look at me." Isabella's gaze was tender and searching. "If that man had killed Quinn, the fault would have lain with the vile creature who thought it was all right to try to force himself on you against your will. Quinn wouldn't have died *because* of you, but *for* you. Trust me, dear, there is a huge difference. Do you understand what I'm saying?"

Kiera frowned. "I'm not sure that I do."

"A man who's willing to risk his life for you—" Isabella tipped up Kiera's chin—"is a man worth giving your life to."

Chapter 23

WITH THE HUMIDITY AT A FEVER PITCH, unheard of for mid-March back home, the smithy doors were open front and back to catch the slightest hint of a breeze.

Quinn wiped sweat from his brow and plunged the pair of tongs into the slack tub. Instantly, the water boiled; then steam hissed and rose to dissipate into thin air as the metal cooled.

His leg almost completely healed, Weston sat nearby, manning the bellows. The bruises had faded, and he'd taken on a bit of a swagger after the fight with Beckett and letting loose with that cannon the other night.

Patrick came running toward the smithy. "Weston, your *da* is back. I saw him coming down the lane."

Weston instantly let the bellows fall flat. Quinn didn't reprimand him. The lad was anxious to see his father and couldn't be blamed for that.

Quinn followed the boys outside, leaned against a post. A few minutes later, Mr. Caruthers rode around the corner of the house and down the sloping lane toward them. The man looked like he'd aged ten years in the short time he'd been gone. His once neat and tidy coat, stained and even torn in a few places, hung loose on his gaunt frame.

Weston stepped forward and grabbed the horse's reins. "Father?"

Caruthers blinked at Weston as if he'd just remembered he'd left him at Breeze Hill. Then he smiled and, dismounting, clasped his son by the shoulders. "How are you, Son? Your leg?"

"Much better."

"Good." Frowning, he motioned to the bruises. "Your face. You didn't get those bruises when we were attacked."

Weston puffed out his chest. "I was defending a girl's honor."

Caruthers chuckled. "Well, that's never a bad thing, is it, Mr. O'Shea?"

Quinn shrugged. "I suppose not."

Caruthers turned back to his son. "Then you're ready to travel? I want to leave at first light. It's time we went home."

"First light?" Weston put a hand on his father's arm. "But, Father—"

Ignoring him, Caruthers addressed Quinn. "Mr. O'Shea,

may I have a word with you? It's about Miss Young and her sisters."

Quinn straightened, his attention fully engaged. He motioned to Patrick. "Go t' the sawmill and get Connor. He's going t' want t' hear this."

Patrick took off at a run.

"If you don't mind, maybe we could take a stroll that way. I've been riding all day and it will do me good to stretch my legs."

"O' course."

Halfway there, Connor came striding toward them, hand outstretched. "Mr. Caruthers. I trust you didn't travel all the way from Natchez alone."

"No, indeed, sir. I learned my lesson the last time about traveling in small parties. A party of travelers was headed north. Friends of yours, I believe. A Mr. Wainwright?"

"Yes, we know them well."

"Mr. Wainwright said to give his regards but that they must press on if they were to make it home before nightfall."

"Understandable. The Wainwright plantation is scarcely half a day's ride north of here." Connor offered Caruthers a sympathetic look. "Any luck finding your son?"

Caruthers shook his head. "I'm afraid not. As much as it pains me, I've given up and am on my way home."

Weston grabbed his father's arm, turning him to face him. "Father, you can't mean that."

"I do. I've searched all over Natchez, and he's nowhere to be found." A haunted look came into his eyes. "The first thing I did when I arrived in Natchez was to pay James Bloomfield a visit. As he'd written, he still had the money from the sale of the cotton. He'd advanced Reggie and the men with him enough coin to find lodging and a meal for the night. But Reggie never returned to claim the rest of the money. Upon questioning, the last place he was seen was the Blue Heron."

Quinn sucked in a breath. "The Blue Heron?"

Patrick pushed forward, jerking on Connor's sleeve. "Pierre Le Bonne's tavern. That's the man who forced Megan and her sisters to go with him."

"Yes, Bloomfield told me of the matter." Caruthers frowned. "So it's true, then? I overheard another traveler insisting that the girl who runs the stand here belongs to Le Bonne."

"That's not true," Patrick blurted out before looking to Connor. "Megan's sister doesn't belong t' that man, does she, Connor?"

"Hush, lad." Connor placed a hand on Patrick's shoulder. "Let Mr. Caruthers speak."

"Aye. And that's not all. Le Bonne is a boarding master, and he's not that careful about how he fills a ship's roster."

Connor crossed his arms, scowling. "Are you saying that you believe Le Bonne might have kidnapped your son and forced him to go to sea?"

"It's either that or something much, much worse. From what I've been told, it's a lucrative business, and that man of his, Claude, is big enough, and mean enough, to do whatever Le Bonne asks of him."

"I'm sorry, sir. What a nasty business, for sure. But if your son is at sea, and he fares well, he may return to Natchez in good time."

"Perhaps." But from the look on Caruthers's face, he'd lost all hope of ever seeing his son again.

Quinn, Connor, Patrick, and Weston stood in silence. There was nothing else to say. Caruthers squared his shoulders and, even in his bedraggled and bereaved state, gathered his courage to look the part of a gentleman farmer once again. He bowed. "If you don't mind, I'd like to retire for the night. It's been a long day on top of several long weeks of travel. And I want to get an early start tomorrow morning." He stuck a hand in his vest pocket. "I'm pleased to say that I have coin to pay for lodging as well as for Weston's upkeep these past weeks."

Connor waved a hand. "No need, sir. Weston has been earning his keep. He'll show you to the quarters where he's been sleeping."

"Thank you. Your hospitality has been most appreciated." Caruthers turned away.

"Father, may I have a word with you?"

Caruthers turned back, a questioning look on his face.

For once, Weston's cocky smirk was absent. He glanced from Connor to Quinn, then to his father. "I want to ask Amelia to be my wife."

"Amelia? Who is Amelia?"

"Amelia Young. She's the girl whose honor I defended."

"You can't take a wife, Son." Caruthers smiled at his son as if he were addressing a child. "Why, you're barely seventeen."

"I'm old enough to know that I want Amelia for my wife."

Connor stepped forward. "I'm afraid Amelia's not free to marry at this time, lad. There's still the question of whether Le Bonne has any legal claim to her, and even—"

"Le Bonne?" Caruthers's brow furrowed. "This Amelia is one of the girls found in Le Bonne's tavern?"

"Yes, but she isn't—"

"I forbid it." Face mottled red to the point of apoplexy, Caruthers held up a hand. "You will not see this girl again. Think of the scandal, and if not that, think of your poor mother. You are my only son now, Weston, and you must marry well to carry on the family name. I won't allow you to throw your life away on some trollop with no name, no dowry, nothing to recommend her at all."

"Now see here—" Quinn stepped forward, but Connor restrained him, pulled him to the side.

"Quinn. He's only going on what he's been told. I'll explain the girls' situation to him."

"See that ya do." Chest heaving, Quinn glared at Caruthers, then jerked out of Connor's grasp and strode toward the smithy. Connor was right. Caruthers was distraught.

Amelia *was* a little flirt who was too young to get married.

But she was Kiera's sister. And from the moment he'd snatched them out of Le Bonne's grasping fingers, Kiera and her sisters had become his responsibility.

"Amelia, don't cry."

"Why won't you let us marry?" Amelia cried harder. "Weston loves me, and I love him, but you and Mr. Caruthers are determined to keep us apart."

"It's not like that at all, dear heart." Kiera sat on the edge of the bed. "You're both so young and you barely know each other. Maybe in time—"

"No." Amelia clutched her pillow to her, anger twisting her face. "His father will never let us wed. He thinks I'm not good enough for Weston."

"Trust me, darling." Kiera smoothed back her sister's blonde curls. "If Weston loves you as much as he says he does, he'll make a way for you to be together."

Amelia didn't answer, just turned her face into her pillow. "Can Megan sleep with you tonight? I'd like to be alone."

"Of course."

Hours later, Kiera lay in her bed, staring at the ceiling. She hadn't been entirely truthful with her sister. She'd told her that Weston might come back for her, but she knew he wouldn't. He was young, immature, and didn't know what he wanted out of life any more than Amelia did.

Quinn had finally coaxed a bit of work out of him, but the boy had balked every step of the way. Amelia was just as selfish and immature, but Kiera hoped and prayed that she'd grow out of her petulance. Of course, it hadn't helped that

PAM HILLMAN

Charlotte had done her best to corrupt Amelia to her con-niving ways from the moment their father had died. Kiera suspected that Charlotte had done it out of spite.

She thought of Mr. Horne's sermon last Sunday as he admonished his listeners to put their hand to the plow and not look back. She didn't even know what path she was on, what direction she was going. Her life had first been gov-erned by the whim of her father, then George, and briefly Pierre Le Bonne. And while it seemed that she had more freedom here at Breeze Hill than she'd ever had before, the path she was on was just as winding and treacherous as the Natchez Trace itself.

Finally she drifted off, a prayer on her lips for herself, her sisters, and the elusive path that God had set before her.

In spite of tossing and turning into the wee hours, Kiera woke before dawn out of habit. Leaving Megan sprawled across her bed, she dressed quickly and headed toward the cookhouse.

The men had to be fed regardless of Amelia's drama.

She got right to work, determined to serve breakfast on time and keep Connor and the men happy. Not to men-tion that the sooner she served breakfast, the sooner Mr. Caruthers and Weston would leave Breeze Hill.

It was probably a good thing that Amelia wasn't an early riser. If Mr. Caruthers was true to his word, he and Weston would be long gone before she got up. While there would be tears, they would eventually dry. Someday her sister would forget Weston Caruthers, and maybe, in time, she'd forget the teasing, temptress ways she'd learned from Charlotte as well.

She'd just put the first pancakes on the griddle when Mr. Caruthers barreled inside. "Where is he? Where is my son?"

Kiera backed away from his angry tirade. "Truly, sir, I don't know what you're talking about."

"He's gone." He shook his fist at her. "Do you know where that sister of yours is? I'll bet you anything she has something to do with this."

"She's still abed."

Caruthers snorted. "If you believe that, you're not the smart girl I gave you credit for. I'm going after my son. When I find him—" he paused—"and your sister, I will send her back to you, and you can do with her what you will." Red-faced, Caruthers gave her a stiff bow. "Good day, miss."

With that, he clomped out of the cookhouse and headed toward the barn.

Kiera stood rooted to the spot; then she faced the big house on the hill, seeking out the bedroom where she'd left Amelia last night. Had Amelia had ulterior motives for asking that Megan sleep with Kiera?

Surely she wouldn't be that devious. But . . .

Heart pounding, she hurried toward the house, each step increasing her dread of what she'd find. The distance to the house had never seemed so far. Halfway there, she spotted Quinn coming her way. "Quinn!"

He looked up, his gaze capturing hers. "What's wrong?"

"Weston's gone. And Amelia might have left with him."

Quinn took her by the shoulders. "Would she do that? Go away with him?"

"I—" Kiera shook her head. "She might. I don't know."

"Let's go." Quinn turned, helped her up the sloping hillside and onto the veranda. Kiera hurried toward the room, Quinn right behind her. She flung open the sitting room door, then rushed toward the bedroom. Pausing, she put one hand on the latch, closed her eyes, and prayed a simple, short prayer.

Please, God. Let Amelia still be abed. Please.

Her hand shook, and she couldn't bring herself to open the door. Quinn's hand closed over hers, gently pushed the latch down, and the door swung open.

The bed was empty, and Amelia's things were gone.

Kiera sucked in a breath, then smothered the strangled sound with her hand. She closed the door and backed away, her attention darting around the sitting room.

Quinn rested his hands on her shoulders. "We'll find her. They couldna have gone far."

"Yes." She took a deep breath, needing to do . . . something. Anything to keep her sanity. She turned toward the door. "The men. They'll—they'll be wanting breakfast."

"Kiera—"

But she paid him no mind. She hurried—almost ran—across the sitting room, outside onto the veranda, then hiked her skirts as she hurried through the courtyard. Her sister was gone, and all she could think of was fixing breakfast for

Connor's crew. Yes, that was something she could do, something she *should* do. Something she had some control over.

Connor expected it of her. She kept moving, one foot in front of the other, keeping to the one path that God had put her on. The only one that made sense to her right now.

Amelia. What have you done?

One foot in front of the other.

She stepped through the door of the cookhouse to find the men already eating, a simple meal of bread and cheese provided by Mary and her daughters. One by one they finished, quietly picked up their lunch pails, and headed toward the sawmill, some patting her awkwardly on the shoulder as they passed by.

Kiera wrapped her arms around her waist. Tears stung her eyes. They knew.

She turned to the empty sideboard where the pails had been. "What—what did you pack for their lunch?"

"Do not worry. They will be fine."

Kiera moved across the room, started stacking plates, her movements jerky.

Mary reached out, gently took the dishes from her, and stacked them on the table. Then the small, quiet woman took Kiera's hands in hers, forcing her to meet her gaze.

All trace of the meek and mild Natchez squaw was gone, and her eyes burned with conviction and fire. "Mistress, you are busy about nothing. God told Elijah to stand on the mount, and a great and strong wind passed by, but God was not in the wind, and after the wind, an earthquake, but God was not in the earthquake. After the earthquake, there was fire, but God was not in the fire. After that, there was a still, small voice." Mary spoke softly, the accent from her native tongue giving a soothing cadence to her words. She squeezed Kiera's hands. "Sometimes God uses a still, small voice to tell us the way to go. Be still, my child, and listen."

"I don't know how to . . ." Kiera paused as the dam burst and tears streamed down her cheeks. She took a deep breath. ". . . to be still. To listen."

"Just be still, and let Him speak." Mary patted her cheeks with both hands, then turned and walked out of the room.

Chapter 24

"Mr. Caruthers!"

Reginald scowled as the youngest O'Shea raced into the stables. "What is it, boy?"

"They want you up at the house."

He ignored the boy and led his mount out of the stables, not caring that anyone here at Breeze Hill wanted to speak with him. He'd left his son, a mere lad, with these people, and how did they repay him? By letting that strumpet twist him around her little finger, convince him that he wanted to marry her.

He knew what she wanted. She wanted her finger in a piece of the pie that was Caruthers Estates. And when Reginald put his foot down, the trollop convinced Weston to sneak away in the middle of the night. His blood boiled all over again. By all that was holy, he'd catch up with the pair and take his son home.

The girl could do as she pleased. It mattered not to him.

He tightened the cinch, his movements jerky. The horse snorted, and he took a deep breath, trying to calm himself. The boy danced around, making the horse even more nervous.

"Hurry, Mr. Caruthers. It's someone with news from your wife."

Reginald froze. "My wife?"

The boy nodded. "Yes, sir."

"Show me." He followed the boy, saw Quinn O'Shea and two men leading mounts heading toward him. He recognized Wainwright. The other—

Peterson?

The blood drained from his face as his overseer looked up, saw him, and hurried forward. The despair on his face put fear into Reginald's heart.

"Peterson? What news of home?"

Peterson held his hat in his hand, looked him briefly in the eye, then dropped his gaze to stare at his boots. "Your wife, sir. She's ill."

"Victoria?" Reginald thought he might fall dead right on the spot, but somehow he stayed on his feet, gripping the horse's reins, almost like a lifeline to—to something. To hope. To home. To keeping his wife in this world. He licked his lips. "How bad?" he whispered.

"They said to hurry home as fast as you could, sir."

Reginald looked at the reins clasped in his hands. Just two long, thin strips of leather attached to the bridle that guided the horse that would carry him home. He nodded. "I'm ready."

"Sir?" Quinn O'Shea stepped forward. "Did you see anyone on the trail? Weston traveling with a young girl?"

Reginald's heart soared with hope, and he whirled toward his overseer. Yes, Weston would go to his mother, knowing she'd stand by his side in whatever decision he made. Peterson should have seen him.

Peterson frowned, his attention ricocheting between O'Shea and Reginald. "Weston, sir?"

"He took off sometime last night." Reginald's lip curled. "With a girl. Did you see either of them?"

Peterson crushed his hat in his hands. "No, sir. I didn't see anyone. I spent the night at Wainwright's, though, so he could have passed on the trail in the night."

An irrational desire to lash out at Peterson rolled over Reginald. He wanted to rail at his overseer. Ask him why he'd stopped to spend the night when his wife lay sick, possibly dying. When his oldest son had been killed or kidnapped and forced to board a floating coffin, and his younger son had thrown his life away on a flighty little Irish tart.

With great effort, he curbed his tongue. Because somewhere beneath the haze of insanity that bubbled up, he knew it was impossible to ride day and night for a full week without stopping. At best the trip could be shortened to five or six days if one rode hard.

He gathered the reins. He'd do it in four or die trying.

Quinn stepped into the cookhouse, saddlebags clutched in one fist, a flintlock in the other. The room was empty.

He walked to the opening he'd helped Connor cut in the log wall just a few short weeks ago. His heart squeezed when he saw Kiera standing at the dining table, the dishes from the morning meal still strewn about. She held her head in her hands, sobs shaking her shoulders.

In three strides, he was by her side. Her blue eyes, awash with grief and worry, swept up to meet his before he drew her into his embrace. He stood there, holding her, letting her cry, her tears soaking the front of his shirt.

When she'd cried herself out, he held her at arm's length, wishing with all his heart he could take away her pain. "I'm going after Caruthers. I do no' trust him t' do the right thing by Amelia."

Kiera sucked in a quick breath, her gaze searching his. "You don't think he'd harm her—"

"No, nothing that drastic. But he's crazy with grief over losing his eldest son. Now that Weston's gone off half-cocked, and his wife is ill, Amelia's welfare will be the least o' his worries. Tell Connor I'm gone. There's no time t' waste if I'm t' catch up with Caruthers and his man."

"Yes, of course." Fresh tears pooled in her eyes and spilled over.

"It'll be all right, lass." He cupped her face with both

hands, then swiped at her tears with his thumbs. "I'll find her and bring her back."

Closing her eyes, she turned her face into his palm. "I know you will."

Her warm breath feathered across his palm, the softness of her lips turning his insides to mush. He wanted—

"I've got t' go." He stepped away, putting some distance between them.

"You'll need provisions for the journey." Kiera led the way to the kitchen, grabbed leftover ham, biscuits, corn bread, cheese, wrapping the provisions with anything that came to hand. As she laid the offerings on the table, Quinn stuffed each bundle into the saddlebags.

When he thought he couldn't put in one more thing, she grabbed a handful of boiled eggs, searched for something to put them in, then whipped off her fichu, laid them in the center, and bound them up. "Take these. Boiled fresh this morning."

She handed him the bundle, her face flushed from exertion, eyes wide and luminous. Quinn stuffed them in his bag.

"Quinn?"

"Aye?"

She reached out a hand, then drew it back, clasping both hands together in front of her. Lips trembling, eyes shining, she shook her head. "Nothing. Just—"

Quinn reached for her, hauled her to him, and kissed her. No holding back. No permission asked, none granted. Just a desperate kiss of wanting because there was no time for anything else.

He savored the softness of her lips pressed against his. Then she stood on tiptoe and angled her face into his shoulder, her arms sliding up and around his neck, pulling him closer. The perfection of the way they melded together shocked and stunned him until he groaned and settled her tighter in his embrace.

Breathing ragged, he drew back, let his gaze slide over her features, her half-closed eyes, her pale lips brighter, pinker, fuller, and all because of his kiss. His breath hitched, his arms tightened. He wanted one more taste, but he couldn't linger any longer.

Reluctantly he released her, feeling the void as they separated. She blinked, a sheen of tears glimmering in her eyes. "Be careful."

Holding tight the memory of her face and the taste of her kiss, he pivoted and left.

Hardly two miles down the road, Quinn caught up to Caruthers and Peterson. Peterson glanced at him, lines of worry drawing his features, but Caruthers barely acknowledged his presence.

Which suited Quinn just fine.

Caruthers was like a man possessed, pushing northward with a relentlessness that defied reason. They traveled hard all day, stopping at every inn along the way to ask if anyone had seen Weston and Amelia. No one had. Either the youths were being careful to avoid being seen . . . or they hadn't come this way at all.

When night fell and it was too dark to see their way, Caruthers consented to a brief stop. Dismounting, he searched the sky. "The moon should be up within the hour. We'll resume travel then."

"But, Mr. Caruthers, the horses—"

"I said we would continue on." Brooking no argument, Caruthers waved Peterson away. "See to the horses."

"Yes, sir."

Caruthers's gaze fell on Quinn before moving on without comment or acknowledgment. Quinn didn't even know if the man realized who he was. Caruthers hadn't addressed him directly all day. Caruthers paced the edge of the small clearing a stone's throw from the trace as if he'd walk the rest of the way home if need be.

Following Peterson's example, Quinn set about tending his own mount, hoping the horse had enough stamina to keep up with the pace Caruthers set. They made a cold camp, and settling at the base of a massive oak, Quinn rummaged through his saddlebags for the staples Kiera had sent.

His fingers closed around the boiled eggs wrapped in her scarf. He unwrapped them and peeled two. Peterson approached Caruthers and offered him a piece of pemmican, but the man waved his overseer away. Peterson left him to his torment and joined Quinn under the tree. He held out the jerked meat. "Have some?"

"Thank ya." Quinn drew two more eggs and handed them over.

They ate in silence, watching as Caruthers paced, anxious to be on his way.

"This isn't like Mr. Caruthers at all." Peterson sounded completely baffled by his master's actions. "We can't keep pushing our mounts like this."

"Short of tying him up, I don't think we have much choice. How much farther is it?"

"Five days of hard riding. But at this rate, we'll make it in four."

Quinn finished his eggs, took a swig of water. Somehow he could understand Caruthers's distress. All in the space of a few months, the man's life had been torn asunder. One son presumed dead, another who'd run away, his wife deathly ill. It was almost like God was letting Satan test him much the same way he'd tested Job. "Does he have other children besides the two sons?"

"There were two daughters. Both died last year."

More ashes heaped on Caruthers's head.

Quinn finished off the last of the eggs, fingering the soft muslin fichu Kiera had wrapped them in. He crushed the soft material against his nose, inhaled the lingering scent that was uniquely hers. That of laundry soap, baking bread, the faint scent of roses, azaleas, or whatever it was that women stuffed in those little sachets and tucked in with their linen. His mother used to do the same, and her clothes always smelled of heather and sunshine. The enticing aroma reminded him of home, of family, and most of all of Kiera.

Caruthers headed toward them, determination in every step. "It's time to go."

Quinn stuffed the fichu inside his saddlebags, then hurried to saddle his own mount. He wouldn't give Caruthers any reason to leave him behind.

Chapter 25

AMELIA HAD BEEN GONE FIVE DAYS.

With the cookhouse cleared of the breakfast dishes and a pot of stew simmering for the evening meal, Kiera opened the door and peered outside. Shivering, she pulled her shawl tight around her and searched the sky. The temperature had dropped, and clouds roiled in overcast skies, hinting at rain.

The turn in the weather was one more worry heaped on top of the multitude she'd been drowning under for the last five days. Where was Amelia? Was she warm? Was she hungry? She'd taken nothing save a few dresses and her cloak. But a cloak wouldn't be much comfort on a day like today.

Five days.

Surely they'd arrived at Mr. Caruthers's plantation by now. Surely her sister was safe and warm and had seen the error of her ways. But . . .

Had they . . . ? For the hundredth time, a panicky feeling of desperation shot through her chest as the unthinkable made another circle through her thoughts.

She'd tried to avoid thinking such scandalous thoughts, but there was no getting around it. They'd been gone *five* days. Regardless of the fact that marriage at such a young age hadn't been her plan for Amelia, in the wee hours of the morning on the day after they'd run away, Kiera had accepted the fact that her sister's reputation was ruined, and her prayers had changed from praying her home to praying that Weston Caruthers's intentions toward her sister were honorable.

The match wasn't what any of them had wanted, but maybe Mr. Caruthers would come to accept Amelia as a daughter-in-law in time.

Kiera wasn't under any illusion that Amelia hadn't gone with Weston willingly. Of that she was certain. But she also knew that her sister was young, hardly more than a child, and that she would be shocked at what would be expected of her as Weston's wife.

Or his mistress.

Her cheeks flamed. She'd let her sister down. She should have paid more attention to Amelia's comings and goings. Surely she could have prevented this . . .

Around and around and around, her worries dogged her,

like the paddle wheel at a gristmill, the incessant pounding, turning, churning making her head spin.

She took a deep breath.

Be still.

Her gaze rested on the smithy, closed up tight, not a wisp of smoke curling from the chimney. And what of Quinn? Had he caught up with Caruthers? Was he even now on his way back? Was Amelia with him or—?

Be still. Listen.

Closing her eyes, she forced her mind to stop. Then, grabbing her cloak from the peg by the door, she threw it around her shoulders and strode toward the smithy. Anything to put thoughts of her sister out of her mind.

On the morning of the fifth day, Quinn and his companions turned off the main trail and rode down the lane toward Mr. Caruthers's plantation. Caruthers urged his tired mount faster, but the animal had little left to give.

Neither did Caruthers, Peterson, or Quinn.

The moment they rounded the bend and the house came into view, Quinn knew they'd arrived too late. He took in the scene at a glance. Half a dozen black carriages lined the circle drive; servants dressed in black stood in two rows along the walkway. A small contingent of mourners, also dressed in black, gathered on the lawn, waiting.

All eyes were on the six somber men and the casket they carried down the steps toward the waiting hearse.

A tall, sparse man stood on the steps, a black Bible clasped in front of him. His gaze rose, spotted them coming down the lane. He motioned for the pallbearers to stop, even as the mourners became aware of their presence, and one by one cast their mournful expressions on Reginald Caruthers.

Time seemed to slow, though Caruthers continued to ride forward, seemingly unaware of the import of the scene. But suddenly his exhausted mount stopped, and he sat there staring at the mourners, at the coffin draped in black, at—

Like a madman, Reginald Caruthers fell off his horse and staggered through the mourners toward the casket. "No." He shook his finger at the pallbearers. "Take her inside."

Quinn dismounted, took up the reins of Caruthers's horse, and waited. Those nearest him whispered, "He's gone mad."

"Take her inside, I tell you!" Caruthers stabbed a finger toward the house, and the pallbearers cast a glance at the gentleman on the porch.

Compassion stamped across his features, the preacher stepped between Caruthers and the casket. "Reginald, we can't wait any longer—"

"I demand that you take my wife back inside. Put her in her bed." He whirled on the mourners, and several of the women gasped, their husbands stepping between them and the onslaught of his despair. "Go home. All of you. Go home. She's not—"

"Reginald, it's too late. Victoria is dead." The preacher's voice rang with conviction and a strength that not even

Reginald Caruthers could deny. "She died two days ago, and we cannot—we must not—wait any longer. Do you understand?"

"And my son? Where is he?"

"Your son? Weston?" The preacher glanced at Quinn and Peterson. "Weston traveled with you to Natchez. Is he not with you now?"

"He returned home early. Surely—"

"I'm sorry, Reginald, but there's been no sign of Weston."

Caruthers glanced wildly around at his servants, at the mourners who'd come to pay their last respects, and without another word, he turned, staggered up the walkway, mounted the stairs, and went inside, the massive front door closing behind him with an ominous click.

No one moved. No one said anything; then the clergyman whispered something to the pallbearers. They continued on, put the coffin in the hearse, and motioned for the driver to proceed to the cemetery.

Kiera let herself into the smithy, the building dark and dreary without Quinn's presence. Her eyes adjusted to the darkness and she walked around, touching his tools, admiring his handiwork.

She was worried about Amelia, but she was equally worried about Quinn. Without thought for his own safety or the work that waited for him here, he'd taken off after Caruthers to try to bring Amelia home.

Her own brother-in-law would never have done such a thing—well, unless it was to reclaim Amelia because she was worth something to him.

She reached out, touched the shirt he'd hung on the peg so that he'd have a fresh one to change into at day's end. Her finger traced the jagged rip that she'd mended, and she remembered how he'd rushed to her rescue time and time again.

Quinn's help came from the heart, not from some desire to get something in return.

She turned at a noise and spotted Isabella standing in the doorway.

"I thought I'd find you here."

"Did you need me?" Kiera dropped her hand away from the shirt, embarrassed to be caught snooping in Quinn's workshop.

"No, I just wanted to check on you." Isabella searched her face. "Are you sleeping at all?"

"Very little." Tears pricked Kiera's eyes again, and she shook her head. "I try, but I keep imagining the worst."

"That's understandable. It's hard not to dwell on our grief, our worries." Isabella hugged her, then held her at arm's length. "When I lost the baby, I thought I would go crazy. The only things that kept me sane were prayer and reciting Scripture, especially the Psalms."

"Be still, and know that I am God."

Kiera's breath hitched. It was no accident that Isabella and Mary had both led her to the Psalms, to the peace that could be found in blanketing oneself in the Scriptures. She determined to do better.

She determined to be still. To listen.

"I'm telling you, she's in love with him."

Connor scowled. "Wife, you don't know what you're talking about."

"And Quinn loves her too." Isabella brushed her hair, then quickly braided it, readying for bed. "He just won't admit it because he's determined to go off and see the world, or some such nonsense."

"Can ya blame him?" Connor tossed the covers back and eased into bed, sighing when his tired body relaxed against the feather tick. "He's already raised one family."

"Ah, but, my love, Rory and Patrick were just his brothers." A soft smile played over his wife's face, and Connor wondered exactly what he was missing in this conversation. "I daresay that if he'll admit it, he wouldn't mind taking on another family, one that involves children of his own."

"I still think you're wrong. They argue too much t' be in love."

"Truly?" Isabella slid into the bed next to him. "That's your reason for thinking they can't be in love?"

"Perhaps you're right." He laughed and snugged her close. "Reminds me of somebody else I know."

She pushed against his chest. "I'm sure I don't know what you're talking about, Connor O'Shea."

"We argued quite a bit in those early days, didn't we, Mistress O'Shea?"

Connor grinned at his wife's raised brow, knowing how calling her mistress brought out her ire.

"Yes, until you learned your place, sir."

"I do believe I've found my place, madam."

Later, with his wife wrapped in his arms, Connor had almost drifted off to sleep when he heard her whisper, "Would it bother you?"

"Would what bother me?"

"For Kiera to stay here forever, for her to marry Quinn?"

Now why would his wife ask him a question like that? He kept silent, pondering the answer, unsure how to respond.

Isabella's quiet, confident voice came out of the darkness. "She's not Charlotte, my love."

Connor frowned. He'd kept his distance from Charlotte's sisters, but even his limited contact with them had shown that they were definitely not cut from the same cloth as their older half sister. Well, except for the minx who'd run off with the Caruthers boy, causing such a stir.

While Amelia was the most like Charlotte, even she couldn't hold a candle to Charlotte's conniving ways.

He hugged his wife. "I know."

He pondered the thought of having Kiera Young for a sister-in-law. And as he dozed off, he realized that it wouldn't be so bad if such a union kept his brother tied to Breeze Hill and Magnolia Glen.

Chapter 26

As the sun sank in the west, darkness seeped into Victoria's room. Refusing anyone entrance, Reginald sat in a rocker, staring at his wife's empty bed.

He'd banished them all. His butler. The housekeeper. Peterson. Even Victoria's brother, the esteemed Reverend John Muiller.

One by one, they'd all failed him.

They'd let his sweet Victoria die.

The creak of the rocker filled the silence, and he balled his hands into fists.

If he'd been here, she wouldn't have died. He wouldn't have let her. If he'd been here, Weston would still be here.

He wouldn't have been ensnared by that . . . that strumpet at Breeze Hill Plantation.

Even in his grief, Reginald had the presence of mind to know that Weston and the girl had not returned home. Which meant that they'd gone in the opposite direction, toward Natchez.

All that time wasted. Victoria lost to him forever. Reggie lost.

All he had left was Weston, and he wouldn't let some tavern wench take his only son.

He had to get to Natchez. He had to find Weston and pluck him out of the clutches of the wanton who'd corrupted him.

"It's not much, I'm afraid." Peterson eyed the hayloft.

Quinn hoisted his bedroll. "I've slept in worse."

Caruthers hadn't been seen since he'd entered the house. The clergyman, who turned out to be Caruthers's brother-in-law, had continued with the burial, but Quinn had followed Peterson to the stables. He didn't know the family and was too disheveled and grimy to even think of attending the funeral of a woman he'd never met.

"You're welcome to join us in the kitchen for supper. With so many mourners, there's bound to be plenty of food."

"T' tell ya the truth, I can barely keep me eyes open. Sleep is what I need."

Peterson nodded. "Of course. I'll see you in the morning, then."

"Good night, Peterson." Quinn cleared his throat. "And I'm sorry that things turned out this way."

"Thank you. I'll convey your condolences to Mr. Caruthers." Peterson inclined his head and left the barn.

Quinn climbed the ladder, spread his blankets, and stretched out on his back. Sighing, he let his body sink into the soft comfort of the hay. Before sleep claimed him, he tried to figure out how to tell Kiera that her sister and Weston hadn't returned to the Caruthers estate. Not one person along the trace could recall having seen the couple. If they'd come north, they'd avoided the stands and stayed out of sight of other travelers.

He'd start for Breeze Hill first thing in the morning. Caruthers had pushed them so hard that his horse was in no shape to travel, but he didn't want to linger.

Assuming Weston and Amelia hadn't met with foul play—and he prayed that wasn't the case—the only other alternative was that they'd gone to Natchez.

He drifted off, his last thought to find Amelia before Le Bonne did.

"O'Shea, get up."

Quinn jerked awake to Peterson's frantic call. He crawled to the edge of the hayloft, squinting into the darkness. Peterson stood at the foot of the ladder, a lantern held high, the light casting dancing shadows on the walls.

"What's wrong?"

"Mr. Caruthers is gone. The housekeeper tried to stop

him, but he was out of his head, ranting about finding Weston."

Quinn rubbed his fingers over his eyes and pinched the bridge of his nose. "What time is it?"

"A quarter past three."

Quinn rolled up his blankets, tucked his pistol in his waistband, and descended the ladder, saddlebags in one hand. He tucked in his shirt, then splashed his face with water from a nearby bucket.

"There's more. He said that Weston was all he had left, and he wouldn't let some little Irish strumpet have him." Peterson twisted his hat. "Beggin' your pardon."

Quinn eyed Peterson. Over the last couple of days, he'd come to know the man as fair-minded and dependable. "Do ya think he'd do the lass harm?"

"A month ago I would have said no. But today I'm not sure what he'll do. Seems like he's lost all reason. He loved the missus and those boys with a passion that defied reason."

"I'm going after him." Quinn ran a hand through his hair. "He'll head for Natchez."

"My thoughts as well." Peterson nodded. "We'll take extra horses. Mr. Caruthers took an extra mount, and he'll be able to make good time."

Peterson called for two stable hands and pointed out four horses to them. In short order, the boys had two of them saddled, a small mountain of provisions strapped on the spares. Quinn threw his saddlebags over his mount. Lashing them in place, he squinted at Peterson. "Are ya sure ya want t' go? He's bound t' not like it."

Peterson looked off in the distance. "This isn't like Mr. Caruthers. When I was a child, my parents died of the fever. Mr. Caruthers took me in, fed me, and gave me an opportunity to be somebody. I owe him my life, and I'll do what I can to save his."

"Very well." Quinn led the horse out, mounted, and waited for Peterson to do the same. "Ready?"

Two and a half days later, they'd hardly slacked up for riding. They'd passed one small band of travelers who'd seen Caruthers, but he was riding hard and fast and had barely acknowledged them.

They pushed on, changing mounts every few hours. Both had reason to want to catch up with Caruthers. What if, in his grief, he decided to target Kiera? Or harmed Amelia when he found her?

In Caruthers's eyes, the girls were just as much to blame as Le Bonne for the tragedy that had befallen his family. If Quinn didn't miss his guess, they'd come to the Breeze Hill turnoff soon. Would Caruthers detour or continue on toward Natchez? A reasonable man would stop, spend the night, and get some much-needed rest for himself and the horses, but Caruthers had proven over the last few days that he was far from reasonable. If they failed to catch up before they reached the turnoff, Quinn had made up his mind.

He'd stop, make sure all was well, exchange the exhausted

animals for fresh mounts, and carry on. And there was always the possibility that Weston and Amelia had returned. He prayed—

Suddenly Peterson sawed back on his reins. "Look."

Caruthers lay crumpled in the middle of the road. The two horses, heads down, grazed on the sparse grass that grew along the trail. Pistols drawn, Quinn and Peterson eased forward. When they saw no sign of foul play, Quinn nodded at Caruthers's prone form. "See if he's alive."

Peterson jumped off his horse and rushed to his master.

Quinn crouched beside them, and they gently rolled Caruthers over. He groaned. There was no blood, no obvious injuries, but Caruthers seemed disoriented and listless.

"Mr. Caruthers, sir, are you all right?" Peterson held a flask to his lips.

Caruthers grabbed the flask, turned it up, and drank thirstily.

Peterson threw Quinn a worried look.

Quinn pushed his hat back. "I think he's just worn slap out. He hasna stopped for days."

He eyed the trail. They were so close to Breeze Hill. . . . But Caruthers was in no shape to keep going. He grabbed up the reins to the horses. "Let's get off the trail and make camp. We're still a fair piece from Breeze Hill, and we can continue on in the morning."

Peterson ministered to Caruthers while Quinn took care of the horses. By the time he was done, Caruthers was asleep on the bedroll Peterson had laid out for him. Now that they'd caught up with him, maybe Peterson could talk some sense into him. Quinn laid out his own blanket and was soon fast asleep.

Sometime before dawn, a clap of thunder startled him awake. Even the horses were restless, apprehensive of the approaching storm. He lay there for a moment thinking that they should get on the road and try to make it to Breeze Hill before the rain hit. The first few drops of rain landed on his face, and he sat up and pulled on his boots, then turned toward the other two bedrolls.

Only to find the space that had been occupied by Caruthers now empty. The horses snorted, shifted, and he saw the silhouette of a man among them. Quinn rushed toward him, but Caruthers swung something—a gun, a club—Quinn didn't know. Whatever it was, it connected with his cheekbone like he'd been hit with a sledgehammer. He spun, glancing off the horse's haunch before landing with a thud over a fallen log. Searing pain shot through his ribs, still not completely healed from the knifing.

He heard a shout, saw Caruthers had mounted. Peterson grabbed at the horse's bridle. Caruthers sawed back on the reins, and the horse reared and came down on the man. Even in his own pain, Quinn heard the man's scream of agony and the sickening snap of bone. By the time Quinn gained his footing, Caruthers had disappeared in a thunder of hoofbeats down the road toward Natchez.

Quinn crouched over Caruthers's overseer. "Peterson? Are you all right?"

"My leg," Peterson groaned. "I think it's broken."

Kiera sat in a rocker on the front porch, staring down the rain-shrouded lane that led toward the Natchez Trace.

Earlier, everyone had gathered on the back veranda for Sunday morning services, but her heart hadn't been in it. She couldn't even remember what the sermon had been about, let alone what Mary and the girls had sung.

As worry once again rose up within her, she silently repeated the Psalms to keep the turmoil at bay.

"God is our refuge and strength, a very present help in trouble."

The rocker kept time to the mournful sound of Mews's fiddle as he played a sorrow-laden song about a pilgrim wandering through the wilderness. The song and the rain fit her mood. The moss in the trees bowed under the onslaught of rain, as if it wept along with her.

Sunday was supposed to be a day of rest, to build your strength for the week ahead. But how could her body rest when her mind continued to run in circles?

"Therefore will not we fear, though the earth be removed, and though the mountains be carried into the midst of the sea."

It'd been a week since Amelia and Weston took off. A week since Quinn had left with Mr. Peterson to accompany Mr. Caruthers home.

Had they found her? Were they on their way back even now? She had no inkling how far it was to the Caruthers plantation. It could be a week or a month's worth of travel

THE ROAD TO MAGNOLIA GLEN

northward along the trail. There'd been no time—or need—
to ask until it was too late.

*"Though the waters thereof roar and be troubled, though the
mountains shake with the swelling thereof."*

Through the fog and the trees, she saw a flicker of movement. She pushed out of the rocker and moved to the edge
of the porch, watching for another glimpse of motion on
the rain-slick road. There! A horse. Then another. Her heart
pounded when she counted four horses.

Lord, please let one of them be Amelia.

But her hope was short-lived when the horses cleared
the trees and there were only two riders, Quinn and Mr.
Peterson, Caruthers's overseer.

Mr. Peterson sat hunched over, Quinn leading his horse
and the two riderless ones. What had happened? Quinn
skirted the house and headed straight toward the stables in
the rear. The specter of the two riderless horses made her
stomach clutch with fear.

Lord Jesus, no. Please, God.

Uncaring of the mist that fell, Kiera raced to the back of
the house and through the courtyard toward the outdoor
kitchen, where she found Martha, as usual. "Martha, hurry.
Quinn and Mr. Peterson have returned, and Mr. Peterson
is hurt."

Not waiting on Martha to grab her wrap, Kiera then ran
through the light rain toward the cabins, arriving just in time
to see Quinn come to a halt in front of the same cabin Weston
had recuperated in. As Toby Mews and Mr. Horne lifted

Mr. Peterson from the horse, Quinn cautioned, "Careful. His leg's broken."

Martha joined them and followed as they carried him inside. Kiera's gaze landed on Quinn and she gasped. Dried blood covered one side of his face, and his eye was swollen and already turning purple.

"Quinn, you're hurt."

He waved her away. "It's nothing, lass."

The horses quivered nervously at a long roll of thunder and Quinn reached for their reins, wincing when they shied away, fighting against his hold.

"Nothing?" Kiera made an effort to control the rising tone of her voice. She slipped under Quinn's arm, holding him up. He stifled another groan, and she jerked her gaze to his face. "Where all are you hurt? What happened? Did you find Amelia?"

Finally he stood before her, straighter, but still clutching his ribs. "One question at a time."

"Yes. All right." Kiera took a deep breath. "Where do you hurt?"

"All over." He grunted out the words through clenched teeth.

She glanced at the moisture-laden sky as the rain redoubled its efforts. There was time enough to find out what had happened, but now she needed to get him somewhere out of the rain where she could tend his wounds. "Can you make it to the cookhouse?"

"The horses—"

"Never mind the horses." She glanced around, spotted Toby. "Toby, take the horses to the stables."

"Yes, ma'am."

"Come. Let's go."

One arm clasping his ribs, the other draped over her shoulder, Quinn allowed her to lead him toward the cookhouse. She glanced up, and her heart squeezed at the way his face was screwed up in pain, his blue eyes narrowed to slits as he gauged the distance.

Inside, Kiera pulled out a chair and helped him sit before she hurried to the fireplace, grabbed the poker, and punched up the fire. As she filled a kettle with water and put it over the fire to heat, she glanced over her shoulder.

Quinn sat slumped against the table, eyes closed. A week's worth of dark stubble covered his jaw, the grime of travel mingled with the blood from the gash on his cheek giving him a fearsome look. Dark circles pooled under his eyes, and she wondered if he'd slept at all since he'd been gone. She had so many questions, but they could wait.

She tested the water, poured some into a bowl, and carried it to the table along with a washcloth. She touched his shoulder, and his eyes opened to slits. He cleared his throat and sat up straighter.

"My apologies. Caruthers set a bruising pace, and Peterson and I have had little rest." He glanced at her. "We didna find Amelia."

Thank You, Lord. The alternative with the riderless horses would have been so much worse than not finding her sister at all.

"No one on the trail t' the north saw them, but we kept going, hoping they'd kept out o' sight o' strangers." He sighed. "But when we arrived at Caruthers's home, there was still no sign o' them—and even worse, his wife had died."

"Oh no. Poor Mr. Caruthers."

Quinn scowled. "Poor Mr. Caruthers almost killed the both o' us."

"Mr. Caruthers did this to you and Mr. Peterson?" Surprised and not a little shocked, Kiera wrung out the cloth, then blotted the blood on his cheek.

He closed his eyes and tilted his head back. "According t' Peterson, he's gone mad with grief."

His dark hair fell over his forehead, and she gently swiped it back, wincing at the bruising that covered half his face. She dabbed at the grime, sweat, and blood, starting with his forehead and moving down.

"When he found out his wife had died, Caruthers seemed t' lose all reason. He didn't even go t' her funeral, just locked himself in his wife's room. We'd been traveling nonstop for four days, and I went t' sleep in the barn. The next thing I knew, Peterson was calling for me, telling me Caruthers had left, heading back this way."

"And this?" She gently ran her fingers along the cut below his eye.

He squinted up at her, then winced. "Caruthers's calling card, courtesy of a felled tree branch. We caught up with him late last night. He'd fallen off his horse and was unconscious in the middle of the road." He shrugged. "At first I thought he was injured, but he was just overcome with exhaustion if I do no' miss my guess. Peterson took care of him. . . ."

As he recounted what had happened on the trail, Kiera dropped the soiled rag into the bowl, tinging the water a reddish-brown. She rinsed the cloth, then wrung it out.

When she turned back, the same lock of hair had fallen over Quinn's forehead. Smiling and listening to Quinn talk, she threaded her fingers through the damp strands and pushed them back once again.

Her heart twisted with all that he'd gone through for her and her sisters.

"A man who's willing to risk his life for you is a man worth giving your life to."

And in that instant, she knew.

She loved this man. Loved that he'd saved her and her sisters from Le Bonne, had stood by her side when his own brother had almost tossed them out on their ear, and had risked his life to go after her sister when she'd done something dull-witted. Her fingertips slid from his hairline over his temple and down his cheek as she wiped the last of the grime off his face.

Chapter 27

THROUGH EYES NARROWED TO SLITS, Quinn saw the tenderness that softened Kiera's face, the gentle smile that played with the corners of her lips. A smile that had him thinking about hauling her into his arms, crushing her mouth with his, bruised ribs be hanged.

He reined in the thought when she turned away, dropped the bloodied cloth into the water, and swished it around. Suddenly she glanced over her shoulder as if something had just occurred to her.

"Where's Mr. Caruthers now? He's not—" her brow furrowed—"not dead, is he?"

"He was alive and well the last time I saw him. But that

might change when he gets to Natchez and finds Pierre Le Bonne."

"He thinks Weston and Amelia went toward Natchez?" All color drained from her face. "And how does he know about Le Bonne?"

Quinn could have kicked himself. Kiera had enough to worry about without the fear that her sister might fall into Le Bonne's hands again.

"Quinn, tell me. What does Le Bonne have to do with Weston and Mr. Caruthers?"

"Caruthers is convinced Le Bonne kidnapped his eldest son and pressed him into service as a sailor. And in his current state of mind, crazy with grief over his wife's death, Weston's defection, he might—" Quinn clamped his lips together, determined to say no more.

"What?" Kiera searched his face, her blue eyes filled with worry. "What else?"

"Nothing." He stood, groaning at the shaft of pain that shot through his bruised ribs.

"There's something you're not telling—"

The door to the cookhouse slammed open and Connor rushed in. "I just saw Peterson. Are you all right?"

"It's nothing." Quinn held his ribs. "Just a bump on the head and some bruised ribs when I fell. I'll be fine. How's Peterson?"

"Martha and Horne just set his leg. He'll live, God willing." Connor scowled. "And Caruthers is on his way to Natchez, going after Le Bonne?"

"Yes."

Connor paced the length of the cookhouse, then settled his gaze on Kiera, then Quinn. "Do you think—?"

He broke off midsentence as pounding hooves drew near. Grabbing the door, he yanked it open, Quinn and Kiera right behind him. As the single rider halted in front of the cookhouse, Quinn recognized Neville Granger from his previous visit to Breeze Hill.

Granger reined in, doffed his hat toward Kiera. "Miss Young. Gentlemen."

"Granger." Connor stepped forward, casting an eye toward the road. "You're traveling alone?"

"No. My party went on ahead." Granger dismounted, reached in his coat pocket, and handed Connor the note. "Mr. Bloomfield asked me to deliver a letter."

"Thank you, sir." Connor ripped open the letter and unfolded it, frowning as he read.

"I can only stay a moment. Bloomfield also said to tell you that a ship bearing freemen from Ireland looking to indenture themselves arrived this week."

Connor looked up from the letter. "That's wonderful news. I was just telling Quinn that we were going t' need more help, and soon."

"It's good to see Breeze Hill flourishing again. Well, I must join the others before they get too far down the trail." Granger reached for his saddle horn, mounted, then frowned at them. "There's something else you should know. We met Reginald Caruthers headed toward Natchez this morning. He was alone and acting very strange, nothing like he was several weeks ago when he traveled with me to Natchez. He passed by as if he didn't even recognize me. I was quite concerned, actually. Did he find his son?"

Engrossed in the letter, Connor didn't answer. Quinn addressed Mr. Granger. "No. And when he arrived back home, he found that his wife had passed away."

"No wonder he looked like he'd aged so. Poor chap." Granger shook his head. "I couldn't get much out of him. He kept ranting and raving about his son and some girl. Said he was going to make the girl pay for ruining his son's life."

Kiera gasped. "Amelia?"

Granger looked at her. "You know who he's talking about, miss? To tell you the truth, I couldn't make heads nor tails out of what he was saying. I didn't think he knew anything about what happened to his son. It was the oddest thing—"

"He wasn't talking about his eldest son." Quinn's gaze met Kiera's. "He was talking about Weston. And Kiera's sister. They ran away together over a week ago."

A hard look came over Granger's face, and he glanced from Quinn to Kiera, then to Connor. "You folks need to find that girl as soon as possible because Caruthers didn't seem to care one whit what happened to her. All he cared about was finding his son." Mr. Granger tipped his hat. "I'm sorry, miss. I hope you find your sister. Good day, O'Shea."

"Godspeed, sir."

Granger turned his mount and rode away, in a hurry to catch up with the rest of his party.

Connor held up the letter. "That's not the only reason

we need to find Amelia. According to Bloomfield, the ship's manifest from the *Lady Gallant* says ye're indentured t' Le Bonne, as he paid for your passage from Ireland."

"That's not true." Kiera shook her head. "My brother-in-law paid for our passage."

"That may be true, but t' make your passage look like a traditional indenture, he put Pierre Le Bonne down as your benefactor." Connor arched a brow at her. "Long story short, your brother-in-law sold you and your sisters to pay a debt. With Charlotte's blessing, if I don't miss my guess. It's plain and simple as that."

Kiera wrapped her arms about her waist. "Is it possible Weston and Amelia went some place other than Natchez?"

Quinn shook his head. "There's no other place for them to go. Unless . . ."

He didn't have to finish his thought. Kiera knew enough about the dangers of the trace to realize that any number of unspeakable horrors could have befallen the young couple before they got that far.

Kiera's eyes filled with tears, and she looked from Quinn to Connor.

"As hard as it is to accept, lass, it's better if she's in Natchez than—" Connor's voice softened—"than being accosted by highwaymen on the trace."

Quinn straightened. "Then we need to find her before Le Bonne or Caruthers does."

"I agree. This has gone on long enough." Brow furrowed, Connor glanced toward the sawmill. "I have enough lumber to make another trip to Natchez, and it will give us a chance to look for Amelia. We leave at dawn."

Everything became a blur after that. Quinn and Connor left to muster the crews and load lumber.

Kiera found Mary Horne, and they began preparing food for the trip. And all the while, the possibility that Weston and Amelia were in Natchez gnawed at her. Undoubtedly Amelia knew the danger Le Bonne represented. But she'd be safe with Weston, wouldn't she? They wouldn't venture anywhere near the Blue Heron, would they?

Kiera remembered when her mother had died, then later her father. She could understand the paralyzing grief that consumed Mr. Caruthers right now. Surely the man would come to his senses when he found his son. He wouldn't abandon Amelia, would he? And if the two were married already, then he'd accept Amelia as his daughter-in-law and all would be well, wouldn't it?

But what if—?

"'God is *my* refuge and strength, a very present help in trouble,'" she whispered. "God, be Amelia's refuge. Keep her from Le Bonne."

Heart racing with terror over what Amelia would be forced to do if Le Bonne got his clutches on her sister, Kiera didn't even bother to stem the flow of her tears as she labored over the evening meal. *Lord, protect Amelia. Keep her safe. Dear Lord in heaven, protect my sister. Oh, God . . .*

Words failed her, and all she could do was pray, "Jesus, Jesus, Jesus," over and over as she kept busy in order not to collapse in a puddle on the floor.

"Kiera?" She turned, saw Isabella standing in the doorway, arms outstretched. Kiera fell into Isabella's embrace. "Martha told me."

"They—they think she's in Natchez."

"She's going to be all right."

"How can you be sure?" Kiera mopped at her face with her apron. "What if Le Bonne—?"

"Hush now. Don't go borrowing trouble."

She sniffed. "I need—I want to go with them, but . . ."

"But what?"

"Connor would never allow it." She shook her head. "And if he did, he'd probably help me pack and tell me not to come back."

Isabella chuckled. "The fact that he's rushing off to Natchez to find Amelia speaks volumes. He's much more tenderhearted than you give him credit for."

Kiera nodded. It was true. Connor had softened toward her, toward all of them, but she was still a bit intimidated by his ever-present scowl. She pressed the twisted apron to her mouth. "I've been praying, Isabella, but I'm so afraid . . ."

"Just keep praying. God will not forsake you."

Quinn spent the rest of the day repairing broken chains, wheels, shoeing horses, whatever came to hand. As soon as he finished one task, someone would bring him another. If there was iron involved, and it was broken, bent, or busted, he fixed it.

It didn't help that his ribs felt like he'd stabbed himself with a red-hot poker, then twisted it for good measure. He gritted his teeth and worked through the pain.

Connor strode toward the smithy, a piece of broken harness dangling from one hand. He tossed the leather onto the growing pile, the metal rings clanging against each other. "At this rate, we're never going t' get off t' Natchez."

Quinn grunted in assent, his attention on the horseshoe he was forming for one of the draft horses.

"While I hadn't planned t' go t' Natchez this soon, it's for the best. The sooner I get this lumber off my hands, the sooner I can get seed, supplies, and some more workers so Mews can start planting." Connor leaned against a post, watching Quinn work. "You considered my offer?"

"I thought about it."

"Blast it, Quinn, I need you to make up your mind now. Braxton did precious little planting last year, and I can't leave the land fallow for another year, or the forest will encroach on the fields. If I'm to work that land this year, I need to buy enough seed on this trip. I won't get another chance."

The sound of Quinn's hammer rang loud in the lingering silence that hung in the air after Connor's outburst. Could he stay? Should he?

He spotted Kiera heading toward the well, bucket in hand. His next blow missed the horseshoe, his hammer glancing off the anvil.

He jerked his attention back to the job at hand, but he still caught glimpses of movement as she drew water, then the swirl of brown as she lifted her skirt and zigzagged back toward the cookhouse, avoiding the mud puddles left by this morning's thunderstorm.

Arms folded across his chest, Connor cut his gaze toward Kiera as she disappeared into the cookhouse, then back to Quinn. "Is there something I should know, Brother?"

A rush of heat flushed over Quinn, but thankfully, the blaze of the forge and the sweat rolling down his face masked it quite well. At least he hoped so. "Nothing that I can think of."

"I beg to differ." Connor's brow furrowed. "There's bad blood between Charlotte and me, but—"

"Look, Connor, if you do no' want t' search for Amelia, then just say so."

"What do you take me for?" Connor scowled. "In spite of what Charlotte did, Amelia's little more than a child, and she was under my care when she ran off. If Weston has done the right thing by the girl, there's nothing else to be done about the matter, but if he hasn't, then he's going to answer to me."

Quinn gripped the hammer and gave the horseshoe one last tap for good measure. He'd thought much the same thing himself but was surprised that Connor felt responsibility for Kiera and her sisters.

Connor walked to the open doorway, then turned. "This is no longer about what happened between me and Charlotte. This is about finding that girl and keeping her from Le Bonne's clutches."

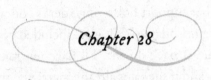

Chapter 28

AFTER ANOTHER SLEEPLESS NIGHT, Kiera made her decision.

When Connor and Isabella walked from the house toward the line of wagons, Kiera gathered her courage and approached Connor.

"I'm going with you."

"No." His eyebrows lowered in a ferocious frown, and her courage almost deserted her. Without another word to her, he turned and stalked toward the lead wagon, where Quinn was adjusting the harness.

Kiera followed, determined that he listen to her. "She's my sister. I won't let Le Bonne have her."

"I said no," Connor all but growled.

Quinn crossed his arms over his chest, his black look a mirror image of his brother's. "I agree with Connor. You aren't going."

"Connor, be reasonable." Isabella stepped to Kiera's side, a mutinous expression on her face. She slid an arm around Kiera's waist, her support bolstering Kiera's courage.

"I am being reasonable!" His glare included both of them, but Isabella didn't back down. "I'll have ten men with me. We'll find her, and if she's not already married t' the sniveling brat, we'll bring her back—"

"Either you take me with you now, or I'll follow behind on my own."

"You'd defy me, young lady?"

"Aye. I would."

She lifted her chin, throwing caution to the wind. Connor wasn't going to let her stay here indefinitely, so it didn't really matter if she burned her bridges with him or not.

Connor raked a hand through his hair, looked at Isabella, then plopped both hands on his hips. "Can't you talk some sense into her?"

"I'm afraid not. I happen to agree with her on the matter. If I were in the same position—"

"Then so be it. But—" he jabbed a finger at Quinn—"you ride with him, and you'll do exactly as I say while we're gone."

"And Megan?" Kiera nodded at the letter tucked in his shirt. "Mr. Bloomfield says that—"

"I don't care what he says." Connor glared at them all. "Megan stays here. The only reason I'm letting you go is it's better t' have ya where I can see ya than traipsing off on your own." He stalked away.

Kiera clasped Isabella's hands. "Take care of Megan."

"I will." Isabella's dark eyes searched hers. "Please be careful and do everything Connor tells you to do. You might not believe it, but he cares about you and your sisters. Trust me."

Now wasn't the time to argue. "What about the cookhouse?"

"Don't worry about that. With most of the men gone, there'll be precious little to do, and I daresay Mary, Martha, and I can take care of any travelers who might come along."

"Don't overtax yourself."

"I won't." Isabella leaned forward. "Truth be told, I'll be glad of a respite. I'm purely sick of Connor's coddling."

Kiera smothered a laugh, the idea of Connor coddling anyone as foreign as . . . as Le Bonne hauling his tavern wenches off to Sunday morning meeting. She threw her arms around Isabella. "Thank you."

"Now, run along and grab a change of clothes." Isabella's gaze strayed toward Connor as he strode toward the sawmill. "I'd better go make amends with that stubborn husband of mine."

Late in the afternoon, Quinn applied the brake as the wagon wound down and around another bend along the trace. The wagon rocked against the ribbon of uneven ruts cut into the trail, throwing Kiera against him. He tossed a glance in her direction, only to see her gripping the edge of the narrow seat, bottom lip clenched between her teeth, a furrow between her brows as she concentrated on keeping her seat.

"You all right?"

"Yes, I'm fine."

The ground leveled off and the road wove across an open meadow, clumps of early spring green peeking through the dull gray of winter vegetation. The sun had come out, making the ride a pleasant one.

Beside him, Kiera loosened her cloak, her arm brushing against his. Quinn cleared his throat and concentrated on the two sets of ears bobbing ahead of him. But it was hard to keep his attention on the horses with Kiera so close. Out of the corner of his eye, he caught her in a jaw-cracking yawn. Her gaze cut to his, and cheeks flaming, she clapped a hand over her mouth. "I'm sorry. I didn't get much sleep last night."

"Or the night before that, I imagine."

"True." She looked away. "I haven't slept much since . . . since Amelia left."

The dark circles under her eyes told their own tale.

"You should try t' get some rest." He shook the reins, keeping the horses moving at a steady pace.

"Sleeping sitting up on a wagon seat isn't easy, you know."

He chuckled, then nodded at Björn in the wagon ahead of them, head slumped down, shoulders rocking from side to side. "Really? Tell him that."

"Some people just have a knack for it, I suppose."

In spite of Kiera's protests, she dozed off more than once as the afternoon wore on. Finally her head dropped to his shoulder as she succumbed to exhaustion. Gathering the reins in one hand, Quinn gently placed his arm around her and secured her against his side.

She murmured a protest, and his heart skipped a beat. But she just sighed, her eyelashes feathered softly against her cheekbones. As the wagon rocked on toward Natchez, she slept, her head lolling against his arm.

Dusk had fallen when she stirred, opened her eyes, and stared up at him, looking bemused. He resisted the urge to drop a kiss on her lips, parted and vulnerable from her nap.

But before he could give in, she sat up, straightened her cloak, patted her hair, then cleared her throat. "I'm sorry. I didn't mean to fall asleep."

"No harm done. You needed the rest."

"How much farther is it?"

"Not far. Connor said we should arrive by dark, and the day is far gone already."

"There won't be time to look for Amelia." Her voice was barely audible.

"Tomorrow will be soon enough."

They rounded a bend and Natchez came into view, spread out on the bluff below them. The horses paused at the crest of the hill and Quinn took in the layout of the city. To his right the Mississippi River snaked southward toward New Orleans, the masts of the ships anchored in port below the bluff easily visible from their vantage point.

Then there was the mass of buildings cobbled together along the waterfront, more clinging to the hillsides here and there, with the town proper perched above the bluff. And in between, Fort Natchez stood sentinel over it all, the Spanish flag waving in the breeze.

The lead wagon moved forward, and the caravan dipped down the crest of the hill into town and wove through the streets. Given the late hour, few people were out and about. And the ones he saw were hurrying home before full darkness descended.

Kiera sat quietly, her face pale and stony. He reached for her hands, clasped tightly in her lap. Her gaze shot to his.

"It's going to be fine. We'll find Amelia, and all will be well."

She nodded, but the worry stamped on her features didn't lessen.

As Connor had predicted, darkness had fallen by the time they arrived at Wainwright House in Natchez. William Wainwright and his wife welcomed them. After a brief greeting, Mistress Wainwright whisked Kiera off to the house.

Quinn watched them go, hoping the other woman's presence eased Kiera's distress.

Kiera jerked awake, blinking at the sunlight streaming in the window. Nightmares of the wharf, Pierre Le Bonne, her sister being trapped in the Blue Heron had plagued her most of the night.

Thankful the long night had ended, she left the bed, dressed, and hurried downstairs. She followed the sound of laughter and found Leah and little Jon in the kitchen with Mrs. Butler.

Leah offered a shy smile from her place on the floor with the baby. "Ah, good morning, Kiera. Did you sleep well?"

"Not much, I'm afraid." Not wanting to sound ungrateful, she added, "The accommodations were excellent. I was just worried. That's all."

"Completely understandable, miss." The housekeeper motioned toward a pot kept warm in a nest of coals. "Would you like some breakfast?"

"Please, don't put yourself out on my account."

"It's no trouble. I have porridge hot and ready." Mrs. Butler filled a bowl with porridge and placed it on the table along with butter and molasses. She patted the back of a chair. "Please, sit."

As Kiera ate, Leah changed the baby, and Mrs. Butler bustled about behind her, humming a soothing lullaby and washing dishes. Kiera dipped a spoon into her bowl, the complete and utter stillness throughout the house and stables palpable. "Where are the men?"

"They've eaten and gone off about their business." Leah glanced up. "Quinn said to tell you to wait for his return."

Kiera frowned. She'd hoped to start her search for Amelia first thing, but she didn't have a clue where to begin. Perhaps Quinn would return soon.

Leah bent over the baby, blowing kisses against his tummy. He kicked and waved both arms, squealing with joy.

"He seems like such a happy baby."

"He is." Leah's milky-white complexion glowed with love, and she smiled down at her son. "You're Mama's sweet angel, aren't you, darling?"

Little Jon's eyes grew wide when he heard her voice, and he pumped his legs and arms as if he were running as hard as he could. They all laughed.

"Oh, I dread the day that child starts walking," Mrs. Butler said, but the tone of her voice said she didn't dread it at all. "I doubt these old legs will be able to keep up."

Kiera ate her porridge, letting the warm scene soothe her troubled heart.

"Oh, look," Leah squealed. "He's trying to crawl."

Little Jon lifted his head, his toothless grin showing his gums, pushing himself up with one foot. Grunting and working hard, he dug his toes into the quilt. Kiera finished her meal, stood, and dropped her bowl in a pan of sudsy water. She reached for a cloth.

Mrs. Butler waved her away. "No, no, miss. I do the work in my kitchen. Sit. Enjoy the baby."

"But—"

"No buts."

"You might as well obey." Leah patted the quilt. "She won't let me do anything either."

"Miss Leah, you have enough to do taking care of that sweet baby." Mrs. Butler tossed Kiera a glance. "She refuses to hire a nurse."

"Now, Mrs. Butler, there'll be time enough for that."

Leah picked the baby up, grasped his chubby little arms, and helped him stand. He squealed and bounced up and down, causing them to laugh.

"When he starts walking, you'll change your tune."

Leah hugged the baby close, kissing his soft cheek. "Perhaps."

The housekeeper opened the pie safe and drew out the dough she'd left to rise overnight. Kiera settled on the quilt with Leah. "May I hold him?"

"Yes, of course."

Leah handed the child over and Kiera cuddled the sweet-smelling baby, remembering Megan as a wee one. Kiera had not been much more than a child herself, but with another child on the way, and *Mam* sickly, Kiera had tended to Megan more often than not. And when *Mam* and the babe had died, Megan clung to Kiera more than ever.

The baby laid his head on her shoulder, rubbed his eyes, and yawned. Kiera's heart turned over at the sweet trust he placed in her, and she patted his back. Leah picked up a blanket and held it out. "Nap time. He'll go to sleep faster with this."

Kiera tucked the soft material around little Jon, cuddled his small body close, and rocked him from side to side. After squirming for a few more moments, he settled down, staring at her; then he stuck his fist in his mouth, his big brown eyes fluttering shut, only to pop open time and again to focus on her face.

Humming, she cradled him in the crook of her arm,

straightened his blanket. He finally succumbed to sleep, his fist dropping away and his little rosebud mouth falling slack.

"You'll make a good mother someday."

Kiera kept her attention on the sleeping child in her arms, even as she felt her face heating up.

A mother?

Becoming a mother would require gaining her freedom, falling in love, marriage.

So far, she'd accomplished one of the three.

Chapter 29

QUINN SUPPRESSED A CHUCKLE as he rode beside his older brother along the wharf.

Connor was like a mule straining against the traces and had been all day. First, they'd spent the morning haggling over the price of the lumber with the contractor named Wicker. That transaction done, they'd visited one shop after another purchasing much-needed supplies for the plantation.

With each stop, they asked if anyone had seen Weston or Amelia, but they'd had little luck. They loaded Björn's wagon with seed and waved him off as he headed back to Wainwright's.

And now they were on their way to see Bloomfield. Connor

threaded the wagon along the crowded thoroughfare toward the wharf. "I've decided to go ahead and purchase enough indentures to plant the fields at Magnolia Glen. Since lumber is at such a premium, we have the funds to do so, and it would be foolish not to."

Quinn nodded, searching each face they passed, looking for Weston or Amelia. "I think that's a wise decision."

"But you're still undecided?"

"I am."

"Fair enough. Mews was the overseer at Breeze Hill at one time. I daresay he can help out as needed. The men at the sawmill look up to Horne. With their help, I can split my time between the two plantations and all should go well." He pulled the horses to a stop, allowing another wagon the right-of-way before slapping the reins and continuing on. "Even though Breeze Hill will be little Jon's someday, Magnolia Glen is twice as big, and I've heard that there is uncharted land beyond my holdings that hasn't been claimed. England is eager for lumber, cotton, tobacco, sugarcane, and indigo."

Quinn cut his gaze toward his brother. "Ya wouldn't be trying to sway me t' your way o' thinking, would ya?"

Connor shrugged. "Is it working? Everything I say is truth. I have the land, so why should I let it go to waste? I'll cut the timber, sell it while there's demand, and plant crops with the proceeds. Natchez and the surrounding countryside are on the verge of something big. I can feel it."

"But you need labor?"

"Aye." Connor nodded. "I need labor."

It all sounded too good to be true. But was Connor simply trying to entice Quinn to stay with the promise of land, property, and prosperity?

Quinn snorted. He'd stayed for less back in Ireland. There'd been no promise of material gain in Ireland, only the promise he'd made to his dying father that he'd see to the little ones.

A commotion along the wharf drew his attention. The clink of chains reached them as, one after another, a long line of Negroes trooped down the gangway onto dry land. Men, women, children, all chained together, their emaciated frames and unsteady gait showing that they'd just reached land after a long voyage.

A woman fell and a slaver lashed her with a whip. He barked an order and those closest to her helped the woman to her feet. Connor faced forward, hands tight on the reins, jaw clenched. Stomach churning at the inhumane display, Quinn was glad to leave the scene behind.

Not too many months past, Connor had been on an auction block himself. But there was no comparison in indenturing oneself for seven years with rights of termination to being a slave, bought and sold as chattel, with no hope of ever gaining one's freedom.

While Breeze Hill's coffers might suffer from refusing to own slaves, Quinn was glad his brother was following in Mr. Bartholomew's footsteps. The O'Sheas came from nothing, and they had no right to put another man in chains and claim him as property. But for the grace of God, he would be the one in chains.

He'd chafed at his lot, but now he knew his prison was of his own making. He could have walked away at any time. He'd stayed because he'd promised his *da*. He'd stayed because he loved his brothers and the lads needed him, not because he'd been forced to by Connor or by Caleb's absence.

He talked a big talk about leaving, about abdicating his responsibility, about turning his brothers over to Connor so that he could see the world, explore and do the things he'd imagined Connor had been doing all these years.

The things that Caleb was doing even now.

But the closer his day of reckoning came, the more he wrestled with leaving. Would he truly be free leaving Rory and Patrick behind? Leaving Kiera?

Freedom without family carried its own kind of bondage.

No closer to a decision, he was relieved when they arrived at Bloomfield's office, and the lawyer escorted them toward the ship that carried a load of freemen who'd left their homeland seeking a better life in America.

On board the ship, Bloomfield greeted the captain. "Captain, meet Connor O'Shea."

The captain grinned. "Ah, a fellow Irishman, eh? 'Tis me lucky day, for sure."

"Perhaps." Connor shook his hand. "You have men with papers for sale?"

"That I do, me lad. That I do." He jerked his head toward the back of the ship. "Follow me."

On the main deck, half a dozen men sat chained together, along with one woman and a small child. Connor bristled, turning to the captain. "Why are these people in chains? My understanding is that they are t' be indentured t' pay off their passage. They're not slaves nor criminals."

"'Tis true, O'Shea, but I've had more than one lad jump ship before I could get me coin for 'im. I'm sure you understand. These blighters sure do." The captain bellowed, and the child burrowed against his mother. "Stand t' yer feet, lads. Show the gentleman some respect."

The chains rattled as they struggled to their feet, as strong and healthy as they could be after three months aboard ship. One man looked pale and sickly, but the man next to him helped him stand. Another struggled to remain upright, his jaw clenched tight, sweat beading on his forehead.

Connor moved in front of him. "What ails you, man?"

"A bit o' rancid meat, that be all, sir."

"Very well." Connor nodded and moved on, turned in a circle, pointing out the five healthy men, including the one who'd spoken up for himself. "If you're willing to work, I can use you all. Seven years at Breeze Hill and Magnolia Glen. You'll have food, lodging, clothing, and your freedom at the end of your service."

"Please, sir, could ya take me brother as well?" The man holding his brother looked up at Connor. "If he dies, I'll take on his time, I will, sir."

Connor's gaze met Quinn's. Something passed between them, something that reminded him of that brotherly bond.

Connor turned to Bloomfield. "Very well. Write it into his contract."

The captain motioned to the woman. "What about her? She be a skilled midwife. Or so she says. Her husband died on the trip over, so I'm out his fare already. But I'll let her and the child go for half the fare if ye'll take her off me hands. She's the last o' the lot."

Connor scowled. "I have need o' men t' cut timber and work the fields, not birth babes."

"Be ya married, sir?"

Connor ignored the question. "Release these men, sir, so we can be on our way."

"Have it yer way. Jansen!" The captain barked orders at a sailor. "Take the wench and her bairn below. She be a bit old for Le Bonne, but he's me last hope t' git rid o' 'er."

Quinn jerked around. "Le Bonne?"

"Aye." The captain winked. "Even if he can't use her in the Blue Heron, he owns other cribs along the wharf what ain't so choosy. Le Bonne will likely take her and her bairn off me hands. Better a wee bit o' coin than none a'tall."

"Release the woman and her child. I find I have need o' her after all."

"Thank ya, Mr. O'Shea." The captain swept off his hat, bowing low. "It was a pleasure doin' business with ya, for sure."

Connor glared at him. "I can't say the sa—"

"Well, now that you gentlemen have agreed to terms, I'll draw up the paperwork, and you can both sign off." Mr.

Bloomfield mopped his brow with his handkerchief and motioned toward the wharf. "Mr. O'Shea, shall we?"

Without another word to the captain, Connor marched toward the gangway. Quinn fell into step beside him. Jaw clenched, Connor growled in a low voice, "Now you know why I avoid Natchez Under-the-Hill at all costs. Men who deal in human cargo are the worst kind of scum."

"Some, yes. But at least these men are willing participants. Unlike the slaves we saw—"

"Look. There." Connor came to an abrupt halt and pointed. "Isn't that the Caruthers boy?"

Quinn followed the direction of Connor's finger, spotted Weston Caruthers loading barrels onto a wagon.

"It is. Come on."

They hurried down the gangway, stepped off, and wove through the crowd. Weston looked up when they were a hundred yards away, saw them, and took off at a run.

Quinn gave chase.

Seated in the shadows on the second-story balcony of the Blue Heron, Pierre observed the commotion below.

A young man ran helter-skelter along the crowded thoroughfare, dodging between carts, pushing onlookers out of his way. As he neared the Blue Heron, Pierre caught sight of his face. He'd seen the gangly youth. It was the same one Claude had recently hired to work on the wharf.

The boy threw a glance over his shoulder and Pierre followed his line of sight, spotting a man in hot pursuit. His hat sailed off his head, and Pierre froze as he caught sight of the man's dark hair and square jaw. The boy's nemesis looked familiar, but the glimpse was so brief, he could've been mistaken. Pierre stood, moved to the edge of the porch to get a better look.

"Weston!" the man yelled. "Stop. I just want t' talk t' ya, lad."

The thick Irish brogue wafted upward. But the boy was having none of it. He raced past the Blue Heron, ducked behind a wagon, and dove beneath the hedges that grew rampant between two buildings down the street. More than one street urchin had made his escape under those same bushes.

Leaning on a corner post and puffing on his cigar, Pierre swung his attention back to the man who'd pursued the boy, chuckling as he turned a full circle trying to determine where his prey had disappeared to.

The man had called the boy by name, so his pursuit wasn't in response to a random encounter. No, there was something else afoot. Probably nothing of consequence.

Another man, similar in build and coloring, joined the first, handing him his hat.

Pierre clamped down on his cigar. This man was no stranger. Connor O'Shea.

O'Shea had stolen Braxton Hall out from under Pierre's nose. Pierre was there the day the tornado destroyed the property and almost destroyed Nolan Braxton. Almost, but not quite. But Pierre had taken care of nature's oversight and ridded himself of Braxton that very day.

Then he'd hauled away enough gold and silver to set himself up for life. Except he wanted more.

With Braxton gone and no heirs, as his closest confidant, Pierre had planned to lay claim to the property. Unfortunately, by the time he made it back to Natchez, he found that the governor had given O'Shea a land grant for the acreage.

Now O'Shea had ventured into Pierre's territory.

Pierre regarded O'Shea's companion. Who was he? Pierre's teeth worried his cigar as he tried to remember where he'd seen him. Then it hit him. This was the man who'd been on the wharf the day Pierre's *bride* had arrived. Not that she'd ever been intended as such, but it amused him to think of her thus.

Regardless, her complete and utter disappearance still rankled. He'd lost a pretty penny on the wench and her sisters. Sobering, he watched as the two men abandoned their search for the youth and headed back down the street. He stood there puffing on his cigar, thinking on the situation.

"Claude?" he called out.

His right-hand man appeared instantly. *"Monsieur?"*

"That boy you hired recently—what was his name? Where's he from?"

"Weston Caruthers, *monsieur.* He didn't say—"

"Caruthers?"

"Oui, monsieur."

Pierre stared at Claude, thinking on the boy. What was

the connection between young Caruthers and the O'Sheas? "Did you also provide lodging for the young fellow?"

"*Oui.* For him and his wife."

Wife?

"Interesting. Very interesting indeed. Find Hugo and bring the carriage around." Pierre took a draught from his cigar and squinted at Claude through a haze of smoke. "I believe it's time we pay young Mr. Caruthers a visit, *non?*"

"Where'd he go?"

"I do no' know. He just disappeared."

"Well, at least we know now he wasn't murdered somewhere along the trace."

Quinn settled his hat firmly on his head, matching Connor's steps as they headed back toward the wharf. "Let's just hope Amelia is still with him."

Connor squinted. "Do you have reason t' think she might not be?"

"I do no' know, but remember Weston worked with me in the smithy—if you can call it work. And Mr. Caruthers went crazy as a loon after his wife died." Quinn shook his head. "I'm no' saying that I blame him. Grief is a powerful thing, but I wouldna put it past either one o' them t' put themselves before the girl."

Quinn eyed the crowded streets, the workers loading and unloading boats, the haggard men and women who sat in doorways, begging for a bit of coin to slake their thirst. "I'm going t' talk t' the men Weston was working with."

"I do no' think you should." Connor shook his head, then motioned to the indentured servants gathered on the landing next to the wagon. "Let's go back t' Wainwright's, and we'll begin our search tomorrow."

"I canna wait. Weston's on the run. No telling where he'll be by tomorrow. Go on t' Wainwright's before darkness sets in. I'll meet ya there."

"Quinn—"

"I will no' argue." Quinn's jaw jutted. "I promised Kiera I'd find her sister."

Connor sighed. "All right. But be careful."

They parted ways and Quinn approached the stevedores, but they claimed not to know Weston's name, where he lived, or anything about him. He made two trips up and down the wharf asking if anybody knew Weston or Amelia and got nowhere.

As the afternoon waned, he spotted Bloomfield walking toward his office and joined him. He motioned toward the stevedores. "Do you know who those men work for? I canna get anything out o' them."

Bloomfield glanced in their direction, then quickly looked away. "Walk with me."

Quinn fell into step beside the portly man, and soon they were lost in the crowd.

"They work for Le Bonne."

Quinn's heart stuttered. If they worked for Le Bonne, that

meant Weston probably did as well. And what of Amelia? Was she still with Weston? Was she safe? They reached Mr. Bloomfield's office, and Bloomfield motioned him inside. With his hands behind his back, the lawyer paced the length of his office, then turned. "Connor said that boy you saw was Reginald Caruthers's son, correct?"

"Yes, that's right."

"Reginald was beside himself the last time he was here, looking for his oldest son."

"You know Mr. Caruthers?"

"Very well. I manage his shipping affairs here in Natchez, much the same as I do for Breeze Hill, the Wainwrights, and several other plantation owners here and about." Bloomfield's brows drew together. "And this young man—Weston, I believe—he's run away with one of the girls Le Bonne holds papers on?"

"Yes, sir."

"Nasty business, that. Do you know how Reginald is?"

"He's no' doing well, I'm afraid. His wife passed away and he returned here, t' Natchez, t' search for his son."

"Reginald is here? How long—?"

"Yesterday, or the day before at the earliest."

"I'm surprised he hasn't sought me out." Bloomfield paced again. "That is odd. Odd indeed."

"Begging your pardon, sir, but Mr. Caruthers isna himself. His man Peterson said so himself. He's crazy with grief and blames Le Bonne for the tragedy that's befallen him and his family. All he wants is t' be reunited with his son."

"And you want to find the girl?"

"Aye. Her sister is worried."

"Of course. A word of warning: Le Bonne won't let those girls go without a fight." Bloomfield shrugged. "And as much as I hate to say it, the law is on his side."

Quinn clenched his jaw. "The law is on his side even though Kiera and her sisters never signed anything? Ya know as well as I do that Le Bonne never intended for them t' be housemaids and cooks."

"I do know that. And I'm sorry. But there's nothing I can do. The only way Le Bonne will give them up is if someone buys their papers or takes their place."

"Takes their place? As an indenture in their stead?"

"Well, yes, but Le Bonne would never agree. I suspect that in his business, the women are worth more than a man would be. And besides, what man would indenture himself for twenty-one years for three women? It would be madness."

"Indeed."

"Come, it's getting late. Let me accompany you back to Wainwright's." Mr. Bloomfield moved behind his desk, picked up a satchel, and started stuffing papers inside. "I keep a carriage at the stable around the corner."

"Thank ya, sir, but I do no' want t' be any trouble."

Bloomfield shrugged into his overcoat. "It's no trouble. I'll enjoy the company."

Before they reached the door, it flew open and a well-dressed man rushed inside. "Bloomfield. I thought I'd missed you."

"Mr. Staton. I was just about to lock up."

"I realize it's late, but if I could have a few minutes of your time? It's a matter of utmost importance." Staton threw Quinn a glance. "I'll make it worth your while."

"Well, sir, I was just about to escort Mr. O'Shea home. And I'm expected at the governor's mansion within the hour."

Quinn shook his head. "Mr. Bloomfield, please, I do no' mind the walk."

"If you're sure?"

"Very sure. I have a lot t' think about." Quinn bowed. "Good day, gentlemen."

By the time Quinn arrived at Wainwright House half an hour later, he'd had plenty of time to think through his decision. And there was no time to lose.

He went in search of his brother.

Chapter 30

QUINN FOUND CONNOR in Wainwright's study, scrawling numbers on a piece of paper, his brow furrowed in concentration.

"Since when did ya learn t' write?"

"I can't. Not much anyway." His brother looked up. "But I know my numbers. And Isabella would have my hide if I didna show an accounting o' every farthing spent on this trip."

Quinn glanced over his brother's scribbling. "I'd be surprised if she'll be able t' read that."

"She won't have t' be able to read it. I will." Connor pushed the papers aside. "Did you have any luck?"

"No. Nobody seems t' know anything about Weston or Amelia, or if they do, they are no' talking."

Quinn rubbed his chin. How could he explain to Connor something that he wasn't even sure of himself? There was nothing for it but to just spit it out.

"Are ya still interested in having me stay on, manage your interests at Magnolia Glen?"

Connor sat back. "Of course I am."

"Then here's me terms." Quinn eyed his brother. "I'll indenture myself t' ya for twenty-one years, seven years each for Kiera, Amelia, and—"

"What?" Connor shot up from the chair. "Have you gone mad—?"

"You need more indentured servants, do you no'?"

"Yes, but—"

"Then I'm offering. Twenty-one years for all three o' them. Provided we can convince Le Bonne t' sign over their papers."

"You're serious?"

"Yes."

"Indenture my own brother?" Connor shook his head. "No, I won't do it."

"Then I'll indenture myself t' Le Bonne instead."

"You'd . . ." Connor stared at him. "You'd do that?"

"Aye."

Connor sank back into the chair, looking dazed. "If— if ya do such a thing, you're going to tip your hand, and

Le Bonne will know that they're with you—with us. Is that a risk ye're willing t' take?"

"I do no' . . ." Quinn took a turn about the room, then faced his brother. "I canna let him hold this over their heads."

"And what if he refuses?"

"I do no' know."

"The lass means that much t' you, does she?"

"Aye, she does."

"So be it, then. I'll agree to your terms." A smile quirked up one corner of Connor's mouth. "On one condition. Marry the lass in exchange for her freedom—and yours."

"Marry her? Are ya daft?"

"Oh, don't give me that, Brother. Isabella gave me fair warning that this was coming. I should learn t' trust my wife's instincts."

Quinn stared at his brother.

Marriage?

To Kiera?

The thought hadn't—

He met Connor's gaze head-on, his jaw clenched tight. "We'll go t' the tavern tonight. We'll confront Le Bonne."

A knock on the door interrupted his thoughts. He turned and came face-to-face with Kiera.

"*Monsieur*, introduce us, *s'il vous plaît*." Pierre smiled, scrutinizing the girl standing behind young Caruthers.

Caruthers and the girl exchanged a glance. "My wife, Amelia."

The hovel they lived in was dark and dank, but even in the scant light from the open doorway, he could tell the girl was blonde, blue-eyed, and lovely. And if he didn't miss his guess, belonged to him instead of the young man who dared to claim she was his wife.

If she truly was.

"Charmed, *madame*." Pierre bowed. "Pierre Le Bonne at your service. Have we met before, Madame Caruthers? Or is it yet Mademoiselle Young?"

Wide-eyed silence met his question, and Pierre chuckled.

"It's Madame Caruthers, sir, and you'd do well to remember that." The young whelp squared his shoulders, his glare as intimidating as a kitten stalking a ball of twine.

Pierre threw his head back and laughed. Claude and Hugo joined in his laughter, although he doubted they knew what he found so amusing.

"*Au contraire*, my young friend. Mademoiselle Young isn't free to wed, I'm afraid, as I own her papers. So you see, you could be guilty of aiding and abetting a runaway should I choose to press charges."

"I won't let you take her." The boy sounded ferociously protective, but oh, so young.

Pierre was enjoying this immensely. "Oh, you don't have a choice. But that is neither here nor there. What I really want from you right now is information."

The boy and the girl both looked at each other, clearly

confused. Pierre looked at the girl. "Where are your sisters, *ma chère?*"

"You don't have to answer him, Amelia," the boy muttered.

Pierre suddenly lost interest in humoring the impudent pup. He snapped his fingers and Claude moved forward. The boy swung, his puny fist glancing off the man's broad chest. Claude cuffed him on the head, and the boy went reeling, slamming against the wall. The girl screamed and scrambled away, across the thin bedding that lay on the floor of the shack.

Another nod, and Claude grabbed the girl by the arm and hauled her to Pierre's side. Pierre wrapped his hand in her hair and jerked. She whimpered. Claude hauled the boy up and sat him in the chair, his knife at the young whelp's throat.

The young lovers really were no match for Claude, but Pierre had known that from the beginning.

Pity they hadn't.

With the girl dangling from his firm hold and Claude's knife at the boy's throat, Pierre twisted his fingers, tightening his hold on her golden locks, until her whimper of pain turned to a breathless sob. "Now that we all understand each other, I'll ask again. Tell me where your sisters are, *ma chère*, if you don't want to see young Master Caruthers's guts spilled all over the floor."

"Breeze Hill," she whispered.

"I see." Pierre held his anger in check. Breeze Hill. Connor O'Shea. "So who was the Irishman who arrived the same day you did, the one who helped you at the docks?"

He knew, but he wanted to hear her say it. He should

have allowed Claude to gut them all right there on the wharf. Then left them for Connor O'Shea to find.

"Quinn. Quinn O'Shea."

"Very good." Pierre twisted his hand in her hair, and she cried out.

"Leave her alone." The whelp surged against Claude's hold. The boy had more guts than Pierre had given him credit for. A thin line of blood trickled onto the knife pressed against his throat, and the girl whimpered. Yes, much braver and hardier than Pierre had anticipated. Perhaps they'd have use for him after all. If Claude didn't accidentally cut the boy's throat.

"I'm afraid that is not possible. Now, one more question. Who else was there that night?"

"I—" she licked her lips—"I don't know what you mean."

"Claude . . ."

Claude grabbed the boy by the hair and jerked his head back, exposing his throat. His eyes bulged out, and he held absolutely still.

"No, wait." The girl sobbed. "The night at the brothel? It was Quinn O'Shea, his brother. Another man—I don't know his name. I never saw him again. And . . . Mr. Wainwright."

"Wainwright? Thomas Wainwright, the plantation owner?"

"Y-yes. We—they took us to Mr. Wainwright's, and then before the night was out, they whisked us away to Breeze Hill. They said we weren't safe here."

"They were right, *ma chère*." Pierre leaned close and whispered in her ear. "You weren't safe then, and you aren't safe now."

Kiera pushed open the study door, relieved to see that Quinn and Connor had returned from whatever they'd been doing all day. Both men jerked around, looking like two boys with their hands caught in the till.

The silence was deafening.

Connor recovered first, gathered a stack of papers, and made to leave. "If you'll excuse me, I need to go check on something in one of the wagons. Quinn, come find me when you're ready to go."

Connor brushed past her. Was that a grin playing across his face? No matter. She faced Quinn, determined to get some answers. "Where have you been all day?"

"Dispersing the lumber and making purchases for the return trip home."

Kiera balled her hands into fists. Did he not know that her sister was out there somewhere, maybe in Le Bonne's clutches even now? She should have followed her instincts and searched for Amelia herself. "I see. And what of Amelia? And Weston?"

He crossed his arms. "We asked about them at every stop today, and . . . we saw Weston."

"You did?" She sucked in a breath. "Where is he? Did he say where Amelia is? What—?"

"I didna talk t' him. He took off before I could get t' him."

"He ran away?" Her heart clutched at the implication. "Do you think Amelia's still with him?"

"I do no' know. Weston was working on the wharf. I asked some questions of the men he was working with, but nobody would tell me anything. Except . . ." He searched her gaze as if he knew the news he had to tell her would be devastating.

"Except what?"

"I think he's working for Pierre Le Bonne."

"Le Bonne?" Her knees went weak. "No. He can't be. Amelia . . ."

"If he truly is working for Le Bonne, that doesna mean anything. Le Bonne has his finger in half the businesses under the hill."

"We have to find Amelia. If Le Bonne gets his hands on her, he'll—"

"Do no' worry. I—we have a plan."

"What are you going to do?" She'd hoped Mr. Caruthers had been wrong and that Amelia and Weston hadn't come to Natchez, but her hopes had been shattered with the news that Weston had been seen. And that he'd run from Quinn spoke volumes. "Please, take me with you."

"It's too risky. If Le Bonne knew you were in Natchez, all he'd have t' do would be t' produce those papers, and any magistrate around would give him leave t' take ya back."

"Quinn, she's my sister. I can't just sit here and do nothing."

"Kiera, please. Listen t' me." He grasped her by the shoulders. "We're going t' the tavern. We're going t' see Le Bonne."

Kiera gasped. "You don't think—"

"No. We have no reason t' think she's there, but Connor—" He broke off.

"What about Connor?" She placed a hand on his arm, urged him to look at her. "What is he going to do? I have a right to know. This is my sister we're talking about."

Quinn speared her with a look, his blue eyes glittering in the flickering candlelight. "He's going t' try t' buy yer papers from Le Bonne."

"Connor would—" Kiera stopped. Had she heard him correctly? "He'd do that for us?"

"Yes. He would. He might hate Charlotte for what she did, but he's not the monster ya make him out t' be. I didna want t' tell you, in case Le Bonne refuses."

Kiera pressed a hand to her mouth, finding it hard to believe.

Quinn cupped her face. "Kiera, I—"

"Horses are saddled." Connor stood in the door.

"I have t' go."

Kiera stepped back. "Be careful."

They hurried away, and she moved to the window, watched them mount, and listened until the sound of hoofbeats faded into the night. Dropping the curtain, she turned away, daring to take it all in.

If Connor succeeded in buying their papers, they'd be indentured to Breeze Hill for seven years. It wasn't what she'd dreamed of for herself and her sisters, but it was so much better than their reality.

And what of Quinn?

Would he be there, or would he leave for parts unknown as he'd planned all along?

Chapter 31

Reginald stood in the shadows outside the Blue Heron.

Somehow in the fog of his grief, he knew that Pierre Le Bonne was at the center of his troubles. He would make Le Bonne pay. He'd make him—

A commotion down the street had him shrinking deeper into the shadows. He watched as two men forced a man and a woman across the darkened street toward the wharf, practically dragging the man.

A fourth man followed along behind.

"Please, no." Even though the girl's crying grated on Reginald's nerves, somewhere in the dark recesses of his brain, he had the urge to stop whatever evil these men had planned for her—but no, he wouldn't interfere. He had one mission to fulfill.

He had to find his son and take him back home. Weston was all he had left.

"Lock them in the hold and post a watch."

Reginald froze. That voice. He approached the man. "Pierre Le Bonne?"

"Who wants to know?"

Holding on to his resolve, Reginald bowed slightly at the waist. "Reginald Caruthers. I have business with you, sir."

The Frenchman chuckled, his gaze skittering toward the four figures who had paused on the gangway. "Indeed?"

"Indeed."

"Please, would you join me?" Le Bonne motioned toward the ship. "I've long desired to make your acquaintance, Mr. Caruthers."

"No." Reginald glared at the man. He wouldn't be lured onto one of Le Bonne's ships, to be taken prisoner and con-scripted as a sailor. "This is not a social call, sir."

"It isn't?" Le Bonne inclined his head, studying him. "*Pardon.* You were saying?"

"I'm looking for my son, and I believe you might help me find him."

"And why would I do such a thing, *monsieur*?"

"I know where the Young sisters are."

"You do?" The Frenchman raised a brow. "Pray tell, who are the Young sisters and what do they have to do with me?"

"Don't play games with me, Le Bonne. Either you want

the girls back or you don't. I want my son, and you can have the women to do with as you wish."

"I see. And what makes you think you're in a position to make demands, Monsieur Caruthers?"

"If you want—"

"It just so happens that I know exactly where the girls are. I also know where your son is." Le Bonne spouted off a round of French.

One of the cutthroats shoved his captive toward them, and Reginald gasped when he saw his son, his battered face almost unrecognizable. Weston groaned and slumped to the ground, unconscious.

"Weston?" Reginald rushed forward, growling with barely suppressed rage.

Le Bonne whipped out a pistol and centered it against Reginald's chest, point-blank. Breathing heavily, Reginald held both hands aloft.

"Now, Monsieur Caruthers, it seems you have misjudged me, and I you. You thought to bargain with me on your terms, but that will never do, will it, *monsieur*? However, I am a generous man." Le Bonne tipped his head toward the girl and curled his lips, the movement more of a grimace than anything resembling a smile. "As you can see, I've recovered a third of my property. Bring me the rest, and I'll consider an exchange."

Reginald looked at his son, lying crumpled on the ground. Was this the only way to get his son back? "It's a good day's ride to—to where they are."

"*Oui*, that is true. The girl told me everything, how the O'Sheas stole my property, took them out to Breeze Hill."

"I'll bring them back. In exchange for my son. But it will take time. Two days, at least."

"You'll be wasting time. The O'Sheas are here in Natchez, and if the older girl cares anything for her sister, she's likely here as well. You should have no trouble finding out where they're staying. Bring her to me, and I might be inclined to forget about the young one."

Reginald backed away, staring at his son's still form. He had to—

Turning, he stumbled down the wharf, his thoughts churning. The Irish girl. The one called Kiera. Le Bonne would set Weston free in exchange for her.

Then they could both go home. Back to Victoria.

But no. A sob clawed at his chest.

Victoria was dead. His brother-in-law had placed her in a cold, dark grave, covered her porcelain face with dirt. Victoria would never welcome him home again. He stopped dead in his tracks, then whirled. Weston didn't know. He had to tell Weston.

Surely Le Bonne would—

They were gone. The wharf was empty, the ships in the harbor rocking gently in the night. He heard the clatter of boots on the ship, the sound of a hatch opening, the girl crying out, voices. Then nothing.

He turned back, squared his shoulders, and focused on the task at hand.

Finding Kiera Young.

And he knew just the man who could help him.

Quinn entered the Blue Heron, and the memories of the last time he'd been in the establishment assaulted him. Nothing had changed. Even the crowd looked much the same.

Rough, vicious, drunk, and disorderly as if they wallowed in the bottom of life's well and didn't know or care that they were drowning in the mire. He followed Connor to a table in a far corner. Soon a tavern wench sauntered over, her silk dress with its flounces and dainty lace oddly out of place in the crude backwater tavern. She grinned, but her saucy smile didn't reach her tired eyes.

"I'm Penelope. What'll ye have, guv'nor?"

"Information," Connor said.

Her focus shifted to his brother. "Information in this place is in short supply, luv." She set one hand on her narrow waist and shrugged. "I suggest you look elsewhere."

Connor pushed a coin toward her with his index finger. The hungry look in her eyes feasted on the money, and with a wink, she slid into an empty chair. "Well, what d'ya know? A boatload of information might have docked after all."

Quinn eyed the woman, something familiar about her. It was the dress. He'd seen it before.

On Kiera.

"Do ya know of a boy named Weston and a girl named Amelia?"

"Never heard of either of them."

She reached for the coin, but Quinn slapped his palm over it, keeping it on the table. "Two months ago, three girls were brought here t' be sold t' the highest bidder. Perhaps ya remember that."

Her attention flickered toward the balcony that ran the entire length of the left side of the tavern, but then she focused on Quinn again, her face a mask of stone. She shrugged. "I don't recall."

Quinn snorted, his gaze running over the shimmering dress again, the very dress that Kiera had worn the day she'd ordered him to keep Patrick away from Megan. "Ye're wearing one of their dresses."

Penelope tossed a lock of teased hair over her shoulder. "I didn't steal it if that's what you're implying."

"Then how did ya come by it?"

"All right, then." She pouted. "They were here. But somebody helped them escape, and their clothes were left behind."

"Escape? Ya make it sound as if they were prisoners."

She huffed. "We're all prisoners in one fashion or another, luv."

"And ya havena seen any o' them since?"

"No." She threw a glance over her shoulder, then leaned forward. "To tell ya the truth, guv'nor, I was glad them girls got out of here when they did. Especially that little 'un. She was too young to be in the likes of this place."

Connor glanced at Quinn. "Tell me, Penelope, where is Pierre Le Bonne?"

"He's usually indisposed at this hour." For the second time, she glanced toward the shadowy balcony. This time she paled. "Excuse me, guv'nor."

And with that she slipped from the chair and faded into the crowd, leaving the coin untouched in her haste.

Through narrowed eyes, Quinn squinted at the balcony, saw Le Bonne looking down at them, but he wasn't looking at the girl or at Quinn. He was staring at Connor, pure hatred in his flat black eyes.

"Miss Kiera, there's a gentleman to see you." Mrs. Butler twisted her apron in her hand. "A Mr. Caruthers. He says it's about your sister."

"Mr. Caruthers?" Kiera rushed to the parlor, found Mr. Caruthers seated near the fireplace. She paused just inside the doorway. She'd known Mr. Caruthers only a short time, but she could see that the events of recent weeks had taken their toll on the man. He looked haggard, but she could hardly blame him.

"You have news of Amelia?"

"I do." He stood. "I can take you to her."

Kiera studied him. He seemed rational enough. She worried her lip. "We should wait for Quinn and Connor to return."

"There's no time." He grabbed her arm but then let go. Stepping back, he cleared his throat. "Le Bonne—"

"Le Bonne has Amelia?" Kiera's heart stopped.

"Yes. And Weston. We must hurry."

"I'll get my cloak."

"Yes, miss."

Mr. Caruthers led her to a carriage out front, helped her up, then climbed in beside her. As the driver carried them through the dark streets of Natchez, she turned to Mr. Caruthers. "How'd you know where to find me?"

"Mr. Bloomfield."

Kiera nodded. Mr. Bloomfield was a business associate of the O'Sheas and the Wainwrights. It made sense that Mr. Caruthers would go to him. Mr. Caruthers didn't volunteer more but sat against the farthest edge of the carriage, watching the streets.

He seemed to grow more agitated by the moment, and his silence only served to increase Kiera's worry. "Where are we going? To Bloomfield's?"

His gaze lifted, speared hers.

A chill spread through her. Did he know anything about Amelia, or had he simply lied to get her out of the house? But to what end?

Too late, she realized she should have heeded her first instinct and waited for Quinn and Connor to return.

"Mr. Caruthers, do you really know where my sister is?"

"I do."

She searched his face again. Had she imagined the darkness she'd seen there? Was it just a trick of the half-moon casting shadows over his gaunt face? Her own worry, fear, and lack of sleep that put thoughts of betrayal where there were none?

The carriage hit a pothole and rocked from side to side. Kiera grabbed for a leather strap with one hand, the other gripping the edge of the seat.

Her fingers curled around something soft and furry. She spread her fingers, feeling the plush warmth of fur. Suddenly, memories of another day, another carriage ride through the streets of Natchez, her sister's chilled skin.

Her gaze ricocheted around the darkened carriage even as her heart pounded against her rib cage in a terror she'd felt only one other time.

How many men in Natchez had a lap quilt made out of luxurious fur in their carriage?

She opened her mouth to demand that the driver halt the carriage and let her out, but fear closed her throat so tight that no sound emerged.

Chapter 32

"I didna think ya knew Le Bonne."

"I didn't. At least not by name." Connor watched with hooded eyes as the man called Le Bonne descended the stairs and threaded his way through the crowded tavern.

The Frenchman hadn't died in the tornado after all. In spite of the jagged scar, this man was one and the same.

He stopped at the table, smirked. "Connor O'Shea. We meet again."

"So we do." Connor eyed the scar on Le Bonne's face. "Trophy from the tornado that killed Nolan Braxton?"

Le Bonne's lips twisted. "You might say that."

"About the scar or about how Braxton died?"

Le Bonne shrugged, motioned to the vacated seat. "May I, *messieurs?*

"It's your table."

Out of the corner of his eye, Connor spotted two men trailing Le Bonne, positioning themselves close to the table, facing the crowded tavern. Le Bonne lifted his cigar to his mouth and puffed, his gaze raking over Connor, then shifting to Quinn. "I don't believe we've met. Officially, that is. I am Pierre Le Bonne, owner of this fine establishment, among other ventures."

"Quinn. O'Shea." Quinn's voice could have cracked steel.

Le Bonne flicked ashes off his cigar. "I should have known you were brothers. You both threatened to knife me the first time I saw you. And oddly enough, both incidents were over women. Beautiful women, at that." He speared Connor with a look. "And how is your lovely wife, *monsieur?*"

"Leave my wife out of this," Connor growled.

"*Pardon.* I see my poor attempt at making small talk has not been well received." Le Bonne stubbed out his cigar. "So to what do I owe this call?"

Connor glared at Le Bonne. "You own papers of three girls by the last name of Young. I'd like to buy their indentures."

"Oh, I have papers on any number of girls. You can take your pick, *monsieur.*"

"Just those three will do."

"But, sir—" Le Bonne spread his hands, looking amused— "I am no longer in possession of the three of which you speak. Someone—" his dark gaze swung to Quinn—"spirited them away the first night they were here. But I am sure you know this already, *non*? Should you know of their whereabouts, I would greatly appreciate the return of my property."

Quinn looked like he was about to jump over the table and tackle Le Bonne on the spot. Connor sent him a warning look. "I do know where they are, but I'm not willing to give them up. Sell me their papers, and you won't have to worry about them."

A seedy-looking character entered the tavern, glanced around, and then hurried to Le Bonne's side. The tavern owner addressed the man. "It is done?"

"*Oui, monsieur.*"

"*Merci*, François. You may go." An enigmatic smile on his face, Le Bonne leaned back in his chair and eyed Connor. "And what if I say no?"

"Then our business here is done." Connor went to stand but paused when Le Bonne waved them back down.

"Please, do not be so hasty, *monsieur*. I did not say that I would decline your offer. As a matter of fact, it pleases me to accept. However, it will cost you triple the normal fare. And since I'm sure you didn't bring enough coins to redeem the *filles* tonight, shall we meet here again tomorrow to complete the transaction?"

"And you'll have their papers?"

"Of course, *monsieur*. What do you take me for? A common thief?"

"We'll be here." Connor stood, motioning for Quinn to follow.

Le Bonne's henchmen trailed them toward the door. As they exited the building, Connor led Quinn down one alley, cut across another, turned back, and then ducked into the shadows behind a stack of crates.

Quinn glanced toward the wharf. "Well, that seemed easy enough."

"Too easy." After a few moments, when no one appeared, Connor eased out and headed down the darkened street toward Wainwright's. There was nothing else they could do tonight. But tomorrow, Charlotte's sisters would be his indentured servants.

Connor shook his head, wondering how that had happened. Never in a million years—

"Listen." Quinn grabbed his arm, pulling him to a halt.

The sound of pounding hooves reached him; then a horse rounded the bend and swept toward them. They ducked into the shadows of the nearest building. The horse and rider raced past, down the narrow street that ran along the wharf, and came to a halt in front of Bloomfield's small office tucked between two warehouses.

"Was that Wainwright?" Quinn asked.

"Maybe. I didn't get a good look at him, but the horse looked familiar."

Quinn stepped out into the street, peered through the darkness. "That's strange. There's a light on in Bloomfield's office. He said he was going home hours ago."

They both sprinted toward the lawyer's office.

The carriage came to a stop, and Kiera clutched the lap robe with numb fingers. Without a word, Mr. Caruthers exited the carriage.

The scream that bubbled up when the same hulking cutthroat appeared who had ushered Kiera and her sisters into the Blue Heron months ago died a quick death when he grabbed her arm and jerked her out of the carriage.

As Claude dragged her down the gangway toward a derelict vessel, she found her voice and turned on Caruthers. "You tricked me. Do you even know where my sister is?"

"I'm sorry, miss, but I didn't have a choice." Mr. Caruthers had the grace to look contrite. "Weston is all I have left and—"

"Ah, but, Monsieur Caruthers, one always has a choice, does he not?"

Kiera whirled, came face-to-face with Pierre Le Bonne. "Where is my sister?"

"All in good time, *ma chère*." Le Bonne's gaze raked over her, a sneer lifting one corner of his mouth. "So you thought you could get the best of me, *non*? Well, we will see who wins this battle of wits."

"You'll never get your hands on Megan. She's safe from the likes of you."

"Don't be so sure about that. I'm aware she's tucked away at Breeze Hill, but she can't stay there forever. Eventually the girl will return to Natchez for one reason or another, and I'll be waiting."

A cold feeling hollowed Kiera's insides. Le Bonne knew where Megan was. She wanted to scream, to cry, to beg for mercy, but she knew it would do no good. Men like Pierre Le Bonne didn't know how to show mercy. They only knew how to inflict pain and suffering on others.

"Or I might just go to the magistrates and present my papers. I do have legal ownership of the three of you, after all." He shrugged. "For now."

"What—what does that mean?" Had Connor contacted Le Bonne already?

"Your friends the O'Sheas paid me a visit tonight. Of course I wasn't inclined to sell the papers, but it amused me to agree." He chuckled. "Especially since you and Mr. Caruthers were already en route."

Mr. Caruthers stepped forward. "You have what you wanted, Le Bonne. Now give me my son."

"*Monsieur*, did you really think you could bargain with Pierre Le Bonne?" He shook his head. "You are a bigger fool than I gave you credit for."

"You can't do this!" Caruthers exclaimed. "You've already taken Reggie from me. My wife died because of you, and now you intend to take Weston. I—I won't let you."

"You won't let me?" Pierre laughed. "Truly, *monsieur*, this time you don't have a choice in the matter."

With a roar of rage and little regard for the two giants flanking Le Bonne, Mr. Caruthers clawed for the pistol at his waist. As his trembling fingers closed around the stock and lifted his firearm, a roar exploded next to Kiera's ear. She screamed as Mr. Caruthers fell to the deck, then stared in horror as a splotch of red seeped through his coat onto the planks.

Le Bonne motioned Claude forward. "Throw him overboard. The current will take care of him."

"And the *fille*?"

"She wants to see her sister, *non*?" Le Bonne shrugged. "Oblige her, *oui*?"

Quinn and Connor reached Bloomfield's office just as William threw himself off his mount and bounded up the stairs. Inside, the lawyer was slumped at his desk, a bloody gash on his forehead.

"Good heavens, Bloomfield, what happened?" William unknotted his neckerchief and leaned over the lawyer, pressing the cloth against the wound. "It finally happened, didn't it? The cutthroats who ply Natchez Under-the-Hill finally robbed you blind, didn't they? It's a wonder they didn't kill you and feed you to the fishes."

"It wasn't thieves and robbers this time. It was someone looking for information." Bloomfield winced, his gaze landing on Quinn. "That's why I sent for you."

"What do you mean, sir?" Fear snaked through Quinn. "You sent for me?"

William glanced at Quinn. "You and Connor were already gone when I received the message. I came as fast as I could, hoping I'd meet you on the way."

"Who did this?" Quinn's jaw clenched tight.

"Caruthers."

"Reginald Caruthers?" William sounded stunned. "Why in heaven's name would he attack you?"

"I was late closing up. Quinn knows. He was here. Mr. Staton had business and by the time he left, it had grown dark. I was just about to lock up when Caruthers showed. I should have known something was wrong, but I was so glad to see him in clean clothes, shaved, and in his right mind that I didn't heed the warning bells clanging in my head."

"What warnings?" Quinn's heart pounded. "About Kiera?"

"Yes. And her sister." Bloomfield's head jerked up, and he glanced around. "The girl? Miss Young? Where is she?"

"Kiera? She's here in Natchez. At Wainwright House."

"Are you sure? When Caruthers told me he'd found Weston and Amelia, and that he needed to find her sister so that the two of them could convince the youngsters all was forgiven if they'd just return home, I told him where Miss Young was. But when I pressed him, he became so agitated that he shoved me out of the way and took off."

"It's a wonder he didn't kill you."

"Aye." Bloomfield touched the gash on his head. "But I don't think he really meant to hurt me. I don't even know if he realized I'd hit my head on the fireplace. He was long gone by the time I came to."

Quinn raked a hand through his hair. Had Caruthers gone after Kiera? He grabbed Wainwright. "Is she still at yer house? Did Caruthers go after her?"

William frowned and shook his head. "I don't know. I had just returned from the warehouse and hadn't even had time to stable my horse when I received Bloomfield's message. I came right away—"

"I need to borrow your horse."

"Certainly." William waved him away. "And get back here as fast as you can with news."

Quinn rushed out the door, mounted, and was gone before William could say another word. As he raced through the night, he prayed that Kiera was safe and sound at Wainwright House.

He was drowning.

Sputtering, Reginald clawed at the wet sand, pulled himself a few inches out of the water. He slumped on the shore, his shoulder on fire. He reached up, touched his arm, and his hand came away wet and sticky. Blood? What—?

Suddenly it all came rushing back. Le Bonne. His henchman. The failed attempt to trade the girl for Weston.

Getting shot.

Le Bonne had bested him. For now.

He crawled up the embankment, then collapsed in a tangle of weeds. He would make Le Bonne pay, and he would get Weston back. He reached for his pistol—

Gone.

He remembered trying to fire at Le Bonne. In his rage, he'd taken chances. But now, in spite of his pain, or maybe because of it, his mind was clearer than it had been in days.

He'd known the man was black-hearted. He'd thought he could bargain with Le Bonne, deal with him man-to-man, exchange Weston for the girls, shake the dust of Natchez off his feet, go back home, and forget about the girls, the O'Sheas, Le Bonne—all of them. But Le Bonne's word was as perfidious and shiftless as the sand along the river.

Now he realized Le Bonne had never intended to release Weston. He'd been toying with Reginald from the beginning.

Was there nothing else to be done? No hope for his son? *Weston.*

I failed you, Son. I failed Reggie, I failed Victoria, and I've failed you. I have nothing left to live for. I should have died in the river.

The ground shook, and he lifted his head. A rider raced down the street that ran parallel to the wharf, passed him, and disappeared up the steep incline that led to the bluff above. He blinked, his gaze landing on the light spilling out of a familiar building.

Bloomfield.

There was one more chance to free Weston. He'd throw himself on the mercy of Bloomfield and the O'Sheas for that chance.

He dug his fingers into the damp sand and began to crawl.

Kiera was gone.

Quinn's heart slammed against his chest when Mrs. Butler told him how Caruthers had shown up and Kiera had gone with him without question. He mounted William's horse and raced back across town, the short distance seeming to take forever.

The horse's hooves pounded on the cobblestones, the staccato beat keeping time with his runaway heart. He didn't even know where he raced to, other than back to Bloomfield's. Then what?

Where would they begin to look?

What was Caruthers's plan? If he even had a plan. Had he been acting on his own or on Le Bonne's orders? What if Le Bonne had Kiera and Amelia even now? If so, it made no sense that he'd agreed to sell their papers after first declining the offer.

Quinn replayed every piece of the conversation with Le Bonne, recalled the messenger—and suddenly everything became clear. The messenger had brought news of Kiera. He'd decided to sell their papers just to toy with Quinn and Connor.

Le Bonne never intended to give them up.

The horse careened down the hill toward the wharf, the light from Bloomfield's office like a beacon in the night.

The only light in a night that stretched bleak and dark before him.

Chapter 33

KIERA'S SLIPPERS BECAME TANGLED in the rope ladder and she almost lost her hold. Shaking, she managed to reach the bottom without breaking her neck. A faint sliver of moonlight shone through the heavy metal grating and kept the space from complete and utter darkness.

Claude slammed the hatch shut and shot the bolt, not even bothering to pull the rope ladder out. She shuddered, knowing it was useless to ascend the ladder again and attempt to push the heavy grate open.

"Kiera?"

The whimper tore at her, and she scrambled across the damp, dark hold toward the gut-wrenching sound, her hands outstretched until they touched fabric. Then Amelia's arms were around her, Amelia trembling and sobbing uncontrollably against her.

"Shh. Shh. Hush, darling. I'm here—"

"I heard shots—"

Kiera's stomach roiled, and she pushed back the urge to retch. "Mr. Caruthers . . . They shot him, then—then threw him in the river."

"Weston's father is—is dead?" Amelia gasped. "This is all my fault. I'm sorry. I—I shouldn't have—"

"Hush, dearest." Kiera smoothed her sister's hair back, crooning into her ear. "It's all right. I'm here. Everything will be fine."

Amelia pulled away and shook her head, the slatted grating offering scant light in the dark space. Even as Kiera's eyes adjusted to the darkness, she could see the outlines of platforms not much bigger than coffins nailed wall-to-wall, end-to-end.

She'd hoped to never set foot on a coffin ship again. She and her sisters had traveled in second class, but the plight of those in steerage hadn't escaped her notice. Even now she could smell the stench of unwashed bodies, refuse, and waste. Her stomach rebelled for a totally different reason, and once again she squelched the feeling and concentrated on her sister.

"Where's Weston?"

Amelia wrapped her cold fingers around Kiera's and pulled her to a corner berth. "Here. That—that monster beat him when he tried to protect me. Then when Mr. Caruthers tried to free us, he almost kill—killed him. He's been in and out of consciousness ever since." Amelia cradled Weston's head in her lap, stroking his cheek. "I don't want him to die."

"Of course you don't, dearest."

Kiera wanted to ask where they'd been the last week and a half, whether they'd married, but now wasn't the time. Her questions could wait.

Amelia laid her head on Kiera's shoulder. "What's going to happen to us?"

Kiera leaned in to her sister. "I don't know. Let's just pray that Quinn will find us before . . ."

She hesitated, blinking back the tears that pricked her eyes. Before what? Before Le Bonne shipped them off to another city, another tavern, another cruel master?

What would be worse: death at his hands or bondage for the rest of their lives? As they huddled together awaiting their fate, she focused on the shaft of moonlight shining through the square high above.

"The Lord is my light and my salvation; whom shall I fear? the Lord is the strength of my life; of whom shall I be afraid?"

Quinn slammed into Bloomfield's office and William, Connor, and Bloomfield looked up. He reached for his hat, then realized it was gone. Without even realizing, he'd lost it somewhere along the way.

"She's gone. Caruthers took her."

"At Le Bonne's behest?" Connor asked, having come to the same conclusion.

"Aye, more than likely." Quinn rammed his fingers through his hair, glaring at everyone and at no one in particular. The blackguard had known it was only a matter of hours, minutes even, before they would arrive back at Wainwright House and discover that Kiera was missing.

"Even now he could have her at the Blue Heron," William suggested.

"No, he wouldna take her there." Quinn shook his head. "He knows that would be the first place we'd go. There's no need t' look there."

But look he would. He'd tear this town apart piece by piece to find her, but even then, there was no guarantee—

Quinn turned at a noise on the steps, whipped out his pistol, and leveled it at the door in one fluid movement. William and Connor quickly followed suit. Caruthers, drenched and muddy, slumped against the doorframe.

An all-consuming rage swept over Quinn, and in three strides, he crossed the room, grabbed Caruthers by the front of his coat, and slammed the man against the wall. Caruthers groaned and wilted under the force of his assault. But Quinn held him up with one hand, the pistol pressed against his temple with the other.

"Where is she?" he snarled. "Tell me what ya've done with Kiera, or I'll blow yer head off."

"Quinn. Don't." Connor's voice reached him, a calm in the storm that threatened to consume him. "He's not worth it."

Quinn breathed in through his nose, then out. In again. Out. He clenched his teeth, then shoved Caruthers away from him.

"As long as he tells me what I want to know."

"Reginald, why are you here?" Bloomfield stood, looking like the effort took all his strength. "Have you come to finish me off, or did you return expecting to find me dead?"

Caruthers lifted his head, his gaze sweeping over Bloomfield's bruised and bloody face; then his shoulders slumped. "I—I don't know what I was thinking. I haven't been thinking, not since my wife died. I've been in a daze. . . ." He shook his head. "I thought I could bargain with Le Bonne, get Weston back, but—"

"Le Bonne has Weston? And Amelia and Kiera as well?" Quinn's heart thudded against his chest.

"Yes. He has all of them."

"Where?"

"A ship." Caruthers staggered toward Quinn, a feverish glint in his eyes. "You have to help me get Weston back."

"Is yer son all ya can think about?" Quinn grabbed the man again. "What about Kiera and Amelia? Do ya not care what happens t' them?"

"Yes. Yes, of course." Caruthers frowned, then nodded as if trying to wrap his brain around the fact that the girls were in as much danger as his son. "I'll—I'll take you to the ship."

"I think ya've done enough," Quinn growled through clenched teeth. "Just tell us the name o' the ship."

"I don't know the name—I never saw it. But I'll know the vessel when I see it."

Caruthers slumped against Bloomfield. Bloomfield's hand came away bloody, and for the first time, Quinn noticed the hole in Caruthers's shirt, the front stained with streaks of fresh blood.

"Reginald, what is this?"

"Le Bonne's man shot me. I suppose they thought I was dead, or they'd have finished the job before they threw me in the river."

"William, see to his wound." Bloomfield held a lantern high and motioned William over. "He'll do us no good if he bleeds to death."

As William probed Caruthers's shoulder, Quinn barely held his simmering rage in check. He paced to the open door and back, glaring at Caruthers. "How did ya convince Kiera t' go with ya?"

Caruthers's gaze skittered away. "Le Bonne forced me to—to find her. He said he'd let Weston go if I brought her to him."

Of all the—

"Ya traded her life for his?"

"Le Bonne played me for a fool—"

"This is getting us nowhere," Connor interjected. "William, how bad is he?"

"The ball went straight through." William bound up the wound. "He'll live."

"Good." Connor grabbed Caruthers and propelled him

toward the door. "Take us to the ship, or Le Bonne will be the least of your worries."

Even in Caruthers's half-crazed, half-dazed state, he was as good as his word and was able to point out the ship. Or at least Quinn hoped it was the right one.

Quinn crouched behind a stack of crates, staring at the narrow gangway. There was only one way on or off the ship. If they got trapped on board, they'd have to fight their way off.

But that's what he'd come for. To fight for Kiera. To rescue her and claim her as his own. Because he wasn't about to let her slip through his fingers now.

He glanced behind him, saw the silhouettes of Connor, William, and Caruthers in the shadows. Bloomfield was in no shape to fight, so he had barricaded himself in his office waiting for their return. Four against who knew how many. Three, given the fact that they couldn't depend on Caruthers's loyalty, never mind his injury.

The ship rode low in the water, even listing to the side a bit. It didn't look the least bit seaworthy, and Le Bonne had secreted Kiera and Amelia away on this floating coffin? Did he also plan to send them out to sea in something that was likely to capsize any day?

"*Pathos* . . ." William grunted as he read the name of the ship or what could be seen in the dark. "Not exactly comforting, eh?"

Quinn crouched, prepared to run along the gangway, when Connor grabbed him by the arm. "Wait."

Ducking back down, Quinn spotted a man striding along the deck. A hulking form materialized out of the shadows and, after a brief exchange, left. The second man remained on guard.

Quinn's gaze met and held Connor's. The changing of the guard had come at an opportune time. Otherwise, they would have walked right into a trap. That Le Bonne had posted a guard gave credence to the idea that Caruthers had led them to the right ship. Quinn considered their options. Mounting a direct attack from the gangway was fruitless. He eyed the myriad of small boats, rafts, and flatboats tied along the wharf. He turned to the others. "I can get on board and find Weston and the girls, but I'll need a diversion t' get them off."

"I can handle that." William nodded.

"What do ya have in mind?" Quinn asked.

"I'll figure something out."

Quinn glanced at Caruthers. "Caruthers, stay here."

Caruthers shook his head. "You'll need help. They beat Weston—"

"Then I'll go with him," Connor said.

"William, we'll need some time," Quinn whispered. "Watch for a raft, a log, something unusual to float past, then wait ten minutes t' give us time t' find them."

William clasped his arm. "Godspeed, my friend."

Quinn and Connor made their way upriver from the ship, located a small rowboat, and slipped it into the water, staying low in the bow.

Once they reached the ship, it was no easy task to climb aboard, but finally they were on and the current carried the boat past, the signal he'd told William to watch for.

Now to find Kiera, Amelia, and Weston.

Kiera startled awake.

Listening, she tried to figure out what had roused her but heard nothing. Perhaps one of the sailors had dropped something on deck.

Her arm tingled. She'd dozed, Amelia still cradled against her. Easing her sister's sleeping form down beside Weston, she tried to rub the feeling back into her arm.

Then she heard it again. Metal against metal. Directly overhead. Her gaze shot to the grate. The hatch creaked open, slowly, the scraping sending panic winding through her stomach. Fully open, the small square revealed the silhouettes of two men leaning in the opening.

She shrank back as one of them clambered down the ladder, the ropes doing a macabre dance under his weight. Her hands curled into fists until her nails bit into her palms. She had nothing to fight with, nothing to protect herself, Amelia, or Weston.

The man reached the bottom, his boots landing with a thud against the rough timbers. Crouching, he turned, searching the shadows. "Kiera?"

A sob broke free as her name fell from Quinn's lips. She stood on shaky legs, rushed toward him, and fell into his embrace, her arms wrapped around his waist as if she'd never let go. "Quinn? You came for me. How—?"

"There's no time to explain." His hands cupped her face, his blue eyes glittering in the faint overhead light. "We've got to hurry. Where's Amelia and Weston?"

"Here."

"Quinn, hurry, man!" Connor whispered from above.

Connor? Connor had come to their rescue?

"Kiera?" Amelia sat up, sounding frightened.

"Shh." Quinn crossed to where Amelia and Weston were. "It's me. And Connor. We've come t' take ya out o' here."

"Weston's unconscious." Amelia's voice broke. "He can't climb—"

"Then I'll carry him." Quinn led them to the rickety rope ladder. He pulled Amelia forward. "You first. Go. Hurry."

"I can't. The ropes—"

"You can. Kiera and I will hold the ladder steady. Now climb."

"Do it, Amelia," Kiera commanded, injecting as much steel into her tone as she could muster. "Now. And be quiet about it."

Stifling a sob, Amelia did as she was told. As soon as she reached the top, Connor plucked her off the ropes.

Quinn motioned for Kiera. "You next."

"No. You'll need me to hold the ladder while you get Weston to the top."

"Kiera—"

"There's no other way."

"She's right," Connor called down. "Bring the boy up first."

Quinn hurried to the corner, hoisted Weston over his shoulder, and headed toward the ladder. As he climbed, Kiera weighted the swaying ladder as best she could. She breathed a sigh of relief when Quinn reached the top and Connor took the lad's limp form from him.

Quinn held out a hand for her. As she reached for the first rung, she heard shouts and pounding steps on the upper deck. Quinn hissed at Connor, "Shut the hatch and get out o' sight! Get Amelia and Weston off the ship if ya can."

Connor hesitated only a moment, slammed the hatch shut; then he was gone. Quinn hastened down the ladder, his boots hitting the planking with a thud. Pushing Kiera toward the darkest corner of the hold, he drew his pistol, light reflecting off the polished iron.

"Can ya shoot?"

Kiera nodded. "If I must."

"Fire only if ya have t'. We do no' want t' sound the alarm."

He palmed his knife and crouched in front of her, ready to defend her with his life.

The silence between them screamed as they waited. The running steps slowed; then the metal grate was thrown back to land with a crash against the deck.

"You down there, gel?"

Quinn shook his head, signaling her to keep silent.

"Iffen one o' ya don't answer, I'm comin' down."

"We're here." Kiera hid the pistol in her skirts and pushed

in front of Quinn. He grabbed for her, but she dodged him and moved into the small sliver of light. "Please, sir, could we have some food and water, some blankets? My sister's cold—"

"Sorry, miss. 'Tis not allowed. Boss's orders." And with that he slammed the grate shut and shoved the latch in place with a foreboding click.

Chapter 34

QUINN LISTENED as the sailor's footfalls faded, the silence broken only by the creak of the boat as it rocked against the current.

"I'm sorry," Kiera whispered, her voice sounding strained.

Easing out from the shadows, he focused on Kiera, trying to see her features, her eyes, her very thoughts. The faint light from above illuminated her shadowy form, but little else. "For what, lass?"

"For letting him know I was here. Because you wanted him to come down here, didn't you? So you could overpower him, and—and get us out of here."

"The thought occurred t' me." Quinn tilted her chin up

and leaned closer, catching a brief glimpse of tears shimmering in her eyes.

"I suppose fighting it out with him would have been better than—" her voice broke, and she motioned toward the bolted hatch—"than this."

"Maybe. Maybe not. But we're alive." He searched her face again. "And I intend t' stay that way. All right?"

She nodded, and he kissed her forehead. "Good girl."

Reluctantly he released her and made a turn about the space. He'd spent three months in accommodations much like these, and he'd learned to find his way around in the semidark.

Kiera sat on one of the berths. "What if they didn't make it?"

"They made it." He grasped a timber on one of the berths and pulled. The post groaned but didn't give. "If they'd been caught, that sailor would've already returned t' see if we were still locked in."

"I hadn't thought of that." The relief in her voice was palpable.

Quinn combed the space from one end to the other before giving up his search for something, anything, to get them out of the hold. They were trapped as sure as rain back home in Ireland.

Kiera's dress rustled, and he caught a glimpse of her rubbing her hands on her arms, her thin shawl no barrier against the chill. He removed his coat, sat down beside her, and wrapped it around her, holding her close.

She leaned against him, and he rested his chin on the top of her head, heart pounding at her nearness and the thought of what was to become of her. He'd give anything to get her out of this mess, but he had nothing to bargain with. Except his life. For hers.

And there was no reason for Le Bónne to bargain since he held all the cards.

"How'd you find us?"

"Caruthers—"

"He's alive?" Incredulity laced her tone. She lifted her head to stare at him, her face mere inches away. "But they shot him and—and threw him in the river."

"Yes. The bullet went right through, and he managed t' get t' shore after he was thrown overboard. He found us at Bloomfield's." He tightened his hold on her. "If he hadna had a change of heart, we wouldna have known where t' look."

"I prayed that you'd come." A sheen of tears glittered in her eyes. "But now I'm afraid . . ."

"Afraid o' what?"

She reached out with trembling hands and traced her fingertips over his lips. Quinn sucked in a breath at her feather-light touch. "When Le Bonne discovers you here instead of Amelia and Weston, he'll kill you."

Quinn tucked a strand of hair behind her ear. "He might. But not if . . ."

"Not if what?"

Quinn smiled. "Nothing."

There was no need to tell her that he would give his life

for hers. Much as Jacob had done for Rachel, he'd indenture himself to Le Bonne for seven years, ten, twenty—forever—if that's what it took to gain her freedom.

"Quinn, I'm scared."

"Shh." He gathered her close, covered her mouth with his, savoring the sweetness of her lips. She wrapped her arms around him and returned his kiss, their hunger for each other fueled by their desperate circumstances.

His thumb grazed along her jaw, and in the few moments they had, he let himself dream a new dream, an adventure that he never thought he wanted.

The adventure of hearth and home, Kiera, and a horde of beautiful blonde, blue-eyed girls that looked just like her, sturdy boys to work alongside him at the forge, in the fields, or in the woods with their uncle if they so desired.

And if they got out of this alive, they could have that future back at Breeze Hill and Magnolia Glen. The future he saw was so bright, it hurt his eyes just thinking about it. He drew back, opened his eyes, and looked at Kiera, knowing he'd come home.

"Kiera, I—"

A blast ripped through the ship, and it jerked violently against its moorings. Grabbing Kiera, Quinn crouched down as the boat shuddered from another discharge. A flash of light and shouts drew his attention to the grate overhead. He caught a whiff of gunpowder and smoke, and fear clutched his chest. He could see the mainmast clear as day, backlit against—

He put Kiera away from him. "Stay here."

"What is it?" Her voice trembled.

"I do no' know." He scrambled up the rope ladder. Pressing his head against the grate, he peered up and out.

What he saw caused his blood to run cold.

The ship was on fire. Even as he watched, another explosion, more deafening than the previous two, shot flames skyward. From this angle, he could barely see the uppermost corner of the poop deck and the flames that already licked at it. The shouts grew more intense as the few sailors on board rushed to fight the blaze.

"What's wrong? What's happening?"

"The ship's on fire."

Kiera stared at him in horror, but there was nothing he could do. Nothing. Not one thing he could do to get them out of here. The interior of the ship, dry as kindling, would go up in flames in a matter of minutes, and without any hope of escape, they would be roasted alive inside the hold.

A fourth blast rocked the boat, followed by an ominous crack. The mizzenmast teetered, straining at the ratlines lashed against it. Suddenly the lines gave way and the mast twisted, started a slow descent, much like a felled tree in the forest.

Quinn let go of the rope ladder and dropped to the deck, grabbed Kiera and shoved her under the nearest berth, tucking himself in beside her. She screamed when the beam, sails and rigging still lashed in place, crashed through the decking to slam with a shuddering blow against the flooring below. The boat shook from the impact, the massive timber coming to rest inches from his head, a gaping hole through the decking.

He grabbed Kiera and pushed her toward the beam. "Come on. Climb."

Hand over hand, they scaled the beam, using the rigging for handholds. Tears streaked down Kiera's face, but she didn't make a sound. Quinn reached the top, swung himself over the edge, and plucked her out of the hold.

Another massive explosion ripped through the other end of the ship, blowing debris into the sky. With a mighty shudder and a heave, the vessel lurched sideways, turning into the current. The ship swung in an arc, the current grabbing the stern.

Quinn pressed Kiera against the broken mast and wrapped his arms around her and the beam. "Hold on, lass."

She buried her head against his chest. "What's happening?"

"The stern of the ship ripped free of its moorings," Quinn ground out through clenched teeth. "If the other end gets loose, we're in for a wild ride down the Mississippi."

"And if it doesn't?"

"Then we're in for worse."

Moments later, the vessel slammed into something with bone-jarring intensity, then with another ferocious jerk, ripped free and spun like a top into the middle of the mighty Mississippi.

Kiera didn't dare look back as Quinn grabbed her hand and pulled her toward the opposite end of the ship, away from the explosions and the fire. But she could hear the crackling of the flames, smell the smoke, and feel the heat as the craft dipped and danced on the river.

Quinn hurried along the main deck toward the bow of the ship, as far from the fire as they could get. Thankfully, the dizzying spin slowed as the vessel settled into the current near the middle of the river.

Her relief was short-lived as the crackle of fire licking at well-aged timbers became more persistent. Shouts from the wharf filled the air, growing distant as the burning ship floated downriver. It seemed as if Le Bonne and his henchmen had abandoned the vessel and them to their fate.

"Come on. There's a longboat." Quinn headed toward the boat, wrestled with the ropes that held it in place.

"Mr. O'Shea, I believe you have something that belongs to me."

Kiera gasped, whirled to see Pierre Le Bonne standing on the forecastle deck staring down at them.

Before she could move, Quinn shoved her behind him, lifted his pistol, and pulled back the hammer. "Stay back."

"So we are at a stalemate." Le Bonne leveled his pistol at Quinn. "You have one shot, so you cannot win."

"Maybe no', but I'll take ya with me."

"Perhaps. Claude?" His henchman materialized out of the shadows, pistol drawn and pointed toward Quinn. The fire dancing behind the hulking giant of a man made him even more sinister than usual. "Two against one. It seems the odds are in my favor. I'll feed you to the fishes, and then I will row ashore with Mademoiselle Young."

Claude circled around behind them. As if from a distance, Kiera watched the scene unfold. There was no way Quinn could kill them both and come away unscathed.

He kept her firmly anchored behind him with his left arm, and she racked her brain for some way to help, some way to even the odds for him, for both of them.

Le Bonne took a step down from the forecastle deck. "Truly, *mademoiselle*, you and your sisters have been more trouble than you're worth. But then a rare jewel is worth a bit of blood, sweat, and tears, no?"

The ship listed as the fire consumed the other end and it started a slow turn toward shore. Suddenly the bow slammed into something, spun, throwing Kiera to the deck. Claude rushed Quinn, and Kiera screamed. Quinn pulled the trigger, stopping the big man in his tracks. He fell dead on the deck.

Without even a glance of regard for his fallen comrade, Le Bonne smiled. "Checkmate. As I said, you had only one shot, and now you have none. I win."

Le Bonne lifted his pistol, took aim.

"Are you sure about that, Monsieur Le Bonne?"

The ominous click of another pistol broke the silence as Mr. Caruthers stepped out of the shadows, clutching a packet of papers in one hand, a pistol trained unerringly on Pierre Le Bonne's chest.

Le Bonne looked like he'd seen a ghost but recovered

quickly. "Mr. Caruthers, I see you survived to fight another day. Well done, *monsieur*."

"I have proof here that you forced my oldest son to sign on to one of your ships." He shook the oilcloth-wrapped packet. "Where is he?"

"Monsieur Caruthers, your son signed those papers of his own free will."

"That is a lie." Caruthers staggered forward, the listing ship and loss of blood making him weave like a drunkard. "The signature on these documents is no more my son's than a washerwoman's."

Le Bonne shifted his pistol off Quinn, aimed point-blank at Caruthers, and pulled the trigger. The ball struck Caruthers in the chest but he held his ground, eyes blazing with rage.

With an aim that was steady and true, he shot Le Bonne where he stood. Le Bonne tumbled down the stairs and landed at Kiera's feet.

Caruthers's pistol dropped to the deck with a thud, and he fell, still clutching the packet of papers. "O'Shea?"

Quinn held Kiera away from him and knelt next to the plantation owner. Caruthers clasped Quinn's hands against the packet. "It's all here. Reggie's forged papers, Weston's, the Young sisters, and more. Take it. Bloomfield will know what to do." His face screwed up into a grimace; then with obvious effort he continued. "Tell Weston that I tried to make everything right, that I died honorably."

Quinn reached for Mr. Caruthers's crumpled form. "I'll get ya t' shore—"

"No . . . no. It's too late. Leave me be." The man batted a feeble hand, pushing Quinn away. "Tell him?"

"I'll tell him."

"I'm sorry . . . miss. I hope—" Mr. Caruthers drew a shuddering breath—"forgive . . . me."

Tears stung Kiera's eyes. In spite of the hurt Mr. Caruthers had caused, he'd saved her life and Quinn's. She knelt beside him and took his hand. "It's not my forgiveness you need to seek, sir. It's the heavenly Father's. I pray you've made everything right with Him."

"I—yes. God's forgiveness." He struggled to get the words out. "Forgive me, heavenly Father, for I have sinned—" His words trailed off, but eyes fixed skyward, his lips continued to move. Finally, he took his last breath and lay still.

Kiera's heart seized tight in her chest, hoping and praying that it was enough.

The fire raged on, consuming the ship.

Quinn tucked the packet of papers ensuring Kiera's freedom inside his shirt and eyed the flames lapping hungrily at the longboat that was no longer of any use to them.

"We have t' go. Now." He reached for Kiera, dragging her to her feet. "There's nothing more we can do for him."

She nodded. Quinn pulled her away, around Le Bonne's inert form and up the stairs toward the forecastle deck.

A bend in the river had the bow of the blazing ship plowing straight toward the shoreline. When it hit shallow water, they would have one chance to jump for it.

He reached the railing, then turned, eyeing the rear of the ship, the mainmast leaning drunkenly to one side, flames licking at the rigging. The poop deck was no more. Even as he watched, the navigation room and the mate's quarters collapsed in a rain of fire and debris. It was only a matter of minutes before the fire would eat through the hull and the ship would start to take on water, then capsize.

He snagged an arm around Kiera's waist, cupped her jaw with his hand, and lifted her face to his. His heart ached at the terror shimmering in her eyes.

"Kiera, do ya trust me?"

Her wide-eyed gaze, haunted, searched his. "Yes."

The ship jerked to a violent standstill as the bow scraped against a submerged sandbar, the force of the impact sending the compromised mast crashing against the main deck. The boat shuddered upon impact, flames and sparks shooting upward, lighting the sky with a fiery display.

For the space of a heartbeat, the doomed vessel quivered in stillness, lodged against the sand. Then the current caught the stern yet again and the ship began its last pirouette.

Quinn calculated the distance to shore, pulled Kiera against him and buried his face in her hair. He whispered, "I love you."

With that, he swept her into his arms, tossed her overboard, and jumped in after her.

Flailing both arms in a vain attempt to slow his descent toward the river, Quinn landed with a splash, his first thought to find Kiera in the murky water.

He grabbed her, even as they went down, down, holding her tight. His feet hit the bottom and he pushed himself off.

They popped to the surface, sputtering and gasping for breath, the flames from the ship lighting up the shoreline. He struck out for the shore.

Finally he hauled them both out of the water onto a narrow sandbar at river's edge. Shivering and freezing, he held Kiera as she collapsed in his arms, sobbing.

Behind them, the ship, engulfed in flames, caught the current once again and slipped away, dancing on the waves, her crew the bodies of the men who'd tried to take their lives, along with the man who'd given his for theirs.

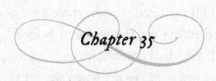

Chapter 35

KIERA LAY IN QUINN'S ARMS ON THE SANDBAR, watching the
ship as it rounded a bend, the flames becoming less visible
with each passing moment until all she could see was a faint
glow, then . . .

Nothing.

She shuddered, feeling numb from shock and cold, but
alive and thankful for it, Quinn's declaration ringing in her
ears.

"I love you."

She was safe. Le Bonne would never hurt her again.

"I love you."

She was free.

"I love you."

She could choose where she wanted to go, what she wanted to do. She could continue to run the stand at Breeze Hill, squirrel away coins for the future.

"I love you."

But none of it mattered save the three little words Quinn had whispered in her ear the moment before he'd thrown her overboard. Yes, she'd thought he was throwing her to her death, that she was going to die when she hit the water, but seconds later, he'd been there, buoying her up, saving her, carrying her to safety once again.

Just as he'd done from day one.

"I love you."

Just as she knew he'd do from now on if she gave her life into his keeping. All she had to do was say the words out loud that her heart already shouted.

"I love you." She tightened her hold on his neck, tears of relief and joy slipping down her cheeks. "I love you."

Between laughing and crying and caressing his face with both hands, she whispered the words over and over, her heart overflowing as she offered her love, her life, her very existence to the man who'd risked his life for hers, time and time again.

He cupped her face, his blue eyes searching hers. And then he lowered his head and kissed her.

She drowned in his kiss, blocking out the horrendous events of the past few hours. They were alive, and Quinn loved her. All else faded away as he pressed her against the sandbar and angled his lips across hers.

A shout from the river drew them apart. A flatboat floated on the current, shadowy forms pointing, waving.

As it bumped land, Connor jumped off and ran toward them.

Quinn and Kiera arrived at Wainwright House as dawn broke over the horizon.

Amelia, Leah, and Mrs. Butler, teary-eyed and smiling, stood on the porch, arms around each other.

Quinn assisted Kiera from the carriage. She gripped his hand, but with a wink, he gave her a gentle shove toward the women. Amelia rushed down the steps and threw her arms around her sister. Tossing him a smile that turned his insides to mush, Kiera allowed Amelia to escort her up the steps, and the women whisked her inside.

William leaned against a post, battered and bruised, his arm in a sling, looking like he'd been tied to the mast as the ship slammed and danced along the river. He attempted to stand up straight, groaning with the effort.

Quinn scowled at him. "What in heaven's name were ya thinking, blowing up the ship like that? Ya almost got the entire lot o' us killed, for sure."

"I'll have you know I had nothing to do with those explosions. Caruthers got away from me, took off for the boat, but he was acting so crazy the guard thought he was drunk. I used the distraction to try to sneak on board, but as you can see, I wasn't so lucky." William shrugged. "I guess they thought I was in my cups along with Caruthers, so they just roughed me up a bit and tossed me on the wharf. The explosions are what brought me around."

"Roughed you up a bit?" Connor barked. "Your arm was pulled slam out o' socket, it was. Luckily, the dockworkers have plenty of experience at that sort of thing. Without blinking an eye, they held him down and yanked it back in place."

"They almost killed me." William scowled.

"They couldn't kill you if they tried, Wainwright. You've got nine lives. But you used up at least three on me." Connor chuckled and winked at Quinn.

"Then it's a good thing there are only five of you O'Sheas." William winced. "Give me fair warning if your other brother shows up. I'll sequester myself at the plantation until whatever scrap he gets into is over and done with."

"Then who set off the explosives?" Quinn asked.

"Caruthers must have found the powder magazine and decided a few explosions would be a good distraction."

"Some distraction." Connor crossed his arms. "By the time I got Weston and Amelia t' Bloomfield's, the ship had broken free o' its moorings and was spinning downriver like a fiery dervish. I thought—" He broke off, the events of the long night making him look as haggard as Quinn felt. "I'm thankful God spared your life, Brother. I want you around for a long time."

"At Magnolia Glen?"

"Especially at Magnolia Glen." Connor clasped his shoulder, his grip firm. "You've decided t' stay?"

"I'm staying."

They shared a look, one that said all was forgiven, that the bond of brothers was stronger than past hurts, past grudges. A sheen of moisture filmed over Connor's eyes, and he cleared his throat.

Quinn fingered his shirt, saturated with the stench of river water. He felt a bit like a drowned rat and probably looked and smelled like one too. "I need to change."

And with that, he strode toward the wagons to fetch a change of clothes, before he and his older brother turned into blubbering *eejits*.

The rest of the men were up, breaking their fast around a campfire, the wagons all loaded and ready to head back to Breeze Hill. He took a hard left and skirted around the group. He wasn't in the mood to rehash last night's events yet again.

Minutes later, after washing up as best he could, somewhat clean and wearing dry breeches and the mended shirt that still showed the stains of his own blood, he headed back toward the wagons.

As he exited the stables, he heard gut-wrenching sobs.

He found Weston Caruthers, arms draped over a stall in the back of the barn, head down. Grief poured out of the youth. Quinn turned, intending to give the young man some privacy, but Weston's head jerked up, raw pain on his face. Quinn hesitated.

What did you say to someone who'd lost father, mother, brother, all at once?

The wagons rolled toward home, Kiera and Amelia riding in the Wainwrights' carriage along with Leah and little Jon.

Leah fussed about William riding astride, injured so. Amelia fretted over Weston for the same reason, and little Jon kept all three of them occupied with a constant wail from teething.

Finally the child quieted and both he and Leah dozed on the seat opposite Kiera and Amelia. Kiera's occasional glimpses of Quinn made her heart sing. But they hadn't been alone together for a single moment since they'd been plucked from the sandbar, and she was beginning to doubt the future, his feelings for her.

What if—?

"You're in love with him."

Hoping the shadowed carriage masked the blush stealing over her face, Kiera gave her sister an exasperated look. "What do you know of love?"

A knowing smile blossomed on Amelia's face. "Well, for starters, I am a married woman now."

"Amelia!"

Her sister laughed, then laid her head on Kiera's shoulder, reminding her of the little girl who'd been barely eight when their mother had died. Tears pricked Kiera's eyes. "I'm sorry, Amelia. I feel that I've failed you somehow."

Amelia twined her fingers in hers. "You didn't fail me, Kiera. I failed myself. I thought I had the world by the tail and could do as I pleased, however I pleased, whenever I pleased. And—" she drew in a shuddering breath—"and Weston's father died because of my selfishness."

Kiera frowned. "Weston bears the blame as much as you."

Amelia jerked up, shaking her head. "No, it was my idea to run away. Weston wanted to wait, to go home with his father, and then marry when we were older. But I convinced him that if we ran away and got married, his father would have to accept me into their family. His father is dead, and it's my fault. I'm sure Weston hates me."

Kiera wrapped her arms around her sister. "I'm sure that's not true."

But was it? Would Weston cast blame on her sister for his father's death, making life miserable for years to come?

She prayed it wasn't so.

The next morning, Kiera woke early, eager to slide back into the routine she had developed over the past several weeks at Breeze Hill. She rushed about serving breakfast to the men, their bickering music to her ears.

"Where's the butter, lass?"

"Are there any more flapjacks?"

"Hey, Björn, quit hogging the molasses!"

In spite of the chaos, she smiled, and a warm feeling spread through her, from the top of her head to the soles of her feet. It was good to be back home, cooking for the men.

Home?

When had she started thinking of Breeze Hill as home? Had it been when the men had combined the two cabins and created a cookhouse? Or when Quinn had repaired the firedogs? Or much, much later when he'd moved heaven and earth to find Amelia?

Her heart thudded against her rib cage as Quinn darkened the door. His brilliant blue eyes caressed her face, landed on her lips, then flicked back to capture her gaze, and his lips tipped up, so subtle it couldn't be called a smile, but her stomach did a slow roll all the same.

Or maybe she'd come home when Quinn's lips touched hers for the first time.

Face flaming, she hurried toward the kitchen, plucked another charger from the sideboard, and piled it high with flapjacks. As she slid it onto the table in front of him, his fingers trailed over the back of her hand.

La! She almost swooned on the spot.

"Something's burning, miss."

"Oh no." She rushed back to the griddle, scooped the last of the cakes up, and brought them back.

"Those are mine," someone called out. As the men all grabbed for one last pancake, the door slammed open, banging against the wall.

Connor stalked inside, a ferocious snarl on his face. "Daylight's a-wastin', men. What are ye dallying for?"

The men scrambled to grab their lunch pails, grumbling at what a hard taskmaster he was. He grabbed a pancake off the platter, speared her with a look. "From now on, cut the

THE ROAD TO MAGNOLIA GLEN

rations in half, lass. Maybe these yahoos will learn to move faster."

Kiera nodded, holding back a smile. Isabella was right. Connor's bark was worse than his bite. "Yes, sir."

Within minutes, the men scattered, leaving her alone with Quinn and Connor. Connor held out the packet of papers Mr. Caruthers had given Quinn. "Your papers, lass. And Megan's, notarized by Mr. Bloomfield."

She drew in a breath. "And Amelia's?"

"I gave hers to Weston, along with his and his brother's, redeemed with funds from the Caruthers estate."

Kiera bit her lip. Weston and Amelia were so young, but they'd said marriage vows, and there was nothing to be done about it now. They'd leave for the Caruthers plantation as soon as Mr. Peterson could travel.

"Thank you." She clasped the papers, trying to grasp the meaning of what he'd said. "This means that—that Megan and I are now indentured to Breeze Hill?"

In spite of Le Bonne's underhanded dealings, she was under no illusion that Mr. Bloomfield could just apportion the tavern owner's property with the stroke of a pen. There would be probate, heirs to locate, property to dispose of.

Connor shook his head. "Nay. You and your sisters are free to come and go as you will. Amelia got the cart before the horse with her marriage t' Weston, but what's done is done. No use in splitting hairs over the matter."

"I don't understand. How—?" She shook her head.

"Let's just say that one good turn deserves another."

Connor winked at Quinn. "All right, Brother, I've held up my end o' the bargain. Now it's your turn."

Quinn scowled at his *eejit* of a brother before risking a glance at Kiera. The sweet softness had disappeared, and she stood with arms crossed, one eyebrow raised in question.

"Oh, and to make it all legal and proper-like, I had Bloomfield draw up some papers." Connor held out another set of documents, grinning.

Quinn glared at his brother before snatching the agreement out of his hand. Connor chuckled, turned on his heel, and walked out, leaving Quinn to explain the crazy scheme to Kiera.

Explain what, exactly?

That he'd bought himself a wife—or more accurately, his brother had?

"What was he talking about? What bargain?" Kiera advanced on him. "The two of you cooked something up, didn't you? Something to get back at me because of Charlotte."

"Now, Kiera, that's no' true." He backed away, hands held out, trying his best not to laugh at her outrage. "As a matter o' fact, this has nothing t' do with Charlotte."

She plopped her hands on her hips, and he wondered where he'd gotten the idea that she'd squelched her Irish temper. If the fire in her eyes was any indication, her Irish heritage was alive and well. His gaze landed on her lips and—

"Then what is it?" She poked him in the chest with her forefinger. "So help me, Quinn O'Shea—"

Unable to stop himself, he reached out and snagged her against him, his lips finding hers, capturing her tirade and smothering it altogether. He'd been wanting to do that from the moment he'd walked into the cookhouse.

Effectively silenced, she snaked her arms around his neck and returned kiss for kiss until they were both breathless. Coming up for air, he released her lips and rested his forehead against hers. She opened her eyes, arched a brow, and he sighed. She wasn't going to let it go.

"Ye're no' indentured t' Connor. I am."

She jerked back. "What?"

"In exchange for yer freedom, as well as Amelia's and Megan's, I indentured myself to me brother."

"Quinn, you—" Her eyes shone with unshed tears. "I can't let you do that. You wanted to leave here. Go see the world."

He smiled, remembering Connor's words about Isabella. He tucked a strand of hair behind her ear, letting the tips of his fingers linger. "None o' that matters anymore. My world is here."

"But—"

"There's more."

"More?" A frown line puckered her brows. "I suppose now that Connor has his way and you're tied to Breeze Hill and Magnolia Glen, he's sending me and Megan away. Maybe we can throw ourselves on the mercy of Weston and Amelia."

"No, Connor doesna want ya t' leave. As a matter o' fact, it's the exact opposite." He pulled her closer and kissed her, then trailed his lips along her jawline to whisper in her ear, "Marry me, Kiera. Be my wife. Like Jacob worked for Rachel, I do no' care if I'm indentured t' Connor for the next ten years, fifteen, twenty. It doesna matter. What matters is that I stay here with you, working, living, loving."

He pulled back, searched her tear-filled gaze. "Say ya will."

She nodded, then whispered, "I will."

Heart soaring, Quinn crushed her to him, his lips claiming hers once again. And he didn't even notice when the papers Connor had handed him slipped out of his hand and fluttered to the floor.

Epilogue

Recorded this 28th day of March 1792

*Be it known unto all men by these present that I,
Quinn O'Shea, a sound and able manservant, do
willfully indenture myself to said Connor O'Shea of
Magnolia Glen Plantation, Natchez, Mississippi,
planter, his executors, administrators, or assignees for no
less than seven years each for a total of twenty-one years
in exchange for the release of the following indentures:
Kiera Young and Megan Young, currently residing at
Breeze Hill Plantation, and Amelia Young Caruthers of
Caruthers Estates, French Camp, Mississippi Territory.*

Without either equivocation, fraud, or delay, and to the true performance of the same well and truly to be made and done, I bind myself, my executors, administrators, and assignees, firmly by these present. In witness hereof I have hereunto set my hand and seal this 28th day of March 1792.

Quinn O'Shea

The condition of this obligation is such that it becomes null and void immediately upon the marriage of Quinn O'Shea to Kiera Young as a token of goodwill from the aforementioned Connor O'Shea.

Connor O'Shea

Sealed and delivered in the presence of
James Bloomfield, Esquire, Attorney-at-Law

TURN THE PAGE FOR AN EXCITING EXCERPT FROM

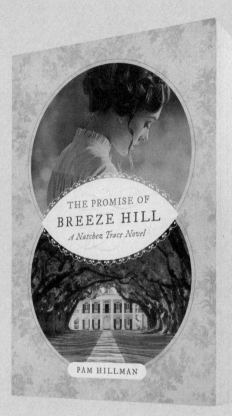

THE PROMISE OF
BREEZE HILL
A Natchez Trace Novel

PAM HILLMAN

"Hillman carries readers to antebellum
Mississippi in an entertaining tale."
Booklist

Chapter 1

NATCHEZ UNDER-THE-HILL ON THE MISSISSIPPI RIVER
MAY 1791

Connor O'Shea braced his boots against the auction block and glared at the crowd gathered on the landing.

Vultures. Ever' last one o' them.

The stench of the muddy Mississippi River filled his nostrils, and the rude shacks along the riverfront reminded him of the roiling mass of humanity in the seaports back home in Ireland. Hot, cloying air sucked the breath from his lungs, and the storm clouds in the sky brought no relief from the steam pot of Natchez in May.

Dockworkers shouted insults at each other. Haggard-faced

women in rags scuttled past as grimy children darted among the wheels of rickety carts. One besotted fool lay passed out in the street, no one to help him or care whether he lived or died. As far as Connor knew, the man could be dead already, knifed in the dead of night when no one would be the wiser.

A commotion broke out at the back of the crowd and all eyes turned as a gentleman farmer shouted that he'd been robbed. The man chased after a ragged boy, but the moment they were out of sight, his compatriots turned back to the auction, the incident so common, it was already forgotten.

Connor ignored the chaos and focused on the high bluff overlooking the wharf.

Ah, to be up there where the wind blew the foul odor of rotting fish away and the scent of spring grass filled a lad's nostrils instead. And be there he would.

As soon as someone bought his papers.

"Gentlemen, you've heard the terms of Connor O'Shea's indenture," James Bloomfield, Esquire, boomed out. "Mr. O'Shea is offering to indenture himself against passage for his four brothers from Ireland, an agreement he had with his previous master."

A tightness squeezed Connor's chest. After serving out his seven-year indenture with Master Benson, they'd come to a mutual agreement that Connor would work without wages if the influential carpenter would send for his brothers. Benson's untimely death had squashed his hopes until Bloomfield suggested the same arrangement with his new master. One year for each brother. Four years.

No, three and a half. Assuming Bloomfield made it clear in the papers that Connor had already worked six months toward passage for the first of his brothers.

But who first? Quinn? Rory? Caleb? Patrick?

Not Patrick, as much as he wanted to lay eyes on the lad.

Having fled Ireland eight years ago, he'd never even seen his youngest brother. He'd start with Quinn, the next eldest. The two of them could work hard enough to bring Caleb over in half the time. He'd leave Rory to travel with Patrick.

Pleased with his plan, he panned the faces of the merchants and plantation owners spread out before him. Surely someone needed a skilled carpenter. Dear saints above, the mansions being built on the bluff and the flourishing plantations spread throughout the lush countryside promised enough work to keep Irish craftsmen rolling in clover for years.

He spotted an open carriage parked at the edge of the crowd. A barefoot boy held the horses, and a lone woman perched on the seat. Eyes as dark as seasoned pecan met and held his before the lass turned away, her attention settling on a half-dozen men unloading a flatboat along the river's edge.

She looked as out of place as an Irish preacher in a pub, and just as condemning.

He stiffened his spine and ignored her. It didn't matter what she thought of him. He needed a benefactor, a wealthy landowner with ready access to ships and to Ireland. And he planned to stay far away from women with the means to destroy him.

The memory of one little rich gal who'd savored him,

then spit him out like a sugarcane chew would last him a lifetime.

"I say, Bloomfield, what's O'Shea's trade?"

"Joinery. Carpentry. He apprenticed with the late John W. Benson, the renowned master craftsman from the Carolinas."

A murmur of appreciation rippled through the crowd of gentlemen farmers. Connor wasn't surprised. Master Benson's work was revered among the landed gentry far and wide. Unfortunately, Master Benson's skill with a hammer and a lathe hadn't saved him from the fever that struck no less than six months after their arrival in the Natchez District. With the man barely cold in his grave, Connor now found his papers in the hands of the lawyer, being offered to the highest bidder.

But regardless, no one offered a bid. Connor squared his shoulders, chin held high, feet braced wide.

The minutes ticked by as Bloomfield cajoled the crowd.

Oh, God, please let someone make an offer.

What if no one needed a cabinetmaker or a carpenter? What if Bloomfield motioned for him to leave the platform, his own man, belonging to himself, with no way to better himself or save his brothers from a life of misery back home in Ireland, a life he'd left them to suffer through because of his own selfishness?

All his worldly goods stood off to the side. The tools of his trade. Hammers. Saws. Lathes. He'd scrimped and saved for each precious piece during his years as a bonded journeyman to Master Benson. He could sell them, but what good would that do? He needed those tools and he needed a benefactor if he would be any good to his brothers.

Finally someone made an offer, the figure abysmally low. Connor gritted his teeth as the implication of his worth slapped him full in the face. But the terms. He had to remember the terms. Every day of his labor would mark one more coin toward passage for his brothers.

A movement through the crowd caught his eye. The barefoot boy made his way toward Bloomfield and whispered something in his ear. Connor glanced toward the edge of the crowd. The carriage stood empty, and he caught a glimpse of a dark traveling cloak as the woman entered the lawyer's small office tucked away at the base of the bluff.

"Sold." Bloomfield's gavel beat a death knell against the table in front of him. "To Miss Isabella Bartholomew on behalf of Breeze Hill Plantation."

Cold dread swooshed up from Connor's stomach and exploded in his chest.

A woman.

He'd been indentured to a woman.

He closed his eyes.

God help him.

Acknowledgments

Having worked with the Tyndale team on multiple projects, I can only say that the process gets better and better. I'm amazed at the level of dedication the entire team puts in to produce a stellar product for the reader. I'm honored to work with a publisher who's passionate about turning out a top-notch product. Thank you all for continuing to help me learn the ropes.

Erin Smith: Thank you for your patience with me. We pulled it off again, even if I got a kick out of "stumping the editor" by making up a couple of redneck Southernisms nobody's ever heard of.

I'd like to thank the Seekers for being ready and willing to answer questions on the fly and to Robin Caroll for talking me off the ledge when I'm on deadline. I don't know what I'd do without you all.

Thanks to my mother, my church family, my readers, and my street team for praying me through writing this book. Your prayers were felt.

Special thanks to my husband for grabbing meals on the go and never complaining about the time I spend tied to my laptop, even editing for hours and hours on road trips.

About the Author

CHRISTIAN BOOKSELLERS ASSOCIATION bestselling author Pam Hillman writes inspirational historical romance. Her novels have won or been finalists in the Inspirational Reader's Choice, the EPIC eBook Awards, and the International Digital Awards.

Pam was born and raised on a dairy farm in Mississippi and spent her teenage years perched on the seat of a tractor raking hay. In those days, her daddy couldn't afford two cab tractors with air-conditioning and a radio, so Pam drove an old model B Allis Chalmers. Even when her daddy asked her if she wanted to bale hay, she told him she didn't mind raking. Raking hay doesn't take much thought, so Pam spent her time working on her tan and making up stories in her head. Now that's the kind of life every girl should dream of.

Visit her website at www.pamhillman.com.

Discussion Questions

1. Quinn O'Shea made a promise to his father to care for his younger brothers, but after nearly ten years of honoring that commitment, he's eager to foist them off on Connor. Do you believe he's fulfilled his obligation? Why or why not? Have you ever made a promise you later began to have doubts or feel guilt about?

2. Kiera Young worries quite a bit about her sister Amelia, whose coquettish ways are bound to land the girl in hot water. What advice does Kiera receive from those around her? What would you recommend Kiera do to keep her sister from harm?

3. Connor O'Shea has long awaited his brothers' arrival from Ireland. How does their reunion go? Are Quinn's feelings toward Connor justified? What does it take to erase the years and distance between the brothers?

4. After meeting the Young girls, Quinn feels compelled to defend them, not only from the likes of Pierre

Le Bonne but even from being cast out by his own brother. Why do you think Quinn saddles himself with more responsibility, just when he's on the verge of relinquishing his brothers' care?

5. When Kiera is given an opportunity to run a hospitality service at Breeze Hill, she finds a new purpose in life. What goals does she hope to accomplish by offering room and board to travelers along the Natchez Trace? Given some of the dangers she exposes herself to, would you recommend that she pursue the venture? Why or why not?

6. Quinn and Kiera take turns doing small gestures for each other—repairing leather gloves, forging a new spit. Why don't they thank each other in words? Given a choice, how do you prefer to give and receive love? Through acts of kindness or physical gifts? With spoken words? Some other method?

7. During the dedication service for Connor and Isabella's plantation, Mr. Horne shares how God gave those two a promising future, blessing the covenant they made to each other and to their nephew. Read Matthew 25:14-30. What similarities can you find between the parable and the events Horne outlines in this scene? What have you been entrusted with, and how well are you managing the responsibilities you have been given?

8. In the middle of a crisis, Kiera struggles to find peace and turns to busy activity. But Mary Horne advises her to be still and listen for God's voice. Do you tend to be a Mary or a Martha (see Luke 10:38-42)? What do you do to quiet yourself, allow God to speak, and find peace?

9. A tavern wench at the Blue Heron tells Quinn, "We're all prisoners in one fashion or another, luv." In what ways are Quinn and Kiera prisoners? What about Connor and Amelia? Pierre and the Carutherses? Are you a prisoner to something? What will it take to break free?

10. For a good portion of the story, Reginald Caruthers tends to be singularly focused and acts in self-serving ways. Is it possible for a person to be so blinded by grief that he lashes out almost unknowingly? What do his actions at the end say about his true character?

11. Quinn initially balks at the idea of committing himself to stay at Connor's plantation for several years. Why does he change his mind and agree to work, much like Jacob labored for Rachel in Genesis 29?

12. Like the father in the Prodigal Son story (Luke 15:11-32), Connor shows great generosity toward Quinn. What other parallels or similarities can you draw between the biblical account and this story?